A Touch of Blood

Sajni Patel

A TOUCH OF BLOOD

SAJNI PATEL

HYPERION
LOS ANGELES   NEW YORK

All rights reserved. Published by Hyperion, an imprint of Buena Vista Books, Inc. No part of this book may be reproduced or transmitted in any form or by any means, electronic or mechanical, including photocopying, recording, or by any information storage and retrieval system, without written permission from the publisher. For information address Hyperion, 7 Hudson Square, New York, New York 10013.

First Edition, February 2025
10 9 8 7 6 5 4 3 2 1
FAC-004510-24346
Printed in the United States of America

Stock images: snake (title page and chapter openers):
1986352829; snake (breaks): 735297934/Shutterstock
This book is set in Garamond Pro/Monotype
Designed by Phil Buchanan

Names: Patel, Sajni, 1981– author.
Title: A touch of blood / Sajni Patel.
Description: First edition. • Los Angeles : Hyperion, 2025. • Audience:
    Ages 14–18. • Audience: Grades 10–12. • Summary: "Eshani, a nagin, is
    whisked to the Nightmare Realm, where she faces terrifying monsters, a
    treacherous court, and a mysterious boy"—Provided by publisher.
Identifiers: LCCN 2024013932 • ISBN 9781368098779 (hardcover)
Subjects: LCSH: Women heroes—Juvenile fiction. • Imaginary
    places—Juvenile fiction. • Imaginary wars and battles—Juvenile
    fiction. • Monsters—Juvenile fiction. • Tiger—Juvenile fiction. •
    Fantasy. • CYAC: Heroes—Fiction. • Imaginary wars and battles—Fiction.
    • Monsters—Fiction. • Tigers—Fiction. • Cat family (Mammals)—Fiction.
    • Fantasy. • LCGFT: Fantasy fiction. • Novels.
Classification: LCC PZ7.1.P37698 To 2025 • DDC 813.6
    [Fic]—dc23/eng/20240729
LC record available at https://lccn.loc.gov/2024013932

Reinforced binding

Follow @ReadRiordan
Visit www.HyperionTeens.com

SUSTAINABLE FORESTRY INITIATIVE
Certified Sourcing
www.forests.org
SFI-01681

Logo Applies to Text Stock Only

For all the girls the world has tried to conquer

A Note from Sajni

THE MYTH OF HADES AND PERSEPHONE HAS LASTED through the ages, reimagined and reinvented, and yet remains as enrapturing as ever. It is a tale of tragedy and desire, of darkness and peace. I've always been drawn to the contradictory nature of this tale, how a man surrounded by death captured the heart of a woman who represents spring. Death and renewal, they are a befitting pair, for one cannot exist without the other.

This myth seemed to fit seamlessly against the backdrop of Indian lore and the ongoing battle between the forces of good and evil as each vies for inharmoniously opposing things.

As a Venom novel, this story deals with several darker topics. Please be aware of the following potentially triggering subjects: war, violence, gore, death, misogyny, depression, creepy-crawlies, and nightmares. After all, this is the Nightmare Realm, where horrors come alive and walk alongside weary travelers.

Beyond that, this is a tale of epic adventure across extraordinary realms where you may find that sometimes...gods are made, not born.

PROLOGUE

HERE, THERE WERE SHADOWS. AN INTEGRAL WEB OF ravenous spectrals upheld by the dakini—the masters of darkness— and ruled by the asuras—those who crossed dimensions in search of conquest.

These were as old as time, beings born during the dawn of the Akash Ganga. When the great sky river writhed in labor, she spawned darkness, poison, jewels, and amrita—the most coveted treasure of all, for it bestowed immortality. Driven by greed, the asuras stepped through hidden gateways and ravaged entire worlds for the immortal elixir, creating pandemonium wherever they went. Leaving death in their wake, ashes in the shadows.

To bring balance, the vidyadhara locked the gateways between dimensions, imprisoning the asuras where they stood. Thus the Nightmare Realm had become theirs, breeding generations of Shadow Kings and Shadow Queens, dark princes and ever darker princesses.

For the first Shadow Princess, in all her spellbinding wisdom, conceived the Court of Nightmares. Through the incomprehensible power of nightmares, she, a dreamreaver, stretched ethereal tentacles across realms, manipulating mortal kings in order to entrap the vidyadhara—to no avail.

Generations failed, but the darkness of the Nightmare Realm had to be fed if its inhabitants were to survive.

The mortal realm sent its dead. Corpses floating along the Blood River, a bank of bones and deadly shimmer, to feed the shadows. The myth of immortality grew, coveted by Shadow Kings and mortal kings alike as they grasped desperately at salvation, which then untethered strings of uttered words that could, and had, destroyed lives.

Prophecy, one of the most dangerous things in all the realms.

THE REIGNING SHADOW KING MARRIED HIS THIRTEENTH bride due to such a prophecy. She was of mysterious origin and beguiling beauty: purple-black hair shimmering like a star-speckled sky; milky skin touched with gray blush; lavender lips that spoke sweet words; ebony eyes with carmine swirls; a pattern of cobalt spirals around her brows. Diti was as cruel as she was stunning, as conniving as she was tormented. For court life was one of iniquity.

To secure her future, the thirteenth bride did the unthinkable for the child growing in her womb. She beseeched the Court of Nightmares—towering, enigmatic statues guarding a pool of unfathomable power—for an anointed heir. Their eyes glowed white, seeing but unseeing. Strange beings locked into place, yet in multiple places at once. Here and in dreams, crossing realms and arching across the cosmos. Fed by the life force of elite asuras.

"Prime Consort," the Court said. "We know what you seek, and it demands a hefty price."

Diti sank into the pool, the waters drinking her in and spitting her out, for she was no dreamreaver. The oracle declared another—the Queen's firstborn—as the future king, for Diti had given birth to a girl touched by nightmares. A gray-tinged infant, quickly discarded and ridiculed, the baby was without a mother's love—for a sickly child would never ascend to the throne. Without concern, the child fell into the pool of dreams but emerged unscathed. A new dreamreaver: a curse named Holika.

When again with child, Diti, still hungry for power, did the unimaginable. She beseeched the Blood River.

Shimmering red mist curled over the potent stench of decaying flesh, revealing the ferry with its ferryman. "I know what you seek," the Ferryman said. "And it demands a hefty price."

One drop lifted from the churning waters. The original poison—halahala. It touched Diti's lips. Her body seized, consumed by hallucinations, devoured alive without death in sight. Her child was a healthy boy. With fangs and wings and horns like the asuras of old. When presented to the Court of Nightmares, they bestowed upon him a name: Hiran, the *Gatekeeper*.

THE FIRST GATEKEEPER WAS SAID TO POSSESS EXTRA-ordinary power and beauty, a nagin who walked worlds—the first of her kind, her talents lost to the stars . . . until the day great suffering befell her people. An era of calamity, of near annihilation.

For the King's search for amrita led him to the naga, and the naga did not bend the knee. They did not go quietly into the night. Their elders did not flee. They took spears and swords and declared, "We fight so others may live."

The war claimed its victor, one side crushing the other without any semblance of mercy.

The vine-laden balconies brimming with gardens shattered in the dusk.

The lotus-filled fountains boiled over with silt.

The serpent-wrapped pillars crumbled.

The naga fell, their bodies sent down the Blood River for the Nightmare Realm to feast upon, corpses cradling secrets.

First, the elders had been slain, a splattering of blood for failure to comply.

Next, the warriors had been gutted, for daring to resist.

Then the men who took up arms had been slaughtered like wild beasts, an example to be set.

Finally, the women and children fought to their dying breath, resilience in their hearts.

In a land stained with tears and blood, their foremothers' voices awakened from the ancestral plane like fog rising from morning fields. A haunting and a promise, they declared, *"You shall rise in garments of ash and venom for blood."*

ONE

ESHANI
(FIVE YEARS AGO)

Specks of blood and ash floated through the air, reaching as high as the twilight sky, choking what vanishing sunlight remained.

Eshani and her family stood in their courtyard, the gardens she'd tended now bruised and wilting around them. Trepidation grew heavy and dire in their hearts. At thirteen years old, Eshani was saying goodbye to her father. Papa was a scholar, but the warriors were no more. So he laid down his scrolls and picked up a shield, exchanged his white-and-gold kurta for makeshift armor.

Eshani had never seen her father afraid. But when he crouched in front of his three daughters and handed them each the last pomegranates from their tree, his hands quivered.

Manisha was the youngest, at eleven. Once the most carefree, she was now filled with sobs. Sithara, Eshani's twin and second eldest by two minutes, was immobile, holding back her emotions. Mama stood behind them, her cheeks wet with tears, determination carving new lines on her face.

Tendrils of despair bloomed around Eshani like datura flowers clamoring to unfurl. Slow but sudden, gently but earnestly. She let her sisters take their pomegranates first, and with trembling fingers, she wrapped her hands around the last of the bulbous fruit. Papa's jaw hardened, but his eyes spoke volumes of fear and sorrow, resolve and pride. He'd hugged all three girls to him. Mama's weeping was stifled by the padded footsteps of Lekha's approach.

The five-foot-tall golden tiger made her way through the gardens that had slowly withered as ash loomed above the city of Anand.

Lekha had been a whining cub when Eshani found her and smuggled her into the city, hiding her in the family estate of stone homes carved into the canyons, connected by gardens. She'd nurtured her and bathed her and stolen milk for the cub that quickly grew. When Eshani's parents had found out, Papa was the first to explain why Lekha couldn't stay—and the second to fall in love with her.

That day, Lekha pressed her large orange nose into Papa's palm, purring and whining because she, too, could not bear to see him go. When he stood to leave, the rising dawn at his back, Lekha wailed, nipping at the edges of his kurta, dragging him back even as the other men marched past on their way to battle.

Eshani wrapped her long, lean arms around her friend and comforted her, weeping into Lekha's fur.

Eshani wasn't a hero like Papa, who freely rode into the Fire Wars on a water buffalo fitted with armor.

She wasn't a goddess like Mama, an architect with a love for gardening who'd turned trowels into weapons, throwing her shears with deadly accuracy.

She wasn't fearless like Sithara, who bristled with indignation.

She wasn't optimistic like Manisha, who had yet to find her footing in this quickly changing era.

WHEN PAPA, AND THOSE WHO WENT INTO BATTLE ALONGSIDE him, failed to return, the women and young ones set out to fight, having trained each day since the looming threat of war.

Merchant carts had long since been stripped for stakes and nails. Metal melted for blades and arrowheads, all dipped in the blood of Eshani's foremothers. The blood, said to be more potent than a cobra's venom, had begun to run dry, and Eshani wondered—with wretchedness—if her own life force was lethal like the naga before her. The temptation to cleave open her own veins, if it meant saving her people, was staggering.

Sweat beaded on Eshani's forehead, mixing with grime as rivulets poured down her temples. Her long dark hair unwound itself from her braid. Soot covered her kurta and leggings. Dirt smeared her dark brown skin. Her lanky body ached.

The last great battle swelled around them, blocking the view of her homeland for the final time. Swords clashed against shields, spears and arrows cut the air, daggers and tridents drove through flesh and bones. Both giants and men fell, the earth soaking up their blood like a parched mouth hungrily partaking of a feast.

Blood and ash freckled Eshani's face, weighing down her lashes and stinging her lips, as she rode Lekha through the frenzy of a tempestuous battle. The tiger shuddered beneath her, a mass of muscle and fury, a death trap for any who found themselves in the path of her razor-edged teeth. The sway of her powerful head knocked soldiers out of the way left and right. Her weight alone was fearsome.

Outraged soldiers aimed for Lekha. *How dare they.* With swiftness, Eshani unleashed arrows bearing winter-steel tips coated in her foremothers' blood. The arrows met their marks, driving venom into soldiers and delivering quick deaths.

Eshani made sure not a single weapon harmed Lekha as the tiger ripped into one enemy after another. Blood dripped from her fangs and fur, and Eshani hoped to properly clean her before any infections set in.

In the near distance, between palls of smoke, Sithara unleashed a mighty cry, driving a spear into a soldier's skull with all her might. The muscles of her thin arms contracted beneath the torn sleeves of her sullied once-beige kurta. Blood splattered her face, a remarkable glistening red against dirt-smudged brown.

This was what the kingdom had become: grown men slaughtering children, cleaving knives through spines.

At her mother's urging, Eshani reluctantly left her family behind, riding Lekha through to twilight to find a safe path, for the army had blocked off all other routes. Lekha sprinted across the plains, a golden flash like a firefly carrying secrets.

There, the marshlands awaited, a shortcut to the jungles beyond with a weighty price. Beyond the precipice, one tree blended into another, a menacing wall of darkness melting into the sky. Eshani trembled as the last drops of adrenaline faded, nearly succumbing to sleepiness. Still she pushed onward, sliding off Lekha and admonishing the tiger to stay put. But Lekha persisted, and together they went, walking side by side. Lekha's warm fur, no matter how sullied, remained a thing of comfort.

Deep inside this strange land, morning light dawned on delicate grass wet with dew. Beyond lay the edges of dark soil and dark trees full of dark leaves. It seemed even light was reluctant to enter the marshlands.

Craning her neck, Eshani stared up at the long, thick trunks and bristling canopy. Feathery clouds and sky were the same, angry concoctions in various shades of gray.

Lekha grunted, pacing back and forth. When it became clear the tiger wouldn't inch closer to the dreariness, Eshani petted her. "It's okay. Why should you fear when you've never feared anything?"

Lekha nudged Eshani, nearly headbutting her. In turn, Eshani ran a hand down her companion's neck, the fur matted with blood and dirt, far from her usual glory.

"You stay here. There's no need for both of us to go." Eshani swallowed, wanting to add that if the shades took her, then Lekha could at least survive and prevent her family from taking this dangerous route.

"I promise, tomorrow we'll get you cleaned up, put a big meal in your belly, and maybe I can track down a melon for you, huh? More refreshing than chewing on soldiers' heads," Eshani said, reminiscing about hot summer days when Lekha possessively pawed watermelons and chomped into the sweet treats.

She climbed onto the tiger, knowing that Lekha would never abandon her. A cryptic silence surrounded them. Snowfall glimmered in the air, a magical intrigue, an eerie beauty swallowed by the chill.

Shivering, Eshani hugged Lekha tight, warmed by the tiger's body heat. Sleep was pulling them both under.

"Stay awake," Eshani slurred, but Lekha's eyelids closed for longer and longer intervals.

Eshani yawned. Before she knew it, she'd fallen off, hissing as the impact jarred every injury back to life. And there were many. When her palms hit the protruding roots of the forest floor, memories and tales seeped through her skin and unfurled in her mind, just as they had with the plants from the city of Anand. In her homeland, the plants told her their final farewells as they suffocated beneath ash. Here, this tree eagerly shared its secrets.

Inky ribbons sprouted along the edges of her vision, pulsating and tightening, ripping back a veil most would never imagine being there. The tree told her tales, weaving a tapestry of stories stretching back to its sapling days many centuries ago. The tree was old—the oldest tree she'd ever come across. In a whirlwind of colors and sensations, it spoke to her. Without sound, because of course trees had no voice.

They knew by sense. Their roots reached far into the ground, touching other roots, communicating. It knew what other trees knew, and it told Eshani.

This land had seen death because it was the *gateway* to death. The tree warned her of the vicious lamprey-type creatures that filled the brook nearby. It showed her a place *beyond* the brook where the darkness had given birth to monsters with gnashing teeth and death-filled eyes. Those monsters had entered this realm beneath a writhing crimson sky agitated by purple lightning, making a brief rush for the gateway between realms—which had been promptly sealed shut.

Dazed, Eshani held her hands to her chest. *The legends were true.* The marshlands were the cradle of darkness, the gateway to the Nightmare Realm.

This was the birthplace of monsters.

Stumbling to her feet, Eshani urged Lekha forward to search the path for safety, but Lekha had stopped moving.

"What's wrong?" Eshani panicked. How far could she drag eight hundred pounds? Worse, if need be, how could she kill the shades?

Ahead, a strange green light shone from the canopy, hitting dark waters in a sickly shade of olive. Campfire stories spoke of the light that came from nowhere, followed intruders, and appeared like a torch showing the way for...

Eshani gulped.

...showing the way for the shades.

She felt them before she saw them. Shadowy apparitions said to kill from the inside. Invincible. Impossible to fight off.

They spilled out into the marsh light, a mist leaking from between leaves and ferns, descending from the branches and prowling toward the girl and her tiger. A tiger that wouldn't move. A tiger who had closed her eyes as if slumbering on her feet.

Something else moved. It'd been so close, but Eshani hadn't seen it. One wrong detour in the path, and she would've walked right into its bladelike talons.

A tall, slender creature emerged. A *monster.* Eerie green light shone on its glossy skin, long arms, and bulbous head with large white eyes. It blinked. Not menacingly, but maybe curiously? Until it snarled, revealing sharp teeth filling a cavernous mouth that stretched from nonexistent ear to nonexistent ear.

It chittered, drawing the shadows toward it. Were they communicating? Deciding how to ration her small body for the entire lot of them?

Eshani's arms were like stones, too heavy to grab her bow and arrow. She nudged Lekha, begging, "Please move. You're in danger."

Could they turn back? The trees all looked identical, with the same bent twigs and the same dark green leaves dusted with gray. The narrow brook had mirrored itself down to the crooks and rocks. Water flowed one way to the left and a different way to the right, but never collided in the middle.

Eshani blinked a hundred times. Her thoughts turned foggy, her tongue heavy, her body sinking toward the ground.

The shades drifted toward her. She dared not look into the eyes of the shades, to behold all her worst nightmares reflected back at her. An amalgamation of true terror so wretched it could tear souls asunder.

Their mist enveloped her twitching frame, the droplets both searing and freezing her skin. She felt herself moving toward them against her will, even as she scrambled to clutch on to nearby shrubs. With all her might, Eshani reached for the ground until her palms hit the dirt, feeling for the roots below, sending a desperate plea for help. The ground rumbled ever so slightly, and the shades paused.

"Please," she uttered. "Let us pass. Allow my people through."

The shades spoke through vibrations pulsating directly into

Eshani's head. Like sharpened nails scratching the soft flesh of her brain.

She screamed, fighting off the pain as they rippled through her thoughts, filleting her mind open. Until the shades knew her down to her molecular level and relented.

"A price must be paid," they echoed inside her skull.

With gritted teeth, she said, "We'll die if we can't pass."

"The price is great," they hummed, the pressure resonating through her skull and prickling down her spine.

Eshani gritted her teeth, willing her body not to implode. They desired *her*.

Papa's encouraging face flashed through her thoughts. He had not hesitated to sacrifice so they could live. She peered at Lekha, whose chest was getting smaller with each weakened pant. Lekha would not hesitate. She thought of Mama who shielded them with her might. She did not hesitate. She thought of her sisters and the others who deserved a chance to live. *She* should not hesitate.

Lekha's eyes grew wide, the whites showing in terror, apprehension. They stayed firm on Eshani, as if she knew what was to happen. Oh, how Eshani's heart ached. Swallowing her sobs, she gave Lekha a reassuring nod.

Bargaining with the unknown was unwise. It was also the path of the desperate.

No thirteen-year-old should have to make such a monumental decision, a choice that could save her people for the cost of one life. A splintering decision with a consequence that her family would have to live with—but at least they would *live*.

With a quiver to her voice, Eshani agreed.

TWO

HIRAN
(NINE MORTAL-REALM YEARS AGO)

"**B**astard child," the other princes would taunt Hiran as they beat him.

"What are you supposed to be the gatekeeper of, anyway?" another guffawed.

"You mean *groundskeeper*. He's no prince. He should be working the fields."

"When I am King," Tarak, the eldest, had whispered, his beady black eyes pulsating like larvae in a soft egg sac, "you and your sickly sister and your whore mother will be the first I'll set on fire. Do you think wings and horns melt like skin...or like bones?"

In that moment, a speck of darkness clawed open a corner of Hiran's mind and drank his will, taking over his body long enough to fight back. He called it the Gloom, what he assumed linked him to the ruthless lineage of his father, and thus the cruelty of his half-siblings, for the Gloom made him crave violence and darkness. He wanted no part of that—it had already resulted in Tarak beating him to near death for daring to fight back. Thus, Hiran locked away the Gloom in a recess of his mind, too afraid to even think about it, much less unleash it.

Only his sister defied their older half-siblings, no matter the lashings she endured. When they humiliated Holika in public, she stole away into the pool at the Court of Nightmares and crept into their dreams, where she practiced dreamreaving, creating nightmares to extract her tormentors' secrets. But because the Court of Nightmares protected the minds of the Shadow King, Queen, and the anointed heir, Tarak remained untouched. For those who wore the crown fed the Court.

Hiran's father was a beastly asura, nearly seven feet tall and fitted with the royal asura fashion of long, uncut hair tied back beneath a crown of shadow and ash. His children had inherited his black hair and were expected to be nearly as tall. He, however, possessed talons for nails and curled claws for feet. He was a strong king, his ripped muscles filling out a navy-blue sherwani with metallic gray threading. He wore a sheathed sword tucked neatly into a scabbard at his waist, a blue ribbon tied to the handle to indicate his status. Items Tarak would one day wear. Not Hiran. Royal blue was never meant for him.

The King gestured to Hiran and announced in a rumbling voice, "You shall escort me to the borderlands and see how dire our situation is. We are tasked with saving this realm, and you can no longer sit idly on your hands like a weakling."

Hiran winced, and at that, his father grunted with severe annoyance. Overhead, lavender clouds spread thin amid a tumultuous red sky, a constant twilight. The royal keshi stomped hooves into the mud and lashed a long, thin tail, one split into many at the end. A monstrosity of an animal with a temperament to match. Feathery lilac antennae sprouted along its form, from an elongated head down a muscular, mauve-tinged body.

Beauty was deceptive.

The royal steed snarled, pulling taut its upper lip to show impressive fangs. It glared at Hiran with its four large eyes, sheltered by purple-and-silver lashes.

"Careful, boy," the King said, the diagonal scar across his face crawling with a centipede beneath his skin. "They smell fear and tend to eat it." He growled, cutting through his flesh and impaling the centipede with one stab. He tugged it from his face. The multi-legged critter hissed and squirmed as Hiran's father slurped it down, pincers and all.

They soon arrived at the borderlands, where dakini, clothed in hooded capes over long tunics, raised dark leather-bound hands to the wall. Mist swirled above them, a monster wailing into the void. Flashes of purple light erupted behind reddish clouds pressed against the dome. The barrier consisted of shadows extracted from beasts and the eternal supply of dead from the Blood River. It was the only thing separating them from Patala, the true realm, which sought to take back.

Cracks in the weakening dome glowed white with a light deadly to those who lived within. If the Court of Nightmares could not find the key to opening the lost gateways between worlds, they would all perish. In the glow of mortality, a beguiling call swelled through Hiran, luring him to the shadow dome. There, a tiny piece fractured. Then he smelled it. Something new, metallic—pungent yet morbidly intriguing.

Death.

Curious, he reached out. A spectral light flickered against his fingertip where it lingered, a petal of light swaying in the breeze. It sang to the blood humming in his veins, as if recognizing something familiar.

A hand snatched Hiran's shoulder, jerking him back. "What are you doing?" a general growled, his nostrils wide, dragging in his next breath.

The spectral petal floated on the movement of air, turning from white light to white ink. Before the general could react, he'd already inhaled.

The distinct smell of new death intensified.

UNLIKE OTHER WORLDS, THE NIGHTMARE REALM WAS A pocket realm within Patala, and thus lacked a sun and moon to indicate the passing of time. Instead, time and history were marked by relevant events: the changing of thrones, notable marriages and births and deaths, and the season of foods. Since Hiran's visit to the borderlands, many crops had come and gone in the fields, cycles of growth and rot. Enough time to see what the new illness could do—kill thousands.

This season had been marked by the white plague, and now the Shadow King lay on his deathbed coughing something wicked. Speckles of death floated from his lips. Even his royal finery and perfumes couldn't hold back the malodorous stench.

Hiran looked up at his father with big eyes, feeling in his gut that the King would die soon. He had an inexplicable sense for death, a calling in his blood that the white spectrals of the plague had recognized, and thus the plague had not infected him. The scent of death drifted around him, and Hiran could tell—without a single symptom—who carried the plague. At least six in this room would die from it.

Holika stood behind Hiran, beside their mother. In their youngest days, the siblings would walk together, his tiny hand in hers, making her giggle. A noise others said sounded like a haunting from nightmares. But to Hiran, Holika was comfort. He was never happier than when he could see his sister, especially after being separated by classes and duties—hers to the pool of dreams.

She had grown taller, prettier, although the court sneered at her ghastly gray complexion. Holika wore a glimmering gray gown gifted to her by the Court of Nightmares. She twirled in her splendor, even as everyone else stood still in mourning. Which made Hiran sick to his stomach, for they were preening her.

"*You* unleashed this curse," the Queen snarled at Hiran and his mother. All turned to glare at them. Tarak, always cruel, had never appeared more unhinged than in this moment.

"Enough," the King interjected, his eyes fluttering. Gill-like wounds on his neck breathed open and closed. His entire body was gasping for air, grasping at nothing. White streaks pulsated along his jaw and mouth.

His eyes lolled, and his head slipped to the side even as he called each child forward to give them their farewells, commanding them to remove their masks so that he could gaze upon what he'd created. To Holika, the King said, "You should smile more."

She blinked at him, cocked her head to the side, and gave a broad smile that swallowed her thin, frail face. Sharp teeth showed beside the sharp contours of an angular face.

"Conquer the dreamscape, open the gateways. Or this world dies. It is the *only* thing you are meant for."

She nodded. Her hand twitched like she wanted to comfort her cruel and unloving father.

"And you, boy." The King turned his glazed eyes to his youngest.

Hiran eagerly awaited his father's sentiment of wisdom and pride.

"You are of poison."

Hiran's heart sank.

"You brought this into our world."

No. Hiran had not brought the plague. How could his father think that? But the King was never wrong. *Was* Hiran the reason they would all die? His eyes filled with tears.

"You...will...bring..." The King's chest heaved with every arduous word. He licked his scaly lips and yanked Hiran close. Hiran flinched, bracing for damnation as his father's spittle touched his ear. "*Ruin....*"

Those were the last words of the mighty Shadow King.

Commotion and chaos ensued, and through it all the Queen's cold glare remained fixed on Hiran. But the thing about this realm was that there weren't many places to hide, especially when the masses followed prophecy and a vengeful Queen. Upon her orders, several soldiers subdued a terrified Hiran, his frail sister, and their vicious mother, who had taken out a throat or two.

"Spare my son!" she lamented, her hands drenched in the blood of those once sworn to protect her.

Holika's face fell; her crestfallen gaze snapped to Hiran. If he could manage any words, he'd tell her that she was more important than him. After all, she was a dreamreaver. Why had everyone forgotten the importance of that? Who would save the realm if they couldn't reach the outside worlds?

Holika stopped struggling against her binds, her glare chilled. "I'll protect him," she said, her voice eerily quiet and alarmingly cold. "And the *realm* will protect *me*. Goodbye, Mother."

The crowds demanded immolation, gathering all the consorts and their children and binding them. *Royal asuras fed the realm.*

For the first time, Ma hugged Holika. Holika, in turn, sprouted her wings free of their binds and cradled Hiran, wrapping her wings around herself and her brother. Hiran, in turn, curled into a fetal position as the mob doused them and lit the flame.

"Sati! Sati!" The demand for widow burning echoed around them in a chorus of barbarity, drowned out by Ma's wretched screams. Holika hissed in the flourish of heat. Hiran whimpered as a flame slipped between the bodies of his sister and mother and singed his wings. He choked on scalding air, his thoughts floundering toward the new king. Tarak. The same boy who had asked whether Hiran's horns and wings would burn like skin or bone.

Everything blistered and crackled around him, the inferno reaching a roaring crescendo.

"HIRAN?" A SOFT VOICE BECKONED. "PLEASE SAY SOMETHING. Anything."

Hiran pried open his eyes, the lashes of which had turned into a mantle of ash. He managed a grunt, his throat and chest sore, his entire body tingling. Holika's body and the wings that had entombed them unfurled as the weight of Ma's ashes crumbled and sloughed off.

The masses were gone; only smoldering pillars remained, burnt sacrifices to a brutal realm. Hiran could not fly with singed wings, so they ran to the only place Holika could think of. They came to a stop at the looming stairs leading into the rotund arena of the Court of Nightmares. A breeze circulated through the enclosure atop the hill. Vines slithered toward Hiran, hungry for flesh, as Holika ran up the stairs faster than Hiran could bear.

"Wait!" he called after her, but Holika had dipped into the darkness of the arching entryway. In another moment, a wall of vines and red-orange flowers separated the siblings, for they would not allow him entrance. The vines snapped and slashed until he tumbled down the staircase and rolled toward the river that had once fed the pool of dreams.

"Little boy," a throaty voice called behind him.

Hiran turned to face a pair of murky sage-green eyes protruding from the water. A matsya. Beneath the distorting waves lurked the upper body of a girl with the lower half of a large fish.

"My name is Netra. I can help you," she said, her voice sweet and mesmerizing. The strange young girl rose from the river as she neared Hiran. Long green hair clung to her chest.

Hiran couldn't look away. That was their myth. The alluring voice and gaze that dragged both asuras and monsters to their watery deaths. But, all things considered, falling into the cold clutches of her webbed hands in this peaceful trance seemed like the best way to die.

So he went with her.

AS HIRAN'S VISION ALIGNED, PIECES OF HIS INNOCENCE floated away like memories shaved off his soul.

Kill or be killed. The Gloom sounded different: deeper, rougher. It *felt* different: thicker, darker. It had burgeoned into a shadow blinking in Hiran's periphery. It sat there quietly, patiently. Terror seized Hiran, for he had never seen the Gloom materialized in his mind before.

"Hiran?" a soft voice beckoned, pulling him away.

Hiran startled to find Holika in front of him, her knees to her chest, her arms wrapped around them as she intently studied her little brother. Her eyes were wide. His sister was scared.

"Are we dead?" he asked.

She pushed back her hair and offered a vague smile. "I don't know."

He went to hug his sister, but Holika scuttled backward. Was she afraid of him? Did she believe what others did, that he'd brought the plague?

"You shouldn't," she said, and gave that small, sad smile again. "Do you know what happened to you?"

He shook his head.

"That girl, the matsya?"

He flinched, not wanting to know how she'd killed him—by drowning or devouring.

"She took you to the end of the river and left you on its bank. You passed out from the speed beneath the water. But you have to wake up. Now. You need to get to the ferry on the Vaitarani. The Ferryman is waiting to take you."

"Take me where?"

She shrugged.

"I don't want to go."

"Then you'll die," she whimpered, biting her lip.

Hiran panicked. "I don't understand. If I'm not dead, then how are you talking to me?"

"You're asleep, and I'm...in the Court of Nightmares. So this is a dream."

"You're alive!" Hiran laughed, relieved.

Holika's sullen expression gave him pause. "No. Not like you. I'm...finally part of the Court. My body is at the bottom of the pool of dreams, and I'm not allowed to leave.

"This," she added with a wave of her hand, "is now my eternal abode. But don't worry. We'll be together when you sleep."

"No—no," he cried.

"Shh, little brother. It'll be all right. I'll always protect you. You see, everyone needs to sleep. And when our enemies slumber, I'll be there to turn the tides of their fate."

A SEASON CAME AND WENT. HIRAN WAS STILL A YOUNG BOY, only a few inches taller, now living on the vessel that ferried the dead. A mass floated down the river, colliding into the ferry. The impact jarred the nest of coiled bodies. Angry dead hissed at the boat, languidly reaching toward the wood-and-metal vessel as segments of flesh peeled off their corpses.

"Gross, but sort of interesting," Rohan said, his big black eyes wistful. The Ferryman's only child, and Hiran's only friend, hungered for excitement.

The Vaitarani—also called the Blood River, for obvious reasons—was a waterway of dead ending abruptly at jagged cliffs. Because the ferry could never go over the edge, it eased itself to a stop, pressing the nest of entangled dead against an invisible wall. A dozen corpses chained to the front of the ferry, fitted with collars to pull the vessel, moaned in annoyance.

Hiran was safest here, even if *safest* wasn't that safe. Below, the vilest of souls floated in the viscous, deadly waters of blood, guts, bones, and the pernicious poison halahala. His gaze darted to the top tier of the ferry, where the comfort of those who'd passed peacefully in good fortune created individual bubbles of shimmering air. These ones glided down the cabin steps to the starboard side, where a ramp groaned open.

Beautiful ghosts with the solidity of real bodies stepped onto the ramp, activating a rainbow bridge. They walked through a white mist to the Vermilion Mahal. The mesmerizing colors of the bridge were beyond comprehension, but such a thing of beauty made sense where the Nightmare Realm blurred and seeped into Patala. Asuras could never venture past this point—when they died, they returned to shadows to add to the dome. And the living weren't allowed.

Then there were the unrighteous on board, tormented by their own detestable deeds. They vacillated between meeting their eternal judgment or trying to make an escape—only there was no escape.

Some went mad seeing the truth around them, for the worse they'd been in life, the more nightmarish things they saw. These ones plunged overboard to their death beyond death, adding to the Blood River. Among them had been a man from the mortal realm called the Famed One, a slayer of monsters who'd killed a daayan. She was merely a monstrous-looking woman, oddly shaped with a slinky body and bent neck, her long hair perpetually covering her face. She'd done nothing but wail in her grief, a sound like a haunting, and he'd mistaken her for a dangerous monster. In retaliation, her kin skinned the slayer while he'd been trapped in his body during sleep paralysis. He could not accept his fate and now floated among the masses in the Blood River.

A short while ago, another slayer and his wife journeyed down the Vaitarani. They'd been slain by monsters and had accepted their fate, crossing the rainbow bridge into their eternity. Albeit with great sadness as they had left behind two children. Hearing this, Rohan commented, "I wonder if they're slayers, too."

"Doesn't seem like a great end for their kind," Hiran replied as the ferry turned course. Up and down the river, one pass after another. No wonder Rohan sought adventure before he was destined to take over as Ferryman. Hiran was already bored.

The wooden railing encompassing the vessel groaned when Rohan leaned against it. Red mist curled around them but never touched the ferry. Instead, it parted like a fog that dared not cross the likes of the Ferryman. Below, in the curdling waters, the dead wailed.

Rohan rolled his eyes and yelled down, "You chose this!" The corpses quieted. Glancing at Hiran, he asked, "Do you still hear them?"

There were few secrets between the boys. Hiran stepped onto his tiptoes to peer over the railing. Another nest had formed, latching onto the ferry like barnacles. They gleefully looked up at him, some with partially rotted faces, others with one eyeball in an otherwise-exposed socket. Hiran winced. When one fell away, caught in the carmine current, another took its place. A message sent along from one corpse to another, never breaking the pattern or the flow of information.

"The Queen Mother is dead..." a corpse called from below.

Hiran looked to Rohan and replied drolly, "Yes. They won't shut up."

Rohan planted his chubby chin in between the bars to look down. "I wonder why. I mean, why you hear them. I imagine they don't have anything better to do than chatter."

Hiran thought back to what Holika had once told him. She'd slipped into their mother's dreams and learned that Ma had consumed hala-hala while she was pregnant with him. Perhaps the poison of the dead had seeped into his mind. Perhaps this was what the white plague had recognized in his blood, for the Vaitarani straddled both realms.

He watched pieces of rot fall off the corpses as another said, "She died in the most gruesome way...."

Another added, "So unlike the royals..."

"You're not supposed to speak to me," Hiran spat at them.

"And you are not supposed to hear," they remarked.

"Yet here we all are," another commented.

"The dead and the boy who hears the dead."

"The Gatekeeper thought to be ash."

"As we were saying..."

"Let us tell you of how the Queen Mother died."

Hiran clenched his eyes shut. He didn't want to communicate with the dead. "Don't you get tired of them?" he asked Rohan.

Rohan pulled away from the bars and massaged his face. "I've learned to drown them out." He cracked a smile. "No pun intended."

Hiran smirked. If halahala had remained in his blood and enabled him to hear the dead, then being born from the Blood River must've given Rohan and the Ferryman the same gift. If it could be called such a thing.

"The royal gutted herself," the nest went on, one corpse falling away and another seamlessly taking its place. "Entrails and blood all over the royal shrines."

"Could she have been distraught over the late King's passing?"

"Did someone kill her?"

"Who could've done such a thing?"

Then they all glared up at Hiran and asked as one, "Yes. *Who* could've done such a thing?"

THREE

ESHANI
(FIVE YEARS AGO)

The shades remained true to their word and let the naga pass, devouring the soldiers who gave chase through the marshlands. The shades had not taken Eshani that day. The bargain hovered over her, a low cloud threatening to burst. There was little time to ponder between battling to survive, escaping a jungle set on fire, and sending Manisha away to the safety of the floating mountains.

The twins had discerned that the King searched for a nagin in particular.

"Do you remember the stories Nani would tell us at bedtime?" Eshani whispered in the evening as they crouched in the canopy.

Sithara nodded, wiping her forehead with a green dupatta. Eshani recalled the tales of old and how their maternal lineage flowed from great serpent queens. Of how the first nagin was born between realms, and thus inherited the ability to cross realms. Among her descendants were a special few: the most potent nagin—girls who possessed ancient abilities to heal and kill. They took to their bosoms one of the most tortured and despised creatures: the serpent. In all its lovely glory, it became a thing to fear. The two became one, an unbreakable bond.

"Do you think the legends are true?" Eshani asked.

"That a nagin with dormant powers would rise during a time of devastation and destruction like no other? Have we not seen such a time already? It's just a story. Only we can save us."

Sithara had outgrown the idea of magic, but Eshani still believed. She felt it when she pressed a hand against tree limbs to steady herself. Ghostly whispers of pain and suffering the tree had seen—what the army had done—trickled into her mind. The tree told her where to find nearby enemies, the ones who had burned the trees with no remorse. The trees grieved.

Eshani jerked her chin toward the east. Sithara followed. Tree limb to tree limb, bows and arrows secured to their backs. When they came upon soldiers, Sithara placed a finger to her lips and indicated they should strike. Eshani set a hand on her sister's shoulder and shook her head. Sithara's green eyes flashed like angry emeralds, but she complied.

That night Sithara asked, "Why did you stop me from killing those soldiers?"

"I don't like how you're so good at this."

"It's either we kill them or they kill us. We didn't start this war, but we will *not* die in it." Sithara huffed, drawing her knees to her chest, her back hitting the tree trunk behind her.

"Please be careful. Don't turn into one of them."

"If we kill them now, they won't be able to come after us later. And for all we know, their hands are bathed in the blood of our kin."

"Just listen to me, sister. Our hearts can't grow dark. Once they do, there may be no coming back. Think of our parents, who taught us to be kind and gentle and loving—to be the ones who turn tides when the tides aim to destroy us."

Sithara sneered. "I think of Papa, who died because of *them*."

Eshani gripped her sister's forearm. "Don't lose who you are because of what they've done."

"We have to be killers *and* healers, fighters *and* leaders. We have to be everything now. Because we *are* everything. We're the last. Do you not understand?" Sithara countered.

Neither girl said anything after that.

Eshani fell asleep sometime later but awoke to the sound of crunching leaves. She immediately sat up, her braid falling from her shoulder, to find her sister cleaning her blade by the firelight. Blood and dirt covered her already-grimy kurta and leggings, her dark brown hair in disarray from its knot. "Oh no. What have you done? Don't tell me..."

Sithara, in all her fierceness, trembled as she met Eshani's eyes. Shadows from the waning fire danced across her long, thin face as she said, "I think Papa would want justice and to know his daughters are strong enough to do this."

Eshani gaped at her sister for a long while, a torrent of emotions streaming through her. She couldn't quite tell what she felt. Disgust, fear that Sithara's heart had grown dark, remorse that she hadn't been there for her, pain knowing that her sister might never be the same, despair that none of them would ever be normal again.

"Are you going to admonish me?"

Eshani shook her head. Sithara was only doing what she thought needed to be done to protect herself, to protect what remained of their family. No matter how hard Eshani tried to remain resolute that killing was wrong, she knew that those soldiers *were* too close to the naga camp. That had things been reversed, the soldiers would've killed them on sight. *This* was their world now.

She slid a comforting hand, speckled in dirt, over Sithara's shaking fingers splattered in red. Sithara whimpered, but never once did she cry.

MANY DAYS CAME AND WENT IN A BLUR OF RUNNING, HIDING, foraging, and fighting. Many times, Sithara lowered Eshani's arrow and took the kill herself.

"It's not because I enjoy this," Sithara promised. "You are a gentle soul, and I am not."

Tears filled Eshani's eyes. She didn't want her sister to bear this.

"I'm strong enough," Sithara promised, her voice sad. "I won't topple into madness. This is the path I've accepted. I am a child no more."

Anguish squeezed Eshani's chest.

What remained of the naga gathered at the great Yamuna River. Flames lapped at their heels, ash rained from the canopy, and the burnt remains of the jungle sent their final wails of pain into Eshani every time she brushed against a tree, a branch, a shrub.

Sithara limped along. Eshani rubbed Lekha's blood-crusted snout. She purred, tilting down from her monstrous height. Eshani led the tiger to the edge of the water and bathed her, unmatting her fur, rubbing salve on her wounds, and promising, "I'll find you some fruit soon, and flowers and soap for a proper bath."

All along the winding river stood scattered naga, exhausted but defiant. Refugees of a war they did not ask for. Survivors of horrors they'd never dreamt of. They were resilience embodied; they were the last.

An auntie looked to Mama and asked, "Where do we go from here?"

Ahead, the Great River glistened as far as the eye could see, north toward the borders and south toward the sea. It was deep and wide, filled with murky waters and dangerous creatures. Eshani could barely make out the trees on the other side, much less anything lurking beneath the deceptively peaceful surface. If only her abilities with nature allowed her to ask the trees and roots and water vegetation to create a bridge.

She closed her eyes and willed such an impossibly marvelous thing. Pebbles quaked beneath her soles, but that was more likely the advancing army behind them. Her shoulders slouched. *Ridiculous* was an understatement. To think such things could happen, much less by her hand.

"We have no choice except to cross," Mama said.

"How?" Another had joined, along with her daughters and son.

Mama stepped into the water. She wobbled as the liquid rose higher, to her ankles and calves and finally to her knees, dampening her torn green leggings.

Lekha lowered her head between the sharp, raised angles of her shoulder blades. She'd stilled, stalking. One ear twitched, arching back and then forward, searching for sound. Warbling birds and skittering rodents, lumbering creatures and swinging monkeys, fluttering insects, rustling leaves, gushing water, and clamoring soldiers in the distance.

But Lekha knew more. Her hair bristled. She snarled, curling her lip over sharp fangs. She paced the edge of the river, around Mama.

A warning.

"Mama!" Eshani lurched toward them, but Lekha stood between her and her mother.

Mama raised her hand, silencing Eshani as Lekha bucked her back out of the water. A gentle motion made by a massive body nearly toppled Eshani.

Sithara grabbed her sister by the waist and held her back. The twins gaped at the ripples in the distance, ridges forming sideways to the current, a triangular movement heading for their mother. Others on the riverbank gasped and muttered, some calling for Mama to return to the safety of the sand, but a woman on a mission to save the last of her people had made her choice.

Something breached the surface several feet away, in the parts of the river that were deeper than a sea. Eshani held her breath, waiting to meet the monsters within. Legends spoke of colossal squids taller than canyons, flesh-eating mermaids, and tiny slugs more venomous than vipers.

Instead, a woman emerged. Long dark sodden hair lay heavy on her head and covered her breasts like a second skin. She rose to sit upright, shoulders back, her discerning gaze sweeping over the river-bank dotted with desperate naga.

She listed her head to the right as if listening to something.

Lekha growled, and Eshani wrapped an arm around the tiger's neck to quiet her. Her eyes darted to her mother, who hadn't shown signs of retreat. Neither twin was fast enough to wade through the river to get to their mother should something attack. Still, Sithara took a breath and placed an arrow in the notch of her bow.

The woman in the water floated closer, and it wasn't until she was well within spearing range that the naga could see the beast on which she was mounted. A broad back of horns in various sizes breached the surface. Yellow eyes glared back, half submerged. There was a giant beneath the surface.

Lekha stood protectively at Mama's side, her head once again low-ered. Her shoulders rolled back, spectacularly smooth, with each methodical step. She paused, one paw forward in prime attack mode. At this, the woman and the beast paused.

She raised her chin and asked, "What do you want?"

"We seek safe passage across the river," Mama replied.

"For what reason?"

Mama hesitated. "We seek asylum from the King's army."

"And you trust us?"

"Are you not the yakshini? Benevolent protectors of the Great River?"

"Come closer."

"Mama, no," Sithara said. But her mother hushed her.

"Lekha, come," Mama said instead, and Lekha obeyed.

Eshani trudged into the river, even as Lekha swatted her back with her tail. Lekha allowed Mama to climb onto her. Sitting atop the golden giant, sunlight breaking over her in a halo, her trident strapped to her back, Mama had truly transformed from gardener to goddess, bathed in the glory of her foremothers.

She gave a reassuring nod to the twins and clucked her tongue. Lekha moved forward until her paws no longer reached the riverbed. She cautiously swam toward the yakshini, steeling herself against the current while keeping a good distance, beast from beast.

The two women spoke for an inarguably long time. Voices and clanking weapons sounded from the jungles, the smoke nearing. The naga prepared for their last battle. Many created a final line in the sand, facing the towering ferns and trees, weapons ready as ash floated toward them, a bitterness carried by the breeze, their backs to the dangers in an already-deadly river.

How best to die? By battle wounds, scorched by fire, or a watery death?

Eshani nocked an arrow on her bow, nodding once to her sister. They stilled. Several sets of ripples disrupted the surface of the river, cutting across the current and slowly heading toward them.

Makara. Water dragons like giant crocodiles pierced the water. First horns, then backs and heads and those glowing yellow eyes.

Mama returned and dismounted to spread the word as naga crowded the river's edge.

"The yaksha will help," Mama declared, a quiver of fear in her otherwise-smooth voice. "New friends in the unlikeliest of places.

Take your last stand now or flee to fight another day. I assure you that day will come."

Behind her, a few makara turned into a hundred floating boulders dotting the river as smoke choked the air. Most had yaksha on their backs. The yakshini who had spoken with Mama came closer.

Those on the shores gasped and backed away as a giant, lumbering makara walked onto land, the movement jostling the woman on its back.

"My name is Kumari," she said, swinging her leg over horns to fluidly dismount. "We'll take you across."

The kingdom's forces couldn't cross the width of the Great River or endure the monsters in its depths. The yakshini, in all their cold, watery glory, were the freest despite being tied to the river.

An arrow whistled through the air, landing in front of the makara. Agitation marked the beast's features as it snapped its head toward the jungles. Before Eshani could grab Sithara and run to their mother, a dozen makara leapt from the river and raced toward the trees.

Monstrous jaws snapped bones in half and swallowed soldiers whole.

There was no time to decide which danger was worse. The twins followed their mother onto the backs of water dragons that sank into the river as deep as a sea.

"Wait! Lekha!" Eshani twisted precariously on a makara's horn-studded back.

Lekha paced the sand, her gaze never leaving Eshani. Eshani's pleading call was returned with a whimper, but Lekha didn't follow. These waters were not for her.

A young yakshini by the name of Vishali sat in front of the twins and commanded their makara to swim.

"She'll ride!" Eshani bellowed over the rapids, but she knew as well as anyone that tigers would not ride water dragons.

"A boat!" Eshani exclaimed. "Someone must have a boat!"

"Eshani, please..." Mama pleaded above the sound of gushing waves, sitting firmly on a makara not far away.

"We must leave," Sithara murmured, sadness heavy in her tone.

"Lekha! Come!" But no matter how much Eshani beckoned, the tiger was a free being. Lekha was not a pet, nor did anyone own her. This was Lekha's decision, and she'd decided to stay.

Eshani hadn't thought her young heart could break even more than it had already, yet here she was, cradling her emotions against her chest. She kept her sobs deep within her, her soul fracturing.

She'd thought losing Papa and having to leave Manisha had pushed her to the very edge, that she was unable to bear any more grief. But she was wrong. Everything was so wrong.

Sithara hugged her sister from behind, whispering, "It's time to go."

Just as Papa had said when he'd left for war, as Mama had said when they sent Manisha to the floating temple. *It's time to go* would forever herald forced goodbyes and shattered hearts.

Lekha swung her head toward the jungle and faced the army. Her deafening roar could be heard for miles, rendering soldiers immobile and easily killed. One swipe after another. One powerful bite after another. Until Lekha, the cub Eshani had loved for so long, was dripping in the blood of their enemies.

KURMA WAS REAL. THE LEGENDS SPOKE OF A GIANT SEA turtle who lived in the incomprehensible vastness of an ocean without borders, an ocean that had swallowed entire homelands.

Long boats were moored to the clifflike edge of Kurma's shell, for Kurma was so big that one couldn't tell where the giant ended and where the sea began. It was a mountain floating in the waves, its back covered with forest and moss. A perpetually moving island.

The naga climbed onto the steplike ridges as the people welcomed them.

"We've awaited your return," a woman said to Mama, her expression one of sorrow and joy. She looked at the twins as if she'd been yearning to see them for years. She touched the tops of their heads in a gentle gesture, the way Eshani's grandparents and parents had done. A simple laying of the hand that conveyed a range of love and longing and pride.

"Do they not know?" she asked Mama.

"They will know now," Mama simply replied.

"Let's first get you settled," the woman said.

The naga shuffled after the stranger, welcomed by Kurma's inhabitants as twilight unfurled across the evening sky. Eshani looked behind her. The land where she'd been born vanished. Kurma was swimming away.

Panic seized her heart. "What about Manisha? Lekha?"

"We'll go back for them," Sithara promised, holding her sister's hand.

Bells chimed all around, a lovely musical cadence bringing out fireflies and the glow of bioluminescent vines and flowers.

"What's happening?" Eshani gasped as water rose to the cliffs. "We're diving!"

Mama rushed toward the twins and hugged them close, saying, "Shh. It's all right. We won't drown. Look."

Ahead, a translucent wall shimmered as it took shape. A dome covered the entire island without ever touching the tops of the canopy. Eshani's stomach roiled as Kurma gently plummeted into the ocean. She held her breath, watching water rise, and, with it, the underworld of the sea. Marine life of all sizes swam around them. Some moved in thick schools with sudden shifts in direction, light glimmering off their scales in dancing motions. Some swam in pairs or alone. They were all sorts of splendid colors, bursts of sunflower yellow and rose red, mango orange and sapphire blue. There were pods of dolphins in the distance, and beyond, a thick murkiness.

There could be anything out there.

If Kurma existed, then sea monsters surely existed, too.

After settling into homes built into large trees, the twins never let their mother out of their sight. They clung to her like they clung to life, and she to them.

"The legends are true," Mama told her daughters as they ascended spiraling steps on the trunk of their new tree home, steps made from sturdy mushrooms growing out of the bark.

The twins followed Mama to the kitchen. Eshani touched her necklace, gifted to her by her grandmother. Manisha had received a bangle, Sithara an arm cuff, and their mother a ring. Each piece had been carved from delicate gold and cradled an oval amber stone. Mama's ring glinted in the glow of bioluminescent flowers growing along the walls.

She went on, peeling root vegetables for dinner, "The naga are from a different place. Centuries ago, our foremothers and forefathers left home to venture into the world. Home is a place of true splendor, with dazzling gems and resplendent palaces, beautiful vegetation and waterfalls, libraries that kiss the sky. Anand is one of the new homes we built because, some time ago, the world flooded during a war between primordial titans, and our true home is now underwater.

"With the flood came sea monsters and giant creatures, like Kurma. Kurma is alive, a floating island, but also a biosphere. Kurma is benevolent and giving, allowing its people to live on its back in order to search for long-lost civilizations and study their ruins. Our true home may be in ruins and the naga thought lost to the oceanic world. But no matter where we reside, we will never be lost. For we will always know who we are."

Here, for a while, they would be safe. But Eshani wept for Manisha and Lekha and Papa every night. She kept her sobs from Mama, so as not to add to her burden, but Sithara knew. Her twin held her hand and let her cry without a word in this wondrous new place.

Kurma was a home between homes, a place where the naga could dip out of existence, away from the fiery reach of the King.

At least for now.

FOUR

HIRAN
(FOUR MORTAL-REALM YEARS AGO)

The Vaitarani had swelled with an influx of dead from the mortal realm due to something called the Fire Wars. The term made Hiran's skin prickle with the remembrance of flames washing over his wings. The season of the Fire Wars had come and gone. The ferrying dead had returned to manageable numbers. On the heels of normalcy came the news of Tarak's wedding, the near last of the royals succumbing to the plague, the increasing scarcity of food, and the worrying speed at which the borderlands were crumbling.

The dakini couldn't keep up their work, and the Gloom inside Hiran bristled with the need to help. While Hiran knew there was nothing he could do, the Gloom grew agitated. The realm was calling to him.

The shadow dome emitted a distant hum that reached across the river like a claw attempting to ensnare him. He did not want to heed the call of the shadows, nor did he want the crown. But the Gloom craved freedom.

"A boy needs to fly," the Ferryman told Hiran. The Ferryman

pointedly looked at Hiran's shoulder blades, where his tucked wings may or may not have been absorbed into his body after so long.

"And take that one with you," he grunted, jerking his chin toward Rohan.

Rohan, taller but still gangly, grinned. No one had to tell him twice to get off the boat.

Thus, the boys traveled far and wide, meeting one villager after another in careful stride. No one recognized Hiran, much less hunted him. Why should they? They'd never seen him as a child to know what he looked like and had no reason to believe he'd survived immolation. Even then, Hiran had grown several feet, his shoulders had widened, and he'd developed modest but strong muscles from working on the ferry. With the gifts inherited from his mother, he was even able to manipulate the appearance of his horns and the color of his eyes. Hiding his identity had become second nature.

Hiran donned a fresh black kurta with matching pants and tied back his royally uncut hair, tucking it into the back of his kurta. He was walking alongside Rohan when something stirred in the pit of his belly. He paused, unsure if the sensation was hunger or exhaustion.

"You shouldn't have eaten those scorpions from the vendor back there," Rohan admonished.

"You ate three!"

Rohan tapped his belly. "My stomach is iron."

Hiran bowled over in sudden, intense pain.

"Are you okay?" a girl up ahead asked. Behind her, several dakini scavenged for material. "Are you infected?"

"No," Hiran grunted.

Unlike the dakini, neither he nor Rohan had their masks activated, as neither could get infected, and it was clear they did not possess the white lesions of the plague.

Swirls of green peered out from beneath the girl's hooded cloak, which concealed most of her head. Plated armor covered her long dark kurta, blending into leggings, and a scabbard gleamed at her waist. Her movements were languid on a lanky body.

"He's fine," Rohan said, awkwardly staring at the girl.

She pressed the corner of her angular mask. The stiff material laced with metal gills pulled back to reveal her face, plump with the roundness of youth. A heavy breeze pushed back the hood from her temple, revealing a perfectly oblong head, bald and covered in intricate green markings, which made for a striking contrast against the glow of her light gray skin. She hurried to pull up the hood, her cheeks flushing.

Rohan pushed back curls from his forehead and grinned so that the points of his short fangs gleamed.

The girl tamped down a smile. "My name's Vidya. And this is my friend Shruti."

A second girl had approached, only to roll her glossy white eyes and tug Vidya back into the fold of the shadow-wielding workers. Both girls were about Hiran and Rohan's age, in the throes of budding maturity.

Despite Rohan's response, Hiran was *not* fine. The Gloom lurking in him sizzled and burned and bubbled up from the pit of his being. He wiped sweat from his brow, glancing toward the purple clouds to the right. Behind Rohan, a forked tongue slithered down from a tree. No, wait. It slithered *out* of the tree. Razor-sharp ridges sprang out from the sides as it darted for the girls.

While the first reaction of a tentative boy like Hiran was to stare in shock, the Gloom inside him, the lineage of a Shadow King, reacted. It slipped into his blood, taking over his movements. Hiran unsheathed his sword, pushing Rohan out of the way, and ran right into the path of the devouring monster.

The girls screamed as its tongue lashed within inches of their heads. Hiran immediately activated his mask and intercepted the tongue with his sword. The long piece of muscle, oozing foul saliva, wrapped around the weapon and yanked it back, sending Hiran flying along with it. He instantly regretted intervening.

In those harrowing seconds careening through the air toward what was undeniably the gaping mouth of a ravenous tree monster, Hiran knew he probably wouldn't survive. Not when he hurtled toward a jaw unhinging to accommodate his size, a mouth filled with oscillating teeth and an expulsion of greenish sludge with a stench that would make the toes of the dead curl and snap off.

He held up his hands to protect his face from impact, an impact that sent his bones rattling and nearly knocked him unconscious. As the tree monster thrashed him about, arrows and shadows pierced the air from behind him, barely missing his head. Several sank deep into the monster's trunk. It wailed and dropped Hiran, who fell to the mossy ground with a painful thud.

Rohan was immediately at Hiran's side, struggling to get him up as the monster curled over them. The boys prepared for impact, a crushing fall that never came—for the dakini were using shadow skill to hold the creature back.

"Get out of there!" The girls yanked them from beneath the massive floating beast.

The boys scurried away and jumped to their feet. Wheezing, Hiran bent over and wiped ooze from his mask. Rohan laughed between pants.

"That was so brave!" Vidya declared but was clearly shaken.

"That was so stupid!" Shruti lamented at the same time.

Vidya shook her head and turned to Hiran. "Thank you! What's your name?"

"He's a nameless boy," Rohan replied.

The girls frowned with understanding and nodded. Many orphaned boys were nameless.

"I should be the one thanking you," Hiran confessed, cradling his ribs. "You saved me."

"We have to help each other out here," Vidya replied.

Behind her, the dakini had already dismantled the beast, extracting shadow from it to repair the dome. Using their wrists and hands in sweeping motions, they drew wisps of dark mist from the monster's pores until a stream of shadow slithered out. The dakini pulled out every particle of shadow matter, handing it off to another team of three who swept the mass into a tight dark ball so that it loomed above their heads and floated toward a crack in the shadow dome. The beast, dried and decrepit, sank into the ground.

"At least we have some shadow mass. We desperately needed it," Shruti said.

An elder dakini approached, her rank evident by her tall stature and the purple stripe down the side of her long kurta and leggings. She invited the boys to stay with them, allowing Hiran to heal. While Rohan relished the attention, Hiran remained quiet, fearful that they would discover who he was and report him to the King.

Shruti eyed him, noting, "Don't see many asuras with horns."

Although Hiran had inherited slight shape-shifting gifts from his mother, he couldn't use them to erase the horns—only to shorten them. "How many have you seen?"

She shrugged. Out here, she probably hadn't seen many. She added, "Interesting blue markings."

His cheeks warmed. How many in the realm possessed the markings he shared with his mother? And how many outside the palace had seen her to know that she had the markings in the first place?

Thankfully, Shruti didn't press. She was no older than him, and even if she had seen his mother, she wouldn't have remembered much.

The elder dakini told the boys, "We could use extra eyes and hands."

"Really?" Hiran asked, glancing at an ecstatic Rohan.

The elder sighed. "But you require a *lot* of training."

Embarrassment flooded Hiran. Still, he had nowhere else to go, and Rohan didn't want to return to the ferry. So they stayed and trained as if their lives depended on it. After some time, the elder dakini presented Hiran a weapon upon open palms. "A fighter must be well equipped."

He took the metal katar, decorated with lines of gold and silver and tipped in black diamond. The triangular blade sat heavy, but when fitted to his wrist, it became a natural extension of his arm aligned with his knuckles. He jabbed the air, his fingers curling into a fist over the handlebar. His punches would now kill with the force of his entire body.

When he jerked, pressing the handlebar with extra pressure, the blade split open, revealing an additional blade inside, slender and sapphire. A triple blade. A scissor katar.

"Nameless boy," the elder dakini said. "You shall remain with us. You will never master shadow, but you can master killing."

A warm sensation crept through Hiran. The Gloom was pleased.

"WAKE UP, WAKE UP, SUNSHINE," HOLIKA CROONED.

Hiran groaned. "What's sunshine?"

"Light from a bright star. Unlike the barbaric light from Patala, it's quite soothing and marks the time for waking up."

Hiran sat up to find Holika merrily studying his face. She slowly smiled, displaying sharp teeth. "You've grown!"

"Where have you been?" he demanded, noting how his sister had subtly aged. She was taller, although still gangly, her hair longer, her face slimmer.

She shrugged. "Wandering a multitude of dreams, lost in the dreamscape, walking into too many minds. I couldn't get out. But I've returned! And I've learned much."

Hiran furrowed his brow. "So . . . the Court of Nightmares knows of you?"

"Of course."

"Then . . . how does Tarak not know that you survived?"

"I made a deal with the Court. I promised to help them if they didn't tell anyone that I'm in the pool. I claimed anonymity alleviates stress. Yes, they serve the crown, and if Tarak specifically asked, they would have to tell him. But why would Tarak ever think of asking such a thing? He doesn't have reason to believe anyone could survive immolation." Her eyes flitted to the corner, and a smile plastered itself uneasily to her face as she muttered, "What's that?"

The materialized Gloom floated off to the side, an ambiguous shadow mass that silhouetted him. Hiran groaned. It had *grown*. "I don't know. Father's bloodline, maybe? Don't you know? You don't have it inside you?"

"No. This thing was but a speck before." Holika shook her head and walked around the mass. It faced her at every step, unthreatening but curious. "I will figure you out."

Hiran explained, "It's growing stronger and feels like a darkness trying to make me do things as Father would. With violence."

"Let's call it a . . . tenebrosity!"

"I don't even know what that means."

"Darkness, shadow, gloom and doom."

Both it and Hiran shrugged. *The Gloom* was easier.

Holika turned to Hiran and exclaimed, "You're traveling the realm,

I see! And no one recognizes you. I don't think Tarak would, either, after all this time. The Queen Mother might, but...well, you know about her."

Holika's eyes shone with triumph and her mouth curled in confession. Hiran's heart palpitated with each word, yet he didn't recoil when she touched his cheek. "Don't be afraid, little brother. The evil Queen is dead."

"You shouldn't have killed her."

"She killed herself."

He grunted, lifting a skeptical brow.

Holika leaned forward. Nothing could steal her joy, sadistic though it was. "She peeled off her skin. Carved out her muscles. Artistically, too, making mehndi designs. So creative, the Queen! She hollowed out her eyes, like those nasty fish she liked to eat while our mother cried."

Holika gestured wildly, as if playing out the gory scene. "She pulled out her entrails like plump, slippery threads, and wrapped them around Father's burial pillars. Poetic, isn't it? Like she wanted to be one with her lover."

She spun and spun, her arms out wide. "Not the usual burning of widows like she enforced upon us."

Suddenly, Holika stopped. Her voice was eerily calm as she said, "I did none of those things, brother. She was wide awake and alert when she tortured herself to death. Her beautiful entrails snaked around Father's pillar as she knelt before it, lifeless. On her knees. As she'd instructed us to be when she set us on fire."

Hiran trembled, but the Gloom chuckled.

"Didn't I tell you that I would turn the tides of the fates of those who hurt us?" Holika sighed dramatically. "One down, but I can't get into Tarak's head to do anything to him." She harrumphed, crossing her arms and scowling off to the side. "The Court of Nightmares is protecting him from me the way I'm protecting you from them. But I did glean news from those around him."

She waved a hand in the air. Colored swirls morphed into distinct details of marble and moss, of mist and malice. Hiran seethed at the sight of the arena, drenched in illustrious gray, brimming with shadows, and beating with the slithering pulse of the flesh-devouring vines that had barricaded him from his sister. A treble of anxiety spiked through him.

"It's all right," Holika assured him. "Cathartic, even, to conjure this place and look it in the eye—the place that severed us and stole me. Feel whatever you want to feel here. Destroy, vent, release it all. This is a safe place for us, brother."

Instead of releasing his emotions, Hiran embraced them. Sadness, pain, remorse, loss, rage.

Ahead, mist floated off the surface of the pool of dreams. The water glowed, revealing an incomprehensible depth. *This* was Holika's watery grave. His heart hurt for her.

He looked up and around. The pool was surrounded by monstrous statues—the Court of Nightmares towered like mighty gods of monochrome gray, still and silent, asleep but aware. They were composed as such: terror, jealousy, anxiety, despair, torment, falsehoods, lust, greed, guilt. The massive marble statues stood guard around the pool, cloaked in saris and flowing chaniyas, in elaborate kurtas and billowing dhotis, encrusted with jewels as old as time.

In between the staggering statues were large, lavish mirrors, deceptively beautiful. Some, broken and fractured, dipped beneath the water. Something moved along the reflections. A twisted limb, a shadow serpent, breaking off as it crossed each mirror and mirror fragments.

Hiran's heart stilled and he immediately looked down. Horrors lived in mirrors. Hiran had no plans to meet them. Even though he knew this wasn't real. His sister's skills were artful mastery beyond anything he could ever think to create.

"I was stuck in those things for a long while," Holika explained. "The fragments are false gateways into other realms where ethereal beings, like me, can traverse dreams. It's why no one sleeps in front of mirrors—that's the fastest way to invite nightmares, you know?"

"Your skills have come a long way. I'm impressed and a bit scared."

"I'm a builder and an artist and a storyteller and a spy all in one. Dreamreaver?" She scoffed, blowing on her nails. "Shall we call it what it really is? I am a *dream architect*. I create entire worlds. And then destroy them if I wish."

Behind them, Tarak ascended the steps, followed by guards and counselors. On instinct, Hiran froze. The mirage of his brother walked past him without seeing him. Although . . . he could've sworn that Tarak sensed him. A twitch in his nostrils, a sway of his gaze.

Hiran hadn't seen his half brother since the death of their father. While Hiran was much taller now, his brother was still taller than him. Tarak was still broader, stronger, more commanding, and terrifyingly like their father. He had the swagger of a royal, the aura of a Shadow King with cerulean centipedes scurrying around his neck. One disappeared into a gill, where Tarak took a deep breath and swallowed it whole.

Tarak was fully grown—married, even—and seeing him brought to mind all those tormenting days from their youth. A wave of trauma churned Hiran's insides. He wanted to cower and hide. His skin prickled with the memory of Tarak beating him nearly to death.

While Hiran looked more like his mother, Tarak took after their father. The six-foot-nine height; the long uncut black hair pulled back beneath the looming crown of shadow and ash; the muscle rippling beneath a navy-blue sherwani; the clawed hands and feet, perfect for ripping apart flesh. Tarak even wore their father's blue-ribboned sword in a gold scabbard at his waist.

Around them, the Court of Nightmares awoke, breathing to life, speaking as one, neither male nor female, both high and low, a mix of everything and nothing. These entities were incorporeal when in the minds of slumbering beings but were tethered to their statue bodies. Their lips never moved, their chests never heaved, but they were alive. A frenzy of energy leaked from their perfectly sculpted folds of cloth and into the pool, causing it to glow with iridescence. A gossamer mist billowed up from the depths.

They announced in an echoing, cryptic voice, "The key to the gateway has been determined: a girl, a nagin, a walker of worlds, a giver of life. With a crown of bramble dipped in red, she is the rise of venom beneath a blood sky."

A counselor added, "The prophecy is at hand! She is ready and must be brought to this realm."

Tarak replied calmly, his voice baritone, "Yes. The oracle said something about a gatekeeper summoning her." His black eyes bulged, his jaw tight with anger. "*Gatekeeper.* The trivial title given to one of my father's inferior children. How the hell does a dead boy fulfill a prophecy? If that runt was even worthy."

The Gloom flickered in Hiran's periphery. Holika placed a hand on Hiran's shoulder and whispered, "Oh, he's in for a reckoning, and ambushes are best served bloody."

The Gloom teemed.

The counselor replied, "He was immolated, and his ashes now a part of this realm, his shadow mass part of the shadow ward. You are ruler of the realm, and thus you can control it. *You* must simply summon her. Nightmares will possess her, and she will come no matter her will."

Hiran scoffed. The royals were so ridiculous to believe they could control the physical realm simply because others referred to them as *Shadow King.*

The counselor went on, "The vidyadhara tried to confine us, and in their haste locked all the portals, you see. While this girl can walk across these gateways, the portal connecting our world to hers has an additional requirement. She can walk through the portal, but only if the Gatekeeper beckons her. And the time has come. All things have finally aligned during your ambitious, anointed reign."

Tarak lifted his chin, as if he'd always known he was special. The *arrogance.*

"But why is her fertility important?" another counselor mused. He snapped his fingers. "Of course! She must conceive your child. She will make you great in many ways."

Tarak groaned, exasperated. "I have no desire for repulsive mortals, but I will do what needs to be done. Although I do not understand what fertility has to do with anything. Will that unlock her full potential? Or is it the child?"

"Prophecy is often a mystery until it has come to pass. Fulfillment unlocks understanding. Taking her as a consort will not harm you. Best to cover every angle just in case, as this means salvation for our kind."

The illusion dissipated as Holika said, "Of all the girls in all the worlds ... how are we supposed to find her?

"Just kidding!" She clapped her hands. "I am a master of suspense, am I not?"

"Yes, you are," Hiran said, humoring her.

She waved her hand, conjuring an illustrious peacock that burped small flames.

"I crafted him from the mayura," Holika explained. "Giant flying peacocks that breathe fire. They live at the vidyadhara's ancient palace in the mortal realm, surrounded by ignorant mortals. They're worshipping a portal and have no idea what it is! But one is . . . different."

Hiran shrugged. In his periphery, the Gloom mimicked him.

Holika batted her eyes. "I was drawn to her nightmares of a war that killed her people. But I didn't add to her nightmares; I erased them." She smiled proudly, a sparkle in her eyes. "Because I am kind! I searched her mind, following the branches of her memories to others like her, and then I searched their minds, too." She gave a dramatic pause. "I found the nagin."

Leave it to Holika to accomplish what no one else could.

She went on, "Oh, foolish girl. She made a deal with the shades to enter our realm in exchange for their help. She's yet to return, but we shall be waiting for her."

"And the Court?"

"They don't know. I am a master of blocking access, after all. We shall slip into her head, gather her secrets, and use them to take back the realm and save it! We will be free." She unleashed a vibrant, maniacal laugh.

The Gloom was loving this plan.

Holika snapped her fingers. The dreamscape shifted around them until it showed sheer darkness cushioning a lit room where a girl slept on blankets.

"Here she is!" Holika squealed. "Although . . . she doesn't look like much."

They crept toward her. Holika bent at the waist to examine the girl, then craned her head to the side. There sat a mirror.

"Oh, stupid girl," Holika whispered, sliding her fingers through the nagin's hair. "You made it so easy for me to find you."

The nagin's eyes sprang open. Her chest spasmed in rapid breaths, but she didn't move.

"What are you doing?" Hiran asked.

"Giving her sleep paralysis."

Hiran stepped closer and looked down at the girl wrapped in blankets, her dark hair fanned around her. Her skin was velvety smooth, rich brown. And her eyes . . . were the most intense emerald. Glowing, hypnotic, perfect.

"She's your age, barely sixteen mortal years old. Her name is Eshani."

Eshani, Hiran mused, oddly and wholly captivated.

Holika stood upright, sweeping scrutiny down Eshani. "I have my doubts. Anyway. Let's reave some information out of her. Mortals fear the daayan."

A tall, gaunt woman materialized in front of the mirror. A dirty dress covered her bony limbs. A mess of hair cascaded over her head, concealing her face, and slithered down an unnaturally bent neck.

Eshani's chest heaved, her breathing labored—fast, heavy, and panicked as the daayan crawled toward her and climbed onto her chest.

Holika hovered over them and asked, her voice low and unsettling, "Where are you, nagin?"

TIME AND TIME AGAIN, HOLIKA WORKED ON ESHANI, BUT the girl withstood nightmares for nearly a mortal year. Holika grew impatient. She couldn't stave off the Court's curious and far-reaching tendrils of communication forever. Soon enough, they would realize that Holika wasn't working for them, but against them.

Hiran was munching on air-filled kernels of corn smothered in ghee and suggested, "Maybe she'd be more open to talking if she wasn't terrified?"

Holika looked to Hiran and waggled her brows. "I wonder if she likes boys."

"Conjure up a pretty boy?" Hiran suggested, not liking where his sister was headed.

She tugged him forward by the arm and pushed him through the dream void so that he stood where the dreamer could see him.

Hiran wasn't sure what to do or say. He scratched the back of his head, bumping his hand against a horn. "You have lovely...um... short fangs."

Eshani blinked, her emerald eyes sparkling back at him.

"Want to see mine?" He grinned, or perhaps grimaced. He proudly revealed two sharp fangs.

Eshani scuttled away.

"This isn't working," he complained.

"Be prettier," Holika suggested. Now she was the one chomping on kernels.

Hiran adjusted his features to what he thought mortal girls might like. Over many tries, he learned Eshani was not a fan of hooves, starry red eyes, talons, scales, or forked tongues.

Holika waved a hand, and an image of a tall boy with lavender eyes appeared. "Try something like this. Her sister is smitten by him. He's what they call a slayer of monsters."

He cringed, recalling how volatile the Famed One had been. And then, remembering the second slayer and his wife that passed, assumed this boy was their child.

"Be like him! Mortal girls fawn over him."

"A slayer," Hiran grunted. Sure, the boy was tall, but Hiran was taller, had a bit more muscle, and better hair. If Eshani's sister had any sense, she'd stay away from monster slayers.

He begrudgingly pulled back his hair into a bun instead of the half-up style of the slayer boy. His eyes shifted from red and starry to brown, matching Eshani's skin (which he rather liked). His horns faded completely away, and with them, his hands became more human and less clawlike.

This time, Eshani relaxed.

The next time, Eshani finally spoke. Over time, she regaled him with stories from the war she'd survived. The Fire Wars. All those passing dead on the ferry had been her kind. His heart ached for her, for he knew what death was like. He knew what the caress of hatred-fueled flames did to a person.

FIVE

ESHANI
(PRESENT DAY)

For two years, he came to her. A terrifying image at first. Episodic visits that turned regular. There was a strange, alluring boy in Eshani's head. She was certain he wasn't real, but she vaguely recalled a series of conversations, a progression of intimacy.

Their time together often faded away once she awoke, leaving floating fragments of his face and the warmth she'd felt in his presence, but she couldn't always recall what they'd spoken of.

He'd been coming to her more and more. He'd first appeared with large wings and claws, and she'd scurried away, terrified. But now? The contours of his angular face softened, his horns rounded and hidden beneath thick black hair, his wings nonexistent, and his claws large hands. His eyes changed often, and then remained a starry mix of infinite black and shimmering rubies, almost as if he'd forgotten to hide them. She didn't mind; she thought they were breathtaking. They sometimes held splashes of deep greens and vibrant purples flecked with gold. They were the cosmos, he'd once said, the colors of faraway galaxies and nebulous star clusters. His eyes were lined with long lashes, which made them easy to focus on and even easier to get lost in. He shuffled awkwardly whenever she stared at him, which was often.

Only Eshani would conjure up a shy boy. Still, dreaming of him was better than dreaming about the war and her father, of losing Manisha and Lekha. He was better than crying and spiraling with anxiety about the things she couldn't control, which were many. And he'd grown with her. First a tall, gangly young boy. Now *much* taller, better built, a young man. In fact, he was so tall—six foot eight—that he had the air raise her to his eye level so her neck wouldn't hurt looking up at him, which she thought was awfully sweet.

He went by Hiran. She whispered his name aloud, to which he always replied, "I like how you say my name." At that, she blushed, which seemed ridiculous in a dream.

He possessed these peculiar yet fascinating cobalt swirls around the corners of his eyes. They shimmered like sapphires no matter the lighting. They were a constant. That's how she knew this was the same boy every time. The swirls. And the way he arched one brow, the other downturned, when he was thinking. And the smell, sweet like burnt sugar. She leaned in and inhaled.

He stilled, clearing his throat. "Um. So . . . where are you now?"

"Why do you always ask me that? You're a figment of my imagination; you already know," she told him.

Red tinged his cheeks. He replied in a deep voice, too sonorous to be his natural voice. "I want to make sure you're okay."

"I am."

"Oh. Good." He looked off to the side and shrugged.

Eshani followed his gaze but only saw gray hills.

"Do you like where you are?"

"Yes. It's prettier than here. . . ." She scowled at the bleak rocky terrain around them.

"Show me what you like . . . um . . . where you are. If it's so pretty."

She tried and failed, and he corrected her: "With your gift, not your mind."

In the real world, her powers were weak. But here, she built an entire biosphere. Hiran watched in astonishment as she wove plants and leaves and blades of grass in a dance of her wrists, with a focus to her thoughts, and a ballad in her steps.

She created meadows with creeping shrubs in full purple and pink and yellow blooms. Ancient trees sprouted behind them, their canopy providing ample shade. The sky turned a deep blue, but a glow of natural light kept everything visible. Gentle breezes swept through, and for a moment, it felt like home, as if nothing bad had ever happened.

"Your powers are growing." Hiran sounded pleased.

Eshani scoffed, running a hand across a persimmon tree beneath a shower of blossoms. "This is a dream."

"Keep practicing, and you'll be the strongest person in the realm."

She smiled despite herself. "Do you think so?"

He nodded with authority. He was always so serious.

"You're . . . deep in the sea," Hiran said with awe, his gaze lifted to the watery dome. A pod of dolphins swam past.

"Yes."

"Nowhere near land?" He glanced at her, chin tilting upward.

"Not for a while."

"Will you return?"

Eshani swayed her hand and the flowers bloomed into fruit. "Yes. To retrieve the rest of my family."

"When?"

"Soon, I hope. I don't have control of where I am. I had no say in this. . . ."

"Ah . . ." He thought for a second, one brow quirked, the other furrowed.

Eshani smiled to herself, and he noticed. He cleared his throat again. A blanket appeared on the grass with a platter of foods Eshani had never seen.

"For you," he said.

She bit into sweet fruits and tart pastries, her taste buds exploding. Hiran grinned triumphantly. He thought it was because he'd come to know her so well, but he was just a figment of her imagination. Still, she let him treat her to decadent food and sweet drinks. He painted her with her family in a field of blue roses, which made her both happy and sad. Blue roses were planted by her people, each for a grave. A field of flowers was better than a field of blood.

With every passing dream, Hiran showered her with attention, intently listening to all her tales, her worries, never once insinuating that she should let the past go and move forward. Instead, he validated her feelings.

"You don't have to keep anything from me," he said.

She nodded and he showed her fashion from "across the realms," which she didn't understand. He gifted her a flowing red lehenga that sparkled like broken rubies, her favorite color despite all the bloodshed she'd seen. And, over time, they became friends. He told her about his world, and how she should visit. At which she laughed and thought the idea nice but silly. Awake, Eshani could never recall what he'd said, though. Just that his world sounded dreary.

Every so often, they'd sit shoulder to shoulder and she'd lean against him, taking in his scent, always of burnt sugar. They perched on a cliff overlooking a shimmering carmine river doused in red mist. Only here, a place he'd often take her to, would he tell her about how lost he felt, and the lingering darkness inside him.

"Madness?" Eshani asked.

He lifted a hand to a shadow boy in the shape of him. "You tell me. Is *that* not madness?"

"Peculiar." For although the shadow boy seemed kind when he smiled, he was a dark force.

Hiran waved a hand and the shadow boy disappeared. "I think it's my father's legacy. He was a cruel man, and my brothers were just as cruel. I don't want to be that way, but the darkness wants me to be. I think."

"You can be whatever you want."

He smiled but seemed unconvinced.

"You're good. Not cruel."

He looked at their hands, pressed into the grass between their bodies. His pinkie touched hers, and her heart fluttered, although she was vaguely aware this was only a dream.

Eshani looked forward to dreaming, no longer plagued by nightmares, and awoke well rested, never remembering much about the boy except his deadpan expressions that made her laugh. And how, when he smiled that crooked smile on rare occasions, he revealed blunt fangs while his joy reached his eyes, crinkling the cobalt designs.

Two years passed like this, and she never told anyone about the deal with the shades, except in her dreams.

During waking hours, Eshani, inspired by the boy's faith, built her skills with plants, finding solace in blooming gardens and observing the underwater world to which they'd been confined. Sithara sharpened her skills with warfare tactics and geography. Kurma breached the surface to breathe and rest, and during those days, Mama and others ventured to faraway lands, building alliances. Time was said to heal all wounds, but time was unbearably slow. The girls were never allowed to leave, trapped on their safe, moving island. Upon every return, Eshani would ask if they had any news regarding Manisha, Lekha, or the others who'd managed to flee before the war.

Nothing.

Had the war never begun, the eighteen-year-old twins would've been well on their way to study for their futures. Eshani wasn't sure what her sisters would've dedicated their lives to, but she knew she would've dedicated hers to agriculture. She imagined telling Papa about her findings. He'd direct her with research, Lekha not far away drifting to sleep in the sunshine and Manisha reading beside her. Manisha would be so tall by now. How different she must look.

Each day proved less painful than the last as memories of battle, phantom wounds, and extraordinary loss wilted away. There were still many things to be thankful for, but every day, the twins circled back to the destruction of Anand and its people. It couldn't slip away without repercussions. The King had to be held accountable for the atrocities against the naga.

"There is always more to learn," the girls' instructor said time and time again. Swati was an older girl who had taken the lead in welcoming the twins and all the children who had come to Kurma. When Eshani felt like a burden, an extra mouth to feed, clothe, and house, Swati made sure the newcomers were anything but. She was, as her namesake implied, a shining star. They were friends, but no one was closer to Eshani than Sithara.

Swati was both kind and fierce, young but mature. She dressed in a forest-green dhoti, a style of loose pants that allowed airflow and full range of movement when kicking and fighting, jumping and running. Her matching kurta ended just past the waist and was much shorter than what the twins were used to wearing.

She advised the class, "Be grateful for every moment, every scar and hard-learned truth. It will make you stronger, wiser, and better prepared."

Sithara leaned toward Eshani and whispered, "For when we return and slit every throat."

Eshani maintained her decorum. She'd had nightmares nearly every night at first, a head full of bloody dreams and haunting screams.

She did not like war, or killing, and yet she had nothing to say to her sister as Sithara turned more lethal, more vengeful by the day. There was simply no forgetting or letting things pass.

Swati added, "You won't live here forever. Kurma isn't meant for permanent habitation. We all will leave at some point. You come from war. You're the last remnants, the new generation—the ones who will reclaim your homeland or move on to build a new one. Absorb everything here so you can be best prepared for whichever path you choose."

While the naga were divided on where to go next, the twins knew there wasn't a choice to be made. They would always choose returning for Manisha and Lekha, rebuilding Anand, and destroying the King.

"Vengeance has a dark side," Swati intoned. "You must decide if it's worth the cost." Her voice fluctuated. "Do you want to increase numbers and strength and find peace, or do you want to—"

"Burn it to the ground," Sithara asserted.

The class of ten boys and girls looked at her. Eshani kept her gaze fixed on Swati. She admired the older girl and her leadership, the way she rarely faltered or lost her patience.

Swati was a good friend who had been nothing but welcoming. But she had lived her entire life in the safety of Kurma's back. She might've heard, or even seen, the devastation across the realm, but she found safety in an impenetrable and constantly moving home. All without feeling like she was moving. There was no packing or running or hiding tracks or carrying minimal belongings. No sending her father off to war or leaving her best friend behind. Kurma might not have been a palace, but Swati lived in luxury. A luxury that the naga didn't have.

Despite all her admirable traits, Swati merely recited what her elders wanted her to teach. "The naga have to find their own home soon, but you shouldn't die off because you choose destruction."

Sithara was, without a doubt, the most fearless of the three sisters. Now she was perhaps one of the most ruthless of the naga. Her opinions caused unease. Mama often told her to subdue her warlike tendencies; the naga were peaceful.

"But, Mama," Sithara would say, "war *made* us warriors. And the war isn't over."

The Fire Wars might have turned from blazing flames to scattered ash since there were no naga left in the kingdom to fight, but the embers had yet to cool. Sithara was proof that those embers would never burn out. She kept them alive, a breath every day in remembrance of loved ones and a promise to avenge them.

"Blood brings blood," Swati warned.

"Yes," Sithara replied, standing with shoulders back and chin lifted. She was the tallest student in the group, taller than even Eshani by three inches. "They drew our blood, and we will draw theirs."

Swati shook her head, her braid falling from her shoulder. "Bloodshed must stop at some point."

"Yes. When the ground drinks their blood the way it drank ours. When the Blood River is brimming with their dead. A kingdom born in blood shall drown in blood."

Swati's lip twitched. Her gaze flitted to Eshani, but Eshani wouldn't step between her sister and her friend when both had valid points.

"Are you going to report me to the elders?" Sithara pressed. "This unruly nagin who will not let ghosts rest? You put a weapon in my hand, and it *will* be used." She twirled her triple-bladed dagger in her hand.

Swati's glance dropped to the weapon. "We're ... trying to prepare you to move on with your lives." She tripped over her words as if doubt had crept in.

"Are you not indignant about the plight of our people? About countless others the King has upended?" Sithara asked, pain and honor dueling in her voice.

Swati nodded and countered, pleading, "Are you not safe?"

"We needed safety then, to heal and regroup and find our strength. But we've healed now, and you said it yourself: We can't stay here." Sithara looked each classmate in the eye as she spoke. "The time is coming, and time waits for no one."

Fellow naga amid the group mumbled. Swati reminded them, "Kurma does not allow violence. If you choose to venture the violent path, Kurma will release you. Is that what you want when you were once desperate for salvation?"

"I want my home," Sithara said, her eyes glistening with rage and grief. "Would you not avenge Kurma if it was destroyed?"

Swati blinked, and Eshani knew that her friend finally understood.

A few quieted, and Eshani gently took her sister's wrist. The twins couldn't fault others for wanting to maintain the status quo, for wanting to put the harrowing past behind them. Sithara lowered her weapon, frustration reddening the light brown of her cheeks. In the jungles, they had to make their own decisions, for it was life or death. Here, everything was determined for them. It was the price of safety.

The twins left class disheartened but not dissuaded. They snuck away from tedious math and astronomy lessons, meandering instead toward their favorite secluded boulder near Kurma's shell cliff. Birds warbled overhead as Sithara unrolled a scroll, setting rocks on the corners to hold it open. Beside the scroll lay Eshani's journal, where she documented all the fantastic findings of Kurma's botanical species, complete with drawings and research. She'd gotten the idea from Papa, for he had been an organized scholar.

Eshani took a bite of her roti and gazed into the watery depths of the vast sea. Kurma was traveling toward the surface, evident by the increasing rays of sunlight breaking the darkness. She had yet to figure out how the biosphere worked.

A monstrous creature appeared in the distance, and Sithara took note. While Eshani found beauty and awe, Sithara was quick to see danger.

"It's a whale," Eshani said. She handed her sister a roti, then leaned her head back to bask in the bioluminescence. Her hair, thick and wavy and loose, touched the grass. "They're no threat."

"It better not be a threat," Sithara said, taking a dramatic bite of food.

Eshani laughed. "What are you going to do? Launch yourself from the canopy, hold your breath as you breach the bubble, and swim all the way out there to spear an innocent creature? And somehow make it back on that one breath? It has young with it."

Eshani watched the whale with a pang in her chest. Did Lekha have her own young by now? Was Lekha as good a mother as she had been a friend? She hoped to see Lekha and her golden brood. One day.

Sithara handed her sister sweets. "I made these for you. Behold my resplendent culinary skills."

Eshani held up an uneven, lumpy ball dotted with saffron and speared with roasted, slivered almonds. She bit back a laugh. It tasted better than it looked. "It's perfect."

"Like its maker," Sithara teased. She smiled at a baby whale, still of monstrous proportions, peering around its mother. They swam toward the surface.

"We'll breach soon," Eshani confirmed.

"Hah, then we leave."

Eshani nodded. "We should tell Mama."

"So she can try to stop us?"

"She won't try to stop us from getting Manisha. It's far past time. Besides, it would be cruel to leave without telling her."

"I disagree. She thinks it's too dangerous. She says as much every time we bring up a plan."

Eshani nodded. There was a sense that Mama wasn't telling them something, and after all the traumatic events, it seemed unfair for Mama to keep anything from them. They weren't children, and by the acts of war they'd committed, hadn't been for a long time. But Mama was still the adult, the parent, the authority. The twins couldn't force her to divulge anything.

Eshani placed a palm against the grass and leaned into her arm. The roots below hummed, sending airy gossamer tingles through her. Her gift with plants was growing, and she spent a great deal of time harnessing her abilities, but she was still very far from controlling the communication. Maybe it was this island. Maybe Kurma didn't want to relinquish any secrets. But then there were times like these where a simple, innocent touch sent flutters of information into her. They were close to the surface—more than that, they were close to the Great River.

"This is what I've gathered," Sithara announced, dragging a finger across her crudely sketched map of the kingdom. "We can take a boat and get to the riverbank—the closer north, the better. At the very least, north of the marshlands."

The marshlands. A heavy dread eased down Eshani's throat and settled in her stomach.

"Are you all right?" Sithara asked. "You look pale. Did you eat that boy's cooking?" She grunted. "I told you he may be in love with you, but he does *not* know how to cook. He's going to kill us all with food poisoning before we see the light of day again."

Eshani forced a smile on her trembling lips. She hadn't told anyone about her bargain with the shades, and instead let her unfulfilled end hang over her head. "We can't return to the marshlands; I don't want to get anywhere near them."

"I wasn't planning on it. I don't remember much from when we passed through, but that place made the hairs on my arms stick straight up. I have that sense, you know?"

Eshani nodded, aware of her twin's uncanny ability to know where dangers lurked.

"Why do you think nothing attacked us? Something was there, but it let us pass; I don't think it let the soldiers pass. None who followed us into the marshlands emerged on the other side. Do you think the darkness helped us?"

With a shrug, Eshani sighed. "Why would darkness help us? It's only ever after things that benefit it."

"Maybe it wasn't hungry when we came through but had an appetite when the soldiers followed?"

"Sounds plausible," Eshani mumbled around another bite.

Sithara watched her sister carefully. "The feeling that I had when we went through the marshlands—that strange but certain knowing? Well, I sense it here."

Eshani croaked, "It's here?"

"No," Sithara added quickly. "A muted, vague version, but the same." She clenched her eyes shut and worked her mouth. "I wish I knew how to explain what I feel."

Eshani reached out and placed a hand on Sithara's arm. "It's all right. I know."

Prying open one eye, Sithara grimaced. "Do you try that tree talk with me? My thoughts are private, you know."

"Oh!" Eshani withdrew. "No! Don't be absurd. I would never invade your privacy—not that I can do such a thing with people. I was trying to comfort you."

"Well, then what do you think about this? I only feel that weaker, distant sensation of the marshlands around you—and usually when you're sleeping."

Eshani swallowed, which did not go unnoticed by her observant sister.

"You have nightmares. And the marshlands are supposed to be the entryway into the Nightmare Realm. Did something happen there? Did something"—Sithara lowered her chin and her voice—"follow you here?"

"I don't think anything can traverse distance over both land and sea like that. We're so far away and have been constantly moving deep underwater."

"The yakshini can traverse land and water and great distance and the depths of the sea."

"The yakshini helped us."

"The point being: There *are* things that can reach us. Is there something you're not telling me?"

"It was a dark time. Don't you have nightmares?"

Sithara gave a slow, sad nod. "Mainly about Papa's—"

Eshani jerked her head and stared at her. Sithara immediately closed her mouth. Eshani would never accept her father's fate until she knew for certain—until she saw his body for herself.

Sometimes, Eshani found it difficult to look at her twin, for Sithara reminded her of Papa. She had a darker complexion like Papa, and she had his height, too. Her features also leaned toward his: a slightly broader nose and sharper cheekbones, and a cunning furrow to the brow. The two of them were always thinking so ardently.

While the bioluminescence of the forest glowed, offering the only source of light they'd had for months underwater, Sithara drew languid doodles on the map.

"Come," Eshani said after a moment. "Let's prepare for departure. We must tell Mama; you know that. Think of how distressed we are not knowing what's become of Manisha. Do you truly believe it's right to add worry about two more daughters to her list of woes?"

Sithara pulled a knee to her chest and flicked away a pebble. "Mama is busy being the new elder. Do you ever wonder why we haven't been allowed contact with others? Why we stay on Kurma like—"

"Prisoners?" Eshani ended.

"Hah. Well-fed, clean prisoners forced to do math."

Eshani snickered. "You will never bend to the King nor bend to equations."

Sithara asked, "When will these equations ever help me? I don't plan on building a house. That's not where my strengths lie. Can you imagine? It would be so uneven, with leaky patches. No one would trust a house I've built. When we're settled—in a new home or a rebuilt Anand—I wish to be an emissary traveling to meet other villages and cities and kingdoms."

"You would make a great diplomat."

"I could've helped Mama on her trips," Sithara said with a scowl.

"She's busy making plans to rebuild our people."

"Without discussing anything with us." The hard line of Sithara's jaw tightened, her emerald eyes flashing as light pierced the ripples above them. "She thinks we're children."

"She wants us to find some semblance of normalcy."

"We are *not* normal. Things will *never* be the same. We stopped being children when we were forced into the war. We have fought and killed and led groups of our people. We're leaders and warriors, and we deserve to know what's going on—to have a say."

"Please don't feel dismissed. She's trying to protect us."

"By subduing our strengths?" Sithara tossed a rock as far as she could with the might of her anger. "I am more than a student needing to increase my grades in math. I know battle and logistics and can see moves before they're made. She knows this. Why is she keeping us at a distance?"

"Maybe because she's already lost so much, and this is her dealing with trauma. I've found solace in the trees, but we all have our own way. Mama needs to take care of herself now."

Sithara scoffed. "At the expense of letting us float away. She's forgotten she has two daughters left."

Eshani gripped her sister's arm. "Then let's fetch Manisha and be together. The time has come."

"If she doesn't want to discuss her matters with us, then why should we discuss our plans with her?"

"We'll leave her a letter. We can't just disappear without a word; that would break her heart. Kurma will reach the surface in a few hours, and then we'll sneak into the elders' meeting to figure out where exactly we are. We'll take a boat before dawn, under cover of night, and sail toward light."

DARKNESS, CONTRARY TO BELIEF, COULD BE ABSOLUTE. Without a speck of light. Eshani had often knelt on the edge of the cliffs and peered down into the endless abyss during her years on Kurma. Frightening, devastating, surreal, the darkness was a monster in itself.

She hadn't expected to face the same maddening abyss in her dreams. Here, she couldn't even see her hands in front of her face. Whispers caressed her neck and feather-light touches danced across the hairs on her arms. She stumbled and flung around, but of course she couldn't see.

She clenched her eyes, although the darkness behind her lids was the same. Absolute nothingness.

Despite the terror in the night, she knew seeing her surroundings was infinitely worse.

"Please don't. Please don't. Please don't," she muttered.

"Do you not wish to see us?" a voice hissed, followed by a dozen chitters and clucks resonating far and wide and all around, stirring in agreement.

"Open your eyes," the voices would say.

"Behold your nightmares."

"Because I didn't uphold my end of the bargain?" Eshani whimpered.

Something clutched her chin and she yelped, gripping the bony wrist to lessen the grip. It was crushing her. Her jaw fractured and cracked, and she howled in pain. Her eyes opened and her vision went in and out, focusing on the glowing, eyeless men. A swarm of them engulfed her, descending on her as vultures would a feast.

"Enough," a gritty voice growled.

The hand released her chin and her bones fused back together, although the pain lingered, a deep, aching thrum radiating to her ears and neck.

Hiran appeared, his face clear and then blurry as shadows broke across his features in a haze. She knew this was a dream, but it felt so real when he reached out to touch her cheek.

"Hi, Eshani," he said, bringing instant comfort.

"Hello, dream boy."

He gave an impish smirk, revealing the sharp points of two fang-like teeth.

She remembered more of him now, and how he'd chased away monsters from her nightmares before and threaded out details to figure out *where* she was. They picked up where they last left off. He'd discerned exactly where Kurma was, her plan to steal away on a boat to get to land, and how close to the marshlands she'd have to travel.

"Everything has aligned. Have you been working on your powers?" he asked, hurried. The chill of his body wafted off his form the way fog lifted off frostbitten forests at dawn.

He held her gaze as he spoke. "You can command plants, bend them to your will."

"No," she whispered. That didn't seem plausible. "I'm not a god."

"Gods are made, not born."

She smiled, falling into his otherworldly charms with a sense that she'd fallen for this boy a hundred times before.

His gaze fell to her lips. The stern line of his mouth cracked into a woeful, crooked smile. "It's time."

"What?"

"The shades are waiting and grow impatient."

Eshani stumbled out of her unnerving stupor, fighting to think straight. *"No,"* she growled.

"Yes," he snarled.

"You can't make me return."

He rubbed the bridge of his nose, exasperated, and she had a sense that they'd had this fight before. "You made a deal. Deals must be honored. If you're not a person of your word, then what sort of person *are* you?"

"You can't manipulate me. This is just a dream."

"Make no mistake, this is *very* real." He took her hands in his, his touch shocking and his tone softening. "Eshani, you have been found. I can't protect you there."

His image began slipping away, though he was holding her tighter, pulling her into him even as his face contorted and blurred. "I need you here. With me."

He looked off to the side, toward the flickering image of a girl giving him a reassuring nod. His chest rose and fell with a deep breath before turning back to Eshani. He looked so deeply into her eyes that she felt him probing her mind.

His expression turned stern, serious, commanding when he spoke: "I am the Gatekeeper. And I summon you to the Nightmare Realm."

She jerked awake, panting and sweating and staring at the ceiling, fighting through the confusion of dreams ebbing away.

Her gaze searched the room, just to be sure, and then landed on the watchful stare of her twin. Eshani jumped. "How long was I asleep?" she whispered, a hand to her forehead.

Sithara shrugged, her motion illuminated by the glow of the large mushrooms attached to the inside of their tree house. A few wayward strands had fallen from the loose bun at the top of her head. "Not long, but I felt the darkness again."

"You're creepy," Eshani grunted.

"I've seen creepier."

"I wish I could sleep like Manisha; she sleeps like a baby."

"She *is* the baby."

"I really miss her."

Sithara reached across their shared bed and squeezed Eshani's hand. "Soon. We won't let anyone stop us. Not Mama or Kurma or an army or a priestess."

"What about the mayura? Sort of need their assistance, don't we?"

As Sithara raised herself to her elbow, a piece of paper fluttered between the two. "I'm sure a blade to an apsara's throat will persuade them. It could be very quick. We're older now, better skilled, quieter, more efficient. We may even be back before Kurma descends into the sea."

Eshani swallowed and glared at the roof, at the shadows that seemed to move. She clenched and unclenched her eyes. They weren't real. The darkness—the shades—had not followed her. That was impossible.

Sithara watched her. She never asked what the dreams were about, but when Eshani's gaze dropped to the sketches on her sister's lap, she jolted upright.

"What is that?" Eshani demanded, pointing at the paper.

"Oh...I have no idea. I wasn't even aware that I was drawing..." Sithara replied, wearing a look of confusion that matched Eshani's. "Maybe, since I can't really explain what I sense, I drew it?"

Eshani crawled toward her and sat on her haunches. A shiver ran down her spine, her skin puckering with goose bumps as if a layer of ice had been deposited on her skin. Sithara knew things, even when she didn't understand. Even if Eshani had never uttered a word of what she'd seen and done in the marshlands.

Her breath caught in her throat as her gaze skimmed across the scroll. Sketches with contoured shading: lanky men with no eyes, slender women with bent necks, inky monsters with talons for hands, and a darkness dripping in blood that used to be fireflies carrying secrets.

Nightmares were supposed to stay in dreams, in sleeping minds, fading away like false memories. They were not supposed to cross over into reality.

But nightmares had found her. She could not outrun a deal made with the shades.

SIX

HIRAN
(PRESENT DAY)

In the dreamscape, the last time Eshani spoke of the Fire Wars, Hiran had asked, "Are you afraid of fire after the war?"

She glanced at him, her eyes twinkling like gems. "No. Why should I let it hold so much power over me? We need fire for life. It's not the fire's fault but the person who used it to harm us."

Yet Hiran felt the heat of flames curling over his skin. He rubbed away the imagined blisters along his arm.

"What's wrong?" Eshani inquired.

He'd never been one to chat; usually he held everything in, as his father had taught him. *Emotions are for the weak, and no one wants to be around a weakling,* Father had often admonished. Yet there was something very cathartic in being with Eshani.

He told her about his father's death and the immolation. Most asuras would tell him to get over it and move on, for there were plenty of woes to focus on. Why dwell on the ones long gone? But Eshani wrapped a hand over his and squeezed. She was so small in comparison.

"It's okay to feel traumatized. Maybe we can work on facing it?" she suggested.

From his periphery, Holika nodded. And gradually, the peaceful jungles dissipated, morphing into that awful event. His hands clenched into fists, but Eshani's hand remained. His breathing turned erratic, but Eshani placed a palm on his cheek, turning to face him.

"Something my father taught me," she said, locking eyes with him. "Control your reaction, ease into the situation, and consider the elements. This is not real. You're not alone. And you can stop whenever you want. This may take many tries—many steps—but the path to overcoming anything begins somewhere."

With her, he could be vulnerable. And being vulnerable, as it turned out, helped sort things out. Hiran thought about that dream often, working his way toward controlled fires. The fear remained, but now Eshani's voice was there, too. He held on to it when Hiran, Rohan, and several dakini handled a raging fire outside their village. This world was drying and dying *and* riddled with plague.

"Some call us heroes," Rohan said, waggling his brows at Hiran as they patrolled the borderlands. Nearby, a group of dakini worked on one of the worst fractures in the shadow dome.

"I think it was you," Hiran replied, ignoring the taste of ash in his throat. "*You* called us heroes, and after endless turns of the prickly fruit seasons, people have begun saying it out of habit."

"I make things happen. You're welcome." Rohan grinned, giving a theatrical bow at the waist. Even as they grew into young men, Rohan's carefree, joking demeanor had remained. It was hard to imagine him as the Ferryman.

"If the court can make everyone believe something by saying it every day, why can't we?" Rohan asked.

Ah. There was no argument there. Every day, the court bellowed about how much their godly Shadow King was doing to save the realm and how close they were to salvation, et cetera. People believed it. They clung to loyalty because they had no other hope.

In the distance, a white streak zigzagged down the shadow dome, having eviscerated any nearby clouds and trees. Below it, the dakini attempted to draw out shadow from a pile of beasts to patch the wall. They stood perilously close to the deadly light of the true realm.

One group worked with elegant movements of swaying arms and dancing wrists, of clawed hands extracting dark mist from the pores, mouths, and nostrils of the dead. In a swishing movement, they sent the shadow to the second group, who in turn lifted the mist high above them in a ball. The sphere rolled and rolled until it became so dense, it appeared solid.

A third group stood on the tallest structure they could find, a rock tower that had been used long ago by the first dakini to erect the shadow ward. There, they moved the compact shadows upward, patching the dome with great effort. Since the return of the white plague, these broken areas had become ever larger and more difficult to repair.

This was like applying bandages to a wound when the body itself was wholly sick. The body was no longer capable of healing. A new form was needed. *A new realm.* Pressure was assuredly upon Tarak to accomplish what the kings before him had failed to do.

The dakini were hard at work, so focused on their tasks that they didn't notice something emerge from the dark forest to the right. A shudder of the branches. A musky smell accompanied the movement, something like pungent earth.

Hiran's gaze swept toward the trees, where a set of multiple eyes blinked at the tower. He removed his sword from its sheath; some things were too big to fight with katars, although they always sat snugly beneath the sleeves of his kurta, ready to spring forward and gut enemies.

He tapped the corner of his jaw, activating his mask, and caught Rohan's attention. Hiran gestured to the dakini. Rohan went to them, his gaze on the tower, and discreetly alerted them. Within moments, the shadow work stopped. Instead of letting the hard-earned matter fall to the ground to be lost, they held it suspended in the air and turned toward the monstrous beast as a long, spiny arm darted out for them.

By now, Hiran was rushing toward the monster. Using rocks and boulders, each step catapulted him higher, faster, until he was nearly running up the partial remains of the building. He'd learned to become more agile, a little more assured, but that didn't mean terror and uncertainty didn't douse his confidence. One wrong move and that would be the end of him. No one would save the realm. Holika would be stuck forever, truly alone. And Eshani would be walking into a death trap. He had too much at stake to cower, too much to risk to not train daily.

The dakini leapt out of the way, using the compact shadow material as a shield. The prickly end of the attacking leg slammed into the barrier and bent in a painful way, sending the beast crumpling forward into the open.

Most of the dakini set up shields around them while a few turned the precious shadow mass into spears. If they dropped the shadow mass, they would lose the valuable substance needed to repair fissures above. Hiran didn't have a choice *except* to help. He swiped his blade clean through the beast's leg. It fell to the ground and caught on the edge of the tower, knocking rocks off. The stench of rot permeated the air. Hiran almost gagged and slipped on viscous fluid, barely missing being sprayed with blood.

One wrong move. And it would be over.

This creature was infected with the white plague, and now infected blood spilled near the dakini. Thankfully, their shields held up, but enough splatter could burn through. That was what the white tendrils did. They pried open the dome, sank into bodies, made beings go mad with rot, turned their blood toxic, and enabled infection to spread. A quickly evolving plague.

Hiran drove his sword into the beast's eyes, one after another, counting thirteen, each stab piercing into the brain. He ignored the pain striking through his arm with each impact.

The creature wailed and swooped its massive head, sweeping one of many legs and knocking Hiran to the side. The crash jostled him, but there was never time to catch a breath. He rolled before a leg crushed him.

The beast did not die as one should when bleeding to death with eyes gouged out.

Rohan came from the side, taking out one leg after another from behind so that the creature was fully on the ground. Hiran pushed through the fatigue and flung himself through the air, sword high above him, and smashed down with all his might, wedging the sword into the monster's head with a few twists for assurance.

Finally, the beast shrieked, collapsed. Its last breaths sputtered out of its chest.

"Damn," Rohan said, gathering beside Hiran. They heaved, glaring at the unmoving monster, a graveyard of its legs splayed out before them. "They're getting harder to kill."

Hiran tapped the device at his jaw, and his mask retracted. "Head kills only," he ascertained. Brain damage was the only way to end the infected now.

"They weren't like this before."

The dakini carefully unraveled their shields and went back to work. They couldn't lower the shadow mass without losing it. And there were too many fractures in the dome to waste a single particle. They shouted out gratitude from where they stood.

Vidya approached, her voice low so her elders wouldn't hear. "The palace does nothing."

Rohan agreed. Hiran didn't respond, for any talk of the palace or his brother made his spine stiffen.

Vidya whispered, "Something must be done. Anything. Or we'll all either be infected by plague or consumed by light. Maybe the dakini should've taken power."

She glanced over her shoulder. Such talk would bring disciplinary action. The elder dakini were loyal to a fault, and they did not tolerate the younger dakini's changing views. "We do everything anyway. What's holding up an entire realm on our shoulders while holding up the entire society as well?"

She grunted. "I better get back to work, but thank you. I don't know why the palace took back the soldiers who once guarded us."

Word around the inner villages was that Tarak had called all uninfected soldiers to guard the palace territory instead.

Vidya jogged off, giving Rohan one more glance. He waved.

Hiran grabbed Rohan's wrist, yanking it down. "Don't be so obvious. Stars, you're hopeless."

Rohan grinned as they surveyed the area for other threats. "You can't have me all to yourself, you know?"

"Trust me, I don't want you all to myself."

"And I have to make connections before I get stuck on the ferry for the rest of my life."

"Your father has been around forever. I don't think you need to worry quite yet." Hiran hurried to a corner where the two kept their belongings while on the move. They each grabbed a towel and water and cleaned off. Hiran had to trash his shirt with the amount of infected blood on it.

Rohan washed his face and arms, scrubbing his skin as if he, too, were covered in blood. "Why else would he have me? Unless he knows his end is soon."

"I don't know. Maybe to share his solitude with? Pass on wisdom? Raise a child and see him do great things? I don't think he asked the Vaitarani to spawn you just to replace him. Otherwise, you'd be at the helm right now." Hiran pulled a fresh shirt over his head.

"Because I can't go very far. And there's nowhere to hide in this realm; it's so small."

They walked around trees, boulders, and the ruins of old homes, checking for other threats. "That's the problem—the realm is too small for all of us."

Rohan scoffed. "One day, you'll leave when the portals open. But I'll be stuck here, no matter what happens to this dome."

"At least you can't die by a blade or a plague or the light of the true realm."

"Neither can you." Rohan elbowed him.

Hiran wasn't going to test their theory about the halahala in his blood. After all, his mother had consumed the poison and still died by fire.

Rohan snickered and Hiran growled, "What?"

"Your kurta is too tight." Rohan laughed at the fabric stretched snugly against Hiran's chest and biceps.

"They're called muscles," Hiran retorted. But true, he needed new clothes. Not that there were many looms working with the plague having killed so many asuras and the change in the realm drying out the fields that supplied fibers to make the threads.

Rohan kicked up a small rock as if there might be something lurking underneath. "I'm telling you, we should team up with the dakini and take down the brother." Rohan said *the brother* as if mentioning Tarak would conjure up the king himself. "I'm sure they're all for it.

In fact, I think the entire realm is for it, including the monsters. Let's take a vote. Creatures included. Isn't this what other kingdoms do in other realms? Revamp or abolish the systems that aren't working?"

"It's not that simple. He has the loyalty and support of every noble because they'll be the first saved. He has the entire army at his disposal, as is their duty. And that crown connects him to the realm itself. Imagine how he can wield it."

Rohan slapped the back of his hand against Hiran's chest, stopping him. Hiran sighed, exasperated, because here Rohan went again.

"If something doesn't work for the brother, or even remotely annoys him, he changes it. All for his luxury and comfort."

"Lower your voice." Hiran checked over his shoulder.

"Do you see where I'm going?"

"I saw before you said anything. You don't even have to say it." Hiran hushed him and turned toward the sound of hooves. Keshi were riding close and fast, which meant they were carrying soldiers. Hiran immediately activated his mask and concealed his eyes and horns as best he could.

The soldiers went directly to the dakini, while Hiran and Rohan instinctively went deeper into the forest. But the dakini had already told the soldiers what happened and pointed into the ruins. Before the boys could quicken their steps to dodge out of sight, a fourth soldier on a fourth keshi caught sight of the two and galloped toward them.

"You there!"

Rohan bounded over logs into the forest, but the soldier had already seen Hiran.

"Stop!"

Hiran was fast, but he wasn't faster than a keshi. He managed to dodge the keshi's tentacle, a mere slap of annoyance that would sting for days. Temperamental creatures.

Hiran's heart raced as the soldiers surrounded him. In a few blinks, he foresaw being dragged to the palace, where Tarak would figure out his identity and torture him. Worse than during their childhood, for now he was the king, and no king wanted another royal threatening his rule.

At least Rohan had a chance to hide. By now, he was surely crouching in the canopy with an arrow nocked and ready.

"Why didn't you stop?" a soldier demanded.

"I didn't hear you," Hiran muttered, averting his gaze in case the red hues in his eyes gave him away.

"You didn't hear us yelling for you to stop, or the gallop of keshi?"

"No." Hiran's heart beat wildly fast, but now it beat with urgency, a sense of rebellion. He didn't want to cower from soldiers, flinch every time he heard a keshi's hoofbeat, or crawl into himself whenever his brother came up.

Hiran knew he should curl his shoulders in to look as small as possible (however improbable considering his six-foot-eight stature) and lower his gaze to display submission (however unnatural) but the Gloom in him, the royal in him, refused to cower. As a child on the run, forever hiding for fear of being caught by the court, melting into the surroundings had been easy.

But why should you, a true prince and a son born from halahala, be subservient to these sycophants? The Gloom in his head spoke louder than his own voice, and it had become increasingly difficult to differentiate the two. Maybe they were one and the same, one manifesting as the familiar voice of a scared child and the other a dark presence of the true prince, an heir so much like his father and brother no matter how much Hiran refused to be like them. But maybe...what Eshani had told him was also true. That he could decide what he was going to be.

"What happened here?" the soldier asked, his voice demanding and haughty.

"The dakini were attacked, and we killed the beast," Hiran replied.

"We've followed these slain monsters all over the borderlands, and we've traced them back to you. The Shadow King has noticed. Come with us."

Hiran felt the blood drain from his face. He glanced around, weighing his options. He could make a run for it into the thicket, but the keshi would only be slowed down. They were slender enough to weave between trees. Then he would be charged for evading the army on direct orders from soldiers.

"No."

Two soldiers readied their arrows.

The blades of Hiran's katars pressed slivers of coldness against the backs of his wrists. He sensed Rohan lurking somewhere close enough to know what was happening. He could only hope his lighthearted, and foolhardy, best friend wouldn't consider this a new adventure to embark on. Another thrill to get out of his system before the ferry locked him into place. Another grand tale to tell Vidya in hopes she'd be impressed and fall madly in love so he could experience romance at least once in his life.

Hell. Hiran knew better than to think that.

One arrow after another infiltrated the air, Rohan's handiwork and precision digging into the ground at their keshi's hooves.

"Don't engage," Hiran warned, even as the Gloom itched for a fight.

The other two soldiers drew their swords.

The Gloom teemed, and katars slid from Hiran's sleeves. *So be it.*

SEVEN

ESHANI

Before light broke the following morning, the twins stood in their dimly lit kitchen and tucked a note underneath a lamp glowing with the bulbs of a dozen fireflies. They thought Mama was asleep. But really, she was waiting at the front door.

Sithara sucked in a gasp, clutching her weapons as if Mama were bent on confiscating them. She was a fighter through and through, but battling soldiers was easier than going against their mother.

Mama crossed her arms and asked quietly, "You think you would make it there and back?"

Stunned, Eshani took a moment before replying, "How did you know?"

"Am I not your mother? Are you not my daughters? I would be set on doing the same thing. How could you leave without a word? Without discussing this with me?"

Eshani stepped forward, her fear of Mama's disapproval fading. "We didn't want you to stop us. Mama, please. We have to go."

"Our plan has remained the same: We must gather allies across the vast and infinite sea and in the forest beyond. Numbers to strike the King with a war he will never expect."

Eshani replied, "That's wonderful and inspiring, and we appreciate all the work you and the others have put into reclaiming what was taken from us. But *we* have to get Manisha. There's no moving forward without her. Not for us."

Mama touched Eshani's head. "I want that, too. But we need our army if we ever set foot back on that land. You're thinking small, the details, while we—the adults—consider the broader spectrum of the situation."

"Manisha isn't a detail."

"I didn't say that. I would never imply such a thing. She is my daughter, my beloved, and I've wept for her every day. The truth remains that we can't risk returning to their land without allies."

Sithara countered, "The army's forgotten about us by now, but she's trapped on that floating mountain. We deserve to be together again. And we're thirteen no longer. We're capable of retrieving one person, especially when we know exactly where she is."

Eshani added, "You continue with the broader spectrum of plans, but *we* will do this."

Mama unfolded her arms, and the sisters stiffened their spines, prepared to go against their mother no matter the emotional pain.

The twins stood their ground, despite how it knotted Eshani's insides to defy Mama. She expected a sheen of pain to flash across their mother's eyes, a pout of betrayal. Instead, Mama grabbed two satchels and handed them to the girls, one bag for each of them.

"What is this?" Eshani asked, dumbfounded as she lifted the heavy bag to her face.

"Food, a water container, and supplies. You have your weapons. Don't be foolish traveling without necessities," Mama replied, her voice curt but full of sorrow, enough to make Eshani regret hurting her.

"Wait. Does this mean . . . ?" Sithara questioned, scrupulously looking inside the satchel.

Mama tilted her chin to Sithara, who now stood inches over Mama. "I will not fight you. You are naga and you are *my* daughters. I know you'll do what you've been planning for months, and even I cannot stop you unless I tie you up. And that, my beloved ones, I will never do.

"I will never silence you; your voice should be heard. I will never impede your growth, and oh, how you've grown much too fast since the Fire Wars. The King has pushed you into being wanderers plagued by fear and fight, constantly sharpening blades and looking over your shoulders. I want you to be free and strong and make determined, confident decisions. That is what your father and I—" She hiccuped on the mention of Papa, her eyes gleaming with tears before she batted them away. "That is how we raised you to be, war or not. That is how all naga are raised, to be independent and fearless, to find your space and fill it without hesitation."

She offered a soft smile. "I supposed we raised you *too* well."

"Mama . . ." Eshani said. "You've raised us right. We are strong and smart because of it. And that's why we must go. We don't wish you any pain, and we'd never wish you any distress if you didn't know what became of us."

Mama released a breath. "If you must go, go with a plan, a map, provisions, and the best possible chance at success. What sort of mother would I be to hinder such an important journey, huh?"

Mama ran her hand down each of their heads in that show of elder affection they'd known since childhood. The twins thought they were too old to be treated like children, but they relished the gesture all the same.

Mama added, "Everyone here knows how capable you two are, and together you make a formidable team. I know better than anyone. No one could bring back Manisha better than you two, and I wouldn't trust anyone else to do so."

She pulled the twins into an embrace, kissing each on the forehead, her voice trembling. "Bring your sister home; come straight back. The yakshini can assist with messages, so you must keep us apprised of any updates. We'll meet you there soon, with allies and weapons. And we *will* reclaim Anand."

"Hah," both sisters concurred, determination buried deep in their bones. They slipped on the satchels, which fitted over both shoulders for easier traveling, secured daggers snug against their hips, and armed themselves with bows and quivers of arrows. For this embarkment, Eshani braided her hair as she had done every day during the war. During the years on Kurma, she'd let her hair loose. It had been a symbolic untethering. Braiding her hair now suddenly snapped her back to days on the run. She felt the ache in her body, and for the oddest of seconds, she thought she would walk outside and see Lekha yawning in wait and Manisha waving her down with that baby smile of hers. They felt like ghosts.

Mama pulled back, gnawing her lip, brows furrowed. "Be strong and cunning, silent and quick. Do not alert anyone to our existence or let them know where we are. Most of all, do not just survive. *Thrive.* No matter what happens to me or the rest of the naga, be naga. Always. Make sure Manisha finds her nagin voice."

She touched the amber ovals on Eshani's necklace and Sithara's arm cuff. "Never forget who we are."

Mama placed a kiss to each of her daughters' foreheads before murmuring a prayer over their journey. "Resilience rises in you. Never let it die. Remember the foremothers before you, the great queens of serpents. Our legend does not end here."

"I'M EXHAUSTED," SITHARA SAID AFTER A FULL DAY OF rowing. "Where are the makara and yakshini when you need them?"

She had set her pack on the boat between them, beside their bows and quivers, while Eshani wore hers just in case trouble toppled them over. Sithara wiped her brow with the back of her hand, pulling taut the short sleeve of her kurta so that it strained over lean muscles.

Excitement gushed through Eshani when she said, "I can't wait to hug Manisha."

"I get to hug her first."

"You don't even like hugs."

"This is different." Sithara scowled, all defiance.

"I'm the oldest."

"By two minutes. You can't use that as an excuse. It means nothing."

"I beat you out of the womb first and I will beat you to Manisha first."

Sithara grinned, and Eshani couldn't help but laugh. She couldn't wait to fight over Manisha's hugs. Behind them, the vast and infinite sea sparkled, a soothing, soft blue melting into the sky.

"Why don't you sleep?" Eshani suggested, although she herself kept rowing.

The canyonlands appeared to the right, so close and yet so far. Many of the larger buildings had crumbled, including the grand library with its elegant spires, once-wonderful arched windows, and flower-covered balconies. The sisters stared idly as they floated past, a deep and relentless ache sprouting in Eshani's chest. She closed her eyes and sent a prayer on the wind, for all those who had lost their lives and for all those who fought to this day.

We fight so others may live.

Sithara hunkered down in the deep, curved pit of the boat. She snored loudly when she was this tired, and it had been a wonder her snoring hadn't alerted soldiers to their location during the war.

Eshani sat on the edge, facing away from Sithara, and pulled her knees to her chest. Listing her head, she glared at the ripples of water, where one ripple changed direction, followed by a dozen more. Something was coming toward her. It had to be a makara. She smiled. Finally. Something she knew, for the makara must be with a yakshini, and the yakshini was sure to help.

The small hairs on the back of her neck stood up, and a chill scratched down her spine. The ripples in the water weren't ripples at all. An inky shadow formed, crawling up through the surface and reaching out for her like her worst nightmare. Vacant eyes returned her stare as light gleamed off its bladelike nails... nails much too close to her face.

She scuttled backward, hitting something hard at her lower back—the bench inside the boat.

In an eerie, cryptic voice, the monster spoke, even though its lips didn't move. "You owe the Nightmare Realm."

"I know. Just...wait.... Let me tell my family goodbye."

"We've waited long enough," it said, its voice distorted.

The beast pressed down on the corner of the boat, the vessel dipping as it crawled toward her like an animal, knees bent so high it must've had extra joints to move in such a way. Stamping one hand after another onto the wooden planks, it left dark, stringy trails in its wake.

Eshani couldn't scuttle back any more. She knew she had to scream, but instead she said, "Please. They'll worry about my fate."

Her voice didn't sound like hers, and she didn't feel the air moving up her throat. Had she said anything at all? Was she dreaming?

The monster looked oddly familiar; she'd seen it once a long time ago, in the marshlands.

Its pace sped up a hundredfold, the way lizards awkwardly moved one foot then another when hunting, like jagged lightning bolts descending upon prey that had never seen their end coming. And just like a predator in deadly pursuit, it was suddenly inches from Eshani. Its face so close that, even in the moonlight, she made out every wrinkle and contour of its writhing flesh.

"Time. Is. *Up.*"

And with that, this already-large creature, part man, part monster, grew to insurmountable size, its back unfolding into inky wings curling over them. An encapsulation of darkness cut Eshani off from everything else in existence.

It was just her and darkness. An *impossible* darkness.

No matter how hard she kicked and punched, Eshani couldn't get through, much less stop this monster from tumbling over the edge with her inside.

She couldn't breathe. Her mind went in and out, floating toward unconsciousness.

Eshani had just enough in her to recall the meditation rites of her people as her eyelids fluttered, trapping her between the realm of reality, where a monster had snatched her panicked body, and the realm of her ancestors, where she opened her eyes to a calm and endless world. Rolling hills of green filled with wonder.

In the middle stood a wide tree with lovely cinnamon-colored bark, and from it stepped forth one woman after another. Beautiful with fierce emerald eyes, their bodies cloaked in shimmering silks, each with a pallu over her head and a long braid across her neck like an elegant slumbering serpent. If Eshani looked close enough, she could see the braids slither.

One woman wore a diadem with slender snakes in serpentine patterns along the sides, meeting in the middle with fangs bared.

"Daughter of Padma, granddaughter of Padmavati," an ancestor intoned.

"What's happening?" Eshani asked, desperate for help, for anything that she could make sense of.

Her ancestor said, "Daughter of life."

"Daughter of death," another added, their voices joining in a soft lullaby.

"The threads of fate, no matter how tattered, will weave together stronger than before," the first said.

"A tapestry you're only now learning to see."

"Behold the fates of time in a land where time does not exist."

The background of soothing hills churned like smoke, turning into towering snakes. Some were larger than a mountain, with seven heads spitting fire. Some were formed by shadows dispersing and coming back together, as black as the ether.

Some, as a third foremother opened her palms to Eshani in offering, were tiny, writhing strings of beautiful vermilion. They shimmered and sparkled like a handful of precious stones meant to occupy a queen's crown.

In an instant, the small beauties slipped through her fingers like blood as her foremother sang, "You shall drown in red..."

Oh, how her voice was hauntingly angelic.

"...the color of crowns and blood. Daughter of ours, walker of worlds, young giver of life...and destroyer of life."

Eshani frowned. How could she, a gentle soul who wanted nothing more than to heal others and grow plants, destroy life?

"From morbid beginnings, you shall rise in blood." Her melodic tone turned into a hiss as the others joined to speak as one: "A reckoning as inevitable as *venom*."

EIGHT

HIRAN

A rmor clanked against supplies, reverberating in the quietude of the pathway lining the edge of the forest. A chill was settling in, heralding a slightly cooler season. Leaves rustled beneath the hooves of keshi in a soft gallop, a swooshing sound following their heels.

Rohan glanced back, asking, "Are we supposed to leave a trail?"

"Monster bait," Hiran corrected him, unconcerned about the ropes dragging the corpses of soldiers behind them.

"I can't believe you killed us," one of the soldiers mumbled.

"You should've walked away." Hiran side-eyed Rohan, who was too busy struggling with his keshi to pay any mind. He hadn't been around the Vaitarani in a while, and not having the dead talk to him had been a pleasant reprieve.

"Did you have to skewer my eye?" another soldier asked.

"This is uncomfortable," a third added.

"I have rocks stuck in my pants," the fourth complained.

Hiran still couldn't understand why the dead babbled so much.

Rohan yelped, slapping away the keshi's tentacles as they stung his arms and latched onto his legs. "Stars, I hate these things. Why the hell are we riding them?"

Amused at his best friend's annoyance, Hiran replied, "Were you going to drag the bodies yourself? I wasn't planning on helping."

"It's debatable."

"Walking over riding? Do you realize how much area we can cover now, and how many things we can carry?"

"Do you realize how much you can cover by flying?" Rohan retorted.

"It would take something dire to unleash my wings," Hiran muttered.

Rohan groaned, gripping the long, thick mane of coarse lavender hair of his keshi to keep from falling off, simultaneously kicking his leg to unlatch the tentacles. His arms were covered in maroon welts sure to sting. The keshi liked him as much as he liked them.

Hiran was glad for his long sleeves. More than that, he'd remembered how to ride a keshi: a commanding presence, showing little to no fear, and looking it in the eyes to assert dominance. A soldier's keshi wasn't as large as a royal keshi, but these were still tall and broad, made bigger by numerous tentacles writhing in several directions.

Ahead, the group of dakini had gathered in numbers, reassembling for the next shift or for some to move down the dome to work elsewhere.

Vidya saw them first and waved them down. Rohan grinned as Vidya and a few others approached, in awe of the acquired keshi and leaning around the beasts to stare at the dead soldiers.

Rohan tilted forward on his keshi, adjusting once or twice, one eyebrow quirked. "We come bearing gifts."

Vidya scowled. "You killed them! You're going to have a bounty on your head for this."

"Do you fret over my fate?"

Hiran rolled his eyes and slid off the keshi to unfasten the corpses.

"I battled for my life. Can I help it if I'm a skilled warrior?" Rohan replied, feigning hurt.

"Are you all right?" Vidya asked him.

"So you do care about me?"

"I want to know so I can gauge how much to beat you," she countered. "The elders won't let you stay with us, you know. They'll have to report you."

Rohan hopped off, less gracefully than he intended, getting stung and slapped by his agitated keshi. Vidya immediately went to his side to coddle him. Hiran thought his eyes might get lodged inside his skull from the sheer force of his eye roll.

"They're so sickening, I can't stand it," Shruti muttered, helping him. "You really shouldn't have killed soldiers. The Shadow King won't let this slide."

Hiran held his hands up. "No one said we killed them."

"But you did kill us," a corpse argued.

Hiran ignored him. "We retrieved their bodies for shadow mass, and possibly monster bait for larger shadow mass."

One of the corpses dropped from the ropes, whining, "Ouch."

Shruti stood upright. "You're a murderous criminal now."

"That's not true. I was a murderer of monsters way before this . . . assuming I killed them at all."

She lowered her eyes to his wrists. "Let me see your katar."

"To see if the blade is still wet with their blood?" He leaned toward her. "To turn in the one who protects your group and provides shadow mass that will save everyone in the realm?"

She huffed and tugged on her top to adjust it at the waist. "That's the only reason we keep you around, you know."

"The soldiers meant to turn me in, as if what I'm doing is a crime."

"And they were given fair warning to let us be," Rohan added. "Very important details."

She glanced at the four keshi. "How did you command the steeds so well?"

He shrugged, evading her implication that only soldiers and royals could command the keshi. Instead, he said, "Let's get to work."

As they toiled with the corpses, dismantling two for shadow mass and using the other two to lure larger beasts, no one noticed a rapidly spreading crack in the dome high above. A white zigzag fracture bolted across the wall, meeting another fissure and then another, until all edges met. The sound was like spices hitting a sizzling-hot pan.

Hiran heard it and searched for the sound. Could no one else hear it?

Then he smelled it. The white plague mixed with something else, something pure and aromatic, almost sweet. He couldn't place the scent, but he could only describe it as the very opposite of rot.

He followed his nose, sniffing and dragging in copious amounts of air, climbing over rocks, and nearly trampling Rohan.

"What's wrong with you?" Rohan asked, shoving him off.

"You don't smell that?" Hiran asked, focused on the growing scent.

"I smell your dirty boots. Ugh." Rohan slapped dirt and caked mud from his shoulder.

By the time Hiran looked up, toward the source of the smell and sound, a rift had exploded.

"Take cover!" Hiran yelled, grabbing Shruti's arms and jumping back.

Large pieces flew past him, inches from his nose, harpooning trees, rocks, stone buildings, and a dakini who screamed in agony. And it wasn't simply the pain of being staked to the ground like an animal. Her body was cruelly bent backward, spine broken, impaled on the long shard of hardened shadow mass bleeding into pure white.

If such a strike wasn't instant death, then the light of the true realm was. Blinding light shone down upon the dakini, leaving only the smoky remains of her burnt body.

Several dakini screamed, and everyone scrambled out of the light's reach. Shruti pushed out from underneath Hiran and stumbled to her feet, standing aghast. Hiran followed, heaving.

A handful of animals and birds had been unfortunate enough to get caught in the light, and they, too, lay as smoldering chunks of burnt flesh.

Every mask went up as the sound of skittering crested the dome. The edges of the opening revealed the dome's incredible thickness—necessary to keep the light of the true realm out—which only begged the question of how the light could penetrate and pull it apart.

"Fix the breach!" the dakini yelled.

Everyone began the formidable work right where they stood, gathering shadow mass from whatever they could, even if it meant leeching it from living trees and animals.

As they worked on condensing shadow mass, the skittering came to a crescendo at the opening. Long fingers, talons, and tendrils curled over the edges. White and feathery.

Hiran's heart went wild in his chest, his thoughts in a frenzy. Rohan looked to him, a silent expression that said, *If there was a time to unfurl those wings, it would be now.*

But what would he do? Was it the white plague? Could it be killed?

A deep, guttural growl rumbled in his chest. Crap. He had to unleash his wings. He had to give the dakini time. He had to do something, even if that something was pointless.

Just as the furled mass of his wings shivered, as the skin on his back crawled and stretched before his wings could rip through his flesh, two dakini shot a disc of shadow into the opening. With their hands above them, their feet positioned to take the brunt of the force, they groaned, keeping the shadow in place as the feathery white creatures piled onto the disc.

"Hurry!" a dakini yelled, her feet sinking into the ground.

There was no time to craft a large shadow mass in their usual ethereal way. Pellets of shadow mass flew to the edges of the opening, hastily molded together, sewing up the breach as fast as the dakini could work. Finally, when the last pebble of an opening closed, everyone fell to their knees in exhaustion. They looked to the impaled corpse of their fallen kin, stricken by their loss.

NINE

ESHANI

Eshani's body was heavy, her mind buzzing. Her neck hurt the worst, and when she opened her eyes, she realized why. She was lying on the ground, her neck over a large rock. She carefully massaged the sore spot, only to discover that every part of her was sore.

Cold tinged the air. Moss grew over everything. The trees were set wider apart than the jungle but were connected by vines like a web entangling prey in a clutch of boughs. Tall grass cloaked Eshani... and concealed things from her.

A low growl percolated through those chest-high blades of grass, forcing Eshani to scramble into a crouch. She gripped the dagger at her waist, grateful that whatever had brought her here hadn't taken her satchel or her weapon. The weight of the dagger was a source of confidence and familiarity, enough to root a bit of hope. She was a fighter. She could defend herself.

Placing a palm against the ground to feel the energy of this strange and unwelcoming place, Eshani dug deep into her bones to unleash the tethered tendrils of touch, invisible and ethereal tentacles uncurling from her palm and seeping into the grass. She felt along the root network extending so far in every direction that she couldn't feel where the grass ended. She was in the middle of nowhere, yet she'd been here before.

In the twilight, the gray clouds stood still, the breeze nonexistent amid the maddening silence. How could she forget this place?

Eshani gathered all her might and determination. The time had arrived, and she needed to face the bargain she'd made so long ago.

Her breath rolled out from her chest, warming her in the chill. Something broke through the grass, and shock overcame Eshani upon first sight. She nearly fell to her knees as the beast rose to full height and angled toward her, sniffing the air, thin lips curled over fangs.

The creature came face-to-face with Eshani and blinked. Large golden eyes took in the girl. The creature could easily kill Eshani with one chomp, one swipe, and yet Eshani nearly sobbed from joy.

She was not afraid. She offered her hand: a scent, and a gesture of peace.

The tiger sniffed, its whiskers twitching. The golden hairs of its coat, the honey eyes, the tremendous height...it could only be Lekha. But would Lekha remember Eshani after so long? It had been years, and Eshani was taller, curvier, a little more filled out with an abundance of food and safety, her hair longer and thicker and tied into one braid that snaked down her back. And Lekha...well, she looked just the way Eshani remembered her. Still standing at five feet tall on all fours, her fur shiny and golden with streaks of white, her honey eyes keen.

The tiger remained intense as she lowered herself to the ground, gaze never leaving Eshani, and crept one paw forward. She stalked Eshani as she'd stalked prey so many times before. Calculating, cunning, *lethal.*

"Lekha," she whispered, pleading, "it's me. Eshani."

Lekha froze. An impasse.

Eshani swallowed. "I raised you from a cub. I kept you hidden in the courtyard and fed you with stolen milk. Mama would scold you when you returned sopping wet from the river and then yell at you when you ignored her and shook water all over the house. Neighbors would complain when we ran through the city and you scared their animals. You taught me how to stalk and ambush when you practiced with Mama's skirts. You let me ride you like a promise of eternal friendship. I treated all your wounds, pulled thorns from your paw, and bathed you with sweet-scented soaps. I comforted you when you wept over Papa leaving."

Lekha pounced, and the sudden weight nearly knocked Eshani back. But Lekha hadn't attacked. Lekha was on her back paws, at an angle so that she wasn't completely hovering over Eshani. She was still much taller, but her front paws fell around Eshani's neck, the pads curling over her shoulders. Lekha devoured her with nuzzles and purred in such a fierce hug that Eshani had to pull away just to breathe.

Lekha didn't let her go, her cheek smashing into Eshani's side, pushing Eshani to hug her back. Which Eshani did, even though she could barely stay on her own feet. Lekha's sheer weight kept pushing Eshani back as she wept against the tiger, her face smothered by fur.

"What are you doing here?"

Oh, how she'd missed her friend. But the reunion was short-lived. Lekha took her protective stance, stepping in front of Eshani, as an inky monster appeared. It was the one who had stolen her from the boat, the same one she'd met years earlier, a witness to her deal.

She clutched her weapon.

It watched them with large teardrop-shaped eyes, unblinking and wholly white. The monster was as tall and gangly as she'd remembered.

The creature moved its mouth, and a series of clicks vibrated the air. Something rustled, a sound that came from every direction.

Eshani gasped, searching every which way. She felt them long before she saw them. A scratch down the back of her neck, a slither down her spine, a cold breath on her ear.

The shades.

Lekha backed into Eshani, but she went lethargic, shaking her head as her paws and legs weakened. Lekha slumped toward the ground, and Eshani stepped in front of her to guard her, to protect her.

"I'm here. Leave her alone."

The shades appeared, those four hovering, shadowy apparitions ambiguous in form and matter. They didn't possess eyes or teeth or claws or limbs of any sort, but they scared her far more than the inky monster who had dragged her here and now stood off to the side. It cocked its chin, urging her forward.

She demanded, "You'll let her leave unharmed?"

The creature nodded.

The shades bypassed Lekha, who struggled to stay awake, and careened straight into Eshani via every pore, through her gaping mouth and nostrils. She felt them in her brain, caressing her thoughts, knowing her secrets, her lineage, her heritage, down to the molecular level that told stories of those before her, of her mother and grandmother and foremothers . . . of the very first shadow-born nagin.

Their grasp on her body from the inside lifted her off the ground, and she could do nothing except stare, unmoving, into the darkness of the shades. In them, she saw the cosmos, the unfathomably black farthest reaches of space, where even light couldn't touch. She saw teeth and eyes and claws and her own worst nightmares. She saw her world drowning in blood and choking on ash.

Then she felt something she'd never sensed before. The shades found it and drew it out, like plucking a delicate anther from its stamen at the center of a tightly closed rose. Part of the flower, yet hidden and unknown until it fully bloomed. Even from that, they lifted pollen fragments and read to the smallest, unseen core. A thread of humanity twined with venom. Something lush and pleasantly dark.

An answer perhaps?

Whatever it was, they seemed placated. They replaced the threads in the core, tucked the pollen back upon the anther, and reattached the anther, in turn, to the stamen, which they then covered by the tightly closed petals of a rose yet to bloom.

It was the only way Eshani could explain what she felt.

The shades released her, seeping out of her mouth and nostrils and pores. Now she knew why they'd bargained with her. All they wanted was to...open a portal, a gateway into their home world. They couldn't return with her until she unlocked it from the other side, and the Gatekeeper would aid her. They'd discerned from the lost memories of her dreams that he had summoned her. He would show her how to return, for only he could reveal the portal from the other side. That was all. And then she could return. The shades had helped her people long ago, and all they wanted was to return to their world. It seemed like a fair deal.

It didn't matter if Eshani didn't possess such fantastical abilities. She had to keep her end of the bargain. They would torture Lekha if she didn't go. They would find Sithara as easily as they'd found her. They could hurt Manisha and Mama and every last naga.

The inky monster grunted and took two stomps toward her. Lekha's breathing turned erratic and labored. She attempted to move, to crawl, as Eshani soothed her with long strokes across her fur.

"Stop. I'll go."

Eshani hugged Lekha, tears streaming down her face. "I thought I would never let you go again, but you must flee. Run fast and far and *never* return. My sweet, sweet Lekha."

She pushed Lekha, but Lekha barely budged. Since Lekha was fighting against the lethargy to stay with Eshani, Eshani hardened her emotions. With a final hug against Lekha's soft fur and solid muscles, she kissed the tiger's forehead, whispering, "I love you. Now leave me."

Eshani walked. And walked. And walked.

Roots curved out of the ground, arching toward the canopy before plunging back into the mud. Creepy things crawled among the rocks, creatures the length of her arm, with a hundred legs and many pincers. Scary things lurked in the brook, slimy backs showing through the water, slashing the air with sharpened hooks like external spines. Menacing things scuttled up the trees, blending into the black bark, so it appeared that the trees themselves had eyes and teeth.

Eshani stole a final breath—her last, she thought. In the end, if she died for her people, for her family, it was the worthiest death that could be bestowed upon her.

She ignored the slight sound of breaking twigs behind her and walked into the thicket. Into the darkness. And not the sort brought by night, but an unnatural darkness. She couldn't see a thing.

Her breathing came harder as she ventured toward the edge of death. But if this was death, then it was a fine way to die.

Eshani stumbled over the uneven ground, dismissing anything sliding against her ankles and arms. On instinct, she reached out, though she wasn't expecting to find anything. She felt the roughness of bark that somehow bent to her touch—a touch that drew in random, violent images of an underrealm, a world below this world. Flashes of crimson water flowing down a river. A black crystal palace sparkling beneath a lavender moon. Extravagant jewels flashing against decadent clothes. A court full of masked strangers. Men covered in golden breastplates and shoulder armor.

Death was eerily beautiful.

She'd never known utter loneliness as she did in this moment.

Complete silence, total darkness. The emptiness tugged her out of her body, pulling pieces of her every which way. Time and space fused into her being, sent fragments of her floating adrift. She rose and fell like petals on the breeze, giddy and lightheaded.

The darkness breathed. Heaved in and out—a living being swallowing her whole. Up was the same as down. Left identical to right. Forward interchangeable with backward. Eshani was petrified in place, her fingers twitching for Lekha, Mama, Papa, Sithara, Manisha. But no one answered her silent call. She was alone.

Willing her feet to move, she counted every feeble step. One, two, three . . . little things that somehow helped by imperceptible measures.

Her eyes widened, taking in what appeared to be ambiguous shapes, shadows amid shadows, cloaked in cavernous shades of black. Maybe she was seeing what didn't exist, or maybe she saw everything. Each tilt and lean and slither.

Whispers swarmed around her, like a horde of buzzing insects, echoing as if they were everywhere and nowhere at once. A coldness fell onto her skin and seeped into her bones, an aching chill stiffening her back.

Eshani clenched her eyes shut, trudging through her thoughts to dig out the sayings of her parents and foremothers.

Be strong. Be resilient. Fear nothing.

She clutched her necklace. Her eyes snapped open, her thoughts incantations forging light through the darkness. Fireflies flashed here and there. First a few dull yellow flickers, never in the same place twice. With each passing second, a dozen more were added to the dance until the sparks lit the night on fire. They were beautiful and unbothered.

Eshani breathed a little easier and walked forward, reaching out for them. There was a sense of calmness associated with fireflies. Maybe because they reminded her of late-summer nights chasing the tiny lights across the city of Anand, watching them illuminate gardens like a beautiful, fantastical world filled with magic. Her grandmothers would say fireflies were special, for they carried secrets and made the terrifying beautiful. In this moment, in this strangeness, those words had never rung truer.

The darkness was still there, still breathing, but it had become beguiling, masking the horrors.

One by one, the flashes flickered off and on, changing from yellow to pale pink. As Eshani walked ahead, she noted how the pink hues deepened to darker pinks, then reds, and finally deep crimson. The fireflies stopped moving but sparkled in suspension.

Eshani, moved by curiosity, placed a finger to a red firefly and jerked back when she felt the wetness. She looked at her finger, the tip glistening with blood. Her breathing turned erratic, her gaze searching the darkness as the hairs on the back of her neck stood up. Goose bumps prickled her arms, and a scourge of terror swept down her spine.

Oh, how she wished she was with Sithara on their way to Manisha.

Upon that thought, ambiguous shadowy doors materialized. Obscure images flashed in those gateways, each one touching and bending the next, until she passed a particular door.

She backtracked, her heart racing as a blurred image revealed a large, opulent hall with pillars of marble and walls of sculpted animals. The ceiling was curved, perhaps a dome? There was a line of orbs near the top, and she could see a girl climbing down. Dim lighting glinted off the metallic threads of her pink-and-pista salwar kameez, her long braid tucked over one shoulder.

The girl turned, hurrying past Eshani, past the diya-lit altar. Was this the temple on the floating mountains? Was that…Manisha? Clean, fresh clothes, with a soft roundness to her face? Signs of prosperity.

Eshani hurled herself at the gateway upon first recognition, calling out, "Manisha!"

Manisha returned, her eyes drawn to the portal, to this shadowy, ambiguous door, one without a frame. Eshani could've wept, laying eyes upon the sister she hadn't seen in years. She covered her mouth to hold back her sobs, reaching out for her, when the dark creatures bristled and shoved her forward.

"No!" Eshani fought against them, against their bites and scratches.

"Take us with you!" the monsters snarled as one.

"Get away!" Eshani snapped.

"Do not fret; they are attached to the gloaming in between worlds," a calming voice told her, a twinkle of lights in the yonder, an embodied constellation.

"Who are you?" Eshani shouted. Was the voice real? The only thing Eshani was certain of was that she was unsure of everything.

"The first."

The first what? This was madness!

Soothing and surreal, the voice promised, "This is kismet and a fate as determined as fury."

"Let me see my sister!"

Manisha appeared like the fleeting sparkle of a star, a taste of both joy and cruelty, for it was not long enough. All the while, the voice had been saying, "This is the in-between where gateways touch, compressing time. What you see has already transpired, and you are not meant to linger. You must proceed or you, too, will be trapped in the in-between."

The voice faded, drawn into the in-between as the darkness shoved Eshani out of this mind-bending gateway and into the Nightmare Realm.

TEN

HIRAN

O nly dakini were allowed near dakini villages, which meant Hiran and Rohan slept outside the village borders, with little protection. It was fine by Hiran. The dakini were in mourning after what had happened, and he wanted to venture south in search of beasts for shadow mass.

"The realm is set up to fail," Rohan said, unrolling his bed. "The King has to do something. He's not even protecting the ones who can hold the dome."

Hiran stiffened at the thought of his brother. "He doesn't care."

"Oh, right. You would know. Better yet, we need a new king. When's that happening, by the way?" Yawning, Rohan settled in and mumbled, "Tell your sister hello for me."

Hiran hadn't seen Holika for many sleeps. He was itching to return to Eshani . . . to see more of her, to know if she'd neared land. He'd actually summoned her, as if he had any power. He scoffed at the thought. As if his imaginary title of Gatekeeper had compelled reality, making Eshani cross mortal waters, face the shades, and find a portal that been lost for generations.

It had been so long. He wanted to make sure Holika was safe. Surely, the Court of Nightmares had figured out what she was doing if they'd been so close to locating Eshani themselves.

Where are you, sister? he pondered as he fell into the tight grasp of sleep.

As if she'd heard his call, Holika appeared.

She wasn't . . . the same.

She appeared as a silver figure made of liquid, dripping iridescence from her wings, eyes white. Golden chains pierced her brow and temple, holding one eye wide open. One side of her mouth was pulled up into a perpetual smile kept in place by thin golden chains piercing her cheek.

"Why . . . why do you look like that?" Hiran asked.

"What? You don't like shades of white?" She pouted, which made her look even more terrifying, her muscles straining against the chains.

"I mean the piercings. They look painful. Why are you mutilated?"

"To look all the scarier. My eye sees all when I walk the dreamscape. And my mouth . . . Well, I went to visit the mortal King, since the Court keeps circling him—an old man on a petty throne—and when I first spoke, he told me to keep my pretty mouth shut. Girls don't speak to him unless spoken to, apparently. He didn't realize we were in a dream. And when I kept speaking, he said I should smile more. Girls should smile more to be pleasant so men will notice them. He's just like Father! I got sick of listening to that."

"So you pinned your lips back?"

Holika patted her mouth and frowned as if he'd insulted her beauty. "Well, first I cut *his* mouth wider to make it look like he was smiling, because if a girl should smile, then an old man should smile back. Don't you think?"

Hiran shuddered, but he tried not to show it. It was hard to keep that visual out of his head, of his sister sadistically leaning over men and slicing their faces open. The Gloom in Hiran's periphery, however, chuckled.

"I let him scream. And as he sat on his throne weeping, I realized I wouldn't get any information from him and left him alone." Her gaze swept to the side. "But I've visited many men, and they all say the same thing. I was so tired of hearing it, little brother. Thus, I pinned my lips back so they had no reason to say it again. Now when they see me, they just scream."

Her smile slipped, held up by the chains now. She added, "I think I prefer screams to belittling."

Hiran swallowed. "Are you all right? All alone in the dreamscape?"

"Oh, I'm not alone. I have friends."

"Really? Who?"

"I meet all sorts in the dreamscape. I can make them do whatever I want, and I want some of them to be my friends. So we're friends."

"Ah..." He lifted his chin and eyed her. The dreamscape was sure to lead to insanity, especially for a girl who had been considered strange all her life, but he hadn't thought the madness would run so deep.

"Some girls in the court, to start. They thought you were cute, did you know? Before the immolation. And some girls in the mortal realm are kind. I like it there. They dream to escape reality, so I give them good dreams."

"Do you really?"

She cackled. "I'm not a monster! I'm there to search for information, but I know the difference between good and bad when I step into a person's dreams."

"Well, you're not evil."

She vigorously shook her head, her brows arching upward. "No.

I'm truly not. Even though the dreamers think I am. Sometimes I have to make them listen, but they see."

"Aside from dreams, you're truly alone in there?"

"Yes," she replied solemnly, sadness evident in her one unpinned eye. "I thought I would find those before me, but they're gone, it seems. Just me merrily prancing from dream to dream."

"I wish I could go there with you."

Her non-pierced brow hiked up, giving her face a more symmetrically creepy appearance.

Hiran frowned. "A giant piece of shadow wall fell through not long ago. It killed a dakini and almost let in creatures from the true realm."

"That sounds bad."

"I wish that our brother would at least—"

"Do *not* call him a brother," she growled. "He's lucky the Court of Nightmares protects his dreams, otherwise I'd pry my way into his gaseous head the way I did his witch of a mother." The tips of her fangs flashed in the dim glow of the fireflies.

Holika shrugged, abruptly returning to a more jovial mood, conjuring up yellow and orange butterflies. Little wings flapped around her face. She giggled so that the pins sagged away from their usual tautness. He wished she would let go of that face, of that perpetual smile, of the anger over their father's comments. But Holika was stubborn, and she wore the insult like armor, turning the thing men demanded into the very fabric of their nightmares.

Hiran watched his elder sister, dissecting her emotions past the energetic facade, beneath the mutilations. Wondering if her vibrancy was a coping mechanism to deal with suffering and loss and pain. If her piercings were a way for her to take control, to show that she could literally grin and bear it.

She *tsk*ed, wagging a finger in front of his face. "I know what you're thinking, remember? I don't harm myself because of others. They harm me enough as it is. Why should I feel sad or depressed because of them? I choose to be happy...even if it is in a wicked way. But fret not, little brother! I assure you that I don't take it out on anyone who doesn't deserve it."

"And you're the judge of who deserves it?"

She dropped her hand. If it hadn't been for her piercings and pullings, she'd have looked deadpan. He sort of missed that flat stoicism she had right before jerking back to grins and wide eyes and excitable chatter. A moment of relaxed facial muscles that conveyed a dozen different things, depending on the conversation. Annoyance, anger, sarcasm, wit, pain, wonder.

"Do you want to know something?" she asked, tearing him away from thoughts she'd already deciphered.

He walked alongside her as the dreamscape changed from dim to bright, moving through an endless world of white. Holika blended in, a flash of iridescence in an otherwise blindingly monochromatic void.

"Huh?"

"The dreamscape is riddled with these little...hmm...I guess... feathers of fire? They flutter around like dust, some small, the size of a fingernail. The sickly girl everyone tried to tear down will live on forever, meandering from dream to dream." Holika gave a short twirl, reminiscent of how she twirled in her pretty dresses as a child.

She continued, "And long after my metaphysical form has decayed, I will continue to exist in these little fire feathers. They are the memories of past dreamreavers. The curse has been around for a long time. It was never you," Holika added softly, touching the top of his head. "The white plague was always going to come. Past dreamreavers saw it before. On a smaller scale, eradicating the shadow dome and the balanced partnership between asuras and dakini."

"One serves the other now," Hiran added.

She hummed knowingly. The Gloom followed them, mimicking Hiran's walk and stance, to which Holika said, "You know, brother, if you merely accepted this darkness, you might no longer feel incomplete."

Hiran sarcastically laughed. "No."

"Don't fight yourself. Accepting it might give you direction, confidence. Look at him; he's full of it."

The Gloom's eyes manifested into white orbs, which he batted innocently. And then he flashed an impish smirk.

"He's full of something, all right," Hiran muttered.

The bright white around them crackled into a vision of one of the outlying towns. In the distance, a halo of light seeped in through a crack in the shadow dome, shining shimmering light upon crumbling homes, broken trees, and demolished belongings.

"What? Is this really what the southern region looks like? A war zone?"

Holika nodded solemnly. "A beautiful thing broken."

Hiran stepped through the debris partially buried in mounds of rising dirt. Wherever the shimmering light touched, things deteriorated faster. Light meant life for most realms, but not this one.

The dakini lay with spears of glimmering light through their chests like physical rods. Roots of light sprouted around the wounds and grew from nostrils and mouths and ears, pushing up through fingernail beds.

"This isn't the white plague," Hiran said, kneeling beside a dakini who gasped her last breaths. Blood pooled in the corners of her vacant eyes, fully white as light ruptured the membrane. Her neck was bent back as if the force of the light rod had broken it.

Her fingers twitched. On her palms glowed a blinding white mehndi pattern, consuming her flesh.

"The light of the true realm is striking back. Quite literally. Patala has had enough."

Hiran stumbled back when a sliver of the light went for him, a snapping of thin tentacles.

"Remember, nothing can hurt you here—well, physically."

He looked up at her from his haunches, heaving out a breath. "So . . . the light is breaking through and . . . targeting the dakini?"

"Yes! The light is smart. And we never knew. Or, if someone long ago knew, that information was lost."

"But the dakini are the ones who hold the walls in place. They're the builders and keepers of the dome. Without them, the walls can't be maintained or fixed." His words spilled out with a hint of trepidation.

"Well, I just said Patala is smart," he deadpanned, standing to glare at his sister.

"The light found a way. Thus, the Nightmare Realm is crumbling. And it's not your fault! See? Good news, eh?" She elbowed him.

He turned in a half circle to find one body after another. Not ones staked by light, but ones that had turned ever darker. Asuras. Men and women and children lay in strange poses. Joints bent in unnatural ways. Some had shredded clothing, the garments of the poor who worked on the outer edges, revealing grayish flesh stripped off bones. Exposed ribs and stomachs, hearts swollen with maggots, crusted wounds from axes and swords and bricks and rocks.

The stench of decay rose from the dead, and Hiran instinctively threw an arm over his mouth and nose in this *incredibly* realistic vision.

Hollow eyes stared up at the crackling sky. Branchlike veins hardened beneath the skin of the dead, thickening and spreading.

In the near distance, a squelching sound caught Hiran's attention. There, shadows manifested as large creatures with gangly canine legs, pointed ears, and lashing tails, consuming the dead and the dying alike.

"I'm sorry," he told the dead and the dying and those being eaten. "This is not a demise I'd wish upon anyone."

"Well, maybe Tarak's insolent face."

"Does he not know?"

Holika scoffed. "He knows. Our conniving half-sibling, unbeknownst to the villages, has left them to fend for themselves. That's why he doesn't send any more soldiers to the borderlands, and why he keeps the strongest dakini at his side. He's building a smaller shadow dome around the palace territory."

"No." Hiran ardently shook his head. "The dakini wouldn't allow that."

She planted her hands on her hip and cocked her head. "Are you arguing with the person who saw for herself inside their heads?"

Hiran raised his hands in defense. "It's just hard to believe."

"Believe it. The powerful will do whatever it takes to protect themselves first. Most of the dakini have no idea. Only the strongest elders, the ones at his side, know about the inner dome. But no one knows the truth—he's told them this is a safeguard to bring all the survivors, free of the white plague, within a more manageable dome. He is a liar. He's fully fixated on getting to the Palace of the Dead and retrieving amrita. He doesn't care if everyone else dies. He doesn't care about his wives or concubines. If his mother were alive, he wouldn't even care about her. Selfish bastard. No matter. Let them die."

"Holika," Hiran warned.

She raised her non-pierced brow. *"Yes?"* The word came out equally sharp.

"Elder sister," he said instead.

"Hmm?" she hummed, chipper once again.

He thought of the dakini, his friends, and all the innocent people in the villages. He had to tell them, to warn them. "Some deserve to live. And what about us? What if the light of the true realm destroys the Court? You'll die with it. And what if the light destroys me?"

She frowned, casting a glance at the Gloom quietly hovering in the corner. "Everything always circles back to one thing: You have to eliminate Tarak and take the crown. He's not fit to rule. This darkness is willing to do what you are not, but if you're truly concerned about the realm, then let the darkness rise."

Hiran released a harsh breath, his hands trembling. Tarak had always been stronger; Hiran could not defeat him without turning into their father, for Father slayed enemies without a second thought.

Holika's face grew pensive. "As for the Court, well . . . I don't think they can die. They're not alive, just entities with the ability to get into dreams, stuck inside statues. Aren't they special? The only thing to survive if Patala cracks open the shadow dome and skewers every dark creature with its unruly light."

Her reflectiveness eased away, and she hummed lightheartedly. "Anyway, the nagin will open the portal. You will be ruler and savior, do things your predecessors never could. All you need to do is get the nagin to help us instead of being used by Tarak."

Right as Hiran thought of how much he did not want to go against Tarak, and how much he did not want the crown, Holika snapped her eyes toward him. A warning. For there was no other way, and even the Gloom knew it. It stood with hands clasped behind its back, chin high and haughty. A *royal*. It was darkness and greed and violence and cruelty and all the things Hiran did not want to be, but things the realm perhaps needed.

A flicker of cobalt on its face matched Hiran's inherited markings. He wished the Gloom would just disappear and stop silently nagging him to control the shadows and darkness around them, the essence of the realm—the very thing the crown was supposed to control.

Instead, the Gloom grinned. Fragments of shadows swam toward it. The entity was becoming stronger, and Hiran felt it struggling for control.

Holika, oblivious to the quiet battle, pulled her hands behind her back in a stretch. She then steepled her fingers and added, "Oh. There's one more thing you should see...."

Hiran stiffened. He had a way of knowing when even worse news was coming.

ELEVEN

ESHANI

The darkness had swallowed Eshani whole and regurgitated her into a world more chilling than the marshlands.

She stumbled over rocks and logs and fell to the ground, her palms hitting the dirt before her face made impact. She turned over and scurried away, gaping at the absolute darkness she'd been tossed from. There was nothing there. Which meant no way back, and there was no one in sight to help, no Gatekeeper as the shades promised.

No.

Standing, Eshani took in her surroundings, a mirrored image of the marshlands but without the gray sky. Instead, the sky was a deep red color. It boomed with thunderclaps and streaks of purple lightning. She jumped at the sound, clutching her ears.

A dull fog crept up from the marshy land, bathing the ground in obscurity and trickling up black-bark trees draped in mossy vines.

Panic rose through Eshani, a frenzy of thoughts, a deadening of her limbs, a surge in the pit of her belly. She gripped her satchel straps and stepped toward the unseen gateway. Bewilderment rose as she searched frantically, tossing aside vines and pushing away branches.

It couldn't just disappear! Bile rose in her throat. The wild was one thing, but an entirely other realm?

This is impossible. There is no way out. There is no way out!

Breathing harder, Eshani walked through every area, hands groping the air, hoping to find the unseen portal. Somewhere, deep inside, she knew that it wasn't as simple as walking through. What had the shades said? She searched her jumbled thoughts. Ah! The Gatekeeper had to open it. She spun on her heels. Where was he, then?

Something slithered beneath the fog, and Eshani jumped just in time to escape a giant lamprey's deadly bite. It raised itself up, opening a large, circular mouth. While Eshani was focused on it, another appeared to her right. She sensed a third behind her.

Her dagger was too short; she'd be no match for them in a fight. She ran, barely missing their lunges. The ground shook beneath her as they chased her off. A series of clicks and chitters ignited the air as trees shuddered to life. They were monsters made of vines, multiple limbs reaching for her, and thorn projectiles that barely missed Eshani's flesh. The thorns pierced the ground and released something that smelled of sulfur.

Eshani covered her face when vines snapped around her, snatching her ankle. She drew her weapon and sliced the restraints, ignoring the residual sting left in their wake. Limbs reached for her, and more projectiles crossed the air. With every second, the creatures choked off access to the gateway and forced Eshani to flee from the deadly forest, running as fast as her aching legs would take her. Her childhood love of acrobatics, of flips and high jumps, helped her evade the attacks. Nimble movements, despite the pain ricocheting down her arms and the burn in her chest.

Skidding out from the forest and into plain sight, she ran toward—and then around—a group of girls ahead. Tall, muscular beings. They were slated with various shades of gray, armor over long kurtas and leggings with one striking purple stripe down the leg. Hooded cloaks covered their heads as they worked, their slender arms held high to the sky, balancing orbs of dark mist hovering in the air. White eyes flashed at Eshani, the only thing visible beneath their hoods and masks.

"Take cover!" they cried.

Instead of escaping into the fields or the decrepit towers stationed every now and then, the women turned the balls of darkness into shields and braced for impact. Others cultivated spears from the misty balls or drew swords, javelins, bows and arrows, and battle-axes.

Eshani knew that she and the hooded strangers shared a common enemy: The forest creatures lurching into the open had incited screams.

She ran past the group, locking eyes with a girl who yelled, "Hey!"

"Shruti!" shouted another girl at the first.

The group battled the monsters, driving them back into the forest.

"Pishacha!" the first girl lamented.

Eshani stole a glance over her shoulder.

"Hello," a cryptic voice whispered.

Eshani spun on her heel to face what the girls had called a pishacha. She was the very fabric of nightmares, even more so than the shades, who, all things considered, had been benevolent in comparison. This being was strikingly tall and thin, the bones showing like jutting knives in her clavicle, shoulders, arms, ribs, and hips. She wore an onyx breastplate matching her skirt. Her skin was dark green, with veins bulging along her arms like creeping vines. She could easily slip in and out of shadows undetected; even her protruding red eyes could've been mistaken for flower buds.

"Dinner, I see."

Eshani gulped, her chest turning heavy from the sheer terror engulfing her entire body. Monsters who wanted to kill her were bad enough, but ones who wanted to eat her alive?

"No thanks," she grunted, retrieving her dagger. She ducked and swung upward, catching the blade on the pishacha's armor. Metal hit metal, clanging and igniting a spark.

The creature was taken aback, but not for long. She swiped her fingers across the air, fingers that began at her elbows and scissored out.

The talons missed Eshani's arm as she dropped to her haunches and cut across the creature's thighs. The pishacha howled and stumbled back. Enraged, her form shifted to something broader, wider, stonier.

The menacing woman backhanded Eshani with what felt like a boulder, knocking her across the clearing, her back hitting the side of a tower. Pain exploded down her side, and she wailed.

The creature was at Eshani's feet in two wide hops, sadistic glee scribbled across her features. "What a delicacy, whatever you are," she said, her words oddly like a trill that Eshani could understand.

As the beast leaned down to feast, four arrows careened into her head. Eshani immediately went for the throat, rolling away from the cascade of blood and onto her knees.

She gasped for breath as two of the hooded girls neared. A third decapitated the beast. The ground drank its fill of starry-night blood.

Eshani was on her feet before the girls finished checking the creature for life. There wasn't any, unless the head lolling down the hill allowed it. Gripping her dagger, Eshani positioned herself for another fight.

The girls were taller than her by several inches, their white eyes narrowed between their angular gill-like masks and their hoods. They looked from Eshani to one another, perplexed. A chill breeze pushed past them, and the fabric of their head coverings fluttered, showing traces of mehndi-green markings on bald heads.

"We're not going to attack you," one of the girls said.

"She doesn't look or smell infected," another said. She turned to Eshani. "*Are* you?"

Eshani shook her head.

The first girl pressed the side of her jaw, and the mask of gills retracted into a thin, neat row at her ears to reveal pale taupe-gray skin pulled tight on high cheekbones. Her long neck was covered in stacks of beaded necklaces in muted colors. She was both strikingly beautiful and strangely otherworldly. "If anything, we should be thanking you for helping to take down one of them."

The other two girls eyed Eshani as the first scrutinized her with a pause. "Who are you?" one asked.

"Eshani," she said. Not that a name meant anything in a different realm. No one would know of her.

"My name's Vidya. This is Shruti."

Before Vidya could introduce the third girl, Shruti blurted, "What *are* you?" Her voice was deeper, severe.

Eshani blinked. "What are *you*?"

"I asked first, and we saved your life, so let's skip the pleasantries."

"Excuse my friend," Vidya interjected, her tone soft. "We don't meet many new people. We're dakini. But everyone should know that. Which makes me think that you're not from here?"

"Where would she be from? The true realm?" Shruti scoffed.

"True realm?" Eshani echoed. And . . . had she said *dakini*?

The dakini pressed their lips together and quieted, their milky eyes darting away. From this close, Eshani could make out the opaque irises beneath, gray like everything else here. Dakini were myths, stories told to children to keep them from misbehaving. This couldn't be real.

"Don't run around alone in the dark," mothers would tell little ones, "or a dakini will snatch you."

"Don't go thieving in the night," strangers would warn, "or a dakini will feast on you."

Dakini were lore, flesh-eating terrors seeking to devour anyone unfortunate enough to get caught in their path of destruction and bloodlust. But these didn't look so bad. Until Vidya smiled. Her teeth were all jagged points filling up a rather large mouth.

"So, what are *you*, then, and where did you come from?" Vidya inquired.

"I'm from... the marshlands. And I'm a nagin."

The girls snickered. "A nagin? Where are your serpents for hair and snake tail? Your slit eyes and scales?"

"Why would I have those?"

"That's what the myth claims."

"Well, your myth claims that you're terrors hunting people to devour."

The girls glared at Eshani, and Eshani glared right back, her grip remaining snug around her weapon. One by one, the dakini cackled. "You can't trust mythology!"

"Did you really think a half-snake monster existed?" Shruti cawed.

"How can anything have snakes for hair? Do they eat? And where does the food go?" Vidya balked at the idea.

Eshani smiled. She'd never heard of nagin being literally part serpent. How ludicrous was that?

"We don't hunt or feast on people," Vidya assured her.

"Gross," Shruti added.

"We prefer plump grubs on a salad of centipedes, thank you."

Eshani maintained her smile. To each their own, so long as they weren't plotting to consume her. Her family would never believe that she'd encountered all sorts of mythical beings, but she knew one day she would tell them. She would see them again.

Shruti asked, "Where are the marshlands? I've never heard of them."

Pointing toward the forest, Eshani answered, "There. I'd like to go home."

Vidya replied, "Oh, no. We don't go there. It is forbidden. How did you survive the dark forest? It must've been a long journey—the forest is dense."

"Are the marshlands on the other side?" Shruti pressed.

"I'm not quite sure, to be honest." The field around them blurred. Eshani stumbled back.

Vidya caught her, asking, "Are you all right?"

"Must be the fuss of battle," Shruti ascertained as Eshani's eyelids fluttered closed.

She tried her best to stay alert in this unknown and terrifying realm, in the arms of these legendary women, but lack of food, water, and rest, muddled with all the emotionally brutal moments between the boat and now, had caught up to her.

Eshani succumbed to the darkness undulating behind closing lids. She could only hope the dakini were nowhere close to the gory myth spoken of them across the mortal realm.

ESHANI AWOKE WITH A GASP, SCUTTLING BACK ON A BED IN a cozy room with a fire crackling in the corner. A small, bald head with green markings popped up from a low table at the foot of the bed, a young girl with big off-white eyes. Peering into dakini eyes was like looking into a vortex. Hypnotizing and frightening.

The girl grinned a full-tooth grin, displaying jagged teeth. She was a miniature version of Vidya, down to the clothes and stack of beaded necklaces.

Eshani gulped, sitting forward and warily swinging her legs over the edge, gaze locked on the girl.

"Hi. What are you?" The girl hopped up and uncovered the table behind her.

"Manners!" Vidya scolded from the door, carrying a steel pot of water. She didn't have her hooded cape on, proudly displaying the green designs on her head. "Don't mind her. We don't get to socialize often, much less with non-dakini."

"Oh," Eshani said on an exhale, her gaze moving to the table, where a platter of food awaited. But if she recalled, the dakini preferred grubs and centipedes. She really hoped the latter wouldn't be staring back at her. "It's all right. Little ones are curious."

The girl grinned, following Vidya as she set up. "I brought you warm water to clean up with. There's drinking water on the table, and food, too. You passed out. When's the last time you've eaten?"

"I don't know," Eshani replied after some thought.

"Here!" The little girl enthusiastically brought over a bowl.

Please, stars, don't be centipedes. Even Lekha didn't get near centipedes. Oh, how she hoped Lekha had gotten away from the shades unscathed.

Eshani stifled a gasp when the roundness of greens appeared. Then something squirmed underneath. The girl looked longingly at the bowl, handing it to her visitor.

"Do you want the grubs?" Eshani asked.

The girl nodded profusely and gulped them down before Vidya could stop her. "That's for our guest!"

"It's okay," Eshani assured her. "I like leaves."

"Are you sick?" the girl asked around a mouthful.

"Stop." Vidya tugged her out of the room. She returned, patting her leggings while Eshani took a tentative bite, hoping it wouldn't kill her. Starvation and thirst also killed; she didn't have much of a choice. But the greens tasted fresh and delicious, and before she knew it, she'd already eaten half the salad.

"*Are* you sick?" Vidya asked.

"Not that I know of. Do I look sickly?" Eshani panicked, touching her face. Had passing through a gateway disfigured her, infected her with something her body wasn't prepared to handle?

"Well, your skin is . . ."

"What?" Eshani held out her arms.

"*Brown,*" Vidya whispered, as if trying not to offend her.

"What?"

"I've never seen anyone that color."

"It's my normal color."

"Ah. Okay. So you're not sick or infected with the white plague? Although that wouldn't make sense, as the plague makes people pale and gives them white streaks down their faces."

Eshani nodded and ate, asking, "What's the white plague?"

Vidya frowned with skepticism. "Is there no plague where you're from?"

"There's lots of illnesses. Maybe we call them by different names."

"The white plague comes from white tendrils that infiltrated the shadow dome. When inhaled, the host becomes ghastly, with white streaks down their face and neck. Even further if the infection has taken deeper root. It eventually makes them go mad and attack others, or, if they—and the rest of us—are fortunate, they die before then. Of rot."

What a horrible way to die, yet how fascinating. This sounded more like a parasite, and Eshani thought there must be a way to kill it. But how advanced were these people? Maybe there was a plant somewhere with the healing properties to help. She had many questions, mainly about the shadow dome and what awaited beyond it, but she knew better than to probe. The dakini would know for certain that she wasn't part of the realm if she didn't know what the shadow dome was. It was like not knowing what a sky was.

But a dome? What an intriguing concept. What kept it in place? How were there clouds and lightning? Was this a biosphere like Kurma's back? If this were a better situation, she'd love to have her journal and study the realm.

"Why is going into the forest forbidden?" Eshani asked instead.

"The kings of old decreed it."

"Why?"

Vidya frowned. "We never asked."

"You just accept what they say?"

"Yes." She laughed. "The kings would never lie to us. They're the reason we're alive."

"So . . . you just obey?"

Vidya frowned at that, her hairless brows knitting. "I suppose when they've never misled us and no one retaliates, it makes sense to assume they're doing something that works."

Eshani didn't respond. Instead she took another bite to hold back her opinion about monarchs. Maybe Vidya had no reason to think otherwise. Maybe she had a good king.

Vidya added slowly, "If we're not allowed to enter, then you probably weren't allowed, either."

"Please don't report me," Eshani blurted, lurching toward the edge of the bed.

"I won't."

Eshani gradually calmed. She believed Vidya but remained vigilant, keeping her ears open to any sounds and her eyes taking in her surroundings. But nothing appeared out of place. She didn't sense any danger. Perhaps not everything here was bad.

Vidya sat on the end of the small bed, as far from Eshani as possible, and pulled her knees to her chest. "Tell me about the marshlands," she whispered. "What's past the dark forest?"

"You truly want to know?"

Vidya bit her lip and nodded, like a child yearning for adventurous tales. Her gaze flitted to the open door, as if maybe she was not meant to ask these things. Which made Eshani want to share even more. She supposed, no matter the realm, girls had to find the truth for themselves.

Eshani carefully constructed her answer. The marshlands were dark and scary and very much a forest with terrifying creatures and a marshlight that came from nowhere. It fit into this realm. She didn't mention a thing beyond the marshlands, the gateway, or her family, much less the shades.

Every now and then, another dakini passed by, glaring into the room but never entering, never speaking.

"Don't mind them," Vidya said. "We're told naga are fierce, magically destructive monsters."

Eshani almost choked on her greens. She'd never thought of a day when monsters like the dakini would consider naga the actual monsters. "I have to get back. Can you show me the way?"

"I can take you only so far."

"Do you know who the Gatekeeper is?"

Vidya's brow furrowed. She thought for a moment, but before she could answer, Shruti swung her upper body around the door frame, her lower half hidden behind the wall. "You're in trouble."

Vidya immediately hopped off the bed with a shudder. Getting into trouble was never fun. Eshani suspected she was the cause.

"I don't want any problems," Eshani promised, collecting her things, pulling her satchel over both shoulders, and slipping into her shoes. A little voice in her head scolded her for wearing shoes inside someone's home, but she ascertained there were far more troubling things happening around her than poor social etiquette.

"It'll be fine once they meet you!" Vidya tried to reassure her, but the glances she exchanged with her friend said otherwise. She flung her hooded cape over her and followed Shruti.

Outside, a ruckus swelled from a large group of dakini, all women and girls of varying ages. Long cloaks fluttered behind them in a gentle breeze, the hoods pulled low over their faces, making them appear daunting and dangerous. White eyes gazed upon the worried dakini around them, spilling their concerns about the nagin in their mist, the monster from beyond.

Being referred to as a monstrous threat, especially when there were *actual* monsters here, made Eshani pause at the doorway of the house she'd been resting in. In physical comparison, she was shorter, thinner, and didn't possess any skill with shadows. Her skin wasn't as thick as the armored texture of the older dakini. She didn't have their muscular arms and legs. How could they think she was a threat?

The older dakini noticed her the second she walked outside. They lowered their chins and growled. Eshani clutched the hilt of her dagger, grateful that the girls who helped her had left her weapon on her body.

"Don't," Vidya muttered to Eshani, her eyes locked on her elders.

As they approached, Vidya's gaze fell to the ground. She had been an adept warrior earlier. Now she stood still and submissive, enduring the berating from her people. She reminded Eshani of Swati. Both girls seemed about the same age, a year or so older than Eshani. Both seemed incredibly smart and free-spirited, but obedient to their respective authorities. It was clear, once again, Eshani had overstayed her welcome. She didn't expect anyone to go against their elders for her.

Eshani opened her mouth to protest but thought better of it. She knew her place. She couldn't invite their anger, not when she had no allies in this realm. With as little movement as possible, she eyed her surroundings for a way out. There was plenty of room between the small houses, and a clear path led through the village. In one direction, several homes were barricaded.

Shaking, Eshani spun toward the elders who were suddenly in front of her. She blinked up at them, craning her neck to look them in the eyes.

"Why are you here?" one asked.

"I was forced to cross the dark forest," she replied.

"Who forced you?"

"I don't know what they are."

"Monsters?"

"Yes."

The elder scrutinized Eshani as Eshani focused on not trembling, on not appearing scared or vulnerable. The dakini seemed to respect strong girls.

Be the biggest person in the field, Sithara would tell her. *Make them think you're bigger than you are. Make them fear you by the mere presence of your confidence. Back straight, chest out, chin up, and stare them dead in the eye. Show no fear. We are naga.*

Eshani did what her twin would've done. "I am naga, but I'm not an enemy."

The crowd hushed. Every pair of off-white eyes glared at her.

"How dare you speak without being spoken to," one of the elders spat.

Vidya trembled and blinked rapidly. Eshani went on, "I mean no disrespect. I didn't want to come here. I just want to find my way home without disturbing anyone. I'm no threat, simply lost. Look at me."

She dangled her arms out. Though her garment had short sleeves, no one could mistake her for being as brawny as the dakini.

"Send word to the Shadow King," the elder said, unimpressed and unmoved.

Vidya gasped, raising her gaze to the elders, and said, "I'll take her to the dark forest and make sure she returns."

Every dakini head snapped in Vidya's direction. "Now it is you who speaks out of turn? You've never broken a rule, and you begin now? Because of this nagin?"

Vidya nodded. "I've never broken a rule, so you must understand how serious I am. Allow me to escort her back, since I'm the one who brought her here."

"Another rule you've broken."

"She was in need of aid. She fought pishacha. No one fights them except the bravest. No one fights them and *lives* except the strongest."

"Monsters battle the pishacha all the time. The pishacha are, in fact, hungry for them. This nagin—this monster—is the reason our own were attacked."

Eshani had no words. She could deny being a monster all day long, but these elders would never believe her.

The elder jerked her pointed chin at another. "Send word to the Shadow King."

"I'll go!" Eshani blurted. "I'll go to him on my own."

"You are not to be trusted."

"Then take me."

"We don't have the numbers to escort you."

"I can take her," Vidya insisted.

"And let her free?" the elders snarled.

"Have I ever gone back on my word?"

Shruti said, "I'll go with them. I don't have any ties to naga and argued *against* bringing her here in the first place."

The elder retorted, "We have work to do and not enough help. The entire shadow dome will crumble, and everyone will die, but of course, let's mother a lost nagin who happens to be a treat for monsters."

"Then let's go," Vidya snapped.

"Yes. Let's." Shruti fumed.

"Do you take us to be fools?" an elder asked, her arms crossed over her breastplate. "Lock her away while we wait for the army to retrieve her. You two, head back to the borderlands; you left your work unattended."

Defeated, the girls nodded and ushered Eshani back into the house.

"I'm sorry," Vidya whispered, her brow furrowed with such empathy that Eshani wholeheartedly believed her.

"Thank you for helping and defending me," Eshani whispered back.

A different pair of girls led her back to the room and locked the door behind her.

Eshani wasn't a damsel waiting around for her fate. She hurried to the window and climbed out before anyone could secure the back side of the home. Her steps were soft, her breathing steady, her movements just so.

There was no telling if she'd slept an hour or a day, but the same amount of low light illuminated the world. Enough to see well, but enough darkness to hide in between barrels and in the shadows of carts.

Straight ahead, dakini went about their duties. The elders had come from the left. Eshani could only go right. Past the barricaded homes where not a single dakini was spotted. Conversations and noise grew stilted behind her as she sank in and out of alleyways.

Every home in the sectioned-off corner of the village had wooden planks nailed across windows and doors. Every now and then, the narrowing paths forced Eshani to walk closer. When she walked too close to a building, an unnerving murmur sounded from within. It grew louder, catching to the next house and the next.

With quickened footsteps, Eshani glanced over her shoulder in case the dakini had heard the murmurs now turning into wails. She jumped when something screeched inside a home she was passing. She jumped again when a wail accompanied a hard pounding against the door.

She stilled, staring at the door. The wooden planks across the entryway jounced with each pound. Any second, that barricade was sure to fall off and unleash whatever was trapped inside.

Eshani quietly backed away, passing the windows of the next home, where thin, pale arms squeezed out of the windows around the planks, long-nailed hands stretching and grasping at the air, and reaching inches from her.

More keening. More battering. More lanky arms streaked with white lightning.

The white plague. These were the infected.

Eshani covered her mouth and ran.

TWELVE

HIRAN

Hiran's gaze jolted from his sister to the dead. Twitching. Snapping their joints back into place. Sitting up. Staring at him without eyes. Then standing.

The breath in his lungs went cold as he stumbled backward.

The dead rose, moved like the dead moved in the Vaitarani. But there was nothing special here preserving them.

"What the hell . . ." he mumbled.

"Exactly! What do you know about this?" Holika asked, suddenly in his face.

He tilted around her. "How should I know?"

"You commune with the dead, brother. Ask them."

"This isn't real, though."

"Their thoughts are. They never turned off. That's why I came here in the first place. This static buzz of nothing and everything at once. It was driving me out of my mind." Holika pressed bony fingers to her temple, looking at the ground and then to the rising dead. "I was trying to work with the mortals, because *someone* has to find an escape from this crumbling hell, and these things grew louder. Maybe because there were more and more, sharing thoughts? I don't know!"

She was leaning toward them, yelling, "Shut up!"

Except they weren't making noise, at least that he could hear. Hiran supposed his sister was hearing their thoughts and memories in the dreamscape.

Holika growled and then suddenly stopped. Clearing her throat, she recited, "A lady mustn't scream."

Hiran's chest hurt for her as she repeated herself in mutters, echoing the teachings poured upon her during her childhood.

Holika clutched his arm, whining, "They're just so loud."

He wrapped an arm around her frigid shoulders. "I'm sorry. I wish I could ease the voices."

"Ask them?"

"Can they even hear me?"

She nodded. "You're in their dreams right now. They're sort of asleep. I don't know. The dead don't sleep; they don't dream. This is all so new and confusing, and no dreamreaver before me thought to write books for future reference. Ah. Useless people."

Other corpses had risen while they conversed. One after another, until the siblings were surrounded by a dozen standing dead. And a few who sat on their hips or rib cages because they had no legs.

"Um. Hmm. Hello," Hiran started.

"Is that how you talk to the dead?" Holika muttered.

He cleared his throat, pushed out his chest, and tilted his chin, imitating his father as he often had as a child. "I am Hiran. The Gatekeeper. Son of the late Shadow King."

"Our lord," someone mumbled without moving their mouth, a strange echo.

"Well. Not really a lord, per se. I have no title."

"Are you seriously explaining your status to the dead?" Holika asked.

Hiran grunted. "Call me Hiran. If you have to. What's happening here? Does anyone know why you're dead and not staying dead? You're too far from the Vaitarani to be behaving this way."

"Did you just ask them?" Holika whispered.

"Are you going to question everything I say?" he whispered back.

She extended an arm, coaxing him to go on while inviting the dead to reply.

"The last thing," one said.

"White plague," another grumbled.

"You killed me," someone accused a random pair of legs. Who knew who they belonged to?

Bickering erupted in jarring jabs of who killed whom and who hit whom and who failed to help whom.

"That's my leg!"

"You took my arm!"

"You bludgeoned me with a pot!"

"You ate my face!"

Hiran groaned, running a hand down his own face.

"Shut up!" Holika yelled. Right in his ear.

Hiran flinched, covering his ears as his sister apologized.

"Look what you made me do," she snapped at the dead. "Now quit your bickering. I don't care about *how* you died or *who* did *what*." She gesticulated wildly with her hands for emphasis. "Answer his question."

Silence ensued. One corpse spoke up, asking, "What was the question?"

"Stars help me," Holika grumbled.

"Why are you not staying dead?" Hiran asked, patting his sister's shoulder to soothe her rising irritation.

They shrugged. "The plague?"

"But the King died and stayed dead," Hiran said, more to himself than to them. "Lots of people died from the white plague and stayed dead."

"What do we do?" A dozen confused undead faces stared at him.

Holika replied, "Go to the Vaitarani or walk into a fire."

"Holika!" Hiran admonished.

"What? Brother, a fire takes care of everything. Kills plagues and the undead alike. Well, except us, but you know..." She waved her hand around.

Such was true, but what was the point if the realm was deteriorating? Maybe they'd survive, unless...

"Are you craving flesh?" Hiran asked.

"Ew." Holika gagged.

"Maybe?" someone answered.

"That sounds like an idea," another said.

"Where's the closest flesh?"

"I *am* a little hungry."

"I could eat."

"No," Hiran snapped. "Don't go eating flesh. What are you thinking? If you're going to walk around undead, then you can't cause more chaos. I swear. I will bring the Vaitarani to *you* and take care of this whole mess."

Those with eyelids intact blinked at him; those with eyes stared. The others...he assumed were gaping through literal gaping eye sockets.

"Tell us where to go, great lord," one said.

"No. Stop that," Hiran reprimanded.

"The King didn't help us," another added.

"Even when we sent word."

"We should eat the King."

"Oh my stars. *Stop*," Hiran hissed.

"I thought the royal counselors were worthless, but you guys are picking up the ball," Holika commented.

A screech pierced the second rise of convoluted comments, startling everyone.

"What is that?" Hiran asked, searching through the darkness, where shadows and ruins and monsters blended in and out.

"I don't know. . . ." Holika turned toward the direction of the screams, where everyone was now curiously staring.

"How do you not know?"

"This isn't fully the dreamscape, remember? It's all turned around and twisted because of these . . . whatever they are." She sneered over her shoulder at the alarmingly innocent-looking expressions of the undead returned to her. She scratched her head, muttering nonsensical things to herself.

"Help!" a girl screamed, sounding achingly familiar.

"Can we go there?" Hiran stepped forward, one thought away from taking off.

"In real time? Only if these go toward her."

"Well?" Hiran snarled at the undead. "Go toward the screams. I need to see what's happening."

The undead grumbled and staggered forward.

"Probably just someone with the plague," one muttered.

"Bludgeoning hurts," mumbled another.

"Peeling faces, too."

"Getting your face eaten is the worst."

"Don't forget the monsters."

Hiran dropped his head back in full annoyance. "They are *so* slow."

"Try pushing them," Holika suggested but stopped short of shoving a shoulder herself. "Ew. I don't want to touch them. No offense."

A man beside her grunted.

"Actually, I mean all the offense. You're disgusting. This coming from the person who gives people nightmares."

Hiran shoved several ahead of him. "But you're not *really* touching them."

"True. This place is growing weirder by the dream." She delighted in shoving a few ahead of the first, using a stick, of course, conjured from her powers. "Not sure how all this works, but I feel like we might be unraveling the threads of the dreamscape. Crossing metaphysical boundaries, different levels of reality bleeding into one another. That sort of thing. Could be creating a new world. Or this is the beginning of a catastrophic end."

Jerking his head back, Hiran gave his sister a quizzical look. To which she shrugged. "As I said, nothing makes sense anymore, brother. I hope this girl can fight. At this rate, she'll be dead and then undead by the time we reach her."

Holika suddenly stopped, her lashes fluttering. She was receiving information from another dream. She held her breath, her body going perfectly still, before heaving out a breath and clutching her chest.

"I hate that. I feel like one of those people who stop breathing in their sleep and jolt awake gasping for air. One minute I'm pulling strings in a magnificent nightmare and the next they're jumping out and all my hard work dissipates."

"Was it important information?"

"Hmm? Oh...Ah. It's from Meet."

"Who?"

"Oh, the creature who lives with the shades. I named him Meet, and I attached a trail to him so that I'm apprised of the nagin. Oh no." She looked past Hiran and into the ambiguous darkness.

On one hand, the screams grew louder, which meant the girl behind them was getting closer. On the other hand, the moment Holika mentioned the nagin, Hiran realized who was screaming.

His heart dropped into his gut, his veins surging with adrenaline. Without thinking, he took off into a sprint, his wings ripping through his back to full breadth, and off he went. Leaving behind the impressed gasps of the undead, who moved faster to keep up. But not much faster.

In reality, they wouldn't have been able to keep pace, and Hiran could go wherever he pleased. Here, apparently, Hiran couldn't go faster than them. No matter how fast this felt, no matter how hard he pushed himself. Because he and Holika were still in the dreamscape, tied to these undead.

The girl sprang from the darkness. Her green eyes wide, filled with horror and confusion. Her lips parted, panting, her dark hair coming undone from its braid. Her clothes sullied and torn. Scabs and dirt crusted on her skin.

Eshani. She was truly here, in the flesh. And, thankfully, alive. He couldn't believe it. He wanted to touch her face, to feel for himself, to understand . . . when a monster leapt after her.

"*Kill* it and save her." He growled the command, and the undead did just that.

Eshani skidded to a stop as the lurching army of undead seemingly went for her. She sank to her knees from exhaustion and terror as they rushed around and past her, like a river of bodies moving around a rock.

Hiran landed on his knees in front of Eshani, his wings whooshing around her, but she couldn't see him. She looked right through him. Her emerald eyes glistened with fear and anger. She huffed and looked behind her at the horde, then at her hands as if she couldn't understand why they hadn't attacked.

She licked blood from her lip, and Hiran went to touch her cheek. He could feel her, but not the real her. And she had no awareness of him as she scuttled away and rose to her feet.

"Wait," he told her, but she couldn't hear him.

Eshani, in all her frantic movements and exhaustion, ran away. Toward the palace territory. She disappeared into the darkness, out of sight of the undead.

Eshani. The beautiful, the brave, the breathtakingly resolute. He'd never seen a stronger mortal.

He heaved out a breath. A *mortal.* In this realm! Everything could smell her. Everything would want to either eat her or drag her to the King. "I have to get to her."

"Wait." Holika snatched his wrist. "I gleaned another bit of information from Meet about your girlfriend."

"She's not my girlfriend."

Holika dismissed him with a wave of her silver hand. "Okay. Your dream lover. Whatever you prefer."

Hiran grunted.

"She communes with plants."

"I know. And?"

"You don't follow. That's how she can cross the 'nothing' past the Bloodfall. She can build a bridge of bramble and roots, connecting both sides. Tarak and his counselors didn't figure that out. She's a giver of life, but it's not about her fertility! Plants! She can grow them, command them. She just doesn't believe it yet."

"I'll slit his throat if he tries to sire a child with her."

"He'll slit yours first. Can't save anyone with a slit throat, hmm?" She tapped a finger against her chin. "I know you've become attached to her during your...dream dates...but stick to the plan: get her on the ferry, cross the Bloodfall, convince her to create the bridge and bring back amrita, and then get her home before someone else uses her to open the gateway. This is it," Holika added with a fist to her chest, with fight to her voice. "The time to dethrone Tarak is upon us."

A growing dread lurched in Hiran's gut. "I don't want the throne."

Even as he said those words, the starry darkness in the shape of him pulsated to life. The Gloom shuddered as if it had been waiting all this time for this moment.

Holika smiled at it and waved. "Tenebrosity believes otherwise."

The Gloom grinned and nodded.

"No one else can defeat Tarak," she added, walking around the Gloom, studying it. "He can't be restrained and imprisoned, either. He's too powerful and has too many allies who believe only he can save this world. Take the amrita. Allow this darkness—this subdued lineage, whatever the tenebrosity is—to lead you. It's the only way."

Again, the Gloom nodded. And Hiran knew he had no other choice.

"Shit," Hiran began. "You sound just like Tarak and Father and all the kings before them."

She glowered, but Hiran knew this was madness. "They wanted it for personal gain. The second he has the nagin, Tarak will escape this realm, not save it. And he'll use her to conquer other worlds. You need amrita to become stronger, invincible, unkillable. To take the throne, to take control of the realm and the shadows. And then, Gatekeeper who has partnered with the walker of worlds, you can find a habitable realm for everyone. It's that or death. Hers and yours and mine."

Holika slipped away, and with that, Hiran jolted awake and shoved Rohan, gathering their supplies.

"What?" Rohan groaned, sitting up.

"Hurry. The nagin is here."

Nearby, the keshi neighed with unease. In the distance, above the dark forest, the skies crackled red with purple lightning.

THIRTEEN

ESHANI

Reality was a puzzle of pieces continuously being torn away with an unforgiving force. Here, time seemed to stand still in a perpetual gloaming. It moved between dusk and dawn with a lingering promise of daybreak—but full light never arrived. Eshani couldn't tell if she'd been in this realm for days or weeks, her rations gone and her energy fading. She hadn't seen a sun, but there was just enough light to see clearly. Just like on Kurma.

She slept when she was exhausted, never knowing if night would descend or if day would break. Never knowing if she would awaken or what she would wake up to. Monsters, creatures, impossible things. Even the trees wouldn't answer her, as if wrought with caution. They wouldn't speak to her, much less show her the way out. And the ground absorbed her tracks. There was no way back.

Forcing herself to think, Eshani wiped away tears. She thought of her family. She had to return to them, save Manisha, and soothe Sithara's worry. Her twin was full of bravado and wore a facade of being strong and unaffected, but Sithara was sensitive. She held things heavy on her shoulders and would blame herself for Eshani's disappearance. But what would Sithara do in this situation? For that matter, what would Papa have done? Surely he'd found himself alone and on the run at some point during the war.

Eshani closed her eyes and grasped the necklace around her throat, searching for the wisdom of all those before her.

Always have a plan when in distress, Mama had taught her.

It eases the mind and soul and gives you a more linear route, Papa added. *To focus on a plan means less time to wither into anxiety.*

She needed a plan. The shades wanted her to open the portal from this side so they could enter, but she had to get the help of the Gatekeeper. Was he the one who approved who could come and go? Did that mean he had approved of her coming?

She clutched her head. This made no sense. It was like learning equations all over again!

She needed a map to get her bearings and figure out where to go. She had no scroll or view from above, but she had something better. Pressing her hands firm against the ground, Eshani strained to read the grass. Grass was a marvelous plant, small blades connected underground by a devastatingly vast network of roots, each string reaching deep into the soil, touching the roots of other plants. The web beneath her knew endless, forgotten things. It created a visual in her mind as she studied the unseen.

She didn't think she had such power, but she pushed herself to try. She had no other choice, for this was the only map she could obtain. A map that could not lie or be manipulated. Eshani poured herself into the roots. Sweat beaded along her temples and arms. When exhaustion took over, she rested. Then tried again. And again. A warrior never gave up, and neither did scholars. She would come to know this world, and it would yield to her.

At first, she learned a trickle of smaller details: the type of grass and its properties; the surrounding plants and fields and forest.

Then the grass unfurled greater details about the world. There was no day or night here, and measuring the passing of time didn't benefit the beings in this realm. They lived according to season. Some plants went into hibernation while others thrived. Some plants died while others grew from saplings. The cycle of ripening and rot was faster here.

When the grass had become accustomed to her, giving her information in a torrent, Eshani changed tactics. Until, finally, this world yielded to her.

A smile broke her focus. The information flowing through was riveting.

This was a pocket realm, enclosed by a dome. She couldn't see past the dome, as the root network stopped there, but she knew there was a vast river on the other side leading to ... what? The roots did not know.

She searched behind her. Perhaps they could locate the gateway now that they were willing to communicate so freely, but they only gave a fuzzy image, too wide to pinpoint even if she could return. It appeared farther and farther away, and the roots pleaded with her not to return.

Something sickly mixed with the roots. Tree monsters. So many of them, lurking around the portal.

Eshani pressed for a clearer image, and the roots buzzed in her head. And when she returned to the end of the vast river, they again gave her the same sort of fuzzy image, the buzz in her thoughts. Could this be another gateway? Would the gateway return her to her world? The roots did not know. She would have to see for herself.

The network showed her roads and villages and a large, central plot that must surely be inhabited by too many for her to contend with. She marveled as the tingles in her hands whispered, pointing out drinkable water sources and food and warning her what to avoid—what was toxic. She had to stop herself from delving into botany, even as the call of research lured her to new and exciting plants. But there was one discovery she could not ignore.

Ahead was a strange source of botanical power, something she'd never thought could exist. Strong and wholly . . . *sentient*. It sensed her beating pulse of communication and responded, hungry and possessive. Eshani couldn't decipher if the plant was dangerous or beneficial, not from this distance. She had to get closer.

Eshani had never pushed herself to know her powers to this extent, hadn't known she was capable. But that was the thing about woes; they forced one into ingenuity. She searched for other things, another way out, the original portal, but the botanical power interfered at every turn. It wanted her, promised her answers if only she would come near. Perhaps Eshani had no other choice.

She headed west. The botanical power loomed on the path toward the river that led to other gateways. As Eshani journeyed as quickly as she could, every crunching leaf or scraped pebble put her guard up. She sank to the ground to check her surroundings. Part of her wondered if Lekha had followed her, but of course she hadn't.

Eshani marveled, perplexed, at the structure all around and above that appeared both solid and mistlike, both sturdy and constantly moving, breathing like a living thing.

In this wall of fluctuating gray, something stood out. A brilliant stark contrast. A shiny white tendril holding steadfast. The white plague? But it was so beautiful, this tendril of white that sat like a ray of afternoon sunlight breaching a crack in a dust-covered window.

"What are you doing here?" a high-pitched, scratchy voice asked.

Eshani spun on her heel to come face-to-face with a small boy.

Although she was bigger and wielded a dagger, he seemed undeterred. He was a child. Dirt covered his torn, ash-colored clothes, and soot was smeared across his pale, bluish face, his eyes cavernous and dark with no whites, his stringy hair messy. In his hand was a stick. Not thick enough to fight someone, but something he dragged along the ground. Behind him was a trail of figures and shapes.

"I'm trying to find my way to someone called the Gatekeeper."

He shrugged, returning to drawing figures in the dirt. "Never heard of them."

Eshani took several careful steps away from the tendril, asking, "Is that the white plague?"

He crinkled his nose at her. "Yes. Everyone knows what it looks like."

"Right." She glanced at the light fluttering in place, curiosity digging into her thoughts. How intriguing. She was more certain than ever that the tendril was a parasite. She looked to the boy and asked, "What's your name?"

"Chintan," he replied. "Are you from the palace?"

Hmm. The palace had to be the large, central dwelling the roots had shown her. "No."

"You look different; I thought you might be a princess."

She smiled.

"But not a pretty one."

She scowled. "Well, that's not nice."

He smiled, revealing the sharp tips of a few teeth. Either some of his teeth had fallen out, yet to be replaced by adult teeth, or they simply no longer existed.

"Where are we?"

The boy looked quizzically at her as an older girl quickly approached. "We're in Amreli."

"Chintan," the girl chided, holding him back and fastening a mask around her face before securing one around his.

"I'm not sick," Eshani reassured them.

"We don't know you." The girl's hand fell to the boy's shoulder. The tug of his shirt lowered the collarless neckline, exposing a white patch of lightning across his chest.

The boy was sick. Eshani should be the one covering her face.

The girl narrowed her eyes and looked past Eshani. Eshani, on instinct, turned. The clouds were brutally red in the direction she'd come from, with a spectacular burst of lavender lightning. Breathtaking and dangerous.

The girl raised her brows and her horn-rimmed chin. "You should go to the palace."

"Why?"

"We were given word that if that sort of thing happens in the sky, we're to send all newcomers to the Shadow King."

A royal wouldn't want to help her. Especially not one with such a frightening title.

"You can't stay here," the girl pressed.

"I'm not any sort of trouble."

"Everyone's trouble."

Eshani nodded and hurried on her way. She gave the village a wide berth, noting how so many homes were barricaded like the ones she saw fleeing the dakini. A ghostly silence from the village rang in her ears. Eyes watched her through the windows.

The village, with its strange quietude, had long vanished. A call—a combination of mewing and a growl—jolted Eshani alert when her eyelids had grown heavy. She'd been foraging for food, communicating with plants to ascertain the safety of their fruits as she neared a shallow stream where the moss on the rocks assured her the water was drinkable.

With dagger in hand, she turned and crouched, but there weren't many places to hide unless she went into the dark forest. Amid the various shades of gray and black landscape, dark green bushes and grass, something golden shimmered in the twilight. A burst of color in the dullness, honey eyes and golden fur streaked with white.

The tiger's ears twitched, each pointed in a different direction. Her head was low, prowling, cautious. Her eyes flickered, wide and panicked, until they landed on Eshani.

"Lekha?" she croaked.

The tiger slowly blinked, a sign of trust and openness that Lekha rarely showed with anyone outside of Eshani's immediate family. In another moment, her head quirked up and her tongue rolled out of her mouth in a pant before she dashed toward Eshani. Lekha was too fast to outrun; Eshani barely had time to stand before the tiger knocked her back onto her haunches.

Eshani laughed and wept into Lekha's fur, petting and hugging Lekha as she purred, nudging Eshani with her forehead and gently pawing at her shoulders as if she were hugging her in return.

"How did you get here?" Eshani asked through sobs. "Did you follow me? I told you to go."

Lekha gave a soft call, a response that they were together, and this was nothing more than a new adventure. Eshani had not felt this sort of overwhelming joy in a long time. She relished hugging Lekha, and Lekha allowed it. She then held Lekha's face in her hands, searching her eyes, then body, for signs of wounds. They were minor.

"You look exhausted, my sweet girl. Here." Eshani gave Lekha her food, most of the fruit and gourds she'd found. Lekha devoured the bounty while Eshani pondered how to feed her. She hadn't seen any animals here, just monsters. That didn't stop her from using her communication with the plants to secure Lekha sufficient food.

A six-legged animal that resembled a small deer with fangs wove in between trees and wandered too close to the forest border.

Eshani was tucked close to Lekha, who prowled low to the ground. "It's safe to eat."

And with that, Lekha made the kill. It was a measly meal, but it was meat. She nudged the limp head toward Eshani. The deerlike animal stared at her with grape-colored eyes and a tongue lolling out between its fangs.

"That's okay, you eat," Eshani said, grabbing a piece of fruit. "I'll have this. Yum."

Lekha purred and devoured the rest of the small creature. While she was distracted lapping up blood from the carcass, Eshani tended to Lekha's wounds. Lekha snarled and whipped her head toward Eshani.

"Well? Would you rather get an infection?"

Lekha grunted and dramatically turned her head away. She sank to the grass, her chin on a rock, and moped. But she allowed Eshani to clean the cuts along Lekha's sides and leg. In her wandering, Eshani had found marvelous plants with healing properties. She stored away the information in her mind and hoped she could transcribe such interesting findings later.

"There." She cleaned her hands against the front of her kurta, the lower part that gathered in her lap.

Lekha chuffed, a sign of contentment.

Eshani drew in the dirt with a stick. She created a map, dragging the stick along ambiguous edges as she explained, "This is what I've gathered. We follow the dark forest to the Great River of this world, but never go into the forest. It's deadly. Here"—she prodded the stick into a small corner where the river and forest nearly met—"is where this realm ends, so it must be better than where we are. There should be gateways there. Surely the Gatekeeper must be there as well. He's supposed to show us the way back. I'm not sure what he wants in return, but we have to find him. Are you paying attention?"

Lekha rested her chin on the ground and puffed. A cloud of dirt flew up.

Eshani sighed. "Rest for a bit."

She yawned and drifted to sleep, slumped against the nostalgic warmth of Lekha.

"YOU NEED TO GET TO THE RIVER," A SILVERY GIRL SAID AS Eshani drifted in and out of sleep. She jerked awake. She'd fallen over, her hands hitting the ground to save her face, and with it, a tingle of information coursed through her palms. The forest to the left wailed.

Eshani's lips parted as shallow, harsh breaths screamed out of her chest. The call of the dark forest was wild and thirsty. She'd always believed that vegetation was inherently good, or at the least adiaphorous. She'd only ever felt pain and joy and memories. Never ambition or evil. Until now, as some of the trees were sentient. It was another tree monster.

She nudged Lekha, pleading, "Wake up. We must flee."

Lekha was heavy with sleep, prying open an eye only when Eshani grabbed her face and coaxed her awake. The ground rumbled. Lekha was immediately on her feet, but Eshani knew her friend was still weak.

"*Run,*" Eshani ordered, and this time, Lekha listened.

Eshani ran after Lekha, dodging a blow from the tree monster.

She ducked and jumped, avoiding a number of pendulous limbs scratching the air for her. Eshani clutched her dagger, slicing the limbs closest to her. The winter-steel edges cut sharp and clean. She ran for her life, following Lekha, who led the way, a golden blur in the distance. She ducked into thickets of trees knowing the monster couldn't maneuver through them with much speed.

Thorns and branches cut her clothes and pricked her skin. Her knees took the impact of uneven terrain, sometimes solid with rock and other times softer with dirt. Her legs screamed and her chest burned, but there was no slowing down.

The crunching of leaves and snapping of branches sounded behind her. The monster sustained pursuit.

She couldn't go left toward the forest, but there was a clearing to the right. She took her chance, fervently hoping there would be somewhere to hide.

She leapt through the small clearing, tucking her knees to her chest to make the jump, and nearly crashed into a boy wearing a hooded kurta.

He wielded a sword and swung. Eshani, unable to slow her momentum, slid beneath his arm and weapon. His blade went through the beast, felling it in one hard swoop.

Eshani didn't stand by to thank him. For all she knew, he was a loyalist to the Shadow King, and she didn't want anything to do with him.

"Wait!" he called after her.

No. She was absolutely *not* going to wait. She met Lekha, panting in the near distance, and together, they fled. Let this boy endure the monster.

An animal galloped across their path, a tall creature resembling a horse in various shades of purple and gray, with multiple eyes and many feathery tentacles lashing about. It whipped its head toward her and snarled, baring fangs.

Stars! Does everything in this world have fangs?

Another horselike animal trotted after the first, this one carrying the most normal-looking person she'd seen here, from his dark brown skin to his curls. "Please, stop," he said. "We're here to help. My name's Rohan."

They skidded to a halt. Lekha's head dipped low, and a vicious growl reverberated out of her weary body. Eshani herself was desperate for space to breathe and for her screaming muscles to settle. She wiped her brow, clutching her dagger dripping with amber blood so the boys would know that she was armed and not afraid to fight.

Rohan slid off the animal while the first boy slowed his pace to approach them both. He had his sword tucked back into its sheath, his hands in the air in a gesture of peace. Behind him, the slain tree monster lay in a pile of limbs.

Eshani stepped back so that the two were in front of her and nothing was behind her. Lekha's gaze first darted between the boys, then settled ravenously on the horselike beasts. In turn, the animals sensed Lekha's hunger and—no matter how vicious-looking—trotted backward. The boys struggled to keep control of the steeds.

The first boy—the one who'd slain the monster—pulled back his hood, revealing a mess of long black hair, light bluish-gray skin, and drowsy red eyes. His lips parted, as if he meant to say something but had forgotten the words. He looked at her as if he knew her. Somehow, she felt the same way about him. Familiar yet not. Welcoming yet dangerous. So many opposing emotions warred alongside the vague question of whether he was friend or foe.

Of course he was foe. There was nothing friendly in this entire realm, aside from the few dakini she'd met before.

There wasn't a single thing about the boy that didn't demand attention, if not immediate acknowledgment. He exuded intimidation, with the height of a giant compared to Eshani; he stood over a foot taller than her. The expanse of his shoulders made him broader, stronger, like he could carry water buffaloes on his back without ever grunting. His body, though clothed in a black kurta, revealed a life of labor. He wore a matching black dhoti, pants loose enough for combat. Clothes sprayed with dirt.

He was a boy emerging as a man. He wasn't a gangly kid toiling away on a village farm, but he wasn't quite a seasoned warrior. He seemed too young for that. A vague line ran down the middle of his face. He possessed very familiar cobalt markings around his eyes, a beautiful contrast against his bluish-gray skin. Purple and black spirals with sharp edges peeked out from his kurta to meet his collarbone. But it was when he arched one brow, the other low, that recognition flickered like an ember struggling to reignite.

Of course Eshani did not know this boy; how could they have met? But how deeply frustrating to be so close to remembering him and yet unable to place a finger on it.

"Wh-what are you?" Eshani stuttered, hating that she showed any signs of fear. He could not be dakini, for all dakini seemed to be female.

He stilled, taking her in, when he replied, "I am asura."

Worse than the myth of dakini!

Her breath hitched. Never had she thought, in all her years, that she would come face-to-face with a demon.

"Who are you?" Eshani demanded. Her knuckles were white over the hilt of her weapon, and she prayed he couldn't see her shaking.

He watched her silently, studied her as she fought to avoid unraveling. A voice in her head whispered of danger and disguise, but she knew. She was in the realm of nightmares, in the world of the asuras, and he was most definitely a demon.

Eshani's shoulders curled in, centimeters at a time, underneath his scrupulous stare. She knew it was happening yet couldn't quite push them back.

She'd heard an odd saying while scouting the jungles below the floating mountains. Soldiers came and went, and generals and nobles had begun visiting the temple that Manisha had been sent off to. These men often used stoicism and hard glares to coerce others.

Men who stare don't like to be stared at; it's an intimidation game with one winner, a commander had said.

Eshani steeled herself and did what very few people would do—she stared a demon in the eye.

The boy didn't budge. He didn't even blink. All the while, Eshani focused on not breaking eye contact first. Was he gauging her naivety? Discerning her strengths? Was he gathering information on that deep inhalation? Or maybe he was distracting her.

She fell into the cavernous eyes of this strange boy. At first glance, they were cold but discerning. But the longer she looked, the more his eyes showed her. A deep blue appeared in the center, pulsating outward into the carmine irises, turning into clouds and speckles of gold, always changing and ever beautiful. They reflected the cosmos, vast and infinite, bold and beguiling... yes, she... remembered him saying this.

When he shifted the angle of his face, cobalt swirls glimmered around those eyes, spanning from his temple and brow to beneath his lashes.

His brow arched again, his lips parting as if he longed to say something. Somehow, he made her feel comfortable, safe, secure. And memory struck. Hazy, but still a memory.

Eshani's lips parted, and for a second, his gaze dipped to her mouth. "Do we know each other?"

"Where would we have met?" he countered stiffly.

In my dreams, she wanted to say. But that sounded ludicrous. She eyed him suspiciously. She knew those eyes and those horns. Thick at the base where they connected to his head in that mess of hair, curled once and tapering off to points. Asura. Demon. More demon-looking than the boy and girl she'd just met in Amreli.

Rohan tapped his head, and the tall boy's hand immediately went to his own head and felt the horns. "Oh. Shit," he muttered, as if she wasn't supposed to see them.

In a blink, they diminished to a much smaller size.

Eshani didn't question the change, assuming anything could happen here, including a boy who could alter his appearance at will. Maybe all asuras did that.

"Well? Who are you?" She pushed out the words, finding courage in her voice. She stood up straight, hoping to project confidence.

He carefully replied, "Hiran."

She repeated his name. How it rolled off the tongue so effortlessly, as if she'd said that name a hundred times before. Familiar, safe, pleasant. The memory struggled to surface, as if her brain was purposely keeping it from her.

He was studying her, waiting for a response. When words failed her, he said, "How about a thank-you for killing that monster back there?"

She scowled. Words never failed an annoyed girl. "You killed it easily because I'd already wounded it. Don't think so much of yourself."

Hiran brooded.

Rohan cackled.

She looked to Rohan, since Hiran wasn't much use. "You said you were here to help. How? And why should I believe you?"

His gaze slipped to Hiran, as if seeking approval to speak. "You're from the mortal realm."

"I think that's obvious," she stated.

Rohan cocked his head toward Hiran, mouthing, "Well?"

As Hiran cleared his throat, Lekha growled. She was shaking, staring at the steeds.

"What's wrong with her?" Hiran asked.

"She's hungry," Eshani replied.

The boys exchanged glances.

"I need to feed her. So let us pass, or she'll devour your horses. And probably you, too."

"What are horses?" Rohan asked.

"They look like those things."

"Ah. Keshi."

Of *course* demon horses existed!

Lekha pawed the dirt, shifting forward. Hiran raised a hand to her, promising, "We'll find you something to eat. Not our steeds."

Lekha's ears perked up. The world broke into trills and chittering, the flutter of wings and creeping vines. The air grew chilled, sweeping down the back of Eshani's neck in an icy breath. She jumped, but there was no one behind her.

"How do we get out of this realm?" Eshani demanded.

"Did you try to return the way you came in?" Hiran finally spoke, his voice deep, raw.

"Don't you think that was the first thing I tried? The entrance disappeared into the darkness, and then monsters chased me out. Pishacha tried to eat me! The Nightmare Realm is horrible."

"Ah. Mortals still call it that?"

"Isn't it?"

"What? The place where nightmares are born?" he teased, cracking his serious facade. "That's only one component. As a whole, this is Patala. Some call it the underworld, the netherworld, the place in between."

"So, what is Patala, then?" she questioned to see whether he would lie to her. Plants didn't weave tall tales, but asuras did.

"It's a realm where multiple worlds cross, where one dimension touches another. I'm sure it's confusing for a mortal mind to grasp, but—"

Rohan covered his face and groaned.

Eshani snapped, "I'm not stupid."

Rohan interrupted, holding one hand out to Hiran. "I apologize on behalf of my friend. He doesn't have the best social skills, especially when speaking to such a lovely girl."

Eshani felt her expression fall flat.

Rohan cleared his throat. "I mean no disrespect, but he does think you're pretty."

Hiran threw a rock at his friend, who ducked just in time. Eshani simply didn't know what was happening.

"We can help you figure this out. Mortals shouldn't be here. How are you alive, by the way?"

She shrugged. "No one killed me."

"But mortals can't exist here."

"Yes, I get that." She released an exasperated sigh. "I was told to find the Gatekeeper. He's supposed to help me."

Hiran and Rohan gave one another a curious look.

"What?" Eshani pressed. "Is he hard to find?"

Hiran scratched the back of his neck, letting his hand linger there. "I'm the Gatekeeper."

"*You're* supposed to help me?"

His rigid posture stiffened, his focus on Lekha now. The tiger had shifted her glare from the keshi she hungered for to something in the nearby brush to the left. "Come with us."

"Where?" Eshani demanded.

"To the river."

The words reverberated through her thoughts. Hadn't someone recently told her this? "Why? What's there?"

"Another way."

"Why not the dark forest where I came from?"

Hiran softened his tone. "I've never gotten close to the portal in the dark forest. There are too many monsters and traps, all vying for access to the gateway themselves. There's another portal, at the end of the river. It's a long and arduous journey, but no monsters lurk there."

She watched him carefully, but he showed no signs of lying. His words matched what the grass network had shown her before.

Papa had taught her to trust her gut, her instincts, the inexplicable pull deep in her bones that told her how to respond to a situation even when she didn't know all the facts. In this moment, amid the strange landscape filled with danger, her instincts were at ease with Hiran. She would go with him.

A gurgled moan sounded nearby, where the shadows broke and splotches of white glowed. Both Lekha and Hiran swiveled toward the brush. Hiran snarled, a clear warning to whatever was approaching. The strange light glinted on a fang.

Eshani gulped and took a step back, although Lekha stood in front with Hiran, combining defenses.

"What is it?" Eshani searched as far as she could see, her fist still holding her sullied dagger.

"We're about to find out." His hand went to a sword tucked in a scabbard strapped to his back.

"Move behind me," he ordered. He and Rohan shifted into fighting stances, their steeds bristling and hissing and walking backward from danger. The keshi moved farther to the right to distance themselves from the still-ravenous tiger.

Eshani moved farther back as the breeze shifted. Hiran's scent bombarded her senses, unexpectedly taking her back to the days before war, before this surreal journey.

She recalled sitting in the shade of a tree, her knees to her chest, when she smelled something comforting. Something like burnt sugar.

"Be careful where you sit, beta," Mama had said, her gaze rising up the large tree.

Eshani had expected to see venomous red ants or centipedes.

Instead, there were only clusters of small, pale greenish-yellow blooms on the tall, ancient tree. She had eased away and gone to her mother, who explained, "Saptaparni, or the Devil's Tree. It's toxic."

The smell had been intoxicating. Sweet and surreal and so strong that it felt like a seductive kiss. That was what this boy smelled like.

A boy emerged from the brush. A child, really. Clothes torn and covered in dirt.

"Oh, for the love of stars," Rohan cried dramatically, throwing his head back. "Why must you be creepy?"

Hiran hadn't returned his sword to its sheath. Eshani was on the verge of telling him to stand down. The boy was but a child.

Hiran spoke first. "I smell death."

The child took another shaky step forward, blotches appearing around his lips. Blood and a piece of flesh hung from his mouth. Eshani's skin crawled. Because if this wasn't unsettling enough, the chunk swinging against his jaw was his own flesh. The pale piece had splintered off the child's cheek, dangling over his jaw.

Eshani cringed, averting her eyes. It didn't feel right to judge a child by such odd looks, yet this didn't seem normal. Even for this world. And by Rohan's reaction, she ascertained none of this was right.

The small child tottered toward them, one labored step after another. His bony knees were bent, his feet angled, his hips wobbly, and his partially exposed jaw chomping at the air.

Three more appeared. They were much older but equally horrific. Like one being, they sucked in a breath, taking in the scents around them, and focused on Eshani.

"Get her out of here," Hiran ordered.

Rohan walked backward toward Eshani, his sights firm on the trio as they lunged forward. The boys had no choice but to engage. Grotesque squelching and gurgling filled the air along with the nauseating stench of death as Hiran and Rohan engaged in battle, swiping limbs and necks.

"Head kills only!" Hiran shouted.

Eshani almost vomited.

"I thought you said they listened to you!" Rohan shouted just as six more appeared from in between the trees.

"They're not dead yet!" Hiran yelled, as if that made any sense.

This could only be the white plague, and Eshani wanted no part of this, especially when all eyes locked on the two beings from another realm. The herd headed straight for Lekha. And these weren't as slow as the first. These meant to devour her, and Eshani wasn't going to let that happen. She wished she had a sword, a bow and arrow, a spear—something long-range. But a dagger would suffice.

Eshani called Lekha to her. "This isn't a fight we want to be in."

Lekha snarled, chomping the air between them and danger. Eshani feared Lekha would succumb to her natural instinct to fight. She called for her to come.

Something tickled the back of Eshani's neck. She spun, slicing her blade across a prickly vine. She grabbed the remnant; it was nothing. Although this would make a fine whip. When she turned around, a pair of white-streaked arms came out of the brush and went for Lekha.

Eshani snapped the prickly vine across the air, jabbing the arms with a hundred thorns. Foul blood splattered into the air and onto Lekha's fur. Eshani had meant to drag the beings toward her, tying them up even as their snapping jaws went for Lekha. But Lekha was in an attack frame of mind, her body already raised upon her hindquarters, her front paws smashing down with her full weight.

She'd crushed the infected beneath her. Their arms dislodged from the sockets. Lekha gave a mighty roar, her face inches from the asuras.

The second infected, the one whose hands Eshani had managed to bind, pulled away from her. She struggled to keep him under control, tugging on the vine and hoping it wouldn't snap. He was dragging her, his focus on Lekha. The tiger snarled in response, dipping her head low in warning and waiting for Eshani to tell her what to do.

His eyes were white. White lesions branched down his jaw and neck and ran along the length of his arms. Chunks of his flesh had fallen off, displaying rotted gray muscle and snippets of bone. Half of his skull had already been eaten by illness—his face was mainly teeth and eye sockets.

He was slowly chomping at the air, leaning toward Lekha like he wanted to eat her. And with that, Eshani used every bit of her strength to tug the boy toward her. She drove her dagger into the back of his head. He crumpled at her feet and Eshani sighed, panting, but when she looked back to Lekha, her entire world changed yet again.

The asura beneath Lekha was still moving. He opened his ear-to-ear mouth so that his head was nearly split in half, gaping up at the tiger. A twisted croak came out of the boy. White tendrils emerged, like long, stiff worms crawling out of his mouth toward Lekha.

Eshani's vision went in and out as she called to her, but the tendrils snagged on a current of air, the labored breath of Lekha. And slid inside her nostril.

Eshani's scream could've shattered eardrums. Hiran was immediately at Lekha's side as she stumbled away. He drove his sword into the boy's head. Rohan slayed the last infected asura behind him.

And then all three stood in horror around Lekha. She staggered backward, violently shaking her head and groaning. As if she knew what was happening, she gave Eshani a look of dread, her eyes so wide that the whites showed, and it absolutely crushed Eshani's heart. Her ribs tightened, threatening to puncture her organs.

She went for Lekha, but Hiran grabbed her by the waist and hoisted her back. She fought against him, punching and scratching and screaming. She was going to kill him if he didn't let her go.

"She's infected," he kept saying.

Eshani did not care. All she could see was the frightened little cub she'd sworn to protect. The friend who waited for her after long days at school. The one she'd run with along the streets all the way to the river because an angry neighbor chased her for stealing food. The safety that allowed Eshani to sleep in the fields with her sisters as they told scary stories around a fire. The animal she'd comforted when Papa left. The one she'd cleaned and tended after battles. The one being who fought harder than the naga themselves.

The one whose woeful expression spoke of apologies and love, who knew she had to leave before she passed on the infection to Eshani. Or worse. What if she became a mindless predator like these corpses around them? What if she tried to eat Eshani?

Eshani couldn't fight against Hiran's grip, even as Lekha skulked away. Her head low, her ears back and down as if she'd done something terribly wrong.

The shadows in the near distance drank her until she was a shadow herself. Rohan stood off to the side, gulping, a fist to his mouth, muttering, "Oh, shit."

Both he and Hiran seemed truly apologetic and pained. Hiran, for his part, hugged Eshani against him, turning her head from Lekha's direction and into his chest.

She didn't want to cry but found herself weeping against this strange boy in this wretched land.

"I'm sorry," he whispered.

Eshani shoved away, anger roiling against her insides like a tidal wave threatening to drown her. "*What* is the cure?" she demanded.

His expression fell, and she knew there wasn't one.

Her lips quivered, but she couldn't stand here crying all day. Lekha was family, and Eshani would find a way. She *had* to. She could *not* lose another soul.

In the next moment, they were surrounded by a new herd of these...*undead*...as she understood it. The infected.

"Stay behind us," Hiran told her. Or maybe he said, "Stay with us."

Eshani couldn't tell, and she would do no such thing. She ran after Lekha, into the darkness, into the shadows, into this unbearable world.

FOURTEEN

ESHANI

Eshani had been chasing Lekha's tracks for hours. The ground appeared parched yet had quickly absorbed the prints. She leaned against a tree and pressed a palm to it, exhausted but demanding to know if Lekha had passed through. Instead, the communication was intercepted by the botanical power from before. If regular plants could cure many things, surely this insatiable power could do much more. It might even be a cure for Lekha.

It is the amrita you need, to save yourself and all. Come to us and we shall aid you.

But amrita—the immortal elixir spat out during the churning of the galaxy—was lore. It had always been a far-fetched myth. . . . Then again, so were dakini and asuras and this entire realm.

Plants didn't lie. And that was why Eshani ended up approaching a rotund structure that seemed important yet abandoned. There was no one guarding or tending to the edifice that disrupted the skyline, its pillars and archways of black marble lined in gold like frozen, weeping trails of gilded liquid. A rock wall enclosed the property, carved in great detail: demons with staggering large wings and horns, dakini raising shadows, lotuses and roses, centipedes and eels, three-eyed birds and three-eyed fish, keshi, monsters in the shape of enormous spiderlike birds, and a throne above them all. Upon the throne sat the largest, most intimidating sculpture. The Shadow King.

This place was reminiscent of fabled foreign cemeteries—where the dead were buried beneath gravestones—perpetually swarming with nightly fog. Here, the ground was moist and sticky beneath her feet. Wings fluttered overhead, out of sight. Things slithered across stones, the sound like strained gurgling.

The place was alive, beating beneath her feet, breathing around her, and stretching into the sky like a giant awakening from sleep.

Eshani walked with trepidation. The walls were made of pillars and archway openings to an inner wall, which was carved with intricate details of the cosmos, the stars and planets, beasts with many tentacles and numerous eyes, dripping in red and gold and blue, as if someone had poured color from the top and the liquid had stilled at various distances from the ground.

Thick vines with large clusters of tiny red-orange and orange-yellow flowers grew around the structure like a bowl arching outward. They were riddled with thorns and droplets of blood. Eshani kept her distance, but a vine snapped at her leg, the sharp tip of its thorn biting into her ankle. She yelped, hobbling away with a lingering sting. She didn't think she'd been anywhere near the vines.

A drop of blood hit the ground, and the ground drank it like it was the elixir of life. The botanical power surged around Eshani. Was it the vines? These climbers moving in and out like tentacles, growing, expanding, and then retracting?

Wandering around, with the air noticeably cooler and humming, Eshani came across a grand staircase of cracked stone. Tufts of tall grass had sprouted along the edges of the steps like little bushes.

Something called to her, luring her inside. A warm sensation placated the warning in her gut, enticing her forward. She wanted to know what this place was.

Up she went, like an ant scurrying underneath the massive pillars and their arches.

The main hall, drenched in ethereal beauty, stole Eshani's breath. Here, the air sparked with bitter cold. Otherworldly fog rose and crashed above the center of the vast, rotund room. Breaks in the mist revealed water—a pool.

Flames flickered all around, from as low as the stone floor to as high as the crowns of the thirteen looming statues. They were as tall as towers and carved with great detail, down to the wrinkles in their dhotis and the bells in their payal, in various shades of gray.

Eshani raised her gaze to their faces, her awe at their beauty fading into terror. Such ghoulish statues. She thought back to the legends of old declaring that at the center of the Nightmare Realm sat the Court of Nightmares. She imagined this might be them.

Between them were gilded mirrors, the surfaces cracked and fractured, some dipping below into the pool. Something skidded across a reflection, and Eshani jumped.

It was said that mirrors were gateways to other dimensions, openings to nightmares. She knew this was true, for some of her worst nightmares came when she'd fallen asleep in front of a mirror and a cryptic daayan sat on her chest, squeezing the air from her lungs.

One reflection showed her the Fire Wars, where her people were burned alive. Shadow wraiths crossed the mirror fragments, lamenting, "Look at us. Behold your nightmares."

Eshani averted her eyes, her heart pounding. She didn't dare look at the reflections again.

The sting in her ankle throbbed, branching out into her heel and up her calf. Eshani glanced down to examine her leg when she noticed the vines, with their clustered flowers and jagged thorns, spilling into the room like moss covering stone.

She backed away. The vines lashed at her ankles and calves. They were alive! And fast. They chased her up a statue, the only direction they hadn't already cut off. They curled in through the windows and spread across the walls, avoiding the flames, mirrors, statues, and pool.

She scampered higher, grunting and slipping but staying just out of reach. Panicked and feeling the effects of their poison, Eshani desperately clung to the neck of a statue with one arm. Catching her breath, her face hot, she watched the nefarious plant consume the stone in a blanket of palpitating vines, glossy leaves, and shimmering flowers.

These *were* the botanical power!

Vines rose to meet her as Eshani fought the poison that made her drowsier by the minute. "What do you want from me?"

The vine stilled, as if contemplating its next move. With nowhere else to go, Eshani swallowed and reached for the plant in a desperate effort to communicate. At first, the vine cautiously rose over her, swaying from side to side, easing toward her gesture before snapping back.

"It's okay," she said, heaving, straining to reach out. "You called me here."

A blunt end of the vine touched her finger. Unlike so many plants of this realm, this one had no barrier to keep secrets from her. It wanted her to know.

One second had never felt longer than in this moment. Eons. A burst of bloody darkness exploded behind Eshani's eyes, an avalanche of information filled with screams and nightmares snaking beneath the frozen ground and toward a wide, vast river filled with thick, sanguine fluid. Lumps of flesh and bones and the dead. Such poison, riddled with primordial toxins birthed in agony when the great sky river, the Akash Ganga, spewed creation and all its secrets.

Eshani gasped. This was the mythical halahala. A drop of which could destroy entire worlds. Yet these plants fed from that river, gorging on primordial poison. They were one root system yielding to many arms that grew and retracted as they saw fit, a botanical form unlike any other but wholly one sentient entity. This amorphous, singular entity—made of vines, capable of expanding and growing and retracting—was separate from the Court of Nightmares. While the plant had autonomy, it served whoever could save it.

We. Are. Ashoka.

In Eshani's realm, the ashoka was a sprawling tree, its name meaning *without sorrow*. It possessed the same vibrant flower clusters as these vines. Beautiful but brimming with sorrow.

The blunt end twisted away, and a thorny end struck Eshani like a viper baring its fangs. The vines rose around her, gathering into a ball, like a massive sphere of twines, snaking in and out and around. They *thirsted* for her.

Special girl, they sang against her touch, *let us taste you.* The sound of wet limbs sliding over another filled the air, the smell of sulfur and salt on the breeze.

Like fine needles, deadly thorns deposited particles into her pores, into her veins, filling her body with primordial poison so that she burned with the intensity of a hundred suns. Her body seized, every muscle tightening and cramping. She couldn't move, couldn't scream. Tears streamed down her face. If one could die a thousand deaths, this would be it. Seconds and minutes expanding into eons, the beginning and the end.

Eshani's chest seared hotter than coals; her breathing stopped. Her heart clenched in its final beat. Her organs curled into a tight knot.

Her bones felt like they were turning to dust. And, finally, when the poison penetrated her brain, it didn't kill her. Instead, the particles infused her memories with their own, showing her the faraway darkness where the monsters and asuras had originated centuries ago. Beyond that, the birth of the galaxy where halahala had been created. Beside the gloomy cloud of potent poison were the legendary gems . . . and amrita. The thing kings killed for, the thing she was told would save her.

For a blink of an eye, she knew these things were real. She knew how they came to be and where they now sat. She knew these were the items of extraordinary legends, of timeless myths, and the sort of treasures monsters and mortals would kill for. They *had* killed for them; it was why she was here. Everything started with amrita, and everything led back to it.

In another blink of an eye, the truth vanished from her thoughts as her body swelled with venom.

One drop could destroy worlds. What would happen to an entire body filled with it?

Eshani gripped the statue for dear life. A fall from here would shatter bones, but she was losing the fight. At long last, the thorns ceased their attack. Instead, the ball of vines watched, waited.

Her mind transported her to a calmer place, the ancestral plane, where her foremothers once again appeared, stoking the furthest state of consciousness to life. It breathed around her, awakening her soul even as her body teetered on the edge of death.

The shadows split apart, revealing a woman dressed in elegant swirls of fabric. Others appeared behind her, gliding across green meadows. The shadows turned into large serpents floating across the skies behind them. Their scales were iridescent purples and greens, golds and reds.

"Daughter of Padma, granddaughter of Padmavati," her fore-mother hissed, her features contorting like a broken dream.

"You shall fear nothing," another said. The serpents rose higher and higher, piercing a gray sky.

"For you thought you were the hunted, the weak."

"But I am," Eshani muttered, defeated and ashamed.

A gust of wind hit her, shoving back her hair so that her necklace fully showed. It writhed and untwisted its coils until it was a fully formed cobra raising a hooded head. Its emerald eyes glowed, and a small forked tongue darted out.

"You are naga," her foremother corrected her.

Eshani remained transfixed by the necklace coming to life. The scales of gold and silver ruffling and skittering into flesh.

"You were never the prey," another said.

"You were always the predator."

Traces of defeat and shame withered away.

"This is not your end. This is merely your beginning."

"Know the blood in your veins. Know the new venom it's creating."

"Potent."

"Deadly."

"Inevitable."

"That is what you are, daughter of the first."

The serpents in the distance flew faster, higher, increasing the winds. Eshani had to shield her eyes. Her serpent necklace coiled around her neck once more, burying its head in her hair. The coldness of its body slid across her skin.

"The touch of blood to save and to destroy."

Something crashed in between Eshani and her foremothers, star-tling her and ending the gust of winds.

She stepped toward the hovering item. A crown. With spikes and brambles tipped in blood. *Her blood.* Where deadly venom met the deadliest poison.

Eshani furrowed her brow. Was this what she was now? A host for a new toxin?

Reading her thoughts, her foremothers hissed, "*Yes.*"

"But I don't understand," Eshani began. She'd never had venom, and halahala should instantly kill her. Never in her schooling had she learned that mixing two poisons could create a deadlier one, and certainly not mixing them inside a body.

"You think, at your young age, you should know so much?" a foremother chided.

Another added, "Rare beings can absorb rare poisons."

"And convert them into something new."

"What am I to do?" Eshani cried.

"Wield your weapon." In the next second, her foremothers screeched, "Breathe!"

Eshani jolted alert, her eyes wide, desperately searching the darkness for a way out. The waters of the pool below rose in a tidal wave, unnatural and conniving. The vines pulled back and then shot forward, screeching and gnashing. One brief touch and a scream from the vines echoed in Eshani's mind. *No!* A cry of desperation as the statue in Eshani's slick grip came to life. It breathed, eyes glowing white, demanding to know what was happening. In her fright, in her pain, in her exhaustion, Eshani fell.

She fell a long way as the arena lit up with glowing eyes, one statue after another coming awake, all turning to her. A chorus of voices.

"It is her."

"She has arrived."

"Finale to the prophecy."

"Walker of worlds."

"Bringer of immortality."

"Liberator of the realm."

"Summoned by the Gatekeeper."

"Alert the King."

Eshani plummeted, narrowly missing thorns and smaller vines reaching for her. She couldn't tell if they meant to devour her or save her, but they were no match for the rising waters. She took solace that at least the poison had blurred her thoughts. Perhaps she wouldn't feel as much pain when she died.

The pool and its cloud of fog welcomed her into its embrace, softening the impact as it took her under. Her back hit the icy water first, a crackle down her spine. The cold splash rose above her. The vines, with their weeping thorns and illustrious leaves and surreal blooms, stopped short of piercing the surface of the water. They would not touch a drop. Their tips splayed over the pool, darting one way and then another, as if considering how to enter.

All Eshani could think about was Lekha, who would die here with the plague, and Manisha, who would never see her again, and Sithara, who was surely out of her mind with worry, and Mama, who would never know what became of her eldest daughter, and Papa—whom she'd disappointed.

MANY BELIEVED DEATH TO BE CRUEL, A STATE OF inconceivable fear cradled by pain. Some thought death freeing. Others believed it to be a compelling journey.

It was all in one, or perhaps none.

Eshani awoke to nothing. There was no pain where the thorns had whipped her, no soreness where the poison had spread, no ache where her back had hit the water, no burn in her lungs from taking in water.

She lurched up, eyes squinting in the glare of brightness. When her eyes adjusted to the vast landscape of endless white, she slumped, accepting the fact she must've died, and this was the inevitable hereafter.

Resigned and surprisingly underwhelmed by emotion, Eshani drew her knees to her chest and rested her chin against them. She would never see her family or friends again.

Someone cleared their throat to her right.

A girl was sitting not too far from a perplexed Eshani. Her long, stringy silver hair covered her temple and draped over her shoulder. She wore a plain white top over white pants, blurring into the landscape. Her stare was unnerving. Her mouth pulled back into a toothy grin that only made her creepier.

Eshani blinked as memories fluttered around her like raindrops wetting a dried image, bringing back parts but not yet the whole.

"Hello, Eshani," the girl said, her voice throaty.

"Am I...dead?"

"Not yet."

"I've seen you before."

The girl lifted her arms out, as if welcoming this strange world. "In your dreams. Literally."

Those restless nights struggled to return to Eshani. A trickling of demons and demands to know where she was and what she could do. Her hand slipped to her side.

The girl, perhaps a few years older than her, tilted her chin up. "Your satchel and daggers aren't on you."

She was correct, and there wasn't a single item in this white void to be used as a weapon.

"I mean, they *are* on your body...but your body isn't physically here."

Eshani lowered her hand, taking in the surge of past nightmares and dreams and...the boy. *Hiran.* That *had* been him! He'd lied to her!

Holika clucked her tongue, already knowing Eshani's thoughts. "My brother didn't lie to you."

"Why did you make me forget my dreams?"

"Most don't remember dreams anyway, but I did indeed lock yours. We needed your help."

"Why didn't you just ask?"

Holika barked out a laugh. "If you knew we, *asuras*, were real, communing from this realm to get information and ask for aid, you would not have helped."

"You don't know me."

"Ah, but you see, I do. Better than most. No matter how good a person you believe yourself to be, you would not have willingly helped asuras." The girl shook her head. "This is a moot point now. I have unlocked our dream encounters. You will remember everything we've said and done."

Eshani took a breath, and upon that breath came all the dreams and nightmares this girl had constructed. Eshani's skin crawled with images of the daayan crouching on her chest, of Hiran's first startling appearance, and how the siblings collaborated to push her to sharpen her gifts and return to the gateway.

"Make of that what you will," Holika was saying. "But you'll know I am not lying. And before you ask, I can only manipulate dreams, not memories."

"You were *inside* my mind!"

Holika nodded, as if Eshani was referring to nothing more than a visit.

Eshani scoffed. "Do you . . . do you not understand how disturbing that is? Invading my privacy, violating my personal thoughts. It is *wrong*. And now you expect me to trust you—to help you?"

Holika blinked absently before she cracked a smile. "I am asura. We manipulate to get what we want. I am a dreamreaver. Entering your dreams is the only thing I know. We can go around and around, but your time is"—she made a ticking noise—"away."

Eshani bristled, but she knew Holika was right. She was going to die. Eshani also remembered how young the siblings had been during the dream visits, how often they'd stumbled but had tried anyway. All in an effort to get her help. Help from a girl who was truly no one. "There is nothing special about me—"

"You are everything," Holika interrupted. "Walker of worlds who can bring salvation. We just want to survive. You know that feeling."

Of course Eshani knew that feeling. She would have done anything to save her people.

"Exactly," Holika said. "Let's start over."

Holika crossed her legs, her back straight as if she might go into a meditation pose. She cleared her throat and announced, with great theatrical adroitness, "I am Holika. The mighty reaver of dreams. You fell into the pool at the Court of Nightmares, the birthplace of . . . well, nightmares. Your body is sinking, but you're somehow alive. The pool of dreams is unnatural. You like to know how things work, but don't ask me to explain the details because I don't know. Now I need you to wake up and get out of the pool."

Holika waved her hand as if she'd explained such things a million times before.

Nothing made sense. This felt so real, so lucid. How could she be drowning and dreaming at the same time? "How do I wake up?"

"Your will. I cannot do it for you."

Eshani thought back to dreams where she'd fought to wake up. Prying open her eyes or thrashing around, or calling to herself past layers and layers of sleep. All the while, Holika watched her, fascinated.

"What makes you want to live?" Holika pressed. The air trilled with urgency.

Family. Mama and her sisters made Eshani want to live. Curing Lekha and getting back to their world made her want to live.

As if reading her mind, Holika spun like a dandelion in the breeze. The white void morphed into an opulent room with detailed carvings and plush pillows and a girl with a beautiful long braid of glossy black hair speckled with jasmine blooms. She prepared sweets at a table, adorned in the finest pink-and-jade silk.

Manisha.

Eshani's heart palpitated as she reached out for the mirage. Her eyes swelled with tears. How Manisha had grown. She was tall and lovely and healthy.

Holika said, "Ah yes, that one. You keep dreaming of her."

The illusion wavered to show Manisha's sadness swelling in her dreams where she wept. Billowing emotions from the war and losing her entire family, of not being able to leave the temple, of feeling hollow and worthless, and the cruel intentions of some of the priestesses. Eshani's soul ached with every passing vision.

"Poor girl has been through some terrible things," Holika ascertained.

Eshani watched with longing, feeling every one of her dear sister's tears in her own eyes. "She has."

"Well! Welcome to the not-so-exclusive, cosmos-crossing, realm-traversing, erringly infinite sisterhood of suffering girls. No admission fee required." Holika swept her head toward Eshani, studying her mourning. "You've suffered a great deal, too, and yet you will suffer a great deal more."

Eshani blinked out of the trance. "Is that a threat?"

"You're very defensive."

"Consider where I'm at."

"Such intrepidness." Holika clucked her tongue and looked at Manisha. "What makes you think she needs saving? Is she not well?"

"You've been in our heads, so you must know. She doesn't belong there."

"But you *do* belong *here.*"

"I absolutely do not."

The girl floated toward Eshani like a ghost. "Then tell me, my dear mortal, why have you walked through realms? How have you survived this world and found your way to me? How did you not drown?"

"Is this not a nightmare of a dying girl?"

Holika placed her chin on her fist. "I'm not a god. This is new. No one is allowed into the pool, and if you're like me, you'll probably drop to the bottom, preserved, and your consciousness will be put to nightmarish work. But it is a long drop. Let me know if you find my body." She lifted her hands, and the temple, along with Manisha, disappeared. Replaced by a watery depth surrounded by broken mirrors.

"Bring her back." Eshani rushed to where the image of her youngest sister had been, her hand reaching out. She came to a staggering stop in front of a mirror fragment where someone else dreamt.

"You need to wake up, Eshani. You haven't got all mortal day."

"Bring her back. Please."

Holika's expression fell. "How about, if you wake up, I'll do you a favor?"

"What favor?"

Holika revealed moments where Manisha had been terrorized and humiliated by a priestess, a second-in-charge, a woman named Sita. Eshani vaguely recalled seeing her take Manisha from the jungle the last time she'd seen her sister.

The imagery changed to Sita's bedchambers. Holika traipsed toward the sleeping woman and leaned over her, blowing out a breath. The woman squirmed. Eshani imagined the breath to be a caress of nightmares.

"What would you say to her? The one degrading your sweet sister?"

Eshani stumbled through her thoughts, a mind-bending sensation of cold against her skin and a yearning to free Manisha. Her chest was burning, her skin frigid.

Holika hopped up from the bed. "You're awakening! Quickly, tell me what vile things you would say to her, and I'll make it happen. Do you wish for the daayan to crouch on her chest? Plague her with so many restless nights that she'll perish from lack of sleep?"

No. Eshani wished no such harm on someone who merely treated her sister poorly. As her senses returned in interrupted patterns of consciousness, Eshani wished for one thing. "Sita has authority in the temple. I demand that she release Manisha."

"Fine." Holika rolled her eyes, her shoulders slumping in obvious disappointment, but she obliged. In a blink of an eye, the pale girl with stringy hair and sunken eyes was suddenly in front of Eshani, a ghost fading from view.

Her haunting voice echoed against the inside of Eshani's head. "Now *wake up.*"

"And then what?" Eshani screamed into the void.

"Get to the river," Holika's fading voice whispered. "Trust Hiran. And no matter what you do, stay away from the Shadow King."

FIFTEEN

HIRAN

There were few things as alarming as a clearing littered with infected corpses that had tried to eat their own kind. It made Hiran's skin crawl. There was barely enough time to catch his breath as he and Rohan searched for Eshani. She and her infected tiger were long gone.

Hiran growled into the forest, a roar reverberating off trees and boulders. What if the tiger infected Eshani? What if it turned on her, devoured her?

"Hey," Rohan said, cocking his chin toward the sound of approaching keshi, forcing the boys to take cover. Except keshi were attracted to other keshi. Their beasts whinnied and snarled, alerting those approaching. Hiran and Rohan had no choice except to slink into the shrubs to avoid detection. They didn't wander too far. Their keshi had been hard-earned.

"Why are these things going this way?" a girl's voice complained.

Another girl grunted, tugging the reins of her keshi back. "They don't listen. No wonder we never ride them."

"What good are they, then?"

Rohan elbowed Hiran. "It's Vidya and Shruti."

Rohan slipped into the open and cockily declared, "Looking for us, I assume?"

He quirked an eyebrow, smirking like a romantic hero coming to save the day. Hiran rolled his eyes.

Vidya's eyes skirted toward him first and stayed there. She smiled, relieved. "There you are."

"Why are you here?" Hiran emerged, dodging a keshi's lashing tendril. "What happened?"

"Why must you think something's wrong?"

"Because you don't leave your service. And keshi... did you steal these from your elders?"

She shrugged. "I don't recall you gifting the beasts to them specifically."

"Are you all right?" Rohan asked, worry creasing his brow even as Vidya jumped down and caressed his bandaged arm, asking him instead, "Are *you* all right? Why are you injured?"

"Worried about me, huh?" He waggled his brows and stood a bit straighter, immediately flinching from the unseen bruises on his back.

Vidya clutched his wrist. "Yes. You're reckless and are newly hurt every time I see you."

"As much as your undying concern pleases me, tell us what's happening. It's not like you to travel this far, much less alone."

The dakini proceeded to spill their story in hushed tones, about the nagin who walked through the dark forest, battled a pishacha, and had been sentenced to be taken to the palace by decree of the King. But it turned out the nagin escaped.

Hiran said, "Don't tell me you're hunting her."

"We're not hunters. But we *are* looking for her."

"Why?"

"She was lost and needs help. I don't think the King wishes to help her, not if the murmurs are true. That he's hunting her."

Rohan exchanged a glance with Hiran, one that requested Hiran tell their friends the truth. Half-truths would do for now. Hiran explained, "She's a nagin from the mortal realm. The oracle said she would walk through the gateway, and the Shadow King believes she'll open it for him. Except she doesn't know how. Not yet. The King will torture her until he has his way." He took a deep breath to calm the rage that stirred within him at the mere thought of Tarak hurting Eshani. "The nagin was here, but she ran off during an attack. We must find her before the King does."

When the shock subsided enough for Shruti to speak, she asked sharply, "Why would you ever go against the King? That's treason."

"Isn't it treason to rise against his call to send her to the palace?"

"We weren't going to go against our elders."

"Yet here you are."

Rohan took Vidya's hands in his, saying, "There's something you should know about your elders. Please believe me. I only speak the truth."

She watched him, concerned, while Shruti remained as skeptical as ever. Her perceptiveness always unnerved Hiran, as if she knew his thoughts, knew who he was, that she wouldn't hesitate to dismantle him for treason hiding among her kind. But Shruti was shrewd and observant, which meant she would not dismiss logic forever.

Hiran said, "We've traveled the realm and have seen a lot. We lurk in shadows and hear everything. The most powerful dakini elders are not at the borderlands. They're around the palace territory building a smaller wall around the King and his court."

"It's true," Rohan confirmed, although he took Hiran's word based off Holika.

Vidya snatched her hands back. "You're lying."

"Why would I lie to you? Why would I ever say anything to hurt you? Come with us to the palace territory and see for yourself what your sisters are doing."

"You know I'm not allowed to go."

"And why not?" Hiran questioned. "Why do you think there's a rule that you can never venture into the inner realm? Never approach the palace unless called on?"

"It's called hierarchy and order."

"Is that what they tell you?"

"It's obvious. Listen to yourself," Shruti intervened.

"No, *you* listen to yourself," Hiran said. "If you're restricted from an area, it means there's something there they don't want you to witness. If this were about order, then you could request to go to the palace, even if you weren't allowed in—which you should be. You're uninfected and you're a dakini. They should welcome you."

Vidya scoffed, shaking her head. "No. No. No."

"Have your village elders ever gone?" Rohan asked.

"Well, no. You've seen our work. They're busy."

"Too busy to see the heart of this realm, the place where all orders and supposed salvation come from?"

"The shadow walls are crumbling!" She lifted her hand above her to emphasize her point.

"I know! Yet the strongest of the dakini are called to the palace and remain there. The King doesn't send soldiers to help you anymore. They all stay in place, every last uninfected person of power and lineage. All the mighty soldiers and endless supplies. They hide food from the border villages. Things have changed, and you never wonder why? Why are you risking your lives in the borderlands with every breath while the strongest dakini and nobles stay at the palace? The strongest among you should be with you. The soldiers should be with you. Everyone able to rebuild should *be with you.*"

"You speak nonsense."

Hiran interjected, "He speaks the truth. We've seen it with our own .eyes. The strongest are protecting the palace, the Shadow King. If the walls crumble, and they sure as hell will, those in the inner dome will survive. They're protecting the Court of Nightmares. They'll be able to pave a narrow path to wherever the gateway opens, whether it's the one in the dark forest or the one at the Bloodfall."

"What gateway in the dark forest?" Vidya narrowed her eyes.

Rohan replied, "My love, have you never known about the portal that was within your reach at the borderlands all this time? The one deep in the dark forest?"

She pressed fingers to her temple in apparent turmoil. "We were just assigned to that area. Told never to leave, even if there were no patches to be done. And..."

She whipped her head toward her sister, her eyes wide voids. "And inform the King if there should be anyone who comes from the dark forest."

Rohan snapped his fingers.

She grabbed his hands, holding them in hers. "The nagin! The area past the dark forest we're never allowed to venture to for fear it'll awaken the monsters... She really did come through a gateway."

He solemnly replied, "Yes, my love."

"She lied to us!" Shruti bellowed.

"What would you have done had she told you the truth?" Hiran asked defensively.

She groaned. "Reported her immediately to the King."

"There's your answer. Why should she trust anyone in this world? The King is going to use her in malicious ways, and don't think for a second it's to help everyone. He's already left all of us outside the palace territory to die without even a word to inform us. Dakini risk their lives every minute to patch the dome and villagers work to provide the palace with supplies, but we've been abandoned. This is the truth. What are you going to do now?"

The girls looked at each other. Vidya seemed troubled and Shruti roared with anger.

"Save the nagin to save the realm?" Vidya asked.

Hiran nodded.

She groaned but added, "Then let's save the realm."

Thank the stars his friends were true to the end. Even if it meant going up against the Shadow King himself.

They each climbed onto a keshi. Vidya took her reins and told Rohan, "Don't think I didn't notice you referring to me as your love."

Rohan grinned.

THE NAGIN HAD LEFT A TRACE OF HER SCENT, A TRAIL THAT only Hiran seemed to notice, which was odd because she wasn't dead. Was it because the dead were on her trail, too? Or was it because she was following the infected tiger? She ventured along the northern edge of the dark forest. He feared that she'd ventured too close to the palace territory. If Tarak had her, then the inner walls of the dome would soon be sealed off completely.

Their band rode as fast as they could toward the inner territory, a sprawling area encompassing fields and water sources, homes and courts. They stayed off the main road and slowed their pace as they advanced. Death tinged the air, tickling Hiran's nostrils.

Returning home was strange. Hiran still knew the scent of orchards and moss, hing and sulfur clinging to the air. Nostalgia and trepidation. He could be killed on the spot, imprisoned and interrogated, or, most likely, slowly tortured by the brother who had always hated him.

The girls didn't want to believe the truth about their elders, but the evidence was undeniable. There, surrounding the palace territory, was a second, smaller shadow dome. Remorse snapped at Hiran. There was nothing quite like seeing your world dissolve before your eyes, even from this distance. The people the girls had respected all their lives had become traitors and deserters to their kind, to this realm. There was no joy to reap from this.

"How could they?" Vidya asked, staring in disbelief at the concrete walls rising into shadows stretching toward the red sky.

"People are dying!" Shruti bellowed. "*Our* kind are dying!"

Vidya pulled her back, quieting her before they were found.

The area around the wall was littered with corpses staked to the ground by arrows and spears, the bodies of villagers arching backward, spines broken, and rotting.

But some weren't infected. Villagers wept over an impaled man. Rohan rode out to meet with them and returned with answers. "Some of the impaled didn't have the white plague. They were begging for aid, for medicine, and when they realized why the shadow wall was going up, they pleaded to be let in. They were killed on sight with burning arrows."

Rohan inclined his chin toward the charred heaps.

Hiran's skin instinctively prickled, as if set on fire again. He knew all too well what it felt like to burn alive.

"The late Shadow King would *never* have allowed this," Shruti declared.

Hiran wanted to agree, but even at a young age he knew how the late Queen Mother had had his father's ear. Not only would she have encouraged the action to safeguard herself and those who dwelled within the palace, but she would've sat on a dais to watch them all burn.

"We have to go north, closer to the Court of Nightmares," Hiran said, following the stench of death. "I have a plan."

SIXTEEN

ESHANI

With legs kicking and arms pushing, hands grasping and lungs burning with the absolute terror of drowning, Eshani launched herself from the first thing her feet touched. Whether a boulder or a pile of bones, she couldn't tell. It was solid enough to offer leverage, momentum when she'd been sinking.

She wouldn't unlatch her satchel with the few items left—the last things from her mother. She wouldn't remove her dagger—her only defense in this cruel realm. Nor did she have time. Every second counted, a sweeping of fate coming to consume her life.

Only the ghastly mirror fragments decorating the sides of the pool offered light, reflecting from an unknown source. They gave glimpses of other worlds and dreams and gateways, a labyrinth of realms.

The water was murky below and clear above, the only indication that Eshani was swimming in the right direction. The pool's cadaverous cold prickled at her skin, sharper than ice spurs razing her numbing flesh. Each second more arduous than the last, her limbs flailing, her arms reaching for the mist curling over the surface.

She called out to roots, anything, to help her. But not the vines. Never those vicious, vindictive vines ever again.

There was nothing alive in this pool lined with mirrors and stone. Nothing slept in these waters except corpses at the abysmal bottom. This place was truly nightmarish.

Then her hand grazed something slick against the gilded frame of a mirror, something bright green and soft. *Moss.* Moss that reacted to her pleas as if awakened from sleep, jubilant to meet another living thing. It lit the way to the top like an emerald waterfall along crooks and nooks in the stone, places Eshani gripped to catapult herself higher and faster. Using not just the speed of her desperate limbs, but the physics of underwater movement.

She breached the surface with violent gasps of air, her body weak, simultaneously on fire and frozen. Her teeth chattered uncontrollably. Nothing could be seen aside from the rolling fog gliding over the water, which meant neither could anything see her.

With a final gulp of air, she swam as quietly as possible until she reached the edge. Hoisting herself out, she crawled under the cover of the fog, around the giant feet of statues and claw-foot mirrors to the entrance.

When she reached the steps, she ran.

A hiss snapped behind her. A vine snatched her ankle, and down Eshani fell. Her body twisted to brace for impact, to save her head from injury, and in turn sprained her ankle. She screamed, her knees and wrists scraping the stone steps. Clambering onto her side, thorns lashing at her back, Eshani grabbed her dagger and cut the vine from her ankle. It lurched away, writhing and screeching in pain.

Don't leave, the vines begged, but how could she possibly trust them now?

Lashing out in every direction until she was free, Eshani jumped to her feet and winced at the shooting pain from her ankle. She stumbled away, limping as fast as she could go and fighting vines along the way. They sprouted like venomous weeds to block off her path, cocooning her and closing the gap ahead. Eshani was not going to make it through the narrowing opening.

He's coming for you. They created a dome, digging deep into the ground.

"Why should I listen to you, Ashoka?" Eshani meant to scream the words, but they came out hoarse, throwing her into a coughing fit.

Ah...So you can *understand us?* She felt their longing through ethereal tendrils against her palms, so intense that it made her heart ache. *No one has spoken our name aloud in eons. How sweet it is to be known. We are devourers of sorrows to those who know us, from sorrows carried on halahala weeping from the Vaitarani to the ones embittering the beings of this realm. But they have forgotten us. You, however, truly know us.*

"You just tried to *kill* me," she panted, shaking off the headiness of poison blooming in her blood.

It was necessary.

Eshani did not believe them and stumbled away, crumpling near a stream. Could she swim? Where did this water even lead?

She pressed a hand to the ground and felt the grass network, her powers surging, growing. The stream led south, around the palace. The river Holika told her to reach was farther east. It wove toward the north, cutting off the roots, but she pressed them to stretch past the unknown, toward the blank space north of the river so she could see. At first, they hesitated, refused, pleaded that they couldn't. But her power took control. Through them, she saw...nothing. There was nothing there. In fact, this realm called that northern expanse the nothing.

Flickers of something touched the ends of the roots, even as they—for some reason—wilted and died. There *was* something there. Neither Holika nor Hiran had lied.

A head rose from the stream before her, cradled by a headpiece of coral, a headband like a crown. Eshani jumped away, staring at the girl's gaunt face covered in long green hair. Her sage-green eyes were wide like a fish's, curious and intelligent. Was she . . . a yakshini? No, she looked different.

"Come here," the creature said.

"I don't intend to," Eshani replied, upset that she was clearly out of breath and most likely showcasing her injury.

The girl rose, revealing sharp collarbones and gills down the sides of a long, slender neck. "I heard about you, nagin. From someone who might be a friend."

"I have no friends here." Eshani searched for another way out. Behind her, the vines of Ashoka grew and twisted toward her. Trepidation clung to her like her soaked clothes.

"Someone who wants to see you live sounds friendly enough. And you're in no position to turn away from help."

"How would you help me?"

The creature pushed away from the bank and smirked. "Come here and I'll show you a way through the stream, beneath the vines that seek to devour you so. I've never seen them so hungry."

"You want me to get into the water with you?"

She nodded and dipped lower. The dark liquid hid most of what was beneath, but there was enough light to catch the luminous parts of a very long tail and the ends of very sharp nails.

Eshani would do no such thing. She hobbled away as fast as she could, even as the creature yelled at her to stop. Her head was groggy, and everything begin to blur.

The mass of vines suddenly squirmed in agitation. Voices sounded on the other side of the closed-off exit. The blade of a sword cut clean through, forcing Ashoka to retreat. The overarching dome of amassed plant retreated into the bushes around the arena. Not just from the brutal swing of a sword, but from the command that came from the man wielding the weapon.

Eshani had frozen in place, a pillar of shivering flesh wrapped in drenched clothes.

A man a few years older than Eshani appeared. He towered over her crumpled body, sliding his sword back into a sheath at his belt. The blue ribbon around the hilt of his weapon disappeared against his blue-and-gold brocade sherwani, matching a sash across his chest and loose dhoti-style pants. His presence matched his clothes, commanding and unparalleled, both silencing the vines and sending the water-bound creature on her way.

A breeze swept through his long, glorious hair—a mass of waves in pigments of black and navy blue—beneath a crown of shadow and ash. His perfectly smooth, bluish skin shimmered like stardust, the color of his eyes. His face, strikingly angular, looked like those of the gods of ancient times, with an aura to match.

He watched her carefully while Eshani struggled to remain alert. He squatted a few feet away, tilting his head as if to examine this foreign girl. Those eyes were an entrapment, shifting in the slightest into pitch-black. And that voice a vat of honey immobilizing her.

He glanced at the welts where blood had, not too long ago, bloomed like a hibiscus unfurling in the cool shade of night.

"You shall fear nothing, my delicate moonflower," he assured, his voice mellifluous and alluring. "For I am Tarak. The ruler of this realm. And you are under my protection."

Eshani's breaths turned arduous, her lungs seizing, her skin heating, her body wilting. With palms flat on the dirt, Ashoka secretly sang to her as they cowered behind the arena. *Do not trust the Shadow King*, they pleaded.

But she had no further strength to fight the halahala. She slipped in and out of consciousness, sweat beading on her brow. She couldn't tell the difference between dream and reality when the statues broke away from their stone facade and spoke with her, demanding answers about how she crossed realms and how to cross back. When Holika shook Eshani by the shoulders and warned her not to say a word. When her body was jostled and placed onto a steed, the warmth of the Shadow King against her back as they rode.

Between here and there, Eshani captured glimpses, her mind too languid to fit anything together. There was another man riding ahead of them, smirking back at her from his keshi, his face contorting between human and asura, a flash of jagged teeth and onyx eyes. Or perhaps the poison was taking over.

Towering stone walls beneath a shadow yawning into the red sky. Looming gates with massive, cracked statues of asuras—one on each side like stone guardians—who blinked at her. Gently rolling hills of grain and orchids that reminded her of home, of channa fields and mangosteen orchards.

A resplendent palace of marble and granite, balconies and glinting jewels winking through the darkness. Carved statues and towers. Hooded, masked soldiers helping the Shadow King as he carried her past eel-filled fountains and trees shimmering with vines of diamonds fracturing the light. A court of elegantly arrayed robes and gowns of glittering threads, mirror work, and metallic designs. Balconies of people whispering like faraway ghosts.

Between lumbering dreams and dark oblivion, Eshani lifted heavy lids in drowsy bouts of consciousness. Sometimes she saw obscure figures in the room, and other times it was voices that stirred her. She muttered, weakly reaching out. There was no one to comfort her—only strangers to watch her.

"THERE YOU ARE!"

Eshani groaned, pushing herself off the pristine white floors, and raised her head toward the cheerful voice. "I never thought I'd be so happy to see my nightmare."

Holika grinned and took a bow. "It wasn't easy finding you. Once you left the pool—brilliant job on surviving both drowning and the vines, by the way—the Court of Nightmares barricaded you. As soon as they realized who you were, the Shadow King had them lock you away in your dreams to reap your mind."

Eshani had never known there could be so many violating her mind.

"*I'm* able to barricade you now." Holika grinned with great pride. "I'm stronger than they think. Your mind is also strong. They didn't get what they wanted. I sent them in circles."

"Let me guess." Eshani pulled her knees to her chest and stretched her neck. It was nice not to feel pain or hunger. "They want to know how to open the gateway into my realm?"

Holika nodded.

"It's because I don't know."

Holika scrunched her nose. "They want two things from you, and they both lie at the end of the river."

"What does that *mean*?" Eshani groaned, frustration riling her insides.

Holika fluttered toward her with large, translucent wings. She appeared to Eshani like a mortal, but with flight. She imagined this was to put her at ease. "I have been working on this for much time. Mapping it all out, logistics and power requirements and outcomes. You can commune with plants. I think you can create a bridge to the Vermilion Mahal...or what you mortals call the Palace of the Dead."

Eshani winced. Her heart flooded to even think of Lekha's fate, if she had fully succumbed to the white plague. Anguish filled Eshani as her mind filled with one death after another. An endless cycle. "No more dead. Please."

"It's supposed to be a peaceful place, where the dead go to get sorted for their next life. What you've heard of it probably isn't all true. But who knows?" Holika shrugged.

Eshani vaguely recalled bedtime stories of a marble palace that healed the dead as they walked toward their next life—depending on their deeds. There was an abundance of amrita for the taking, if only one could get there and back, which was impossible, as one had to be dead to reach the Mahal. There was said to be an eternal library that collected all the knowledge from those who passed through, from this realm and every realm. A library of infinite knowledge had always appealed to her, which was why Papa embellished that part. There were magical guardians and endless halls, and the palace itself was encrusted with jewels. She'd thought it a fairy tale to lull children into sweet dreams or to alleviate grief.

Holika drew a map in the air, piecing together what Eshani had learned from the roots. "See, at the end of the river is the nothing; only the dead can pass through because only the dead can activate the bridge over a vast area of . . . well, nothing. There's a gateway on the other side, one that leads to many realms. Also, amrita is there. And the Shadow King vies for both."

Eshani's hands clenched into tight fists at her sides. "The immortal elixir that the Shadow King and mortal King razed *entire* civilizations for?"

"Yes."

"Smells like a trap. Maybe *you're* the Court of Nightmares appearing to me as Holika to reap my secrets."

"The Court doesn't know everything. They don't know that I've been in your head all this time. You have two choices." Holika raised one finger. "You can try to get back to the borderlands where you came from and find the gateway that's protected by darkness and insidiously hungry monsters." She held up a second finger. "Or take the ferry down the Vaitarani—what you call the Blood River—to the Bloodfall, and use your naga powers to create a bridge."

"I have many questions."

"Well, you're practically unconscious right now, so we have time."

Eshani jumped to alertness. The blankness around her wavered like heat off hot summer stones.

"Calm down. Don't wake up just yet. Your body is safe...enough."

Eshani did *not* like the sound of that. "Quickly. Tell me, then, and be forthright. We don't have time to play games. Who knows what they're doing to me?"

Holika nodded.

"How do I get to the Blood River?"

Holika snapped her fingers in the air. The space to the right wriggled into color. Four people appeared. The two dakini Eshani had met at the borderlands, Vidya and Shruti, and the two boys outside the forest, Hiran and Rohan. At first sight of Hiran, her heart beat like a hammer attempting to break her ribs. She now saw him with a full recollection. Buried memories rose to the surface. From times when he manipulated his appearance to get her to speak, to times when they emotionally connected, to dreams where he'd gotten adamant about learning her location and abilities.

Eshani wasn't sure if she should hate him for being in her head, too, or understand him for all the layers of himself he'd unveiled in her company.

"They're coming to rescue you," Holika was saying. "Let me explain: This handsome one who lacks social skills—I'm sure you remember him—is my dear brother, Hiran. He wants to save the realm. That is why we were in your head, but honestly, *I* only wish to save him. I don't know if this realm *can* be saved, but he needs to survive. He is the only person I've ever cared about. *Please.*" Holika's voice had never been softer, had never been so desperate.

Eshani saw in Holika what she felt for her own family. The dedication that had led Eshani to make her deal with the shades all those years ago, the decision that had brought her here. "I—I don't even know how. Everyone thinks too much of me."

"You'll figure it out. You must." Holika dropped her head back and gave a dramatic sigh. She then locked eyes with Eshani and admitted, "I never apologize. I stand by my actions, et cetera. But don't hate him because I pushed him into your dreams. You need him."

"To rescue me?" Eshani scoffed, crossing her arms.

"Yes, yes. You are a woman roaring into the night, who needs no man to help. But he's the Gatekeeper."

Eshani sucked in a breath. "*He's* the one?"

"Well, he has yet to figure out how. . . . Hiran is willing to go against the Shadow King, the strongest asura in the realm, which means he's willing to die for you—and I am willing to perish for him. It is the best we can offer."

"What if I find amrita?"

Holika's gaze darkened, her mouth curling with lust. "We are vicious creatures who desire great things, and we are capable of irrefutable destruction. Give it *only* to Hiran, or do not return with it at all."

The air wavered again, a sign that Eshani was trying to wake up, distorting her thinking process. She wanted to know *why* Hiran needed it. All she wanted was for him to open the portal so she could fulfill her bargain to the shades and return home. The question lingered on the tip of her tongue, but it faded away. She shook her head and asked instead, "Will it cure the white plague?"

Holika gawked at her. "You . . . want to make everyone who is ill immortal?"

"No. I want to save my friend the tiger. She's infected."

"Tiger?" Holika scoffed. "Best to move on if she's—"

"No," Eshani snapped. "She is my family. Just as you would raze this world for yours, I will do the same for mine."

The mirage of the band of friends fell apart, and Holika raised her eyes skyward. "The Court of Nightmares is trying very hard to breach your dreams. I can't hold them off much longer. So you need to push through this poison and wake up." Holika tapped a long silver nail against her chin. "Although I do wonder how you're still alive after the vines pricked you."

"I don't know. What about my friend?"

"Yes. Obviously. Amrita would heal her because it would make her *immortal.*"

Iridescent green vines bloomed around them. Eshani asked, "Quickly. Can you tell me if my sisters are safe?"

Holika craned her neck back, then from side to side, cracking it. The air shifted to show a place Eshani had never seen. In the corner, Sithara hunched over a slab where a girl lay entombed in glass. Her twin looked so . . . different. One side of her head was blurred, as if her hair had been sheared off. She appeared gaunt and sickly. What in the realms had happened to her?

Eshani's breath caught in her throat. "Can you reach her? Can you tell her where I am? She must be so worried."

"She knows." Holika smiled so broadly her cheeks squished her eyes. "We're practically best friends now."

Eshani scowled. That was hard to believe. "Let me speak to her."

"She's not asleep."

"What about Manisha?"

The air quivered, and Holika gritted her teeth. The Court of Nightmares was getting stronger, but Holika held on. The space around them changed to that of the temple, of Manisha with her splendidly fine clothes and silky hair.

Eshani pressed a hand to her mouth. "I was supposed to rescue her with our sister. Sithara must be searching the waters for my body still."

"Time works differently here. It goes by a bit slower than the mortal realm. Something to do with this being a pocket realm near a cluster of realms. And, of course, most realms have their own sun and moon and gravitational orbits to calculate years, et cetera."

"Huh?"

Holika grunted. "I am an educated reaver. You've much to learn. In short: Nearly a month has passed in your realm since you've left. Although I'm showing you a recurring dream of Manisha's, drawn from a moment that happened months ago in your realm."

Eshani gasped, unable to breathe. Oh no. Her family had to have been worried to their ends over her! And Sithara obviously wasn't on Kurma or with Manisha, which meant their mother had no idea what had happened to either of them. Panic rose within Eshani. She had to return! Her gaze drifted toward her youngest sister. So much time had passed already.

Eshani watched as Manisha spoke with a boy on her balcony. Oh, how healthy she looked! And the boy appeared kind, even handsome. Eshani was grateful to know that Manisha was alive and doing well. If Manisha had time to think about a boy like this, then things must not be too bad. If he made her feel normal and adored, then Eshani approved. But there was something about him . . .

"He's the slayer of monsters," Holika said, sitting on the balcony behind him.

Eshani sputtered, "*Slayer?* Oh no. No, no, no. This will not do."

"Would you rather have a poet capture your little sister's heart? Well, too bad. I've seen this one around. He's enamored with her. A match, I think."

"Well, no one asked you."

Holika guffawed dramatically. "Yet I know better than most. Trust me, if you want someone in your sister's corner, this is him. Just look at him...." She turned toward the slayer and smirked. "So tall and strong and good-looking...for a mortal. He's a born fighter. Literally. It's in his blood. Just observe how he looks at her. Adoration. Like a queen. This warrior boy is full of unending respect and love for her. Doesn't matter that he's the mortal King's errand boy."

"What?!"

"Oh, are you now suddenly interested in what I have to say?"

"If he touches her, I'll end him from even this realm."

Holika's half smile stretched into a full one. "Now you sound like one of us."

"I sound like a concerned sister. I'm nothing like your kind."

"Ah. *Our kind*. Who murder and destroy and toss everyone into politics? That's *every* civilization, across all realms. *Our kind*, who would kill for our loved ones? Why...yes." Holika laughed, a haunting sound that sent a chill down Eshani's spine. "Nothing is black and white. Life is vicious; only those living a privileged life can afford to have clean hands. *Murder* is bad, but killing for vengeance, or accidentally, or to save a life? Well, then suddenly you're hailed as a hero."

Eshani groaned. "I have morals."

"But you kill."

"I-if I have to," Eshani stuttered.

"Killing is morally wrong. Thus, a true hero doesn't kill."

"No one said I was a hero," Eshani refuted. "And it's different if I'm killing to save myself or my family from attackers who chased us." Her statement startled her, reminding her of Sithara and that night in the jungle when her sister had slipped away to slit the throats of soldiers who had neared.

Eshani had thought, at the time, that they had to mark a balance or otherwise cross a line there was no returning from. She didn't want to become a killer for the sake of killing, much less enjoy it. But to kill out of necessity? Well, that was when lines blurred.

Holika shrugged as the air pulsed around them. "So, let's say the Shadow King isn't actively on your trail, would you kill him?"

"No."

"What if you knew that he and his father caused the massacre of your people?"

The words rang in her ears.

"In case this realm crumbles and I never see you again, you should know what happened."

Words could be lies, but what reason was there for Holika to spill this information? Eshani found herself leaning toward the girl, anxious for answers as to why the naga had been nearly wiped out.

Holika groaned, her eyes clenching shut as she pushed the pulsating air away. With labored breathing, she explained, "They search for amrita and a way to open the portals to leave this realm for a better one. The oracle foretold a nagin would be the key."

Eshani's heart palpitated with every word.

"They used the Court of Nightmares to get into the heads of the mortal kings, driving them to do their bidding. Long ago, they used the mortal kings to manipulate the vidyadhara into opening the gateway between our realms, and when the vidyadhara realized what had happened, they locked every portal from us, preventing asuras from traversing realms, from fleeing one dying world to conquer the next." Holika's head dropped and she let out a haggard breath before she sat down.

Eshani's energy was draining, but Holika went on, "Our kind

pressed harder for a way out, and the nightmares drove the first mortal king mad. He tried to ensnare and kill all the vidyadhara, thus losing the key to opening the portals. When all hope had been lost for your mortal centuries, the oracle gave a new prophecy of promised deliverance. A nagin. A walker of worlds."

Eshani's breath left her lungs and she stumbled backward. This couldn't be true.

"The mortal King was supposed to take the nagin and test them at the portal, for there was one who held the power of her ancestor deep in her blood. The gift of the first nagin. Never mind that they needed the Gatekeeper to summon you, allowing you to pass. Our kind are not always the brightest. It didn't matter; the mortal King misunderstood. That is why he hunted your kind."

Eshani's throat went achingly dry. She heaved with her next words, anger boiling her insides. "Did you . . . tell the King to hunt us? Did you give him those maddening nightmares?"

Holika slowly shook her head. "The Court of Nightmares *stole* me. I don't want to be trapped here. My quest has always been to find a way out for my brother, and yes, hopefully myself. I would *never* help the Shadow King—the one living then or the one in power now."

The fire in Holika's eyes burned with truth. She went on, "Now the Shadow King has you, and you, my dear walker of worlds, are the only thing that stands between him and total control of every portal accessing every realm. What he did to your people, he will do to entire civilizations a hundred times over."

Eshani's breath caught. Images and emotions from the Fire Wars rained over her.

"Now tell me . . ." Holika floated toward her. "Would you kill the one responsible for destroying your kind, eradicating your people, and torturing you, all in an effort to take over other worlds?"

Eshani sucked in her next breath; her hands balled into tight fists that didn't go unnoticed by Holika. Eshani had always wanted peace and enjoyed adding to a place where plants and people and creatures could thrive. She'd been called the little goddess of spring for her rare gift that enabled the dry canyonlands to flourish.

Sithara was the one who craved vengeance. Eshani tried her best not to think less of her sister because she couldn't understand why a young girl would want to spill blood. But in this moment, knowing the truth, Eshani wished for nothing more than to raze the palace to the ground and soak it in the blood of the asura. It was not wrong to kill a person who had caused so many to die, and who, if given the chance, would kill thousands more...was it?

"I see your thoughts piling on one another in your head, defending your reasoning. You, my dear walker of worlds, both savior and destroyer of this realm...are neither hero nor villain. You are far past any rudimentary labels. You are a storm no one prepared for. You are Eshani. Nagin. And that is all anyone needs to know."

An ember of vengeance flickered somewhere deep inside Eshani. Once a flame caught fire, it was set to burn.

The air shuddered harder than ever.

"It's time," Holika said with a respectful bow of the head. She lifted her eyes and raised a brow. "I wonder what sort of storm you herald."

ESHANI OPENED SORE EYES TO A BEDROOM DRAPED IN FADED tapestries, a chandelier of flickering lights hanging above and a hard bed beneath her. She searched underneath the covers to find that her clothes had been changed, her skin cleaned, and the welts left by the vines healed.

"You're finally awake."

Eshani startled to find the Shadow King sitting on a chair near the wall. Beside him was a table with a washbasin and a damp washcloth.

He'd been reading through a scroll and leisurely walked toward the bed, sitting beside her. When she scurried to sit up, he took her shoulders and pressed her back into the mattress.

The assertive strength in that touch made her skin flare. Fear lit her veins on fire. She managed to glower at the imposing asura, though he did not respond.

"You fought the poison from the vines. It seems to have passed," he told her, his features blurring. "So interesting how a *mortal* like you ended up in my world, survived vicious beings, and endured this potent poison," he added, as if she were a frail miracle.

She blinked hard, her thoughts pinned to the fact that she'd been cleaned while unconscious. "Did you take care of me?"

"Of course."

Eshani's skin crawled.

His finger slid across her arm where the welts had once been. "Such smooth skin. Just a mortal. All over."

She pulled away, and his brows knitted. "I would not harm my delicate moonflower," he insisted, his voice like honey. *Too* sweet. "I've taken great care of you. Your clothes are clean. Your pack and weapon are on the chair beside the bed."

"What do you want from me?"

He paused, his affectionate smile slipping for a mere second. "My world is dying. The gateways have locked us here for your mortal-realm centuries. But you have managed to cross. Now I need you to help me open the portal so we may leave."

"Into my world?"

He nodded. "Until we find another gateway. There's a reason why you came, why you were allowed here. It is to heed the call of the realm. I summoned you here. To save us."

"You summoned me?" She furrowed her brow, trying to follow along.

"Yes, for I am both Shadow King and the Gatekeeper."

Eshani's pulse raged. He couldn't be the Gatekeeper. "Where is the gateway I came from?"

"Oh, some secret place along the borderlands."

No. It was in the dark forest. "Th-that's all you want from me?" she asked, stalling for time.

"It's a bit more complicated than that."

"I—I can't walk back through the gateway. It vanished." If he were the true Gatekeeper, he could find that gateway.

He solemnly nodded, as if he knew that would happen. He took her hand in his. Eshani recoiled but couldn't pull away for fear of inciting his anger. "No. At the end of the Vaitarani is another gateway."

"Why can't you open the one where I came from? What if the other one goes to a different realm?"

He waved off her comments, a flash of anger in his tight jaw. "Never mind that one. The one at the end of the river is more important, but we must be united to reach it."

"What exactly do you mean?"

He merely smiled. Her gaze fell to the sharp points of his teeth, a pair of upper and lower fangs like a wolf. He was a predator. "The white plague is upon us."

"Is there a cure?" she blurted, thinking of Lekha. He was the king. He had to know of a cure.

The dejection on his face gave away his answer. Tears prickled her eyes. He caressed her cheek and said, "You care so much. We can end the plague. However, you must comply. Now let the maidservants prepare you, moonflower. We have waited long enough for this moment."

"I have questions."

"We have no more time to waste on frivolous things," he said, dismissing her.

She dared to protest anyway. "My questions aren't frivolous."

He chuckled. "An ant thinks so much of itself, even in the presence of a giant." He kissed the back of her hand, taking in her scent as a hungry wolf would.

Eshani shrank into the bed as he left, glancing at the bowl and used washcloths on the bedside table.

SEVENTEEN

HIRAN

Shruti was perched on her keshi, sneering at the horde of undead. "*That's* your plan?"

Vidya added, "They'll tear everyone, including us, to shreds. And I mean so shredded that no dakini could even pull a speck of shadow mass from the piles."

Even Rohan cast Hiran a concerned look that said, *But you couldn't control the last bunch!*

"We stay ahead of them," Hiran said. "All we need is to lure them into the palace, use them as a distraction."

Vidya worked her lower lip before asking, "You're going to allow the infected to attack everyone inside that border? We'll be responsible for their deaths."

Hiran pointed at the impaled. "Look what they did to our kind. They abandoned yours. And if we don't get the nagin, we all die anyway."

Shruti nodded to Vidya, adding, "We would be at the borderlands working ourselves to the bone, never knowing we're about to die no matter what we do. We always had questions. What do we do now that we have answers?"

Vidya replied, "Okay. Okay..."

"You can stay here," Rohan offered.

"No. I will fight for our kind."

Hiran surveyed the wall between watchtowers. "Can you break through the wall with shadow skill?"

Shruti replied, "Does it rain sulfuric acid in the southeast?"

"We can't undo someone else's shadow skill, especially if they're still holding the wall up," Vidya argued. "But we can squeeze our own shadow into the barrier like pliers and spread open a passageway. It requires great effort and skill."

"Which we have," Shruti assured him. "But it'll only hold for as long as we can physically keep it open."

"In other words," Vidya clarified, "you can't get out without us."

"I'd never let anything happen to you," Rohan said, kissing the back of Vidya's hand as Shruti made a gagging noise.

"Aw. You're so sweet to think that I need your protection," Vidya replied with a wink.

The plan was set. Once the dakini carved through the wall, they were relieved to find there wasn't a need to create shadow pliers. It made sense for the elders not to waste shadow mass or effort, and they certainly weren't expecting any borderland dakini to abandon their posts and drop by.

To control the flow of infected, the dakini formed a narrow slit. They slipped through first with Rohan. Hiran secured the attention of the slow-moving horde, then followed, running to meet his band, dipping behind trees and crouching amid tall grass.

Elder dakini stood in waist-high towers spread across the top of the wall, adjusting the finishing seals and capturing the girls' attention.

Their disbelieving eyes went wide. Vidya balled her hands into fists, shadow mist squeezing out from between her fingers. They'd already accepted the truth and seen the wall from the outside, but the pain and betrayal of witnessing their elders wielding shadow against them cut deep all the same.

"We have to go," Rohan said, taking Vidya's hand.

She'd been heaving, close to tears. "We can't trust the ones in charge. The realm is not at all what we thought it was."

They moved swiftly underneath natural-looking shadows erected by Shruti, staying low to the ground, hiding behind trees and brush, sliding behind rocks and structures.

Once they'd entered the fields, they no longer needed to hide. They moved freely but kept their pace and dodged anyone that might spot them.

Hiran's chest thrummed with recollection—sights and smells and whispers. How long had it been since he'd treaded these grounds, with a mix of joyful and brutal memories?

They stayed a great distance from the palace, but it loomed before them.

He could still recall those towering trees surrounding the palace, with jewel-laden vines, and the bushes of large, deep amethyst flowers and small, lush indigo blooms. The earthy smell, unlike the rot of the Vaitarani and the acidity of the borderlands. It was the cleanest smell he'd ever known. Fried food wafted from small homes, and incense plumes made their spices known all the way from the shrines. And then there was the hint of hallucinogenic sage. What his mother had used.

"It's so impressive," Vidya said, marveling at the impending palace.

Seven stories of black granite pushed against the clouds, as tall as they were wide with plenty of room to spare. The walls were scalloped with massive, curved balconies larger than entire borderland homes. The palace was adorned with grand lattice windows and domes of gold and silver, painstakingly etched with depictions of birds and keshi, teeth and claws.

Each level had two fewer balconied rooms than the one directly below, creating an angled side. The top floor was the private chambers of the Shadow King and his family, as it cast the largest shadow in the realm, dwarfing all others. It was almost as wide as the uncrossable Vaitarani.

An architectural feat.

As a small child, Hiran had played on these grounds with Holika. They'd chased one another around pillars and trees, avoiding scolding from counselors and nobles who couldn't be bothered by inferior children.

For a brief moment, nostalgia hit Hiran as he was thrust back to those young days. Warm food and clean clothes, festivities and Holika's laughter. Those memories flickered like a painting set on fire, the edges wilting and burning, turning colorful scenes into ashes and eventually into nothing. The way Ma would tuck him behind her to protect him, but also, how she hadn't done the same for Holika, leaving her exposed to be teased for her looks and frailty.

His stomach turned sour as the image of his mother boiled and blistered, her black-and-silver silk lehenga turning to ash and floating away.

Memories were fragments of lost time, a haunting in his head. Every memory with Holika made him miss her so much. Every memory with his mother, now that he could see with an older mind, decayed. It was a strange emotion. He wanted to love her, to miss her, but the more he thought about it, the more he saw how cruel she'd been. Especially toward Holika.

He'd wanted vengeance for his mother. But she was gone.

Now he just wanted vengeance for his sister. His nails grew into talons. The darkness inside him rolled awake. There was something unsettling and unkind about this place, and he wanted to watch it burn. Set it on fire the way it had set him and his family on fire.

He tamped down the embers of rebellion that sounded too much like Holika, who, if given the chance, would set the palace in flames and walk away laughing. Yet he loved that about her.

And then his thoughts curled toward Tarak. Hiran was so close that his brother could probably smell him. He could still feel every punch and cut and emotional scar Tarak had given him. He could still hear his brother's conniving laughter, see his eyes pulsating with cruel intentions just like their father. Hiran would never be like them. He would never be ruthless or selfish. He would never be filled with unfounded hatred.

Yet those were the things that made Tarak and their father formidable. How could Hiran accomplish anything unless he became more like them?

He was shaking now, just as he shook in the dreamscape confessing such things to Eshani.

"I know," he'd snapped, disgusted with himself. "I am a child, a weakling." And with that, he'd jerked his hand from hers and walked away.

Eshani had run after him and taken his hand so that they walked alongside one another. He'd stiffened, hating himself even more. How could she stand the sight of someone as inadequate as him?

"You're not weak," she'd told him. "Vulnerability is not a flaw."

"I'll never be strong enough to do what needs to be done," he'd replied, resigned.

"My father said strength is like a building. It takes time to grow, but you must start somewhere and keep building. Sometimes, you must focus on one area longer than others."

Eshani had smiled up at him, her emerald eyes sparkling beneath the glow of string lights. "When you think there's no progress, step back and see how much you've built."

Now Hiran let out a breath as he faced the palace, where his past horrors and present traumas converged. But he remembered what Eshani had said all those dreams ago.

You've come so far. Keep going.

THE BAND FOLLOWED THE RIVER TO THE COURT OF Nightmares, as it was the safest route to the palace grounds with the least number of guards. And this was where Holika had last spotted Eshani. But before they got anywhere near the structure, something rippled in the water. A shadow beneath the surface followed Hiran. The river was wide and deep and filled with snapping fish and fanged turtles and electric eels. But this creature was large. It didn't take long for the group to notice.

Hiran slowed and faced the river, taking several steps backward, pebbles crunching beneath his steps. He steadied his breathing and laid a hand over the hilt of his sword. Normally, things lurking in the water were only dangerous if one ventured too close. But when that something was following him, he had to assume the danger would come to him.

"What do you want?" he asked, his friends checking their surroundings.

A head slowly emerged from the water, tentatively breaking the surface as if ensuring the air wouldn't hurt them. A head full of sopping-wet green hair rose out of the water, revealing sage-green eyes. The creature blinked at him.

Hiran didn't move, his hand gripping the hilt of his unsheathed sword. He had a sense for danger, for monsters. He didn't get the same sense with this one.

The head rose a bit more, revealing an entire face. A girl with a diadem of coral. She offered a slight smile that pushed up her gaunt cheeks.

"Well? What do you want?" Hiran repeated.

The girl frowned. "I expected more excitement."

Hiran scowled. "What?"

She rose higher, exposing jagged clavicles and bony shoulders. "Don't you remember the girl who saved you?"

Relaxing, Hiran let his hands dangle at his sides, stepping closer and looking down at her. It had been ages since he'd seen Netra, but yes, she looked and sounded like the matsya who had aided him so long ago.

She swam toward a boulder and hung her arms over the smooth, round surface. She rested her cheek against it, eyeing his friends. "Don't worry. There's never danger in the water when a matsya is near. Unless you count us the threat."

"You're always a threat," Shruti countered.

The matsya shrugged.

"It's been a while, Netra," Hiran said.

She beamed, revealing sharp teeth. "You remembered my name?"

"Of course."

"So sullen."

"I'm on a mission. Also, do you realize where we're at?"

She tilted her head. "Close to where we first met."

"Hurt and terrified."

Her joy slipped. "I remember. But look at you now. So tall and big and definitely not terrified."

He looked over his shoulder at the arena in the distance, knowing Holika's body was at the bottom of its pool.

"She's still there," Netra whispered, her voice soft and soothing. "I watch for her, but she's never come out."

He knew this, yet it hurt to hear the words. "Is there a connection underground?"

She shook her head. "I searched. It's a *very* deep well, and thickly enclosed. I used sonar to try to locate her, but the walls are solid. Which makes sense, considering what's there. I'm sorry."

He shrugged. "I never expected her to walk out. It's been too long. I've accepted the facts." He swallowed hard, imagining his sister's remains stuck in a watery grave. He'd known her fate for so long, and yet it never ceased to gut him.

"Who are they talking about?" Vidya muttered to Rohan in the near distance. Hiran couldn't make out Rohan's response but knew he wouldn't tell anyone about Holika.

"Are you looking for the nagin?" Netra asked, her long, iridescent tail moving sinuously in the water.

He nodded. "How did you know?"

Netra's brows tilted up as her long fingertips skimmed the surface of the river. "I saw her a while ago, and *someone* told me to fetch her." She subtly glanced at the dakini, and Hiran was grateful for her discretion. "I tried to get her to come with me, but she refused."

"Yeah, I wonder why," Shruti said.

The matsya hissed, baring fangs alongside a mouthful of jagged teeth. Shruti didn't react. She knew she was safe that far from the water, but that didn't make the matsya any less frightening.

Hiran's stomach dropped. He knew the answer before he even asked. "Did the guards get her?"

"The King himself found her."

"Shit," he mumbled, his fingers hardening into claws.

Netra's eyes flashed to his hands. "He shouldn't be king," she said, dragging her eyes back to his. "But only an heir can wear the crown. Literally. And there is no other."

"I don't desire that burden," he mumbled.

"Maybe you should, and take a matsya as queen," she mused, her gaze flitting away and her pale cheeks reddening.

"Maybe you should be a matsya queen anyway," he countered.

She beckoned with her finger, and Hiran lowered himself into a squat. He didn't trust many people, but Netra was the reason he was even alive.

"Yes?"

She smiled. "Has anyone told you that you're handsome? For an asura."

"All the girls tell me that," he joked dryly. *No one* told him that.

She splashed him. "Careful or your head will explode."

Grunting, Hiran wiped water from his face and arms.

"You know we're planning an uprising," she whispered.

"How's that going to work? Your kind can't walk on land."

"So you think."

"If you could, there would've been an uprising long ago."

"I don't know the details, but my father is on the council, and they need to do something. We hear all. Sound and secrets carry so well on the water. We know the white plague is getting out of hand and the border walls are falling apart. We're well aware of the inner dome. We may survive if the realm crumbles, below in the deepest labyrinths, but we'll be stuck so far underwater and, honestly, that's simply no way to live."

"Is there a way out down there?" Hiran pressed.

"There are endless tunnels and some we haven't explored, but nothing we can call an escape."

"Have you seen the true realm?"

"I've seen the light. It's so bright, and it penetrates miles—there's no way we could near the surface."

Hiran sighed, his shoulders slumping. "Isn't that some sort of freedom? To move between this world and theirs?"

She scoffed, hugging the rock. "No."

"I'm trying to help."

"We know what you do."

Hiran jerked his chin toward her, startling at how close they were. He knew not to look into the eyes of a matsya for too long, for they hypnotized prey and asura alike. "What do you mean *we*? Do your people know about me?"

She placed a cold, wet palm against his cheek. A calming hum washed through his mind as she locked eyes with him. "My people know you hunt monsters for shadow mass and protect the dakini, to help save the dome."

"Is that all?" Every word was becoming harder to say. Every passing second made it more difficult to think.

Netra's voice turned melodic with a soothing cadence. "Who you are and what happened is between you and me. No one needs to know, for yours is not my story to tell."

He swallowed hard, forcing his thoughts into order, knowing he needed to look away. He'd never felt danger from her, but right now, he felt . . . nothing.

"I wish you could come with me." She clenched her eyes shut and looked away, breaking the trance.

Hiran gasped and fell back, Rohan at his side. All emotion and sensation returned to Hiran in a surreal ball of overstimulation. His skin crawled and his insides bubbled, and his mind screamed. He'd heard tales of how matsya lured prey and asura alike, striking with claws and teeth and dragging them down into the waters in a vise grip. Typically, the victim was eaten before they drowned. But sometimes, they were drowned to be eaten later.

He'd heard how others had saved some, snatching them before the matsya could get them. They said coming out of their trance was like coming down from a brutal high. They wanted to return. They hungered for the feeling of utter contentment.

"Be careful!" Shruti admonished, either to Hiran or the matsya, he couldn't tell.

"I'm sorry," Netra murmured, pushing away from the rock. "I didn't mean to . . ."

"It's okay," Hiran said, his throat aching. "I know you wouldn't do that."

She bit her lower lip.

"We need the nagin."

"She's in the palace. Fourth story, west wing, center room between balconies. She has no balcony of her own, only a wall."

"Thank you."

Netra moved away and slipped beneath the water.

EIGHTEEN

ESHANI

Eshani didn't have much choice except to wear what the Shadow King sent her. She couldn't incite his anger until she figured out how to escape. Maidservants, silent and covered from head to toe, came and went, leaving Eshani to stand bewildered in her sequestered room, adorned in a crimson-and-black lehenga with maroon mehndi stamped across her palms and feet, partially covered by glass bangles and anklets.

Her hair had been combed and adorned with a red hibiscus. Heavy earrings hung from her lobes, below ear cuffs that fanned out like flames against her hair. A thick necklace enclosed her neck and spread across her breasts in branches and blooms. It pressed her mother's necklace and the little amber oval against her skin, a stone that had grown since her arrival. Her nails were cuffed with gold.

She looked like a bride.

Whenever she could, Eshani would press her fingers to a multitude of surfaces, particularly near the window, to feel for botanical life. She found none.

The maidservants motioned for her to follow them. "Where?"

Eshani asked, but they did not look at her, much less respond. They had not said a word this entire time.

She glanced at her clothes on a drying rack in the corner, her satchel and dagger beside them. She couldn't get close to her weapon without the maidservants warning the guards, but she could use her jewelry. She broke a glass bangle, clutching the shards in her fists as she was escorted down dimly lit halls. Torchlight sconces were tucked neatly into the marble-and-stone walls. Every door was closed, making the palace even darker. She dropped a shard at every turn, a trail of glass. She timed her steps to drown out the slight *clink* of glass hitting the marble.

Each turn derailed her nerves in this dark labyrinth. They went down several flights of stairs, and no one would respond when Eshani inquired about where they were going and why. They remained silent. They wore coverings over their mouths and noses, decorated in accordance with their rank. The maids had plain gray coverings, easily blending into the walls. The guards' were darker, with painted teeth. The soldiers' were garnished with spikes. The nobles'—she assumed—were adorned with gems.

They led her into a courtyard—a sizable rectangular yard with trees in each corner, trees with jewels instead of leaves. Between them were slender, murky waterways filled with sleek black eels. The area opened to several stories, each level cut into sections by arches and pillars, each section with a rigid, armed guard watching her.

In passing, Eshani pretended to stumble and braced herself against a tree, her hands pressed hard against the smooth surface where the bark had been peeled. It was in pain, for no tree welcomed the stripping of its layers.

I am sorry, she told the tree, then sent a blast of power to its roots where the strings touched the roots of the grass, which would connect with the vines from the Court of Nightmares.

Ashoka, she beckoned, *help me*. Her fingers slipped from the tree as the guards urged her along.

She spun left and then right, but there were so many doors. She'd at least counted the steps from the stairs to have some sort of grounding in this vast palace. Finally, the maidservants ushered her through towering pillars where guards indicated she enter looming doors studded with what appeared to be bloody spikes.

The silence and emptiness of the palace faded behind her as Eshani entered the throne room, where elegantly dressed asuras, all masked, were gliding beneath low-hanging chandeliers lit with a thousand diya. Upon her arrival, they paused and watched her.

Eshani swallowed hard as a man with glossy black eyes approached her. She recognized him as the asura who rode ahead of her on the way to the palace and from the way his face contorted.

"I am the High Lord of this court," he introduced himself, taking her hand, which she vehemently jerked away.

The crowd gasped and muttered, and the High Lord hardened his jaw. But then he gave a smile. His teeth were sharp and far too many in a mouth that seemed too big for his face. She shuddered, and he appeared pleased.

"Follow me, *little mortal*," he sneered, his chin high as he glared down at her.

An ant among giants.

Eshani couldn't move yet felt every breath brush down her neck. They were predators, the lot of them. Stronger than her, in positions of great power. They knew this and made sure she knew it, too. The inquisitive crowds flocked around her, a wave of shimmering navy blues and forest greens and every shade of gray and black and in between.

"Suit yourself," the High Lord replied, his gaze raking down her body in a way that made Eshani want to curl into herself. It was wholly degrading, for he thought so little of her.

How could he so immediately have such power over her? He wielded an authoritative aura, one that snuffed hers out, one that said he could do horrible things to her should she not comply. It drew visceral memories to mind, gossip spreading during the Fire Wars of how men of the kingdom knew they could terrorize girls with a single glance. A glance that promised awful things of torment, emotional abuse, and mental stripping. They thought it so easy to carve a girl into a hollow shell. Eshani wanted to fight it, but terror seized her. And oh, how he knew it.

Giants easily stomp ants.

The asura smirked and added, "Did you know . . . red is the color of glorified whores?"

Eshani bristled. It was her favorite color, one that represented love and passion for the naga. Even a bloody war could not pry her from it.

The crowd parted for the Shadow King. He approached in fine silks and brocade, bedecked in pearls and jewels. The illusion of civility masked the danger. Behind him, on a dais fashioned from bones, a woman in a gown of black diamonds sat on a throne, her face veiled with an elegant muslin fabric. She sat morbidly still, her face turned toward Eshani like an angry ghost.

The King announced, "My moonflower, the nagin. Walker of worlds and my newest consort."

"What?" Eshani choked out, her question lost in the sea of applause and clanking glasses and boisterous chatter.

"You are mine."

"I—No."

"You," he said, touching her chin and forcing her to look up at his intimidating height. Pain spiked down the back of her neck from the angle, but she dared not move. "Do not disobey me, for my patience will run thin. Prophecy has foretold our union. What better balance to death than life?"

"No," she repeated weakly.

"Should a giant show an ant what it is worth?" He released her. "Now be compliant."

Eshani backed away. The Shadow King was quick to snatch her wrist, his free hand grabbing a garland of lustful red blooms. The crowd snickered at the only red in the room being placed over the only girl wearing red. The garland fell over her shoulders, a symbol of betrothal or marriage, but she couldn't simply be married to the king of demons just like that!

"We will consummate our union and fulfill the prophecy," he grumbled with a roll of his beady black eyes, as if touching her was beneath him. "Now *drink*," he demanded, shoving a cup into her hand. She refused to take it. It fell to the floor, releasing thick, sanguine liquid with a distinct metallic scent. *Blood.*

The Shadow King groaned. "I tried to be pleasant. Perhaps I am too kind to an infantile mortal?" he asked the court. The crowd praised him. "No more. You are tiresome," he said to Eshani.

He snapped his fingers, and the veil of this world flitted away. The air changed just then, chilling and thick.

One by one, the Shadow Court removed their decorative masks, revealing pale, broken skin and ear-to-ear grins filled with sharp teeth and reptilian tongues. Some had centipedes burrowing in and out of their cheeks and eyes that bled crimson rivers down their faces. Others had gnashing gills on the sides of their necks with worms peering out, oscillating mouths in search of flesh. They were horrors wrapped in fine threads and shimmering decadence.

The servants around the room had hollow, carved-out eyes and mouths sewn shut. Was that why they never responded to Eshani? Because they couldn't speak?

Bodies were strewn across the walls and around pillars like carvings. Some hung from the ceiling with backs arched toward the ground, swinging with candles stuffed into their eye sockets and mouths. The main chandeliers were made of bones, some with flesh still decaying on them.

Eshani gagged, her breathing wretched and ragged. She caught her reflection in a dusty mirror and whimpered. All this time, she'd been wearing a diaphanous gown, with only her jewelry providing any coverage. Jewelry that now crawled over her skin. The cuff of blossoms squirmed over her ear. She screamed, batting it off. A nest of centipedes fell to the floor, red-and-purple antennae and pincers raised to her, unhappy to have been exiled from her body.

The branches and blooms of the thick necklace fanning over her neck and collar turned into choking fingers. She gasped, struggling to wrench the necklace free and glad that it didn't clasp in the back. She threw it across the room. She started peeling off the remaining jewelry—the bangles and bracelet connecting to her finger, the ring and nail cuffs, and anklets—as they turned into burning coals that left welts on her flesh.

Eshani turned to flee, recounting how many guards she'd passed at the doors and how many soldiers stood in the courtyard. She froze when the woman from the throne suddenly appeared in front of her. She could only assume this was the fearsome queen of this world.

A woman of great presence, and an eldritch horror to match. If a person could wear emotions the way they wore clothes, then this queen was exquisitely arrayed in ghastly fright. Not the emotions she felt, but what she incited—the fear she fed on.

One look at her and terror slithered down Eshani's spine, turning her rigid and gooey at the same time. It was an impossible sensation, but it was also impossible to be so frightening.

The Shadow Queen was dressed in a gown of lavender and gray that seemed to move with her, as if the fabric was a part of her body, melting into her skin. She wore a veil across her nose and mouth. Her reptilian eyes were visible in hypnotizing gray and gold shades. She lifted her fingers to delicately remove her face covering. Eshani stifled a gasp and stared at the scissored teeth taking up the space between her nose down to her long chin, from mid-cheek to mid-cheek. A gray landscape of sharp features and keen eyes.

In a throaty voice, she commanded, "You will comply. I tire of this realm."

Eshani let out a whimper when the Queen snatched her by the jaw, running a long nail down her cheek. Eshani's hands went to the claw, but the Queen was unbearably strong. Eshani clenched her eyes shut as pain radiated down her jaw to her ears, the back of her skull, and down her neck, certain the Queen would crush her face in this unyielding grasp.

"You're a weakling. Your people couldn't even manage to keep their lives, and *you* are the one who survived? How pathetic your kind must be if you're the strongest. Your dead must wail at the injustice."

"Careful," the Shadow King growled.

His Queen snarled, her teeth gleaming sharper like fleeting ghosts. She shoved Eshani away, adding, "Your lineage was once great. That greatness is buried somewhere in your bloodline." The Queen sneered. "*Deep* in that bloodline."

Eshani trembled, caressing her aching jaw.

"The prophecy proclaims your fertility... a *giver of life*. Breed quickly."

Eshani's hands flew to her mouth. They misunderstood. She could give life, but to plants.

"You can enjoy what little kindness I give... or not," the Shadow King said amid salacious jeers. "Although it is customary for the court to witness the consummation."

"No," she managed to say. She would *not* just lie down and take this.

In one breath, he was standing in front of her, taking up every inch of space between them. His eyes bored into her being, clawing into her soul, mimicking what the shades had done. Just as the veil had been removed from the ballroom, so the veil lifted from him.

His skin crawled, ridges rising on his face and wriggling with the outlines of centipedes—legs, pincers, and all. His eyes were gelatinous black voids. He raised a hand to her face, his nails growing into talons, the sound like a blade scraping rocks. When he snarled, curling back his top lip, he not only had fangs, but every tooth ended in sharp points, and there were a lot more teeth than before.

Eshani could barely breathe. Her entire body hurt with a dull ache.

The Shadow King slid a nail across her cheek. She winced. Wetness cooled on her skin above a delineating sting. If he'd cut her, she dared not move to touch her wound. Yet he was the one who recoiled. He ... loathed the feel of her.

His nail ventured to her lips, the cool wetness following. Her mouth twitched. He raised her chin. Higher and higher until her neck was fully stretched and she was staring at the ceiling, where shadows crawled along the stone and chandeliers.

Then he released her. He was laughing with his court. "The things I must do for you!"

Bile rose in Eshani's throat. She thought of her mother and fore-mothers and the war where she'd slain soldiers and the years of training on Kurma. She was not weak. She would not cower. But she *would* run.

The Shadow King's laughter faded behind her as he called out, "There is nowhere to hide!"

No one stopped Eshani when she bolted from the throne room. Ahead, guards blocked off access to certain halls, turning her around in the labyrinth of corridors. Her hands, gliding across walls and sealed-off windows and doors, desperately searched for vegetation, but nothing returned her call, not through such thick stone. Instead, she rushed down corridors, each like the last. Dreary and cold, dizzying and identical, until she spilled into an unusually wide hallway, the ceiling of which was swallowed by darkness.

"What is this place?" she rasped, catching her breath.

Her question was for herself, but a groan answered her. She jumped, searching the area to find no one.

"The Passage of Bones," several voices groaned. "Where the court fishes out the wandering dead from the Blood River and stakes them to the walls."

The walls writhed in stilted, short movements like decorations of perpetually glistening rubies and onyx. Corpses, molded right into the stonework, wailed and moaned and jerked, arms and legs pinned but fingers stretching toward Eshani.

She held a hand to her mouth to keep from screaming, to keep the stench of rot that permeated the air from choking her. With morbid curiosity, Eshani walked onward. The hall was wide enough that nothing could harm her.

The bodies were strewn along the corridor, one beside another, one above the other, but not on top of each other. Some had decomposed to grimy bones tinged in dusted blood. Some had threads of muscle and skin but were otherwise skeletal. Fully naked, exposed. Some had chunks of flesh clinging to legs and arms and chests and faces, yet the floors were clean. There was no blood spatter or morsels of flesh littering the hallway. And still, some looked as if they'd just arrived from battle, recognizable as who they'd been in life.

Gashes in their throats, slits in their skulls, missing limbs, entrails spilling out . . . tales of how they'd died.

The corpses were terrifying, yet Eshani felt a deep sense of sorrow for them. How could the Shadow King do this to the dead?

Eshani walked on, embracing the depth of sadness from the corpses who watched her, futilely reaching for her, until she noticed a familiar face.

Her heart caught in her throat as she backtracked to a naga boy. He'd lived a few streets over from her house and had picked up his father's sword after his father died in his arms.

Her heart spasmed as his lifeless eyes glazed over, his mouth plopping like a fish.

Farther down, she recognized another naga. The uncle from the library who had traded books of invaluable knowledge for daggers and shields.

Eshani hurried onward, searching all the faces, no matter how rotted.

The older girls from school who left behind dreams of studying astronomy to cleave enemy hearts. The secret lovers who pushed past their fear of war to fight for their future. Even the most scared, the most vulnerable, who died within steps on a battlefield.

To her horror, this wall was filled with the dead of her people.

Eshani's knees went weak, wobbly. Her legs refused to hold her upright, and she crumpled to the floor. Her chest ached, her heart twisted, her lungs clenched, caught between releasing her sobs and holding them in. Tears flooded her face. She was surrounded by death, *her* dead, and overwhelmed by the insidious disregard of one enemy King who had sent her kin here and another enemy King who had strung them up like ornaments.

Whatever food and drink she'd had in her stomach spewed violently out of her, leaving Eshani lightheaded and nauseous. As she lay on the floor, her shoulders slumped. Defeat had grown into a monster crouching on her back, slowly winning the fight until Eshani had nothing left to give. It would sit with full weight on her and crush her until her bones were ash, her blood a dusty smear, and her existence eradicated.

She trembled as she slowly looked up, as if she were afraid of what she might face. Even though she knew. Her heart splintered at the sight of the fallen. Her body ached as if overcome with sickness, fatigue. Her breaths were short and labored. But she forced herself to look. They deserved that much at least, acknowledgment.

They'd died for their lives, for their home, for others, for her. Eshani pushed herself up and stood, cleaning her face with the back of her hand. Her arms dangled at her sides as she tilted her chin and breathed in their presence.

"Naga," she uttered.

As if the word were an incantation, they stirred and then abruptly stilled. A hundred heads turned toward her. A hundred pairs of hollow eye sockets watched her.

She gulped and glanced around, to the high ceiling swallowed by darkness, and turned. They were all watching her.

"I'm sorry this happened to you."

One or two twitched, a spasm of the fingers or arms or face.

"I'm sorry this is where you ended up."

The wall of bones began to breathe as one, eerie yet nonthreatening.

Her eyes flitted away for a second, but she returned her gaze to them, steadfast. "I will make this right."

Eshani took a guarded step toward the wall, freezing when a body groaned. What a haunting sound, one that wove up and down the hall, piercing the darkness only to return.

She approached the uncle from Anand's grand library, a labyrinth of treasures that she'd once loved dearly. He was a person she'd seen in passing, a caretaker of knowledge. She lifted her hand and retracted, but then lifted it once more. Her fingers quivering, Eshani touched his calf; he hung higher than the first row of half bodies missing large portions of themselves. Eshani wasn't sure why. Perhaps a gentle touch could ease his suffering, comfort him, acknowledge him so that he would know he was more than a corpse to her. He was a victim of a war that they had not asked for, and he did not deserve this.

Then something unexpected happened. A connection she had not felt outside of plants. At first, the multiple visions startled her, but Eshani persisted. She wanted to know.

She licked her lips and closed her eyes, drinking in the memories of this naga. She whimpered as he relinquished his hold on his life. She felt the sun in the canyonlands warm her cheeks, heard warbling birds in the morning trees, felt the stone beneath her feet on the way to the library. The push of air as he opened the double doors to a multistory complex filled with scrolls and books and art and trinkets. The smell of old paper and new ink. He'd loved the library so.

Then she felt the anguish of his last goodbyes to his beloved, his children and family and friends, the infant in the basket. She flinched as he thought how that infant might not live to see another month. She felt his eyes swell with tears and then his chest expand as he reined in his loss and concentrated on the war.

The terror of his first steps onto a field rose around Eshani like an outstretched hand curling over her. He'd never seen such horrors, a field overrun by dead bodies and warring soldiers. A new terror washed over him as he tried to step into battle. He was a scholar, not a warrior. But the warriors were dead, he knew, and he would die anyway. So he would die a valiant death. He would die fighting. He would die slaying his enemy and giving his family and friends a chance to live. He dug deep into his soul, calling upon the strength of the naga before him, of the naga fighting around him, of the naga who had been slain.

Eshani felt the wetness of blood that he wiped up from the ground. He swiped his fallen kin's blood across his daggers and looked death in the eye. A dozen upon a dozen of the King's soldiers marched toward him. He would die, he knew this. But he found the resolve to die bravely.

"To my last breath, I am my forefathers and foremothers," he whispered with trembling lips.

"To my last moment, I will not fear death." His voice rose to a mutter, the army advancing with the gleam of the King's best weapons.

"To my last, I will not bend a knee to a tyrant." His voice was louder.

"To my last, I will not tolerate evil!" he yelled as the soldiers came toward him. He clenched fists around the daggers.

"To my end, I am *naga*!" he cried, and swiped and dodged and fought.

Eshani felt every cut and hit, ones he delivered and ones he took. She felt sweat trickle and mix with blood. She felt the power of the naga roar through his veins. She felt the smallest moment where he thought he might live. Then the moment he thought he could at least kill a few more so that a few less would attack those in Anand. Then the moment he realized this was the end. And finally, the moment when three long blades drove into his stomach, splitting him open so that his entrails spilled, coating the ground with his remains.

Eshani clutched her necklace, her link to their people, and wept. "Uncle..."

The man swept his head from side to side, his mouth widening and closing. He seemed so inhuman this way, both dead and undead. His eyes were white and cloudy, and he was missing several teeth.

"Na-na-na..." he muttered.

Eshani pressed a palm to his calf and tried to relay comfort the way she had done with trees. The man sighed, a shallow movement of lungs and ribs accompanied by the stench of rot. She tried not to vomit, tried to clear the nausea so he wouldn't know.

"Na-na-na..." he tried again.

She assumed he was making his best efforts to utter the name of their people, to feel the blood of their kind again. But no matter how hard he tried, he failed. His body couldn't grasp the words.

"Shh," she cooed at him. "You don't have to say anything. I'm here."

Oh, how she wished she could remove his sorrows like Ashoka. She wanted to move on to others, to learn their stories despite how agonizing it was for her. They deserved to tell their last moments, and pain was a sacrifice she was willing to bear. It was unfair not to mourn someone because she was too tired from having mourned so many before them. They each deserved her tears, her thoughts, her prayers.

The hallway groaned, stone grinding against stone and coming to life. The bodies writhed, agitated, as a dark presence spilled into the corridor.

The dead didn't appear angry, despite their gnashing teeth. They seemed more pleading. Heads swayed back and forth, from the darkness to her, telling the darkness where she was or perhaps telling her to flee.

She gazed into the depths of shadowy black and gray. This was not the way out.

The hallway was long, longer than one should be. The bodies... they were endless.

A breath skittered down the back of her neck. Her skin instantly puckered, all the way to her legs.

"Little mortal," a voice sneered.

Eshani spun around to face the High Lord.

"Your fear leaves a trail, and it is *delicious*." His gritty voice made her want to fall to her knees and vomit. She hated that he'd turned her immobile with fear, that anyone could affect her so.

He stepped closer so that he took up her entire view. The bodies wailed. Had they been silent all this time? Or had they been warning her all this time? It didn't matter. Nothing mattered other than the fact that he was here.

He lifted his arms. "Do they make you feel more at home? Your kind, are they not?"

She couldn't tell if he honestly believed this or if he was taunting her. He was cruel enough for either.

He lowered his arms. "Not the sort of gratitude I was expecting."

Gratitude? For this grisly, inescapable place?

"What? Too macabre? You are a weak creature, aren't you?"

Eshani blinked as the High Lord advanced.

"I've come to fetch you for my king. A word of advice, hmm? Simply submit. He is our way to freedom, and we are all willing to hunt you for him."

Eshani couldn't breathe when he gave a sinister smirk that made the veins in his neck pulsate. He *chittered*, an unnerving sound that sent chills down her spine.

No, a voice said, tearing through cloudy thoughts. She yanked off a glass bangle, broke it in half, and stabbed him in the throat.

It wasn't a strong weapon and didn't cut deep into his thick skin, but it was enough to distract him. He cursed, snatching her arm as she made her way past him. She slashed his wrist and turned, lifting her foot to kick him in the chest, taking him by surprise.

Eshani ran, glancing over her shoulder to find him licking his wounds with sadistic glee. The darkness consumed him until he was nothing but white fangs amid the shadows. She glanced at the bodies of her slain kin as they tried to reach out to her.

She was a fool. How could she save them—save *anyone*—when she couldn't even save herself?

"It's in your blood. Never forget," they howled.

In her blood? Did they mean like her foremothers who had venom in their veins, or did they simply mean that she was a fighter like those before her?

Hugging walls, Eshani ducked into dark corners. Ahead, a wild ruckus flooded the courtyard. Soldiers and guards raced across the open space, lamenting, "The white plague has breached the walls!"

Others cried, "Secure the nagin!"

As Eshani ran to her room to get her things, she noticed the throne room had been sealed off. She followed the glass trail she'd left, hunching low to catch the slight sheen reflecting off fractured segments until she found her room. There was no guard posted. He must've heeded the call of battle or joined the search.

She rushed inside, closed the door, and quickly changed into her own clothes. A subtle sense of comfort washed over her. She flung her satchel over her shoulders and adjusted her dagger at the waistband of her leggings.

Something skittered past, and Eshani yelped. A centipede rose in front of her, over a foot long. The centipede's blue-yellow antennae tested the air, its mouth pincers opening. The centipede chittered, and when it attacked, Eshani struck first. She stabbed it with her dagger. Over and over, filled with rage and hatred and everything that this realm stood for.

She hated every king she'd ever known.

She hated the war that had brought her to this terrible realm.

She hated the shades for allowing Lekha to follow her here. Hated that Lekha would soon perish and Eshani was trapped in this labyrinth like a worthless mortal, an infantile girl unable to do a single thing to help.

Tears cascaded down her cheeks. Oh, what a foolish girl she was!

Stop that, a voice said, sounding perhaps like Swati? No . . . not quite.

Eshani gasped, spinning on her heel to find her room empty. "Who . . . who said that?"

Swati, hmm? Do you really not recognize your own twin?

"Sithara?" she croaked, wildly perplexed.

Yes.

Eshani clutched her hair. She was going mad.

You're not. I'm really in your head. I can do that now. We'll talk about it when we meet again.

"I miss you," Eshani murmured, unconvinced Sithara was truly in her head. It made no sense to believe such a thing. But it was comforting. "I miss you so much. You would've driven a blade through his chest. I wish I was—"

As vengeful as me? Sithara laughed that throaty laugh of hers. *Bloodthirsty? Vicious? Do you truly think that of me?*

"No! But you rise to the challenge; you do what must be done. You're brave."

Sithara's voice went in and out, strained. *Let yourself go. We'll never be carefree children again. War changed us, but we are braver. We know what we can truly do. Look at me! I'm in your head. I can do amazing things now, and so can you. Don't turn away from that. Embrace it. Be who you're meant to be and nothing less.*

Eshani clenched her eyes shut.

Sithara's voice faded. *You are naga. Rise to your calling.*

NINETEEN

HIRAN

A patch of trees concealed the band of four. Rohan and the dakini sluggishly leaned against the trees, their eyes drooping.

"Stay here," Hiran told them. "I'll go alone."

In an instant, Rohan bounced into alertness, his movements jittery. "And let you hoard all the swashbuckling glory?"

There was no glory to be had, only bloodshed. Hiran placed a hand on his friend's shoulder. "I thank you for being at my side all this time, for having been my companion and confidant since childhood."

Rohan swung back his head. "Oh, stars. Not *this* again."

"I'm serious."

"As am I. You're not the only hero," Rohan refuted.

"I'm not any hero. I need to get in and out. If they find me—"

"I know. Which is why I should be there to watch your back."

"You need to stay here and protect them." Hiran glanced over Rohan's shoulder at the dakini.

"We don't need saving," Vidya assured him.

"I know, but without you we can't get out of here. I need you to be rested so we can flee as soon as the nagin is secured. It'll be a battle, plus the strength needed to get through the wall."

"Where's the horde?" Shruti inquired, searching the area behind them.

Hiran took in a deep breath, skimming the air for death. "Not close enough." He straightened his back, spine rigid, shoulders broad, chin tilted, and said, "I'm not asking you again." The words rumbled out of his chest in a voice even Hiran didn't recognize. His friends stared at him. "If you're caught breaking in, much less helping me, the King won't have any mercy on you. Ferryman or not. Dakini or not. He *will* make an example out of you."

He'd never seen Shruti shiver, but fright sparked around her. From his tone or the truth, he didn't know. Still, she said, "Are you going to just walk in there?"

"I won't be walking in."

"Do you mean you're going to unleash *those* things?" Rohan pointedly looked to Hiran's shoulders.

"What things?" Shruti questioned.

All this time, Hiran had kept his wings—much like his identity—to himself. Out of necessity. Out of fear. Aside from Hiran and Holika, there hadn't been an asura born with wings in ages, and there hadn't been another born with them since. Once his wings were revealed, everyone would know that he was the brother to the Shadow King, a rightful heir, a prominent threat, and the only family member sent to burn who had survived to walk the realm.

He never thought that he would unleash the powerful appendages ever again, nor had he planned to. But something about being this close to the palace stirred the Gloom. It rattled inside his skull, telling him, *Live your truth. You are the Gatekeeper.*

Hiran no longer cared to cower in the shadows, to hide like the terrified child he'd once been. He was grown and powerful, and the royal asura lineages gushing from his marrow could no longer be contained.

Tarak couldn't use Eshani. Her powers couldn't fall into the wrong hands. Hiran had a right to this realm—and more importantly, he had to rescue Eshani. She hadn't asked to be here. She hadn't asked to be caught amid prophecies and desperate attempts at salvation and glory.

Hiran clenched his jaw to trap the cries of agony as his flesh split open. It had been so long that the skin had grown thick. The sensation and pain like someone digging fingers into a tiny cut and expanding it by brute force. He heaved as a scorching burn charged across his shoulder blades, crackling down his back and curling over his sides in a death grip. His spine cracked as his wings writhed underneath his skin, the membrane and bones re-forming, the pointed tips edging out of the opening, until, finally, they sprang open with a behemoth wingspan. They were not only healed from the immolation burns, but fully formed, larger than ever.

Hiran arched his back, feeling the pleasure of their weight, and slowed his breathing. His wings ached to fly, to stretch muscles he hadn't used in far too long. Such a maddening, glorious sensation that overpowered even the matsya's hypnotizing headiness.

Shruti sucked in a breath, shaking her head. "I *knew* it."

Vidya jumped back, exclaiming, "What are those! Why do you have wings?"

"I'll explain later," he promised, even as Rohan walked around to take in the blue shimmer skimming down the membranes of Hiran's wings, grunting with admiration.

"Damn," Rohan said, giving a soft whistle. "Never thought I'd live to see the day."

Vidya punched Rohan's arm, and he feigned pain, rubbing the spot. "Did you know all this time?" she snapped while Shruti hounded

Hiran for an explanation. But there was nothing to explain. There was only one asura in all the realm with wings like these.

"Brother to the King," Shruti whispered. "I'd heard about the consort who had blue swirls around her eyes, but I thought she and her children were all burned."

Hiran nodded, activating his mask so that the narrow planks slid across his face, once again hiding his identity. "We were."

"That just raises more questions," Vidya said, looking at him as though for the first time. "All this time, the nameless boy was... *Hiran.*"

TWENTY

ESHANI

"Eshani," a voice called from the window, a cold current in the air carrying hints of saptaparni blooms, stirring Eshani's memories. Nostalgia and warmth and tender moments growing with a dream boy. Only one being smelled like this.

Hiran was masked. He smashed through the glass. The breadth of powerful wings eclipsed them both, and Eshani couldn't help but to be in awe of such magnificence. Even the Shadow King didn't possess wings, and this boy—with dirt-flecked hair and bruised cheeks—appeared like a raptor with the leathery pinions said only to be bestowed upon lore's most worthy beings.

"How—how did you find me?" Eshani stuttered, stepping away from the shards littering the floor. Part of her wanted to run to him, hold his hand as they'd done so often. She knew his touch would be soothing, protective. But she also knew he hadn't revealed himself to her when they met in this realm.

Hiran swung his legs inside first, the shards crunching beneath his boots, his wingspan taking up much of the room.

"We don't have a lot of time," he said, taking her hand and leading her to the window.

She pulled away. "What are you doing?"

"Come with me."

Eshani eyed him suspiciously. She could understand why the siblings had done what they'd done, but there was still mistrust between them. He hadn't earned her faith, but he was her best hope. "Hiran."

He sucked in a breath at the sound of his name.

"I—I remember it all. You were in my head! For *years*."

Hiran's stiff shoulders relaxed. He closed his eyes. His voice emerged soft, pleading, despite the gruff and hurried undertone. "I am sorry. I truly am, but if you remember all the dreams, then you know it was the only way. We were children when we started."

"And now?"

He gazed into her eyes so that she saw what she'd seen a hundred times over: Hiran's vulnerability. "Now we are desperate. Now we hide nothing."

"You had so many chances to tell me the truth."

"And then you would not have trusted me."

"But you knew I wouldn't remember. You didn't even tell me when we met in the forest."

He swallowed, working his throat. "Can we please discuss this when we're safe?"

"There's no safe place in this entire realm!"

"Shh," he said, holding a finger to his lips, his gaze darting behind her.

Eshani knew she should be quiet, but having a boy shush her only made her angrier. "Don't you shush me!"

She stormed toward the window, not knowing how high above the ground she was, but she would leap.

"Are you going to jump four stories? I have wings, you know." He was right.

Eshani grunted. "Insufferable."

When she turned toward him, Hiran was suddenly inches from her. His height and breadth took up the entire space. Her heart raged, with anger or attraction, she couldn't tell. But then all their dream conversations spilled into her. The way he created scenes for her during their outings, bringing her decadent foods and flowers and showing her things she couldn't imagine existing. For years, they'd grown up together. She told him so many personal things—her struggles, her ambitions. And had he, even once, told her the truth? No.

But he had revealed pieces of himself as well. His favorite things, his goals, his loss, his pain. She had not seen animosity or cruelty in his vulnerability.

"There is a safe place, Eshani," Hiran said, his voice rumbling out of his chest. His hand slid down her arm to her hand. "We've prepared for this. Let us go before—"

An arrow pierced Hiran's wing, simultaneous with the sound of the door ricocheting against the wall and the guards calling for the soldiers, announcing to the entire palace that the nagin had been located.

In that moment, Hiran's features shifted. His horns grew much longer and his fingers changed into claws as he swung his head and growled. He pulled the arrow from his wing, dropping it to the floor before rushing across the room to attack two guards while his wings sank into his back. Eshani picked up the arrow and, without hesitation, stabbed a third guard in the throat before guards apprehended her, clutching her by the hair and dragging her into the hallway.

"Eshani!" Hiran roared as soldiers tackled him. It took more than one might think. He shoved them away with a mighty push, with slashes and kicks.

Pain screamed through Eshani's scalp as the asuras continued to drag her away and as the fight drew Hiran out of the room. She unsheathed her dagger and stabbed the guard. Hot blood sprayed across her face. Two groups of soldiers emerged from the darkness, one from each end of the hallway, descending upon Hiran as he tried desperately to reach her. He raked his claws across faces with a roar that reminded Eshani just how inhuman he truly was.

Eshani, for her part, couldn't fight off the soldiers much longer. She only had a dagger and knew her physical strength was no match for towering asuras. They swallowed her beneath a wave of claws and punches.

She sucked in a breath as a guard smashed the hilt of his sword into the back of Hiran's head. Then they shoved her into a room. The sound of a locking mechanism rang in her ears.

TWENTY-ONE

HIRAN

The resounding ache at the base of Hiran's skull had him slipping in and out of consciousness as they dragged his body away, his hands bound by excruciatingly tight cuffs. His clothes snagged on cracks in the floor, the stone crude against his shins. The guards had confiscated his sword but had not detected the katars beneath his sleeves, sheathed in leather forearm bands.

Was that a collared scorpion the size of a child lounging in the corner, or was he seeing things?

The hallways were wide, but not as gaping as they'd seemed in childhood. The palace was large enough that a scuffle in one wing, an escape, wouldn't alert the entire place. But of course, the palace was in an uproar. Servants rushing around, soldiers called to arms. The sound of running feet, armor and metal clanking. The distraction had worked, but Hiran needed the horde closer.

His father's voice didn't haunt the halls or reverberate off the smooth marble walls. The Queen Mother was but a pile of ashes on his father's coffin. And the families of Hiran's time were long forgotten.

This was a new age. An era ready to meet its end.

Like muscle memory, the layout returned to him, no longer an endless labyrinth. Ahead, to the left, was a domed arena. The throne room was past a pair of arching doorways. Inside, massive chandeliers hung overhead. From each of them, strings of light flowed to the sconces on the wall. Dim lighting over a throne he'd never wanted. A throne of bones fitted with white gold, the back rising and expanding like a curled claw of skulls with sapphire eyes, complete with a cushion of blue thread and gold zari. Blue was the color of the Shadow King, and only he could wear it.

The throne room was no brighter than the outside realm. It was enough to see the two thrones on an elevated dais ahead. Enough for light to glint and dance against a million stitched jewels and mirror work and glittery thread of very expensive and rare clothes made just for the ruling royals. And then there was his father's crown of shadow and ash hovering atop Tarak's head.

The Gloom thrashed around Hiran's skull at the sight.

For the briefest of moments, Hiran almost expected to see Father. He even felt the uprising of a flutter in his stomach wishing that his father would say even one word to him. But the feeling fell away. This king was not his father, but his brother. His tormentor.

Beside Tarak sat a veiled Queen with a smaller version of his crown on her head, a crown previously worn by the Queen Mother. Hiran despised it.

The court of officials and nobles and ladies was present, those who must've been Tarak's consorts, and maybe even a few surviving royals who did not pose a direct threat to the King. They nibbled on food of tentacles and pincers as if a horde of the infected hadn't just breached their walls. They thought Tarak would protect them; Tarak would protect himself first. They were merely a shield in case the horde made it to this room.

There was an uproar of muttering and chattering. An onslaught of staring. Many maintained the high fashion of elaborate piercings—chains between nose and mouth and ear—feathers in ornate hairpieces, centipedes around throats, and sleeves made of crawling spiders. Some ladies wore veils with edges delicately dipped in blood, while others showed faces of tattooed swirls and carmine lips licked by long tongues.

Still others, with slender talons for nails, scooped food from overflowing platters. Some gobbled drinks with dull beaks, some with fangs, some with forked tails, others with hooves, and so on. The asura came in many forms, and in this moment, they all stood to intimidate the boy walking among them.

The guards threw Hiran to the floor. He grunted, his hands sliding over smoothed stone.

"What is this?" Tarak snarled. "And where is my moonflower?"

Moonflower? If Tarak knew anything about Eshani, he'd know her favorite were persimmon blossoms. Hiran scoffed, immediately earning his brother's contempt. He dared to peer up through his disheveled hair at the man his half-sibling had become.

The sight of his brother made Hiran stiffen, his body ready for a beating that never came. His abdominal muscles twitched with the phantom sensation of being punched, his back with the sting of being whipped, and his face with the burn of sliding against rocks.

"She has been secured in a guarded room awaiting your orders," someone replied.

Hiran willed his heartbeat to slow down, willed his limbs to stop trembling, and focused on maintaining his false features as he stood on the command of the new king.

Tarak dragged in a long, deep breath, no doubt taking in Hiran's scent. His nose twitched as a flicker of recognition sparked in his eyes.

"Approach," he said, his voice deep, guttural, commanding, and so much like their father.

The sound of his brother made Hiran want to cower and return to hiding. It sent a chill down his back, prickling at the scabs over his tucked wings. But the Gloom fought the residual trauma infiltrating his thoughts.

We will not stand for this, the Gloom hissed.

The hushed conversations quieted, and all Hiran could hear was the raging pulse swooshing through his ears, his harsh breaths, and his footsteps. He lowered his chin as the Shadow King approached.

"Remove your mask," Tarak ordered.

Hiran shook his head.

"Now," Tarak growled, his anger palpable.

Hiran gulped, afraid to speak for fear of being recognized. Just as strongly, he hated the fact that his brother still incited such terror in him. After all this time, why was Hiran afraid? This was fairer a fight than ever before.

The guard behind Hiran nudged him. He stumbled forward. Laughter filled the room. Tarak smirked, inhaling the humiliation and rejoicing in his ability to decide the lives and deaths of others like they were puppets he dangled over the fire.

His father had told him never to show weakness, to own the room the way he owned anything else. With an undeniable, commanding presence.

Hiran growled beneath his breath, his lungs hot, so that when he replied, his voice rumbled out of his chest. His true voice, deep, resonant. "I wear this to protect myself from the plague."

"He's not part of any of the palace-territory families," a guard discerned.

"I come from the borderlands," Hiran said, contorting his features to seem less like the little brother Tarak might've remembered, making sure that he couldn't see Hiran's distinct cobalt markings. He turned to the guard as he deactivated his mask and coughed into his face.

The guard yelped, jumping back. Hiran just as quickly replaced his mask.

Tarak's rigid jaw twitched with annoyance. "*What* is your name?"

Hiran silenced the Gloom struggling to take control. Now was *not* the time.

"Answer your King," a guard said, shoving Hiran with a spear.

Hiran swerved his head toward him and said, "Don't make me remove my mask again."

The guard stifled his fear, but Hiran could smell it.

"Actually, I don't care," Tarak said. "What are you doing here?"

"Your Highness," someone spoke from behind Hiran. "The horde of infected has reached the gardens. We're unable to keep them at bay; the white plague is spreading."

Fear rippled through the court in a wave of mutters, fracturing this semblance of normalcy. A court would not support, much less protect, a ruler who couldn't safeguard them.

"Great," Tarak said dryly. "The dakini will have shadow mass from the dead to rebuild the wall."

Hiran's eyes drifted toward Tarak. The absurdity and ignorance of such a statement!

A dakini elder spoke. "Shadow mass can't be extracted from the infected."

"Why the hell not?" Tarak growled.

"The plague warps the body and thus the shadow mass. It's worthless."

More than that, the shadow mass of the infected would infect the shadow mass in the wall. The white plague continued to destroy long after the host bodies died. How did Tarak not know this? Or did he simply not care to know?

Tarak's lip curled upward to flash his fangs in a hint of temperamental annoyance. "I'm surrounded by incompetence. Gather the dakini to fix the wall. Gather the soldiers to eliminate the threat. Kill anyone who even looks like they've been near the infected."

He ordered the servants at the far wall, "Take my Queen to her quarters and set up security. Secure the nagin on the top floor as well, and guard her with your life."

"What about us?" A noble stepped forward.

"What about you?"

"You promised to protect us."

"This is where you take up arms like your lives depend on it... because they surely do. Make yourselves useful for once. I can't do everything." Tarak cocked his chin at a soldier. "Prepare my armor."

Tarak walked around Hiran, sniffing, snarling, fangs bared. "Take this one to the dungeon."

Perfect. Hiran could easily break free and rescue Eshani.

Before Hiran could turn to follow his guards out, a powerful blow cleaved across his back. Talons sliced through his flesh, scraping his ribs. A cry of agony escaped Hiran.

"*This* is for daring to enter *my* home."

Tarak's fist clutched Hiran's hair and slammed his head into the stone with brutal force.

"And *this* is for daring to take what belongs to *me*."

TWENTY-TWO

ESHANI

The bare stone floor was cold and scratchy, cutting Eshani's cheek when the soldiers shoved her into the room. She sneered, wiping the blood from her face. Without thinking, she smeared the red drops over her dagger blade the way she'd done with her foremothers' blood during the Fire Wars. A quick and potent death, if only she had the same venom. It didn't matter; if she was going to stab an asura, they would know naga blood.

It took several moments to adjust to the darkness, only a little light trickling in through the barred window at the far end of the room. She stumbled toward the bars, ignoring the searing pain across her face and stomach, her arms and fists, and her scalp where she'd been dragged. With a sniffle, she grabbed the bars and peered out, at freedom, gathering her thoughts, compartmentalizing her emotions. Once every so often, a display of purple and red illuminated the sky. The light touched her necklace, and the amber stone reflected a glow. She touched it, a thread connecting her to home and a reminder of what she was fighting for. Her sisters, her mother, and Lekha.

The stone felt soft, but before she could consider it, she noticed a thin, curling vine near the window. The sort at the ends of pea plants and ivy. Eshani reached for it, but the bars held her back.

Grunting, she willed the tendril to stretch toward her. In another moment, it unfurled and twisted toward her in jerky spasms. Finally, it touched her fingertip.

Do not fret, Ashoka is on their way.

A breath skittered down the back of her neck, a light chuckle. She swallowed hard, sensing not one but *many* things behind her. A paralyzing presence.

Eshani's grip on the bars stiffened. These were plentiful nightmares that she wasn't ready to see.

Her fingers twitched, calling out through the climbing plant now curling around the bar. The long-healed welts from the sentient Ashoka prickled her skin. Finally, it answered. She felt Ashoka's vines slither like serpents, vast and hungry, toward her.

"*Look,*" the voices muttered behind her, a vibration in the air.

"*See us,*" they hissed.

"Turn around, mortal girl who shall not resist our King."

Bony fingers curled around Eshani's right shoulder. She gasped, unable to move.

Another hand pressed padded fingertips into her left shoulder. She exhaled.

Pointed knuckles dug into her back. She shuddered.

A talon dragged down her spine. She whimpered.

A breath caressed the back of her neck, near her left ear, but when a voice spoke, it whispered into her right ear.

Eshani clenched her eyes shut, her fists burning at her sides.

More hands, more fingers, more voices wrapped around her, forcing her to curl into herself.

You are naga, her mother's sweet, determined words rose through the cacophony of voices.

You have the blood of great queens, an ancestor's voice chimed in.

The life force of fantastical beasts, another ancestor reminded her.

You are a goddess emerging, yet another ancestor said.

A seedling breaking through the dirt.

Once nourished by darkness.

Now reaching for greatness.

A reckoning as inevitable as venom.

A force as inescapable as nightmares.

A foundation as deep as blood.

Eshani trembled as the voices of her family struggled to be heard amid the noise from the creatures around her.

Beta . . .

Eshani froze, desperately searching her thoughts to hear her father's voice again.

My love, Papa said.

She could almost feel his final embrace before leaving for war. He'd given her the last pomegranate from the tree in the courtyard. The tart red seeds were a favorite shared between them.

Nightmares can be real, but your mind is strong. Let no one control it. Let no one take that power from you. And when you're ready, allow your mind to unveil great things. For the world will hurt us, beat us, manipulate us, anger us, scare us . . . but we rise. There is a diya in your mind, a flame of immeasurable courage. Unleash it. It is the one fire that should always burn bright.

Eshani opened her eyes, glaring at her white-knuckled hands covered in grime and dirt. She worked through her tremors, releasing a breath on quivering lips, and slowly turned to face the room of demons. Her gaze started low and traveled up. Skeletons stained in blood, cracked bones, crevices filled with maggots and centipedes slithering in and out of eye sockets.

She stared at the one directly in front of her. It was so close their foreheads could touch.

Skeletons. They weren't so terrifying.

But the tall, faceless men behind them were, with their crooked smiles of razor teeth. Blood darkened the indentations where eye sockets should've been, dripping down protruding cheeks.

And the women with bent necks, half their faces covered in long, stringy hair, mouths oozing with red clots. They wailed, gleeful for Eshani to finally see what had been watching her all this time.

A faceless man crawled upside down on the ceiling while some of the long-haired women skittered along the walls in a showy display of rotating necks and widening eyes and gaping mouths. Blood dripped from the walls, a pattern of carmine tears and smudged handprints.

Eshani recalled all the times these things had haunted her dreams. She would run and run and yet never get anywhere. They'd laugh at her and scare her some more until she sank into the ground, petrified and begging. She knew they weren't real in her nightmares. They couldn't physically harm her. But here? They could. Which meant... she could hurt them, too.

The skeletons were just bones, no muscles, ligaments, or tendons holding one piece to another.

The one in front of her cackled, inciting raucous laughter from the others until the sounds reverberated against the stone walls, slapping her already hypersensitive skin. Some keened, shrieked.

"We've been in every room with you, all this time. You just never saw us," a woman said.

"We watched you sleep and bathe, whispering down your neck," a man added.

Eshani clung to the memories of her parents and ancestors for strength. She was weak and afraid, but she could reinforce the strongest parts of her. Her mind, her determination, her resolve.

I am nagin. I am nagin.

I. Am. Nagin.

Eshani sucked in a breath, her skin hot as coals and yet as chilly as midnight dew.

The skeleton swaying directly in front of her sang, "Welcome to your nightmare." Then it proceeded to throw its head back in skin-tingling laughter, rattling the others to do the same. A chorus of cackles, a cadence of clattering bones.

Behind her, she sensed Ashoka slithering up the tower. The vines spilled into the room, caressing her knuckles, sending out tendrils of longing. They no longer wished to consume her. No, now they were one with her and rose behind her in a curtain of deadly thorns.

Narrowing her eyes, Eshani gritted out, "Welcome to yours."

The skeleton's head clamped back into place to glare at her. Before it could even utter a sound of surprise, Eshani grabbed its upper arm, jerking it toward her with all her might and snapping it from its shoulder blade. The sound of fracturing bones stabbed the air. The skeleton howled, cutting off the others' laughter, as Eshani used the arm to sever the head from its body in one fell swoop. Its neck bones cracked, splintering, and the skull clattered to the floor. But there was no time to think, or to react to the pain shooting up her arm. She decapitated the skeleton beside the first, and the one next to it, and the ones rising from behind them to stop her.

Alongside her, the vines struck like cobras, piercing skulls and prying apart entire bodies. The horde of terrors fell into a heap of decayed nothingness.

Yes, Eshani was exhausted and weakened, but fighting skeletons wasn't so hard. No muscle or organs to saw through. Bones were fragile. They were easier to break than she was.

Adrenaline set her body aflame, momentum growing as she ignored the incessant ache in her arms and back. The fact they came to her made it easier. She rammed her bone stake into the face of a faceless man, jumping back as putrid blood gushed from his wound. She immediately snatched one skeleton arm after another, ripping them apart, impaling the faceless and staking the bent necks.

"You stupid girl!" a woman screeched, lunging for Eshani, hands curled and aimed for her throat.

She knocked Eshani to the ground. Eshani yelped when her back slammed against the stones, struggling to fight the woman off.

"We can kill you in this realm!"

"Which means," Eshani grunted, "I can also kill *you*!"

With one hand, Eshani searched for several shattered bones cluttered around them, using the opposite arm as a barrier between her and the woman's snapping jaws and long, clawing nails.

The vines snatched the woman back, stifling her scream, and continued on Eshani's behalf. And when there was no other living thing left, the vines hovered in front of her. It wouldn't be long before the soldiers noticed a mass of plants on the side of the palace where there had previously been none.

A vine carefully nudged Eshani's hand until she pressed her palm against it. Tendrils of information leached from one being into the other, requesting Eshani's forgiveness and understanding with great earnestness.

"You're forgiven," Eshani replied to its plea.

We did not mean for you to fall into the pool, they said against her palm. *Healer who can heal our world.*

"You attacked me."

It was necessary.

Eshani scowled.

To unleash the true potency of your blood. To thread your power into this realm so it may bend to your will. To free us all.

"You should've just told me."

Our apologies. We did not know that you could hear us.

"Where is Hiran? I can't leave him."

We do not know. But the tiger . . . your friend?

"Lekha!" Eshani gasped, staring at the hovering vines as if looking a person in the eye.

We've felt the clash of information within the roots, plant to plant, grass to tree. The tiger fights to live amid the dark things in the dark forest, infected and struggling. There is still time to save her—but not much time, as she is slowly losing her battle.

"How do I cure her?"

Amrita.

The most difficult thing to obtain in all the cosmos. Eshani let out a desperate breath. She squeezed her eyes. "I need Hiran to show me the way."

Safety first. The Shadow King is not far. He comes for you. We cannot harm the one who wears the crown, for the realm feeds on royal asura.

"Is that why you hid from him when he found me? Does he not command you?"

He could if he thought us more than a bloodthirsty plant, but the kings have never asked us and we have never revealed, for nothing wishes to be in servitude to another.

That was fair enough.

Ashoka allowed Eshani to crawl out of the small window, twisting and turning and catching her kurta until she was staring several stories down. She held on to the thickest vine, which did not dare prick her again, and Ashoka lowered her to the ground.

Before her feet touched the pallid grass, a small army was already upon her. A battle sounded behind them, and they seemed, if only for a moment, divided. Alarms rang in the air, shouts echoed, and metal clanked against metal. Cries and screams, both men and women, court and soldiers.

No matter what sort of chaos was descending, Ashoka told Eshani the way, nudging her aside while they fanned out, lunging for the soldiers in their ravenous hunger.

Eshani ran toward the back of the palace and headed for the nearby river. The water was deep and dark, but she pressed her palm against the ground and felt for plants to create stepping pods for her.

"Don't bother," a girl said.

Eshani tumbled back, not having noticed the coral-crowned girl chest deep in the water. She was the same one from the stream at the Court of Nightmares. "What do you want?"

"I need your help," the girl said, her voice ever soft and soothing.

"Why should I trust you?"

"I tried to save you before, warn you about the Shadow King. Just like the vines tried to keep you from him."

"By getting me into the water—your territory—so you could kill me or eat me?"

"No. Why does everyone think I'm out to eat them?" The girl guffawed, perplexed that the sight of her sharp teeth and taloned hands weren't deemed inviting.

"I can make my own way, thank you."

"You're Eshani."

"Apparently news spreads."

"Holika told me about you. That was how I knew you were at the Court of Nightmares. She sent me to help you, and her brother was trying to save you. I told him where you were."

Eshani narrowed her eyes.

"Hiran," she whispered, as if his name were a deadly secret.

"If you wish for me to help you, tell me where he is."

"The Shadow King captured him. He's going to die in an underwater prison, and I don't have the strength to save him. And his friends are unable to work fast enough."

Foolish boy! "No one told him to come for me!"

"That's the thing about Hiran; one never has to ask. But you and I, do we not want the same thing?"

Eshani, crouched close to the shrubs, glanced over her shoulders at a few soldiers who'd managed to slip past the vines.

The girl pointed down the river. "He is there. Where the water meets the palace."

Eshani pressed both palms against the ground and felt along the path of the river to the palace, where the swaying lotus told her about the bound boy halfway underwater. Her powers had indeed grown a hundredfold since Ashoka's attack.

A cry sounded behind Eshani. She spun to find a soldier face down on the ground with a point protruding from his back, gushing blood.

The girl in the water shrugged, tossing a sharpened reed in her hand. "Time is important. You must decide."

"You would defy your king?"

"He's no king of ours. We're trapped here because of him, and he doesn't care for us. He hurt Hiran, who is my friend, and now he's hurting him again."

"Let's go."

"The water is the quickest way," the girl replied in that melodic voice.

Eshani hurried to the riverbed, pebbles crunching beneath her feet, and looked down at the menacing-looking girl holding out her webbed hand with taloned fingers.

"My name is Netra. I am a matsya."

Matsya? Of course there would be vicious mermaids in this realm! Then again, she'd been wrong about some of the dakini and some of the asura.

Netra went on, casting her gaze over Ashoka's long-reaching

tentacles, "I know that you tamed the vines of halahala. I won't even think of betraying you."

"See that you don't."

Eshani stepped into the morbidly freezing water, clenching her jaw and her fists from the cold. The bottom was deeper than she'd suspected, her feet quickly losing touch with the ground. She floated in front of Netra, who said, "Hold your breath. This might hurt."

Eshani sucked in air and nodded.

Netra took her hand, and together they sped through the water faster than lightning. Swift turns left Eshani's body whipping back and forth with absolutely no control. She only managed to keep her breath in and her eyes shut. When they stopped, the momentum in her ears kept going, leaving her dizzy and ready to vomit.

They faced a wall. Only a few inches of the barred window showed above water.

"He's drowning," Netra quietly yelled, searching for soldiers as two other matsya studied Eshani with silent questions. A blaze of explosions lit the sky, and a stampede of keshi jostled the ground. Pandemonium had fallen over the palace.

The water broke around them. Aside from Eshani and the three matsya, two dakini and a boy emerged from the river, gasping for air. Eshani immediately recognized them. Although they'd barely brushed each other's paths, she took comfort in seeing familiar faces. Perhaps even friends.

"Hey!" Rohan huffed, his face blue from the bitterly cold river. "Nagin!" he exclaimed, his voice marked by excitement and urgency.

"Eshani," she told him, smiling at the sight of Rohan, Vidya, and Shruti.

"You're alive!" Vidya said with genuine relief. "Oh, thank goodness. We've been trying to reach you forever now."

Shruti bypassed salutations and went straight to the matter at hand. "You can hug it out later. We've only cut through *one* bar. There's not enough room for him to get through, *and* he's tied up."

Eshani nodded and sank to the bottom, calling for all plants strong enough to help dislodge metal bars. Ashoka also heeded the call.

Eshani returned to the surface, gasping and wiping water from her eyes. "I'd say get out of the water," she suggested.

"Why?" Shruti asked.

Rohan's eyes widened as he pointed down the river, where fierce ripples careened toward them. "What the hell is that?"

"The *vines*," Netra replied. The matsya flung themselves out of the way while the dakini and Rohan scrambled onto the riverbank.

"Don't worry, they've just feasted," Eshani assured the others. Dipping below the water, she swam to the bars.

It was difficult to see, but light from bioluminescent plants illuminated the way, shining upon Hiran and the inside of the dungeon. This place was meant to drown prisoners.

He was holding his chin above water, his wrists bruised and bleeding in the shackles above his head. He bobbed up from the water, clearly exhausted, when he saw her. Concern flashed in his eyes.

"Get. Away." He panted the words between bounces. "Save. Yourself."

The vines slid past Eshani and wrapped tightly around the bars, wrenching and bending. She came up for air, fighting through her lightheadedness and nausea, and sank again. Ashoka worked harder, but the metal was strong, and the water was rising.

On her fourth trip down, while Hiran's friends gathered with bated breath at the riverbank, the vines finally pried out the bars. Eshani rushed in to hold Hiran above water. He was panting and sinking. Blood marbled the water around them.

"I've got you," she said, her hands sliding down the muscular ridges of his sides to feel gashes where he'd been cut. Even underwater, he was heavy. She had to use her body to keep him afloat.

He hissed, then joked, "Now's not the time to feel me up."

Eshani scowled and moved to his wrists, where the vines curled around the shackles.

His eyes drifted toward the slithering mass.

"Gently," she instructed.

He took in sharp breaths, spasming against her. No doubt Hiran had been in this position for far too long. Eshani comforted him the only way she knew how, placing her palm against his chest and sending soothing energy.

His breathing eased; his muscles slackened.

"I couldn't leave you alone for one moment?" she teased, hoping it would take his mind off the pain.

One shackle burst open. Hiran snarled, bringing his arm forward and inadvertently around Eshani's waist. She stiffened, although she knew he didn't mean to. He probably didn't have any feeling in his hands at this point, and it was all right if he held on to her if it meant he wouldn't drown.

The second shackle broke apart, and Eshani grabbed him before he sank, her body flush against his, holding him against the wall of the dungeon.

He hissed, clenching his eyes shut. "The wall is jagged," he grunted.

"Oh!" Eshani pulled him toward her and away from the wall. Ashoka retreated. Netra swam to Hiran and hugged him, flinging her arms around his shoulders.

He flinched, returning the embrace, but his eyes remained on Eshani.

"Let's get you out of here," Eshani told him, happy to see this band of friends safe and reunited. Maybe, together, they could find a way out of this mess.

And with that, the three matsya took hold of the five of them, one for each hand—Netra hugging Hiran to her to ease the sudden thrashing movements—and dashed through the river. They went much farther this time, to the edge of the palace territory and past the inner shadow barrier.

TWENTY-THREE

ESHANI

With the chaos of the palace territory far behind them, the band of five quietly moved around the northern border. Exhausted and shivering, they stayed a safe distance from the dark forest, villages, and dakini.

Eshani couldn't stop thinking about Ashoka's update on Lekha. She was struggling to fight off the infection, which meant she was alive. Was she somewhere in the dark forest now? Following them, watching from afar? Eshani could almost sense her, catching glimpses of honey eyes or golden fur between the shadows.

Every so often, Hiran stifled a grunt paired with a wince. Eshani wanted to ease his pain, but he walked behind them. Vidya and Shruti flanked Eshani, and Rohan took the lead. While Eshani didn't feel any sort of danger from the group, she was glad to have Vidya at her side. And more than that, Vidya wasn't upset that Eshani had withheld the truth when they first met.

"The population, and therefore the white plague, is practically non-existent on this side," Rohan confirmed, stretching as he walked ahead of the rest. "Rocky terrain doesn't make for great farms or settlements."

Less plague, less monsters, less danger. Eshani dared to ask, "Did you see Lekha again?"

"The tiger?" Rohan solemnly shook his head.

Eshani swallowed back tears, her eyes darting to the dark forest to their left. Vidya placed a hand on Eshani's shoulder, giving her a sympathetic nod.

She pushed aside the ache in her chest and, after a while, asked, "Are we headed to the Blood River?" Eshani nibbled on vegetable roots the trees told her were safe to eat. It was kind of Vidya and Shruti to get them for her. Her nausea and headache were finally abating.

"The Vaitarani? Yes," Rohan replied.

While the girls told her what had happened since she'd last seen them and Rohan gave wonderful insight into the new terrain, Hiran remained quiet, observant.

During breaks, Rohan checked on Hiran's back and the dakini scoured the area for food. While Eshani perched on a flat rock, Hiran handed her fruit.

"Thank you," she said, taking the apricot-colored fruit and pressing her palm against one of the few brightly colored things she'd seen in this realm.

"What are you doing?"

"Speaking to it."

He arched a brow. "What...does it say?" His voice cracked, as if he couldn't believe he was asking such a thing.

"That it's safe to eat." She bit into the juicy, tart flesh and relished the nourishment.

"Ah." He nodded, agreeing with the fruit. "Did...he hurt you?"

Eshani looked at him, at his broad frame protecting her from the flashes of lightning overhead. She swallowed and looked down.

"Did he?" Hiran pressed, clenching his fists.

"Does touching my unconscious body, dressing me in a sheer gown in public, and forcing me to marry him count?"

A snarl resonated from the boy like thunder. His friends stilled, casting subtle glances at them.

"Are you all right?"

Eshani blinked away tears. "Physically? Exhausted, but yes. Mentally, emotionally... that might take time." Her breath shuddered at the thought of what the Shadow King might have done to her while she lay in bed. Or worse, what he *would've* done to her had he not allowed her to run out of the throne room.

"I am truly sorry," Hiran replied, his tone genuine.

"It wasn't your fault."

"I'm sorry that I didn't get to you sooner."

"You're not my protector."

"When it comes to the King, I am. He'll raze the realm to retrieve you."

She didn't respond for a while until he flinched and stretched his back. Finally, she asked, "Did my touch actually ease your pain in the dungeon?"

He blinked at her, the skin of his throat—beneath his mask and above the tattoos on his collarbone—reddening against the bluish-gray tone of his skin. She immediately realized that she had no such power. He'd only been humoring her.

"Your touch soothed me," he said quietly, shyly.

Heat burned her ears. Ahead, the group moved on. Eshani and Hiran followed. Now the two walked together, following the others.

"They're going too fast for you," Eshani said.

"I'm fine."

"You're still hurt."

He grunted. "They're making sure the way is safe for you."

"Do you know what he wanted from me?" She watched him for any hint of what he might know, and more importantly, if he knew anything she didn't.

"He needs you to open the gateway so he can escape into the mortal realm, but not the one you came through. A different one, where he believes the amrita awaits. With you and immortality, he could conquer your realm and every realm beyond."

She bristled at the idea of being used in such cruel ways. If the prophecy was true, the fate of every creature in every realm rested on her shoulders. "And you're not stealing me for yourself?"

Hiran looked straight ahead, impassive, and Eshani couldn't determine if that meant he *did* want her for himself. She stopped him, her hand firm on his wide, muscular forearm, as cool as morning dew. The contact startled Eshani as much as Hiran. His gaze dropped to where their skin touched. His chest heaved.

"I would never steal you," he promised. "I've only wanted to protect you."

"Since the first time you came into my dreams and deceived me?" she couldn't help but prod.

"We will discuss this when you're safe on the ferry."

She removed her hand. "We certainly will."

He grunted.

She furrowed her brow as she pondered the immortal elixir, since so many believed she would lead them to it. "Could amrita heal the white plague?"

Hiran listed his head to the side, as if this question were one of the complicated equations Sithara had yelled at her during her studies. "It means immortality, so I suppose yes, it could."

"When I asked you in the forest if there was a cure for Lekha, you said there wasn't. That was a lie."

"No," he replied quickly, looking directly into her eyes, forcing her to stop. "I would not lie to you. The truth is, I've never considered using amrita to heal others."

"That makes no sense. When I think of something that grants immortal life, I think of how it could cure the illnesses that cause death."

Hiran's gaze never left hers. His shoulders curled as he hunched down to be at her eye level, his tone smooth. "Everyone I've ever known—all the kings and royals who've sought it—have been after the thing that grants *them* immortality. It is a selfish pursuit of power for them alone. It never crossed my mind that amrita could be used for others in a selfless act. It is why kingdoms and realms have gone to war and destroyed so much in the process."

Eshani considered his words as she searched those strange eyes that had never left hers. She believed him, for in every amrita legend she'd heard, it had only been sought by those seeking power, never by those wanting to save others.

She nodded. Hiran gave a great sigh of relief and ran his fingers through his hair, muttering, "Why has no one before you thought to use amrita for good?"

Something golden shone in between the trees past him, nestled in shadows. Eshani's heart faltered, her breath hitching. "Lekha."

Hiran turned, his hand going for a weapon. Eshani placed a hand on his to stop him. "She won't hurt me."

"Eshani." He spoke with a level tone, his eyes never leaving the white eyes glowing amid the leaves. "She is infected."

"Maybe she's still herself? She hasn't attacked us." Eshani mused on what Lekha was eating and whether she'd lost weight. Had she found water? Who would clean her and comb her fur if not Eshani?

"We can't risk it."

Eshani released a shaky breath, taking a step forward. Lekha sank into the shadows. Eshani heaved out a breath and ignored the splinter in her heart. She had to save her. She needed the amrita as desperately as everyone else.

"She still lives. She is strong, just like you," Hiran stated.

Eshani nodded, biting the inside of her cheek to keep from crying. Somehow, Hiran knew how close to the emotional edge she lingered. He nudged her shoulder with his and handed her another fruit. "Sweetness makes the bitter less alarming."

Nothing could ease this pain, but she took the fruit anyway. "Thank you."

"Do you want to talk about it?"

Eshani gaped at him, suspicious of what he was trying to do.

He cleared his throat. "In your dreams, you often sat beside me and just talked. You told me about your worries and anxieties, and how you couldn't tell them to your sister or mother because you didn't want to burden them."

She looked at his hands, large and curled. "You would take my hand in yours and I would lean against your side. You always made me feel better."

"I'm glad."

His hand tempted her, and Eshani wondered if it was just the dreamscape or if his touch would reassure her the same way again. Instead, she spoke quietly about her feelings and Hiran listened with great interest. She could at least let him think that her guard had lowered with him so he might tell her anything that he might be hiding. But the truth was, it was nice to talk with Hiran like this again, to share her burden with someone else for a moment. After all, she wasn't spilling secrets, for she had none left.

The dark forest faded as it veered toward the right, leaving Lekha's sliver of this world. Hiran never left Eshani's side, matching her stride, which meant if she slowed her pace, he wouldn't argue.

Suddenly, Eshani remembered his wings, which were absent once again. "Where are your wings?" she asked.

"I don't know what you're talking about."

She poked his arm. "Oh? Did you not fly into the palace?"

Hiran raised one brow, amused. "They're inside my back."

Eshani leaned around to check his back before realizing his friends had caught her in that moment. What that must've looked like!

"Enjoying the view?"

The idea that something as large as his wings could fit inside his back amazed her. "Can I see?"

"You mean . . . you want me to remove my shirt?"

Her face burned. "No!"

He smirked. "I believe you do. How else could you see?"

Eshani huffed. "If you're trying to save me, can't you fly with me in your arms?"

Hiran deadpanned. "Can you run with me in your arms?"

"What is that supposed to mean? Are you calling me so heavy that you can't?"

"Wings are meant to carry the creature they're attached to and their much smaller prey. If you were a tiny child, perhaps. You, my beautiful but full-sized being, are not small enough for me to fly with, much less in my condition."

Her skin hummed.

Hiran quickly looked away. "I didn't mean to make you uncomfortable."

"You didn't. I know very well that I'm a beautiful full-sized being."

His lips twitched.

"Speaking of wings!" Shruti called from ahead. "I haven't forgotten. *Why* do you have them?"

"Later!" Hiran snapped, and then flinched.

"Was the wall you were shackled to that rough? Did it shred your back?" Eshani asked.

"Are you concerned for me?"

"Maybe I can help."

"Do you have a magical salve?" he asked in a tone both sarcastic and saddened.

Eshani reached out to shrubs as they walked past, letting her fingers glide over their leaves.

⚬〜

A NAUSEATING SMELL FILLED THE AIR. ESHANI CRINKLED her nose, but the stench was so strong that she could already taste the foulness hit the back of her throat. Hiran and Rohan cast sideways glances at each other as the dakini gagged.

"*What* is that?" Shruti asked.

"Behold, the Blood River," Rohan said with a theatrical wave over the hill.

Eshani had only heard vague legends about the river where the dead floated toward their afterlife. She never understood why they came here and had to travel such an unsightly journey. Had Papa and countless other naga been through? Was she seeing something her father had seen years ago, a surreal place connecting them across time?

Nothing could've prepared her for the endless, winding river of red. It went on forever in both directions, shrouded in a mist of sparkling scarlet droplets. The air shimmered, its beauty a stark contrast against the smell of rot.

Here, the sky was marbled in rose and crimson without the agitation of lightning.

Eshani had been so enamored by the unique swirls above her that she wasn't watching her steps, ignoring the crunch beneath her feet. She slipped, and Hiran caught her with an arm around her waist. He flinched from the abrupt movement stretching the wounds on his back.

"Careful," he chided, his jaw clenched.

Frowning, Eshani pushed away, only to skid again. *What* was so slick? She finally glanced down, only to gape slack-jawed at the bones beneath her feet, the resonating crunch of skulls as the others trod carefully ahead.

Bones. That was what was crunching with every step. Eshani gripped Hiran's wrist, her stare affixed to the blood gushing over the shore ahead.

"This is the right way?" she asked, her voice trembling.

Hiran slipped a hand over hers, although she didn't loosen her grip. His touch was a cool whisper against her warm flesh, his hands callused but comforting as they had been so often in her dreams. "It's where you'll be the safest."

"Are you lying to me?" She searched his eyes, those strange pulses of color that made their surroundings flicker out of existence. As if only she and he existed.

"I would not lie to you."

She scowled.

"*Outside* of your dreams," he corrected. "Although I never lied."

"Circumvented," she grumbled.

Eshani allowed Hiran to lead the way. He caught her several more times when she slipped, the bones even slicker closer to the shore. She cringed when she stepped onto the first fragment covered in sticky blood, her heart racing, her nails biting into Hiran's wrist. All she could do was stare at the blood lapping at her feet. She'd never seen so much.

"Before we get any closer," Hiran told her, "be aware of the dangers in the river."

"Like what? Snakes and eels and vicious fish?"

"The river is filled with halahala."

Eshani trod carefully. How wrong this felt, to slowly shatter ribs and broken skulls.

Hiran said, "No matter what happens, never fall into the river. It will kill you."

How awful a death that would be, seeing as a mere sting of halahala from the vines had knocked her unconscious.

She rubbed her arms as they waited several moments, turning toward the sound of something behind her and to the left. Crunching bones? Breaking twigs? She looked longingly into the dark forest. Was Lekha still there? Watching? Could she come onto the ferry? Was that permitted?

Hiran listed his head toward the forest, but he didn't speak. He merely squeezed Eshani's hand, conveying so much that words were not needed. She wondered if Hiran knew her pain or if he was merely comforting her enough to get her onto the ferry. Perhaps both.

A cloud of glittery fog parted over the river, revealing a massive ferry of extraordinary height and length, set aglow by flickering firelight from sconces placed at intervals. How unimaginably haunting. Made of ancient wood and brass interrupted by large circular windows along the side. A cabin reared up from the center of the ferry, a long structure two stories high, but she could not have known how deep and generous the area belowdecks was.

A ramp unlatched from the side and groaned open, connecting the ferry to the shore. Rohan ascended first, giving the dakini a reassuring nod. Although Shruti and Vidya seemed skeptical, they followed. Eshani went next.

The wood creaked and bent beneath her weight without a handrail to clutch. She didn't intend to look down, but she did, startled by the eyes peering back at her and the hands breaching the surface reaching for her.

Hiran pressed a hand to her lower back and urged her forward. "Also, there are corpses in the river."

Eshani couldn't get on the ferry fast enough. Once Hiran was aboard, the ramp lifted, and the ferry disappeared into the glittery fog.

She walked around, but carmine footprints did not follow. Her shoes were clean of blood. Hiran remained close behind. She dared to peer into the river at the head of the boat, where more corpses—collared and chained—wailed as they pulled the ferry forward. The boat lurched as it trudged through blood, guts, skeletons, and halahala.

Chunks of flesh and tattered clothes hung from the corpses' bodies, much like the naga bodies hung on the walls of the Passage of Bones. Such ghastly things juxtaposed against the nostalgic firelight. The glow from the flickering flames reminded her of nighttime festivals where she and her sisters ran about, eating and singing and twirling.

"Why are they imprisoned?" Eshani demanded.

"They're not." Hiran stood beside her, his hands curling over the railing, wind sweeping through his hair. "No one on this vessel, including the Ferryman, can interfere with the dead. This is simply a passage to the other side. Some don't accept their death, or fear their fate, or decide they want to return to the world of the living to finish matters. They willingly go into the river. Once in the waters, they can't leave. They're bound to the river, where they slowly rot. Their bones wash up onto the shore. These ones . . . well, they offered to pull the ferry in hopes of getting others to the end faster so that others don't face the same fate. They can request to be unchained. There's always another willing to take their place."

Oh, he's cute, Sithara's voice crooned in Eshani's head.

Eshani bit the inside of her cheek and turned from Hiran. She was no longer on the brink of starvation and exhaustion. *Why* was she still hearing her sister?

Because I am *actually in your head. I needed to make sure you were safe and on your way.*

Eshani clenched her eyes shut.

Although I won't fault you too much if you take your time for Tall, Dark, and Terrorizing over there.

Eshani willed the voice to go away and hoped no one noticed her cowering.

TWENTY-FOUR

HIRAN

Eshani had wandered the ferry for a short while. She seemed to need space, and Hiran gave it to her. She was safe here.

He drew in a breath, his gaze casting across the expanse of the unknown, when Eshani walked toward him and leaned against the wall of the middle decks. She tucked her hands behind her and looked off to the side. They were alone.

He knew it was far past time to confess. "We came into your dreams to find you, to know what you could do—to get you here to help us before the Shadow King could use you. It was not right to be in your head, or to hide the truth, but we didn't have a choice."

"You could've just asked me."

He quirked a brow. "And you would've helped the demons from your lore?"

She shrugged. "I went over this with your sister, but I'll tell you the same. If you'd told me the truth at *any* point—showed me this world, educated me—I'd like to think I would've helped."

His right eyebrow rose as he took in her words. "You are right. But to be fair, we were young, and the ability to simply ask for help was not a thing we knew of. We've always been taught to take what we want. We're still learning."

"Be honest with me, Hiran. Are you using me?"

"I *need* you." He closed his eyes, recalling all the dreams where they chatted and took long walks and learned of new games. He had never felt more like himself, had never felt so free. He needed Eshani in ways that he could not explain and would not dare admit.

He went on, "You made a deal with the shades to save your people. That was your choice and there was no fault with it. You did a brave and selfless thing, for that is who you are. Your deal brought you here, but we all need you. The Shadow King tried to bend you. Yet I'm here to finish the journey without a blade to your throat. Make of that what you will."

"Do you also think my womb is magical, like a factory producing fairy-tale children? Don't tell me that you don't want me to open the portal for you." She glared at him, her eyes wild, defiant, and glossy with hints of anger. "You can use a person without a blade to their throat."

"That's not it," he growled, and closed the space between them, flinching. His wounds were bleeding again, leaving a wet and aching trail across his back. He clenched his teeth. Maybe Eshani mistook that for his own anger, for her next words came out fiery.

"Tell me the truth, Hiran. Or I swear I will jump into this river and leave this game without a winner."

He braced himself against the wall beside her head to lower himself to her eye level again, his face inches from hers. In part to have something to lean on, for he was so very tired. And in part for her to fully see him, to know he was not lying. His every breath was more labored than the last. "Listen closely, then, girl who commands plants. When we get to the Bloodfall, you are to create a bridge. Not one of wood and rope, and not one as easily destroyed as shadows. A bridge of bramble and thorns."

Eshani's breaths quickened. Her cheeks flushed. "To get to amrita? So that *you* can become immortal?"

"*Yes*. It's the best chance I have at defeating the Shadow King and saving what little life we have left here."

"What if I refuse? What if I just want to return home?"

His muscles went slack. "Then destroy the bridge once you cross and return to your realm. I will allow all gateways to be known to you if it is within my power. Never cross the shades again."

She blinked. He was so close that he felt her breaths crash against the skin of his neck.

"I will not force you, Eshani. I am not the Shadow King. I am asking for your help."

"For a place that terrorized my realm and led to the slaughter of my people?"

He dropped his head. How could he ask such a thing of her? "Maybe we don't deserve help. For so long, I've just tried to survive and believed what I was told. That we asuras are great and superior. You perhaps don't know the truth about us."

She shook her head.

"Using portals, my ancestors came from the faraway darkness at the edge of the cosmos, seeking power and destroying everything to get it. This world is a parasite in this realm. It is a tumor that burrowed deep alongside the Vaitarani and tried to expand far past its limits. Within its shadowy borders, endless chaos ricochets off the walls. The true realm, Patala—the one outside these shadow walls—has had enough. It's reclaiming what belongs to it. My kind and the monsters who breathe in this darkness had no right to be here. *That* is what we are. *Parasites.* Malignancies claiming lives in every realm we invade. We are colonizers. You think your pitiful mortal king is bad?"

Hiran gave a weary sigh and stood up straight, adding distance between them. "We are the breath that gave life to the mortal king's deleterious evil. His and that of his entire lineage back to the first king. We are the reason they eradicated the vidyadhara and brought ash and ruin into your world. We are the voices behind madness and violence; just ask Holika. The Nightmare Realm feeds off my kind. We make it strong so it can branch into other worlds it doesn't belong in and cause chaos. We are the embers of a wandering fire that seeks to unravel and scorch the entire universe."

Hiran scratched the back of his neck. "We are the bad guys. I'm only now beginning to wonder if we deserve you: our second chance."

Distant chatter and a flicker of laughter caught his ear. Vidya was laughing and Shruti's voice rose in conversation. A smile beckoned at his lips.

Eshani touched Hiran's arm and his gaze swept back toward her. Her eyes shimmered in the glow of torchlights. "I would be lying if I said there weren't wonderful things here to save—I would love to understand the Court of Nightmares and the vines. And wonderful creatures...Lekha is still out there. And not least of all your admirable friends."

"They are your friends, too."

She smiled at that, nodding in agreement. Her smile slipped; her brow creased. "I would save endless realms for Lekha."

Hiran gently wiped away a tear slowly streaming down her cheek. "I know."

"Okay."

"Okay?"

"I will help you. An entire realm cannot die because I walked away."

He closed his eyes in the briefest second of utter relief.

Eshani nudged him with her elbow. "Do you see? All you had to do was ask."

Hiran couldn't help but grin sheepishly down at her, even if she couldn't see it behind his mask.

TWENTY-FIVE

ESHANI

Rohan had prepared their sleeping quarters and called the band to the entrance of the cabin. Double doors led to a set of stairs that went down into a softly lit hall.

"Your room is ready with a bath to clean up," he told Hiran. He turned to Eshani. "You have a room as well. You can take rest if you'd like. It'll be a while."

She followed the others belowdecks. Rohan assured her that she was free to go anywhere she'd like except the roof. That was meant for the traveling dead.

Shruti and Vidya stood outside their door at the end of a long passageway. Vidya offered, "You can share a room with us, if you'd like."

"Thank you," Eshani said, "but I'll be fine alone." She needed privacy and space and didn't want to alarm anyone in case Sithara's voice returned.

She glanced over her shoulder at Hiran. He watched her for a second before pushing his door open and disappearing.

Eshani's room was sizable. It held a bed, a bath behind a divider, and a large oval window the width of three people... in case she wanted to view the corpses. Sconces provided plentiful light. Lots of plants grew over hanging pots, but most were in poor shape.

She touched them, one by one, and asked for their stories, to learn about them and this ferry that somehow felt safe. They were so eager to tell her everything, for no one had ever spoken to them before. Eshani was content to listen to them and heal them as they chattered away. And in between, she deciphered what each plant was and its origins. Herbs and ornamentals and food. They originated from neither the Nightmare Realm nor Patala. They just were.

Eshani learned that this boat was just that, a vessel to transport the dead to their next journey. The Ferryman focused solely on his work. Rohan had been created to take over one day in the distant future. And Hiran was an orphaned child taken under their protection. In the veins of the leaves that had been in Hiran's presence, they weaved whispers of all they knew.

His trauma bled from the plants and into her fingers. Her heart ached for the boy who had been through so much.

IT TOOK SOME TIME AND A LONG SLEEP, BUT THE MEDICINAL leaves Eshani had found on the way the river had now taken root snugly in a pot beside other herbs. All the plants whispered and trilled with excitement as the leaves took root and grew at fascinating speeds. Normally, most vegetation couldn't grow from a mere leaf, but Eshani had a gift. One that had sparkled with incredible augmentation since . . . since the vines had pricked her with halahala. Which made no sense—that was poison that should've killed her, and nearly had.

The plants in the room concurred it was the halahala. A poison, true, but with elements that amplified a person's true nature and gifts.

For example, they told her, *Hiran senses death, and he can even communicate with the dead.*

Eerie.

Eerie, true, but a rare and valuable gift.

Eshani couldn't imagine how. The dead held tales of demise and sorrow. Although she'd communicated with the naga in the Passage of Bones, and now their stories would live on through her.

Wilting leaves, shriveled buds, and stems that had been desperately clinging to life now flourished. Eshani delighted in them all. Not everything about this realm was cruel and terrifying.

She set out for a mortar and pestle, drops of water and oil, and medicinal herbs. Once she'd prepared a paste, Eshani knocked on Hiran's door.

"Yes?"

She opened it and walked in.

Hiran was sitting on his bed, back to the door, without a shirt. Eshani sucked in a breath at the sight of his wounds. Not the scratches from a jagged prison wall or even the welts from a whip, but four wide, deep gashes. Something had clawed him open.

Hiran twisted to view her. Realizing it was Eshani, he jumped to his feet, turning from her, and immediately winced. "I thought you were Rohan."

"I'm sorry. I . . ." Her voice trailed off as she lowered her eyes, realizing how absurdly she was staring at his chest and abs. He wasn't as lean or muscular as the boys from Anand and Kurma, and she'd never noticed the older boys when they swam in coves at the bottom of the canyonlands or trained in the forest of Kurma's shell. She'd either been too young or too engrossed in her own training. This was the first time she'd ever seen an older boy's bare torso, much less one with a great deal of muscle. She imagined living in a world like this—fighting for his life every day—was what made him this way.

He cleared his throat, grabbing his shirt from the end of the bed. "Did you want something, or were you trying to catch me half-naked?"

"No, wait," she blurted.

He froze, one arm inside his kurta. "So . . . half-naked?"

Eshani pushed out an exasperated breath and held up the mortar. "I made you a salve for your back. You're welcome."

"Oh. Thanks. I'll ask Rohan to apply it when he wakes up. I can't reach back there."

"I can do it for you," she suggested. "Your wounds are going to get infected."

"Or maybe you want to see my wings? For which I must be shirtless."

Her head listed to the side. "I am not interested in your nakedness, you ridiculous boy. You asked if I had a special salve. I have it now."

His gaze dropped to the small bowl in her palm. "Where did you get it?"

"I found leaves along the way and made it in my room. Do you want this or not?"

He furrowed his brow and quietly growled. "You may place your hands on me." He turned from her and sat on the bed.

Her skin flushed as she crawled onto the bed behind him, the only way to apply the salve without forcing him to move.

"But no groping, I beg of you."

Eshani grunted. "Get over yourself."

His shoulders vibrated. Was he laughing? At least his back was clean.

"This will sting at first, and then feel cool. It shouldn't burn."

He nodded and tied his hair up, muttering, "I need a haircut."

Eshani had never cut someone's hair short. Trimming Sithara's hair was easy, and even her own. Kneeling behind Hiran, she said, "Ready?"

"Yes," he replied, stiffening as if she might jab his cuts and spread them wider.

Her gut spasmed at the sight of the wounds, clearly cuts from some beastly monster. They ran deep, the wider centers exposing raw muscle, the ends tapering off, and the edges crusted with curled skin and oozing blood. She hoped he didn't have an infection already, although the salve should fight it off.

Using the handle of a clean metal utensil that she'd burned over a flame, Eshani spread the salve over the first cut. Hiran jerked at first touch but didn't make a sound, nor did he pull away. She paused, resuming with light, even strokes for effective application.

"This ferry is cleaner than I imagined it would be," she commented.

"The Ferryman and Rohan aren't animals."

"Of course not. But this realm is so dark and gory—and we *are* floating down a river of blood. I didn't expect an airy room with plants, clean running water, and comfort."

"When you live out your days here, you might as well make it home." He sucked in a breath on the next wound.

"Two more to go."

He nodded.

"How did you get these wounds? These can't be from the dungeon wall."

His shoulders went up with a deep breath and slowly relaxed. He hunched over a bit. "The Shadow King."

Eshani's hand froze, the utensil dipped in the salve. "Just now? Between you breaking into the room I was in and being thrown in the dungeon?"

"Yes."

"Wh-why?"

"For being in his palace."

She gently continued to the third wound. "Because of me?"

"Hah," he confirmed.

"You could've died." Oh, how she wanted to hug him.

"Well, I can die a hundred ways at any time."

"Tell me about the end of the river." She scooped up the last bit of salve, just enough for the final wound. Not having known the extent of his injuries, she had expected there to be leftovers. But she could easily make more.

"Where it ends is a place we cannot see."

"The nothing?"

"Yes. It's part of the true realm where all is connected. There's the treacherous Bloodfall the dead cross, but only the dead can access the way. We can't pass, for obvious reasons."

"How interesting. And that's why you need me to create the bridge? Because no living being could build one by hand?"

"Correct."

"Ah. Does the ointment burn?" Eshani asked, checking for any areas she might've missed.

"No."

"Good. We'll let it work a bit before dressing the wounds."

"I think, if the powers you wield could have chosen a host, they chose wisely."

"Really?" She chuckled at the thought. "Why is that?"

"Your intelligence and desire to learn never cease to amaze me."

Eshani smiled to herself, watching his profile every time he turned his head. "Has anyone tried to build a bridge?"

"The Shadow Kings have tried everything. They've even sent soldiers to jump over in hopes of relaying news, somehow. But everyone who jumped was sent back."

"Sent back?"

Hiran nodded. "If you're not dead, Patala knows. It sends you back to the point you jumped from."

"So...when they're crossing over...the dead jump?" she asked quizzically.

"No. A rainbow bridge appears for them to walk across. Colors I never imagined. It's said to lead to the Vermilion Mahal, or what some call the Palace of the Dead. There, the dead are sorted according to their deeds for their next journey. Or...so I'm told."

Eshani searched her thoughts, asking, "And that's where amrita is held?"

"So says lore."

"Myths and legends stem from bits of truth." Eshani observed the ointment glistening on Hiran's wounds.

"And grow to insurmountable sizes. Who knows what's really there? It's not as though we can pass to search for it, and anyone who goes there can't return."

"Yet the Shadow King searches for it. As does the mortal King," she said, her tone dripping with sadness for the fate of her people. "It's why my kind were slaughtered."

"I know. And I'm sorry for the injustice."

"I loathe the Shadow Kings and this realm," she replied through gritted teeth.

"I would, too."

They sat in silence for a moment, Eshani watching the play of Hiran's back muscles as he inhaled. His breaths were deeper than hers with longer intervals. The wounds shone with salve, crossing over the imprint of wings. Hiran's detailed markings of curved lines and swirls glowed purple and blue.

Without thinking, drawn to the iridescence, Eshani ran a finger over the imprint, above the wounds.

"I thought I said no groping," Hiran admonished, although light-heartedly.

"This is beautiful," she said, tracing the tattoo until it came to a vertical ridge. There were two identical ridges. Scars beneath the beauty of color. "Your wings. This is where they are inside you?"

"Hah," he confirmed.

"Does it hurt when they come out?"

"Extremely painful."

"Why not keep them out all the time?"

"You ask a lot of questions." He reached across the bed for bandages, handing them to her.

"Well, you are a strange boy taking me to the end of a terrifying river at the edge of a horrific realm. I have lots of questions."

Hiran stood and she followed, wrapping the long strip around her palm to make it easier to work with. He was as tall as the Shadow King.

"Why are you shaking? Is my body that glorious?" Hiran teased.

Eshani blinked away tears. "Your perceptiveness knows no bounds."

"Hey." He ever so lightly touched her chin with the crook of his finger. He didn't lift her chin but allowed her to look up at him herself, if she wanted.

Eshani's gaze remained level with his collarbone, skimming across his chest and shoulders and the myriad of scars and bruises.

"What's wrong?"

She didn't want to think of the horrors the Shadow King had planned for her. She shook her head and dismissed Hiran's question. "Hold this." She gave him one end of the strip and walked around to his back, carefully laying the fabric over his wounds.

Eshani worked quickly but meticulously. Hiran held his arms up as she circled him, glad that the bandages were this long.

She didn't really know this boy, yet she welcomed his large frame like a protective force that could shield her from the entire world. She searched his cavernous eyes with their mesmerizing glimmer, always shifting.

His chest rose and fell in rapid, shallow cadence.

Her gaze skimmed the lines of his face, rugged angles caused by his mask. She yearned to see his true face, but did she dare to lift the metallic shield? Was she ready for what lay beneath? He'd been handsome—and very human-looking—during their dream dates, but there was also the face he'd worn the first time he appeared. Which was the real Hiran?

Without realizing it, her fingers traced the mask's cheek and jaw, hooking on the corner beside an ear.

Hiran took her hand, but he didn't pull it away. "Don't," he said in a single breath, as if it pained him.

"I want to see what you look like."

"I am asura. You will not like what you see. Let me be faceless."

"Faceless because you don't want to show anyone? Or faceless because you... have no face?"

He chuckled. "Have no face? Who doesn't have a face?"

She scowled, answering, "The faceless men, for one. They terrorized me in a room."

"Because they have no faces. See? You would be afraid of me. What did you do to those men?"

"Drove bones through their heads."

"Well, now they really have no faces. And I would like to keep mine."

Pressing her palm against his cheek, she reminded him of her request. "Show me."

"Why are you so curious?"

"I want to see you."

Hiran finally obliged and removed his mask. He wasn't grotesque, yet there was something surreal about his features. So . . . human. The parts she'd seen over his mask. Smooth skin with dark blue swirls glinting from the corners of his eyes to his temples, a bold contrast to his shifting red eyes. A strong jaw paired with high cheekbones and rather nice lips. Lips she'd once seen curl up to reveal fangs in her dreams. And a light pattern down the middle of his face.

She reached up to touch it, and he pulled away. "That, you do not want to do," he warned.

"Ahem," Rohan said from the open door, a lazy smile on his face. Vidya leaned around the doorframe to get a peek, Shruti behind her shaking her head.

"I made ointment!" Eshani cried, her face heating to the degree of a sun-drenched midsummer day. She dared to glance up at Hiran as she secured the end of the bandages at his stomach.

"Your friends . . ." she mumbled with a shake of her head.

But Hiran looked out the window, lips pressed together and cheeks as red as hers must've been. He didn't replace his mask.

TWENTY-SIX

HIRAN

T he halls were alive with plants of all kinds visibly growing and winding over the corners where wall met ceiling, draping doorframes with aromatic blooms. Hiran had never seen anything like it.

Rohan and the dakini studied the foliage with great admiration at the end of the hall, where flowering vines crawled up the steps.

Ahead, Eshani walked up with ginger steps. Stems and leaves swayed for her as she walked past, pebbles rumbling in her wake, and droplets of water floating in her presence. Was she aware?

He'd never understood plant life as profoundly as he did in this moment, watching her fingers reach for a fruit ripening from a flower above her. She looked back at him, joy in her eyes and wonder on her lips.

Life followed her wherever she went, bending to her whim, arching toward her graceful touch. Like an entire forest succumbing to her presence. Eshani was spellbinding, and she wasn't even trying. Vines and blooms and hues this world hadn't seen since the arrival of the asuras sprouted along the walls and ceilings, bringing a perfect harmony of color to the dark.

She plucked the fruit to study it. The light from the exit behind her created a halo of her silhouette as she bit into the fruit.

He hadn't realized that her gift was this strong, this compelling. Life would flourish because she was here. Death would reign as long as he existed. Yet they were imperfectly perfect together. Balanced. And inherently stronger. Life was valuable, but death had its place. Both were equally important.

"Did you hear me?" Eshani asked, nudging the fruit in her outstretched hand toward him.

He took the fruit and ate. It was, by far, the most succulent piece of food he'd ever tasted. He watched her watching him until her cheeks flushed. He felt his own warm.

Eshani had once told him in the dreamscape that she wasn't a god, and he'd replied with *Gods are made, not born.*

That had never been truer than in this moment. Hiran was witnessing the rise of a goddess, for Eshani could not possibly be anything less.

His eyes never left hers, and the rest of the world melted away, even as plants clamored for her attention.

On the deck, pods of purple peas and red okra grew. Food for days. The Ferryman was pleased, although he didn't leave his post at the helm to enjoy it.

Along the central building, vines of diamonds shimmered, like the ones in the palace courtyard. They refracted the light from the mist, sparkling pink and red.

"You are simply magic," Hiran murmured.

Eshani grinned back at him, quickly flanked by the dakini and their admiration. If Holika had been here, she'd have conjured butterflies and peacocks, and the ferry of the dead would have turned into a lush floating garden, a veritable—if ironic—thing of beauty atop a river of death.

"We're always so busy with work that we've never had much time to enjoy life," Vidya explained.

"Not that this sort of thing exists where we're stationed," Shruti added. "Might've been distracting."

Tightly wound curls of purple pea vines reached over Vidya's hand. She glanced at Eshani. "You're doing this?"

Eshani nodded. "I gave them a spark back to life and they're thriving."

"Definitely a better smell," Shruti commented, wrinkling her nose. She turned to Rohan. "No offense."

He shrugged. "I'm not the one who smells."

Offended mutters fluttered up from the river, and Hiran stifled a laugh. Why should corpses be offended? They were rotting! And the idea that they could be so sensitive!

In a matter of minutes, even the dead hailed Eshani as a goddess. The beauty, the aroma, the life . . . it was everything to them.

"Mehndi!" Vidya screeched so loudly that everyone flinched. She sniffed the leaves of a short shrub before plucking them off and rubbing the leaves between her hands like she was trying to set them on fire. She squealed at the orange tinge, the earthy scent bursting through the air.

"Truly!" Shruti took Vidya's hands to examine her stained palms.

Mehndi was rare in this realm, reserved for the queens during their ceremonies for engagement, wedding, and birth. It was said to bring them comfort and fortune. It was then that Hiran noticed the mehndi designs on Eshani's palms.

He flinched, taking her hands in hers to examine the details. "Are you married to him?"

She allowed him to hold her hands in his. "I don't know what your marriage traditions are or how binding they are, but no, I did not marry him. In my culture, marriage without consent doesn't stand. Marriage is made with a promise between the couple and witnessed by loved ones, meant to be a union of love and respect and prosperous futures."

Still, the fact that she'd been so close to marrying Tarak, to be fully abused by him, tortured Hiran. "I wish I could erase this for you."

Her mouth tilted into a soft smile. "You wish to do a lot for me. These are merely stamped on, and they'll fade quickly. What he tried to enforce upon me has not tarnished my love of mehndi." She held her hands in the air. Shruti and Vidya admired the designs.

Eshani glanced back at Hiran and promised, "Mehndi is a thing of beauty and joy, and I assure you, nothing can destroy a girl's love of it, much less ruin her fondness for it."

Hiran nodded, pleased that she'd retained her joy. It was the only solace overshadowing his ever-growing hatred of his brother.

He listened from a short distance as Eshani told stories of how her people made mehndi: harvesting and drying leaves, then grinding them into a fine powder, adding water to form a paste, and applying detailed designs on their hands and feet.

"Every girl I've ever known loves mehndi," Eshani boasted as the dakini went to work making their own paste.

"I guess I'll harvest dinner," Rohan groaned. With mehndi around, he wasn't going to get any attention from Vidya.

Hiran helped, and Rohan cooked. He was far better with spices and herbs and had turned giddy with the variety at his disposal. Life at the borderlands didn't lend itself to much time or ingredients to enjoy true cuisine.

Eshani wandered to the right side of the boat and asked, "What's that?"

Hiran explained the desolate, barren land of lava rocks and burnt forest leading into the Eternal Rann: a salt desert with rolling dunes that altered the presence of time. It wasn't part of the Nightmare Realm, but it was dark enough that the Shadow Court didn't need to erect a shadow dome over it. The Blood River was the border. This was where the first asura had found refuge, a dimly lit area during the true realm's darker season.

Eshani remained at his side and took in the endless land, curiosity sparking in her eyes. She had many questions about the ecosystem, to which he had no answers. It saddened him that he couldn't explain much, but the truth was, it was near impossible to know a land that he could never venture into. He saw her mind working and he smiled.

"What?" Eshani asked, casting him a double take.

"You wish to commune with the plants and heal them, don't you?"

A soft smile tugged at her mouth. "You know me well."

For a short and unprecedented time, the ferry was alive with laughter. Very few asuras or dakini ever came aboard; parties like this were unheard of. Dinner featured delicious stews and savory vegetables, ending with mehndi application.

"You're terrible," Vidya told Shruti as Shruti applied a design with a harsh hand. "I want Eshani to do mine."

"Unfortunately, I'm no better," Eshani grumbled as she practiced on Rohan.

"Why are you allowing them to do this?" Hiran asked, keeping his distance from the mehndi-wielding girls.

"It's soothing," Rohan said, his eyes closed and his breathing calm. He was sitting on the floor of the deck as if meditating. "The coolness of the paste, the earthy scent, the light touch on my palms. When shall I ever again be pampered with mehndi, huh? You should try it."

"Maybe you'll be less cranky." Shruti raised a brow at Hiran, wiping away the glob on her palm to start over. She could create shadow mass with precision, but mehndi application eluded her.

"We have some daunting things coming up, in case you've forgotten," Hiran reminded, eager to get Eshani to the gateway or to the amrita or anywhere closer to freedom—his *or* hers.

The closer they ventured to the Bloodfall, the more the Gloom awakened. *Rule the realm that calls to you.*

Hiran shook his head. No, he wanted to save the realm, but he didn't want the crown. Darkness swirled inside his marrow and seeped into his blood, hissing, *Oh,* yes, *we do.*

His grip on the banister tightened, his fingers elongating into claws. *Vengeance. Power. Control. This is destiny unfolding.*

Below, waves thrashed around a corpse who reminded Hiran, "The realm needs a royal asura."

"And you can't save the realm with another on the throne," a second corpse added.

Hiran had always known this. The realm drew power from the royal asura who wore the crown. He could claim he didn't want power all he wanted, but the truth was, it was in his blood. The realm would bend to the one who could save it, and Tarak would rather leave than try. Hiran, the Gatekeeper, was born for this. And the realm wanted him.

They were so close to the end, yet still so far. Could he really take on Tarak? Even with immortality on his side, was he strong enough? Fierce enough?

Eshani had often told him in the dreamscape that he was enough. But what if he wasn't?

He watched her, his gaze sweeping over his friends. His heart, for the first time ever, brimmed with joy. They were enjoying themselves. For once without looming danger or urgent assignments or rigid boundaries of where they could go and what they had to do.

Vidya leaned an arm against Rohan as they lay on the deck and watched the marbled sky. Shruti went to the Ferryman to listen to his stories. And Hiran slipped into his room.

Before long, someone knocked on his door. Eshani entered, a mortar balanced on her palms like a sacrificial offering. "We should change the bandages."

"I can ask Rohan to assist. I need his help washing my back anyway."

"He's . . . having a moment with Vidya."

Hiran rolled his eyes but chuckled. "I'm glad they can have their moment." Even if it wouldn't last long. He removed his shirt, and Eshani's glance flitted to the bowl of water on the table. "Are you sure you want to wash my back?"

She nodded, placing the salve on the table and dipping a square towel into the basin before wringing it out. "You're not so splendid that I'm going to faint at the sight of you."

He took a step toward her so she didn't have to move from the table. Eshani startled when she looked up with nothing but a few inches of space between their bodies. "Why are you blushing, then?" he said, commenting on the pink dusting across her tan cheeks. Why did he want to touch her face? To see if the color would disappear or confirm if her skin was as soft and mortal as it appeared to be?

"I thought naga had scales," he said finally.

Eshani deadpanned, "I thought asura had horns and claws."

His nostril twitched. "I do."

"Where are they? Hiding in your skin like your wings?"

"I don't think you'd like to see them," he replied, sadly recalling how horrified she'd been in her dreams.

"Well, I would." She jerked her chin, indicating he turn around.

Hiran undid the binding at his waist and unraveled the bandages with Eshani's help. Warm water and a rough towel glided across his shoulders and down his back, cleansing his sides and hips. Eshani was gentle.

"Did you have anything to do with the horde attacking the palace?" she asked, sliding the damp cloth across his wounds.

"Yes. We needed a distraction, otherwise we would've been fighting the entire army."

"Smart," she told him.

"Yeah, yeah. I know it was reckless, but desperate times call for stupid measures."

"No, I mean it. It was a smart move."

He glanced over his shoulder with quiet resolve. "I allowed infection into the palace."

"Do they deserve to live?" She blinked at him.

"They made their decision to leave everyone out to die. And to torment you. I don't regret it." He huffed and turned back around.

Eshani patted his back dry, the air cold on his exposed wounds.

"They weren't innocent," he added. "In case you feel bad or think less of me."

"I don't, to either," she replied with an edge to her words. Eshani was not all blossoms and sunshine.

He smirked. He liked that about her.

"Your wounds already look much better," she commented, sliding a finger between sore ridges. Hiran's gut tightened. He felt her touch on the skin over his wings, which tingled, wishing to be free, to wrap around her and press her into him, cocooning their bodies.

"The salve," she announced. "Like before, a sting and then a cooling sensation."

He nodded.

"Tell me about you," she said, surprising him. But maybe she just wanted him to focus on something to get his mind off the sting.

He hissed. The wounds hurt like hell. "My life is a story that unfurls by the minute, a story in which I have not much say. What I've lost, how I end. That is undoubtably a scroll written by the fates. My father died from the white plague when I was young; my mother and sister and I were sentenced to death by fire. My mother died. My sister and I survived."

"I'm sorry for your loss."

"Even though we are asura?"

"Even so." She finished with the salve and began dressing the wounds. "Then what happened?"

He looked down at her head when she moved in front of him, ignoring how she made his skin tingle. "The Court of Nightmares snatched Holika, separating us. Netra, the matsya you met in the water, helped me escape. The Ferryman took me on board and raised me alongside Rohan. After a while, I could no longer sit idly by, watching the realm crumble. It was calling to me to intervene, a compulsion I couldn't ignore—nor did I want to. Rohan and I slayed monsters for shadow mass so the dakini could patch the dome, and we protected them whenever they were under attack. Everyone worked so hard—only to realize that the Shadow King had left us to die while he lived safely inside an inner dome. Shadow Kings before him intended to save the realm. This one does not."

"He's the real monster," she said, reaching around his waist to secure the end of the bandage near his stomach.

Her hands pressed against the binding; his gut clenched. She was so small compared to him but didn't seem as fragile as he imagined mortals to be.

"Asuras are depicted as vile demons in our lore," she said.

"Are you not afraid of me, then?"

"I think you're one of the good ones."

"I'm not good, Eshani. I have my moments, but I don't typically think of the greater good or strive to save innocents, even as their enemy swings a blade at their throat. I let an entire section of uninfected become infected, and I didn't care."

He leaned into her. He could hear her heartbeat quicken, a plucking of strings in the air. "Heroes die for a world that will never bend and will soon forget the selfless act. I'd rather burn the world so it may always remember who I am, no longer the weak thing it tried to burn first."

Eshani held her breath, processing the absolute cruelty of his words. "I'm still not afraid of you," she said, her tone level, confident.

"Are you certain? Your pulse rages behind those delicate ears. Your heart pounds beneath those ribs. You fear me."

"I've faced worse," Eshani remarked. "I came out of war bathed in the blood of my enemies. I've killed more soldiers than I can count. I've fought off monsters in multiple realms."

Hiran smirked. "I suppose naga fear little."

"I know that I agreed to help you, but..."

"Have you changed your mind?"

"No. But I want something from you first."

"Anything," he said, still leaning into her, still so close that he could smell the fragrance of her hair.

"Show me your true self."

He scowled, stepping back.

"Let me see who I'm agreeing to help. When you get very emotional, your face changes just a little. You're keeping yourself from me. Besides, your horns are much bigger than when I first saw you."

"Shit."

TWENTY-SEVEN

ESHANI

Eshani braced for the true Hiran, an asura, like when the Shadow King lifted the veil at the palace. But she was not met with rows of gnashing teeth, a reptilian tongue, extra eyes, gills, or dreadful worms eating his flesh. She saw the boy she'd met years ago in her dreams.

Hiran didn't look much different, but he'd stilled for her reaction. Was he nervous about what she would think of him?

His eyes glowed red and moved like the cosmos, swirling with speckles of infinite colors. Breathtaking. His horns were longer, thicker at the base where they connected to his head behind his hairline. Blue spirals and swirls crossed his flesh like iridescent tattoos. His hands were more clawlike, his talons twitching as she took one into her hands to observe. And the light pattern down the middle of his face turned dark. He allowed her to run a finger down the line, from his forehead down over his nose and lips.

"What is this?" Her words came on a breath.

The line shifted. A ridge formed and spread open, revealing bone underneath. Her breath hitched. Eshani was transfixed by vertical gnashing teeth where the seam had been, over exposed skull. He was a nightmare beneath the beauty. But he let her truly see him for what he was. And she was not afraid.

"Why did you think I wouldn't like the real you?"

He swallowed, the ridge closing and his flesh sealing the pattern down his face. "You were terrified of me in your dreams when I first appeared in my true form."

"That was a dream."

"I'm no longer terrifying?"

"You're handsome," she decided, her skin flushing. She quickly added, "Enough..."

Hiran shook his head. "No. You are brazen. You can admit I am handsome."

"Get over yourself."

He smiled, flashing the points of his fangs, which she found oddly attractive. Heat scorched her skin.

Hiran said, "I am truly sorry we deceived you through your dreams. I assure you, we won't venture here again." He gently tapped a finger against her temple.

"Holika was in my dreams at the palace."

"Oh. Well, once you're safe, or we no longer need to reach you for imperative reasons, we won't do that again. There has to be a better way of communication... but I promise that there will be no more deception and we will not try to retrieve anything without your consent."

"Ah. Thank you for the clarification."

He smiled, and she returned the smile with her own.

Over the next couple of sleeps, Holika left her alone and Eshani learned more about everyone on board. The Ferryman, as grim as he was, had the most stories to tell about the naga he'd carried to the Bloodfall. She missed them so much, even though she hadn't known them all. But it was nice to know that none had passed from the war since Eshani's last battle. Those who had escaped across the Great River that day lived.

Shruti and Vidya told tales of their very non-terrorizing lives in servitude to the realm, explaining how all dakini were women, born in an underground cave from mushroom spores, raised together in a protected nursery, and then absorbed into a village where they would be stationed for the remainder of their lives. They shared a deep sisterhood that reminded Eshani of her own sisters. They didn't always get along, but they loved and included one another in all aspects of their lives.

Shruti explained, "In the beginning, asura kings took dakini as their queens. It's why they were called the Shadow Court in the first place. It was always supposed to be a partnership between the two races. But at some point, the dakini were delegated the task of upholding the physical realm and the asura upholding the metaphysical. There are rumors that the dakini have birthed children with both bloodlines. But those children were too strong, and they wished to give more power to the dakini—which the asura opposed."

"What happened to them?" Eshani asked, finding it fascinating that dakini could reproduce in various ways.

"They were killed. Naturally."

"Asura don't like anything more powerful than them," Vidya specified.

"But aren't the dakini more powerful anyway?" Eshani inquired.

Shruti smirked. "I'd like to think so, but the realm feeds off the royal asuras."

Eshani had heard that saying often. "What does that mean?"

"Dakini create shadow mass from any living thing that dies, including asuras. But when royal asuras die, they fuse into the Court of Nightmares and become one with the shadow dome. This makes both the Court and the dome stronger, and thus allows the realm to stand for a while longer. We were supposed to receive a huge burst of protection when the last King died." Shruti glanced knowingly at Vidya.

"What happened?" Eshani asked.

Shruti replied, "The late Queen Mother immolated all the royals who weren't her own children. But it didn't work."

Eshani glanced at Hiran, who stood in the corner looking off into the distance. Her heart hurt for him.

Vidya added, "If a dakini and asura offspring had been spared, they could've fed the realm without dying. The Court of Nightmares could leech their energy and let them live."

"Well, the asuras are power-hungry and bloodthirsty," Shruti grunted. "Present company excluded."

By which she meant Hiran, who merely shrugged.

As they neared the Bloodfall, Hiran's wounds slowly healed, and both he and Rohan received haircuts from each other. Hiran liked the bottom half of his head cut close and the top half a bit long. He looked more handsome than ever.

"What do you think?" He tilted his head one way and then another.

Eshani touched the nearly shaved sides and he stilled. "Fuzzy," she teased. "I didn't realize your hair had been so long."

"Asura men don't often cut their hair short."

Shruti eyed him, adding, "Especially royal asuras."

Hiran shot her a scathing look. "Having uncut hair used to mean something to me. But the custom was used against me as a form of humiliation when my brothers tried to shear my hair off as a child. I realize now it's just hair."

Shruti grinned and lowered her hood to run a hand over her perfectly oblong bald head. "Hair is overrated."

They laughed.

"Well, I adore yours." Eshani ran a finger along the back of Hiran's head, noting cobalt designs like the dakini's green ones. "You have tattoos here, too?"

"Markings that I inherited from my mother," he explained.

Shruti was still watching and now exchanged another knowing look with Vidya. Eshani didn't think much of it, and no one else noticed.

Eshani later went to the front of the ferry. Ahead, the shadow wall glimmered in a light gray color marbled with white and red. A delineation from this world to the true realm, an end to the Blood River.

"The ferry won't fall over?" Eshani mused aloud.

"No," Hiran replied, appearing at her side along with the rest of the group. "It's like slowly hitting a rail."

"The corpses in the river?"

"No. Nothing falls over except the water."

The dakini watched in awe; they'd never ventured this far. Vidya said, "I never thought we'd see so much in our lifetime. The palace, the Vaitarani, and soon the Bloodfall."

"We'd been confined to one section along the borderlands all our lives," Shruti added. "At least we witnessed this place."

"What was the Shadow King like?" Vidya asked Eshani after a pause.

Everyone stilled. Hiran said, "You don't have to speak of it."

But telling others what happened was part of healing, wasn't it? That was what Papa had taught them. *Don't keep emotions closed inside your heart, where they fester and spread like poison.* Sometimes, things weren't as heavy once spoken aloud. Sometimes, telling another person vanquished what could otherwise be detrimental.

Eshani took a breath and told her friends, who listened, deeply captivated. She released the fear the Shadow King *and* the High Lord had over her. She refused to carry it like stones on her shoulders slowing her down. She did not need the burdens others had placed upon her. She told them about the Passage of Bones and the diaphanous gown she'd been forced to wear, leaving her nearly nude for all to see during her "wedding" to the Shadow King, and how he'd threatened to consummate their union before the entire court.

Vidya gasped. Shruti hugged her, whispering, "What an evil monster."

Eshani nodded, thankful for the support. Some believed the best of their leaders, no matter their actions; they justified them to their last breath. Eshani was glad her friends could see through the curated lies.

"I bet you never thought the day would come when a terror like me would console you," Shruti added, and Eshani cracked a smile.

Hiran slipped a hand over hers, so lightly that it tickled. "I'm sorry he hurt you, that I wasn't there to stop him."

"You're not my personal guard."

He dramatically sighed. "I know . . . you don't need saving. You saved yourself. You even saved me. It's not just you, you know. I try to save all my friends."

She tilted her head back, asking, "Do you also hold their hands while saying so?"

His mouth twitched, his thumb grazing the back of her hand. She rued her breath hitching, and then, through breaks in the rust-colored fog, she caught a glimpse of the bone shore and the dark forest beyond. Eshani felt Lekha traveling alongside them, but maybe she was being foolish. She hadn't decided how she'd use the amrita if she had to choose between Hiran and Lekha.

Hiran leaned over the railing and told Rohan, "We should prepare some weapons."

Rohan nodded and trotted off. The dakini followed.

"What's happening?" Eshani asked Hiran.

"In case the army finds us before you have time to form a bridge. We can hold them off."

Eshani swept her gaze from left to right. The mist was so dense and the river so wide that she couldn't see the shore on either side. "How would they reach us?"

"They have their ways."

"I'd like a bow and arrows in that case."

"Are you a good archer?"

She clucked her tongue. "I'm a phenomenal archer."

"Then a bow and arrows you shall have." Hiran reached over and wiped a lone tear from her cheek that hadn't quite dried. "Tell me about Lekha."

Eshani clutched her necklace, wondering if the amber stone had grown. It seemed impossible, but it sat heavy against her chest— heavier than she remembered. "Lekha found me when I was a child and she a fuzzy-haired cub with the sweetest whine."

Hiran twisted toward her, engrossed in her tales about adventures with Lekha, from destroying neighbors' tapestries to slaughtering enemies. He laughed over stories of the tiger getting tangled in vines, hanging from trees, and whining over fireflies. She was afraid of them for some reason.

Eshani realized she'd only seen Hiran laugh this way a few times, and only in her dreams. She decided that he looked quite nice when he lowered his guard, displaying his fangs. When his grin reached his eyes so they glimmered like rubies and somehow made the cobalt swirls sparkle.

No matter how much it hurt to think of Lekha, she told him more stories and Hiran listened, in awe of the mighty tiger. As she spoke, she clutched her necklace, noting how the stone had definitely grown larger and softer.

ESHANI WALKED AROUND THE FERRY, LOOSENING HER shoulders and wrists in preparation for the impossible. She tried to focus on various methods and scenarios in case the plants wouldn't obey or if the nothing stopped them.

When she rounded the same corner for the fourth time, she caught Shruti approaching Hiran and demanding, "Will you tell us now?"

"You already know," he replied, seemingly agitated as he worked on sharpening arrow after arrow.

"So you *are* one of the King's children?"

Eh? Hiran seemed much too old to be the Shadow King's child, unless the King himself aged very slowly. She already knew time moved differently here.

Hiran didn't look up from his work. "Yes. I thought the wings gave that away."

"Only two asuras in my lifetime have been born with them."

Eshani slipped to the wall and sank to the floor to listen, hidden behind a water barrel.

"Hah." He hunched over a table as he worked. "My sister and me."

"I thought you were immolated."

"My mother didn't survive, but we did."

"Oh," Shruti said quietly. "I'm sorry. I heard all the widows and consorts volunteered for immolation to feed the realm and the children wanted to go as well."

Hiran chuckled at the irony. "You believed that? Who the hell wants to be burned to death?"

"We believed everything the kings told us."

"Immolation isn't how you feed the realm."

"But you are a rightful heir to the throne. Is that why you rescued the nagin?"

Eshani's gut spasmed. *No. Do* not *let this be true.*

"I rescued her for multiple reasons; thirst for power isn't one of them."

She sighed with relief. Of course Hiran wouldn't use her . . . but still, if he took the throne, he would gain power. And no one sitting on a throne had ever been good, at least not for long.

"Come help us!" Vidya cried from the cabin.

Before Shruti ran off, she told Hiran, "You being an heir gives us a better shot at this. I'm guessing your brother doesn't know that you're still alive?"

"Brother?" Eshani asked, rising from the wall.

Hiran jumped to his feet, flinching from his still-unhealed wounds. Shruti cast an apologetic look and ran off to help Vidya.

"You didn't tell me the Shadow King is your brother," Eshani said as she approached.

"It's irrelevant," Hiran replied.

"It's very relevant. Are you certain you're not using me to get the throne?"

Hiran worked his throat. "You have to have known. The realm needs a royal. I am literally the only one left who can do this."

He lifted his hand toward her, but Eshani jerked back. Hiran sighed, adding, "It's not for power, but for salvation."

"You will still receive power. Power, from what I've seen, corrupts."

"*You* are power," he pointed out. "And you are not corrupt. I see in you what I need to be—a balance."

"The Gloom?"

Hiran nodded. "Hah. I finally don't have to pretend."

Yet Eshani feared for him. Dark things wanted him, and he was caving. Could he truly balance power and shadows and the immortality she'd promised him?

A crackling noise ruptured the constant rush of waves. Hiran whipped his head toward the parting fog around them. "Take cover!"

he yelled, lurching toward Eshani and tackling her to the ground. A spray of arrows lodged in the wall above them. The ferry jerked to an unnatural stop.

Ahead, a shadow wall spread across the river. At the same time, a shadow bridge pierced the fog, growing from the riverbed and arching toward the now-still ferry.

The Shadow King's army and the elder dakini had found them.

"Corpses! Don't let them reach the ferry!" Hiran roared, and the ferry tilted from movement beneath the waters.

"Vidya!" Hiran shouted as she scrambled across the deck to reach them. "Go to the other side and take Eshani to the riverbed."

"At the Eternal Rann?" Vidya called back, strapping weapons to her back.

Hiran nodded. "I'll hold them off."

He looked to Eshani, holding her face, and said, "No matter what you decide, this is your choice. But if you do not see us waiting for you on this side of the bramble bridge, return to your world and let this realm die. Never come back here."

Vidya skidded to crouch beside them, concurring, "It's better to seal our fates with no portal than to allow the Shadow King to pass through. He is not here to save us, but to save himself."

"You're willing to die? And let your friends and family die?" Eshani croaked as Hiran released her. Rohan and Shruti slid toward them.

"We were sentenced to die the day the shadow dome cracked," Shruti said. "We just didn't know it. You were our last tiny thread of hope, but the tapestry of this world is burning. What can one thread do?"

Eshani furrowed her brow, determined. She would obtain the amrita, and they would end this once and for all. "One thread can stitch a frayed tapestry into a new one."

Shruti swung her arms around Eshani, muttering, "Of all the

women I've served alongside, you are among the strongest and by far the most powerful. Your thread doesn't disappear here, but we've accepted that ours will." She released Eshani. "Now, go," she told both Eshani and Vidya before standing and gathering shadow mass to create a scythe to cut through the forming bridge.

"My love," Rohan said, kissing the back of Vidya's hand. She shook her head, yanking him in for a deep kiss.

"My love," she replied, leaving them both breathless.

Rohan grinned and crawled away with a set of newly carved arrows, howling into the sky. "I knew it! She loves me!"

This unlikely band of five, who would've otherwise never crossed paths, had become friends. In a foreign realm meant to devour her, Eshani couldn't turn her back on them.

Hiran was stuffing arrows into the empty quivers when he growled, "Eshani. *Go.*"

She looked to Vidya, who nodded, understanding, and then told Hiran, "It's my choice. I choose to fight. Give me a bow."

"Eshani! I don't have time—"

Eshani clutched his kurta and yanked him into her with all her might and rolled. She toppled over Hiran as he roared in pain beneath her. A whirl of arrows narrowly missed his already-screaming back.

She was halfway straddling him as she slipped a quiver full of arrows over a shoulder so that the belt sat diagonally across her chest. With one knee on the deck beside him, she leaned into Hiran and said, "Neither do I. Let's go."

With that, Eshani removed herself from Hiran and unleashed one arrow after another into the breaking fog. The girls wouldn't be able to hold off the shadow bridge much longer.

Many soldiers ran across whatever bridge was available. Corpses harpooned them like flying fish; the air filled with horrid screams as teeth and hands went straight for soldiers' faces. A death by drowning, in poison, while being torn apart by the dead.

Eshani hadn't felt this sort of urgency since the Fire Wars. Adrenaline coursed through her veins with the will to survive. She imagined each of these soldiers and opposing dakini as the Shadow King and his court. If they meant to capture her, to use her against her will, to consume her realm with darkness and greed, then killing them was not so disagreeable to her otherwise-peaceful nature.

Between the skills of their band of five and the corpses fighting on their side, a sliver of hope shone bright.

But the quivers quickly emptied. The fog parted by way of elder dakini in their ceremonial long coats, buttons to their throats and purple stripes down their sides. Their hoods loomed over their heads, their faces covered in angular masks with gills. Only fierce eyes showed as the elders focused on their work.

"What are you doing?" Shruti screamed at them.

The elders startled when they saw Vidya and Shruti on the ferry, and for a moment, they hesitated. The remaining soldiers, however, did not.

Winged beasts rose above them—arachnids with many legs and many eyes—carrying soldiers over the corpses lurching out of the river and depositing them onto the ferry.

Arrows depleted, Rohan, Hiran, and Eshani took to swords. Shruti and Vidya pleaded with their kin to stop, continuing to saw through the shadow structures. But the battle raged on.

Rohan, having mastered his father's ship, bounced against poles and ran up to the cabin, where the few dead above remained oblivious to the war being fought around them. Hiran was outnumbered in a corner, and Eshani went for a soldier from behind, digging her blade into his shoulder.

"There you are!" a familiar voice roared behind her. The High Lord grabbed her arm, spinning her around. He swept low in an attempt to toss her over his shoulder.

"You will *not*," she declared, lunging at him with her sword.

He dodged and slid with quick foot movements, laughing all the while as if she were a child pretending with a stick. She remembered how he ridiculed her, tried to belittle her, attempted to terrify her. Even now, he laughed as if this were a game. Her body wanted to seize up, but surrendering was not a word she wanted to know. Frustration skewed her movements, hindering her fighting skills.

Vidya slammed a shadow shield into his back and muttered, "Still laughing now?"

Eshani gave a trembling nod of gratitude and ignored the disappointment of having failed against the High Lord. Yet again. Even now, as he lay clutching his shoulder and struggling to get up, Eshani couldn't get close enough to stab him. There were too many soldiers surrounding him. He rose to his feet, wiped blood from his brow, and laughed. Taunting her.

Vidya shouted, "Behind you!"

Eshani dropped low to avoid a swing. Vidya immediately went into shadow battle with one of her own, yelling, "Elder! Stop!"

Her elder did not stop. Thus, Vidya did not hold back.

Eshani focused on her attacker, putting her entire force into a blow that sent her blade through his back. She skidded toward Hiran.

"Get out of here while you can," he growled. He wrapped an injured arm around her waist and pressed his forehead to hers. "You will *not* be captured. You will *not* be abused. *Go*."

Several soldiers yanked the two away from one another. Eshani lost sight of Hiran in the scuffle. With her sword thrown out of her grasp, her hands and arms ringing from the impact, she stumbled away. Her back, cushioned by her quiver, hit the cabin. She was trapped.

She grabbed the dagger at her waist. Eshani wasn't the best hand-to-hand fighter, but she drew a breath and put her fists up, blade in one hand. They would have to earn her. "Let's see if you can hit as hard as a girl."

The soldier faced her alone. As he took a long stride toward her, two blades pierced his chest and twisted sideways. He screamed out in agony, blood gushing from his wounds. He fell forward, having been kicked off the blades by Hiran's foot.

Hiran was covered in splashes and speckles of blood, his katar blades dripping with deep crimson. His chest heaved.

Eshani was overcome with the need to embrace him, when something descended from the clouds. One of the flying beasts! It snagged her empty quiver with a talon while three soldiers held Hiran back. He tried his best to fight them off, desperate to get to her as her feet kicked the air. A wave of anger and anguish rolled over his face as wings erupted from his back.

Her stomach roiled being this high up, the bloody river gushing below. She was still clutching the dagger. She stabbed at the leg above her. The beast howled and shifted, sinking, then soaring. It jostled her, but she rammed the dagger into the beast at an awkward angle and dragged the blade all the way down until she was dripping in its inky blood. She began trying to saw off a talon.

The monster shrieked, thrashing from side to side until its talons released her. She fell toward the Blood River. The corpses beneath keened, reaching up for the girl who'd rather die than be taken back to the Shadow King.

TWENTY-EIGHT

ESHANI

Crimson waves gushed up and over Eshani in a torrent of blood and guts. Hands of stringy ligaments and disfigured faces falling from skulls reached for her. As she panicked, her chest burned from holding in her breath. The current knocked her about, muddling which way was up or down.

Bony fingers dug into her wrists and arms and ankles and legs, pinching her skin, dragging her under—or were they pushing her toward the surface? They'd followed Hiran's order to attack the soldiers, but even if they helped her now, the current was too violent.

Her family would face another loss. Her mother would cry for years over her. Sithara would hate herself for letting Eshani disappear from right beside her. She would never see Manisha again. She'd never have the chance to tell Lekha goodbye.

Eshani had let down her father and their people. For all her determination, she wasn't enough in the end.

The fire in her lungs roared hotter than the sun, flames scorching her ribs, suffocating her heart, burning her throat and skull. She couldn't hold her breath any longer. Her eyelids fluttered as the sting of the bloody waters plunged into her eyes, seeping into the backs of the sockets.

Her entire body ached as she desperately searched for anything to grab on to, but the current took her under. A faint recognition of vegetation echoed back at her, responding to her pleas. She sensed long-forgotten roots, hidden deep beneath the bed of a bottomless river, twitch to life. An awakening from an endless sleep yawning into the rocky bottom as the roots pushed aside the pebbles.

But it wasn't enough. Just like *she* wasn't enough.

The current thrashed around the corpses as they reached for her. They were trying to help. She stretched toward them, always close but never close enough. Some came from below and shoved her. She breached the surface and gasped. The din of a waterfall roared to life. There wasn't a single rock or root to grab.

The river took her over a jagged crag—the Bloodfall. In her final, frantic moments, Eshani screamed, calling forth any vegetation that could sense her. An instinct. A silent, volatile plea swept across the waters, rode over the bones and bodies of the dead, and jabbed into the ground, digging through rocks and sand and dirt until finally reaching something that lived.

As the Blood River hurtled her off its edge, somehow keeping the skeletons in its embrace even as they reached out for her, the sides of the great Bloodfall sliced across her shoulders and legs. The deafening, pounding waters silenced her screams, muting her descent as roots erupted from the sides of massive cliffs, entangling her.

The roots were thick and as black as tar, leaving gaping holes in the sides of the cliff. They held her like a mother cradling a child, and just like that child, she'd never felt so secure.

A moment to exhale.

Eshani hung in the gloaming between death and eternity, a strange but marvelous view. High above her, sanguine liquid spilled over the lip of the Blood River, murky but no longer dense. Then a light shimmered just overhead, creating a delineation between itself and the dark realm.

All around, the Bloodfall created a glittering mist in a rainbow of reds and pinks. The air was crisp and cool and clean.

If the dead passed through here, where was the bridge across to the silver haze, that place that shimmered just beyond the Bloodfall?

Below, the mist blurred the infinite abyss, perhaps a hundred feet more or a thousand or an eternity.

The dead weren't supposed to fall, let alone the living. This was not a place meant for any to venture.

Eshani could only deduct these things from where she perilously hung. But she knew for a certainty from the messages found in the fading embrace of the roots.

This place in between was both moving and unmoving. Both up and down, past and future. Both interim and eternal, changing and unchanging.

A jolt of mercy echoed through the roots, reverberating through Eshani with the deepest apologies and the greatest of woes. The roots were suffering in this place where nothing new could exist. In order to maintain the delicate balance, the cliffs grew over the severed cracks where the roots had emerged.

Eshani twisted in the crumpling hold to see for herself. The rock face grew back together, pebble by pebble, crushing the roots before fully choking them off.

Slivers of thinner roots plunged into the mist below and simply disappeared. Evaporated as if becoming one with the ever-looming fog.

A new wave of panic washed over her. The largest roots cradling her decayed, going limp and brittle, until finally the last of the pebbles fused together.

Eshani screamed as she fell, preparing for death. Time and space converged as she fell and fell yet didn't seem to fall far. The roots turned into embers and particles around her, black bleeding into the red all around her.

She heard Hiran calling her name, his face appearing through gaps in the mist, his wings spread wide above him like the largest bird of prey she'd ever seen. Then the wings were gone, streamlined behind him as he dove.

Reaching out for him, she cried, "Hiran!"

He reached for her. But the thing about this place of in-between, this gloaming linking the dead to eternity, was that what should not exist here would not be allowed here.

The mist drew her down, enveloping her in billowing clouds, and shoved Hiran away, sending him back to the realm where he belonged.

TWENTY-NINE

HIRAN

Hiran couldn't reach Eshani in time. There had been too many soldiers, too many blades careening toward them, too much darkness and shadow conspiracy. The entire realm was bearing down on them, crushing the ferry with the might of the Shadow King's hand.

Vidya was pinned to the wall of the cabin with a spear in her shoulder, desperately trying to remove it.

Shruti, in her all her dark rage, had been tackled by five soldiers.

Rohan had been tied up, along with his father.

And Hiran was being beaten down, punch by punch.

An uncanny roar exploded from his chest as his katar-flanked fists sliced and stabbed. Blood covered him. The dead clamored to get onto the ferry, tipping it to the left.

Hiran's wings ripped through his flesh, reopening his wounds in a surge of power rivaled only by agony. Pain seared across his injured back and shoulders.

He launched himself from the ferry, soaring through the pain and following the river where Eshani had been swept away.

She'd gone over the Bloodfall. Everything he'd ever known about going over dictated that the true realm beyond would spit her back up. He would catch her. Still, driven by panic, Hiran's wings tucked behind him and he dove.

There!

"Eshani!" He reached for her. She was so close!

But then the dazzling white mist stole her away, swallowed her whole. At the same time, the wind snatched him up and tossed him back onto the cliff where he skidded, tearing his wings and smashing his head against the ground.

The world went in and out of his vision. Several hands grabbed him, tying him up. The gleam of a royal longsword flashed, a flicker of a blue ribbon tie at the handle, as someone knelt beside him.

"Hello, *brother.*"

No.

"I thought I recognized you in the palace. But these wings? A dead giveaway." Tarak kicked Hiran in the face so hard that his neck almost snapped. "Looks like someone needs a good shearing."

Tarak pressed Hiran's face into the mud with his boot before an inconceivable pain slashed across his shoulder blades, an affliction so grave that Hiran passed out in a pool of his own blood.

FINGERS COMBED THROUGH HIRAN'S HAIR, MASSAGING HIS scalp and stirring him awake. His face was pressed against the softest pillow. There was no searing burn where his wings had once been. He knew he'd lift his head to find Holika cradling his head on the pillow atop her lap.

"Hi, brother," she said softly.

He clenched his eyes shut, pushing back tears, as he remembered his last moments.

"Shh," she cooed at him, calming the trembling air.

"He cut off my wings."

"I know. I know," she whimpered.

"Eshani fell over the Bloodfall. I couldn't save her. I couldn't save anyone."

"She didn't return."

"Because she's naga? Did she make it?"

"I haven't found her," his sister replied softly.

"Does that mean she's dead?"

Holika didn't respond. Instead, she hummed a tune, something she'd learned in the mortal realm. "Rest," she told him.

As a tear slid down Hiran's cheek, the world of white transformed into a meadow dotted with brightly colored flowers, tall grass swaying in the breeze. White butterflies flitted around. Ruby-crowned cranes walked alongside a glimmering stream. The sun shone bright. Hiran had never seen a sun before, had never seen true light. It didn't hurt his eyes.

Second by second, his suffering wilted away, carried off by a soothing breeze. While Hiran withered, the Gloom grew. Enraged, vengeful, and breaking through the bonds Hiran's mind had cast upon him. He'd tried for so long to keep the Gloom separate, as if it were a thing to be despised or feared. But ever so frantically, the two intertwined as one. Or, perhaps, they had been one all along.

THIRTY

ESHANI

Eshani stood in the ancestral plane of her people, surrounded by an unfathomable color. A line of naga materialized in the distant haze, some hues so spectacular that they almost made her fall to her knees and weep.

Surely, she'd died.

Surely, she'd bypassed the official journey along the Blood River, never having crossed the rainbow bridge or been judged at the Mahal for her ever after.

She couldn't say she was sad. This was peace.

Something cool and slender slithered across her neck. Eshani peered down at the necklace gifted to her by her grandmother. Instead of a thin, unassuming gold chain with an amber oval, there sat a serpent. A slender baby cobra moved down her arm and around her wrist, settling on her palm before rising to look her in the eye. The serpent watched Eshani with mesmerizing moss-colored eyes, her shimmering red scales like hundreds of small, multifaceted rubies drawing in and refracting the light.

"Am I finally dead?" Eshani asked, both to the serpent and the naga.

Women stepped forward, the same ones Eshani had seen before.

"This is not your end," one said, her head-covering billowing like a cobra's hood.

"Rather your beginning," another added, a crown of serpents awakening on her head.

"The serpent's return," yet a third spoke, her eyes cutting the haze like an emerald scythe.

"Three for three," another added from behind the others, the hem of her gown touching the ground and turning into writhing vipers.

"Do not fear."

Eshani wasn't afraid.

"Our intrepid daughter of life."

"Our dauntless daughter of death."

"The blood of your foremothers flows through your veins."

"The blood of the first resides in your bones."

The haze shifted to reveal a beautiful nagin, a titan etched into the sky. Pink-and-green nebulous clouds draped her elegant frame in a slitted gown. Stars sparkled like jewels at her ears and nose, a string against her throat and wrists, a cluster at her ankles. Long locks floated around her face in a nest of gloriously magnificent serpents.

The first nagin. The walker of worlds spreading life and death. An incomparable beauty destined for great adventures and tremendous sorrows.

She looked to Eshani, her eyes flashing green. She smiled, her berry-stained lips a decadent and lush color. Her celestial form bent over Eshani's foremothers like a pall of divine stardust. Eshani stared into a long, reptilian slit eye as large as Eshani was tall. The first nagin blinked, sending a soft breeze to Eshani with that one flap of her lashes. The lines and speckles in her irises shone brightly with every variation of green dotted with hazel.

A chorus of giggles haunted the air—her long-gone happiness as she traveled the cosmos. She didn't speak, but Eshani heard the first nagin's voice, a cadence of wind chimes. "You are crafted from my stardust and moonlight; a fleck of my essence rises in your soul. A touch of my blood lives in yours. A touch of blood . . . is all you need."

Eshani's eyes fluttered closed, wrapped in the comforting aura of her ancestor, in an unrivaled tenor. When Eshani reopened her eyes, the titan had returned to the backdrop of the sky, her movements stilling into a constellation.

"But I've failed," Eshani said.

Her foremothers stood around her. The ruby serpent wrapped itself snugly around her arm.

"When you fall . . ." A cloud of dirt billowed up from the ground.

"We shall lift you up . . ." The debris swirled into a tower of serpents.

"Daughter of the first." Their eyes glowed green.

"Stronger than her enemies." Fangs bared and hisses resounded.

"They will know their retribution . . ."

"A reckoning as inevitable as *venom*." Her foremothers spoke as one, a screech that lingered like a fever dream.

PEACE WAS A SOUND. SOFT, GENTLE, SOOTHING. CLEAR WATER lapped at Eshani's arm, tickling her neck. A slightly larger ripple splashed against her face, jolting her awake. She gasped for breath, her body wrought and aching.

The river at her side flowed with crystal-clear water over luminous pebbles. Vibrant apricot-and-cream-marbled koi darted past, jumping into the air and floating down with fluttering wings.

Pink mist concealed the distance in every direction. Above, the skies were endless beneath a trio of amethyst suns of varying sizes.

"Hiran," Eshani murmured, searching for him only to find that she was alone on a grass island with one dead tree in the center.

"Oh, stars." She touched her collarbone in remembrance of her vision, only to find that her necklace was missing. She searched in an exhausted panic, but to no avail. The family heirloom was gone.

Eshani groaned at the wretched loss. Driven by severe thirst, she drank water to her fill and wandered the island. It was small yet endless, always returning her to the wilting, decrepit tree.

Above, one bruised dark red fruit clung to life like a final farewell before the tree's passing. It was food, but Eshani was too weak to climb. She slumped to the ground, her breathing shallow, and let her hand fall to the roots cradling her, wishing for the tree to live as she drifted toward sleep.

ESHANI FADED IN AND OUT OF CONSCIOUSNESS. SOMETIMES it was dark; sometimes it was day. Sometimes she noticed a tiny, moving red speck, perhaps a trick of the odd light. Her ancestors had told her this was her beginning, but she was certain she would die. At least it would be a peaceful death. At least she was already so close to her next journey.

Her fingers twitched; her hand relaxed into a curled bowl. A drop of red hit her palm. Then another. Confused, she looked up to find a sprawling canopy of flourishing leaves and breathtakingly lovely blooms, the petals of which fluttered around her like butterflies, gracing the ground in a blanket of lush red-orange color.

Eshani laughed. The tree had wanted to live.

Another drop hit her palm. Upon closer look, some of the red-orange clusters were bulbous fruit. One convulsed. Another drop fell. A tiny head poked over the fruit. A small serpentine body tightened around the bulb until both the fruit and the creature fell into Eshani's palm.

A beautiful crimson serpent swayed its upper body, as if shaking its head, and looked at Eshani with the most beguiling emerald eyes. Her breath caught in her throat. The snake from her vision! Had it been born from her necklace? Was the heirloom a living, breathing creature?

Eshani lifted her weak arm, bringing the fruit and snake closer to her face. An unprecedented joy flooded her like a monsoon of rain filling a dry summer well to overflowing. Tears cascaded down her cheeks, wetting her dry, chapped lips.

"You are the most beautiful thing I've ever laid eyes upon," she wept.

The baby serpent nudged Eshani's chin with the top of its little head, then squeezed around the fruit. A crack fractured the dark crimson rind.

"Thank you."

Eshani clumsily pulled apart the rind, exposing glistening ruby seeds. *Pomegranate.* Just like the small tree in their courtyard in Anand. The day her father kissed them for the last time was the day he plucked the remaining fruit.

Her father, a scholar of great wisdom, had taken up arms as one of the first to turn warrior. He'd handed Eshani a pomegranate the morning he'd left, dressed in bronze and equipped with winter-steel swords, daggers, and venom-tipped arrows.

She had wanted him to stay. But standing back while others suffered was not the way of her family. She had been young but understood sacrifice, understood hope. And now she understood what it meant to be a warrior.

She held the fruit to her lips, where drops of the sweet, tart juice revitalized her and healed her. As she ate the seeds, the tiny fruit popping in between her teeth and releasing juice, her aches and sprains noticeably melted away. Her drowsiness faded and clarity stepped in. The world was brighter, sharper. Sounds were crisp. It was as if she were emerging from a chrysalis: evolved, better, stronger.

Eshani licked her lips and offered seeds to the serpent. It gladly ate. Eshani guessed the serpent was a female by the slenderness of the gradually tapering tail. "I shall call you Ruhi. For you are soulful and ascending."

Ruhi gave a nod, as if she understood.

"Did you come from the necklace?"

Another nod.

"You are highly intelligent. And alarmingly cute."

Ruhi's scales caught the light, making them shimmer like rubies.

"Are you mine?" she asked, furrowing her brow to make sense of the magical being. Ruhi had been with her all this time, yet the young serpent didn't feel like she belonged to her.

Ruhi shook her head.

"Ah." If Ruhi had come from the heirloom, and her sisters and mother each had an heirloom, maybe they all hatched into mythical serpents? Maybe they all belonged to only one of them.

"I shall bring you to whomever you're meant to be with."

Ruhi gave a cheery sweep of her head and then nestled into Eshani's palm. Eshani leaned against the tree with her free hand. It told her, in soothing whispers, what it was. In one word.

Amrita.

Eshani scrambled to her feet, Ruhi wrapping around her arm, and stared at the once-decrepit tree now restored. She carefully placed a palm against the bark and felt the eons in its veins. Primordial, born along with halahala from the churning of the cosmos.

What the Shadow Kings had killed countless worlds over.

What the mortal King had massacred her people over.

She stood in both awe and reverence. How ironic that even if the Shadow Kings *had* reached this place, the tree wouldn't have had the fruit for them to drink.

Realization dawned on Eshani. She had consumed amrita. She fell to her knees and bowed her head. "I didn't mean to take it; I didn't know."

But you earned it, little goddess of spring, it replied through vibrations in the ground thrumming up Eshani's legs. *You brought me back to full health so that I may see another eon.*

"Thank you," Eshani said, humbled.

In her periphery, the mist parted, revealing an endless field of purple disrupted every now and then by a shadowy, oblong gateway.

The one who can walk my shores to consume amrita is the one who can stir portals to life.

For a fleeting second, she wondered if she could transport amrita to her sisters and mother, to Lekha. Eternity without them was no way to live, but she wouldn't dare risk amrita falling into the wrong hands.

If you wish for another to be healed, take the red stigma from the purple blooms. But only the rarest can survive the journey to my shores and partake of my fruit. And only they shall be granted immortality. Amrita shall not leave my shores.

And while it saddened her to think she would outlive her family, Eshani felt great relief knowing amrita could never be stolen by those seeking power. Immortality was safe.

"Can the red stigma cure the white plague?"

It can cure anything.

Eshani could sob from happiness. Lekha could still be cured!

Ruhi yawned with her fangless mouth as she settled around Eshani's throat, her tail curling around to meet her own neck, close to the head, and stilled. Her carmine scales turned brassy and metallic.

Eshani tapped her. Solid. "How in the realms do you change like that?"

She asked the tree for one more thing so that she could transport the stigma without it falling into the wrong hands. The tree obliged, and Eshani tirelessly worked the tree's leaves and twigs into something she couldn't quite put into words, but her hands knew, and the foliage knew. Braided bracelets turned into woven armbands—the kind archers had worn in Anand. Papa had shown her.

In return for these rare gifts, Eshani helped the tree grow and flourish to its full potential, to what it had been centuries ago. Roots grew strong and deep, winding farther underground than ever before. The branches stretched higher than they had in centuries, a sprawling of leaves and ever-calming red-orange blooms of frilly petals.

She welcomed the sense of renewal, strength, and peace in helping. A symbiotic transaction.

Eshani once again thanked the tree with a palm to its bark, then touched a hand to her chest in reverence. She ventured into the field of purple flowers as far as she could see, the air heavy with a complex aroma of sweet honey and earthy hay. Upon closer inspection, she noticed the stigmas were a red-orange color matching the pomegranate blooms.

Celestial saffron.

With the potency of the stigmas, she could grow this variety across the realm and cure illnesses. No one would ever get sick again! Oh, how her heart rejoiced.

She tucked a few precious flowers inside her armband and studied the floating doors. How would she get back to help her friends and save Lekha? Eshani searched and searched, walking around portals to find new ones, and thought of the only two gateways she knew of. The one at the marshlands, and the one on the floating temple.

"I want to see Manisha," Eshani willed aloud. "Show me the gateway to the temple."

Every portal dulled. Except one. It shimmered with iridescence, and Eshani hurried to it. She paused in front of the haze and stared for what felt like hours before something slowly materialized. The center rippled, a window into the temple. It was the one on the floating mountain. Manisha!

Eshani smiled, stepping forward, but she was abruptly stopped by an invisible force. The crystal pikes on the other side of the gateway glowed, their sharp teeth pointing away from her. No matter how hard she tried, she couldn't get through. Something burned in her thoughts, a reply to her unspoken answer. This gateway showed the past, for Eshani had asked to see Manisha and Manisha was no longer there. Just like the portal had shown her Manisha when she entered the Nightmare Realm.

Her shoulders went slack. How would she ever master gateways?

A woman walked by on the other side of the shimmer, pausing near the inner shrine. Sita. The woman Holika had shown Eshani, the one causing strife for her little sister. Sita was wearing a lovely sari, her head covered, and spoke to a man with a scar across his face.

"Present her in a compromising position, and that is all you are to do to her," the woman said in a low voice in the empty hall. "That is enough to kick her out."

The man chuckled. "You could claim this of her at any time."

"I won't lie."

"Ah. But you'll fabricate a situation. What do you, a head priestess, hold against her, a lowly apsara? She's too young to be a threat and possesses no allies."

Sita raised her chin, her pallu slipping from her head. "The Nightmare Realm comes to me, demanding that I release her. She is cursed by the demons and must be released or be the downfall of the floating mountains."

Was she...referring to Manisha? Had Holika done what Eshani had asked? Sending messages to Sita to free her sister, only for this woman to deem Manisha a curse because of it?

No...What had Eshani done? She screamed into the void, her voice muffled. But they'd heard something. Sita startled, clutching a fist to her chest. "Do you not hear that? That girl is possessed and has brought with her the demons."

The man didn't seem as worried as Sita was. "Then let the deal be made."

She followed him out and said, "Remember, General. Just enough to declare her compromised. Nothing more."

They walked out of view and Eshani screamed, *"Run!"* in futile hopes that Manisha would hear.

She tried harder to pass through the gateway, but the invisible force would not relent. It sizzled and crackled and burned her flesh, little curls of skin that fused back together. She could not step into the past.

The gateway blurred in and out, and Eshani moved on to search for her true path with a fierce purpose.

Think. Be logical.

Somewhere nearby, a darker portal shimmered, one depicting the marshlands. She stood at the precipice of a diverging path. She could walk through, *finally*, and return to her family, warn Manisha...if the shades didn't get to her first and drag her back. And Manisha was still so far from the marshlands.

She lifted her hand to touch the portal. Could stepping through be so easy?

Mehndi shone on her palms. The stamped designs from the palace had faded, but the true mehndi from the paste she and her friends made on the ferry—the designs that Vidya and Shruti had drawn on her—remained. They were ambiguous designs drawn with shaking hands, far from delicate. But they had been drawn by her friends. They'd shared a rare time on the ferry where they could just exist. And those friends were being tortured at this very moment for protecting her.

With fists clutched at the side of her head, Eshani trapped a scream. Her sister needed her, and Eshani couldn't reach her. She mentally called for Sithara and Holika, but no one replied. No one could help.

Emotion can drive one to great things, Papa had told her, *but be astute.*

Her heart ached. How she wished Papa was here. He would know what to do. He would make the decision that felt impossible to make.

And what of the Shadow King? He would kill Hiran and their friends and drag her back into his realm. He could exact revenge on her family and force her to do his bidding.

Through teary eyes, Eshani searched for the gateway back. With her resolve solidified, the window to the marshlands faded while a singular gateway took its place. One that sparkled and whispered with tendrils of information about the most pressing matter.

The Vermilion Mahal beckoned.

THIRTY-ONE

ESHANI

The eternal library was real, and it was magical. The hall was monumental and quite possibly heaven. Tall and wide, filled with shelves of books and scrolls. Some danced through the air, hopping from shelf to shelf. Some giggled and muttered. Others recited elements and science and math and astrology. Some debated philosophy. Many told tales of those who had come through this very place, an intersectional plane between death and whatever lay ahead.

Moss covered bioluminescent mushroom steps winding around shelves of branches, connecting floor after floor. Vines and budding flowers covered the walls. A soft light glowed from the top and through windows. Trees grew from the floor, adding a spray of petals and red leaves, with swinging benches perfect for reading. A magical library made from meadows.

Eshani twirled with delight, her mind thrumming and hungry for information. She was dazzled by all the stories the plants whispered to her and all the knowledge the books and scrolls shared. The mushroom steps glowed purple and pink and green wherever she walked on them. Touching them brought a deluge of information, her head thrumming.

In turn, the self-sustaining ecosystem read Eshani's lineage.

The nagin, they buzzed. *Walker of worlds, little goddess of spring, keeper of venom, adrift with amrita.*

"Tell me what you know," Eshani whispered.

They spoke to her about her lineage, the greatest naga before her, and how all came from a touch of venom. Their stories were accompanied by moving pictures made of colored dust. The first nagin had bestowed power upon the lowly serpent—the cobra, the namesake of Eshani's people—which had, over time, evolved. *Mutations*, the ecosystem explained.

When Eshani wondered how halahala had not killed her, the plants knew her inquiry before she spoke it. An image appeared of a beautiful, bright blue oceanic slug. Minuscule in size but mighty in power. It absorbed the venom of other creatures and utilized it as its own, making it one of the deadliest creatures in all the realms.

"Do all naga possess this ability?" Eshani inquired.

No. In a time of great need, in great distress, three daughters of three crowns will rise from venom.

"Who else?" Not many had survived the Fire Wars.

You will know when the time comes.

"Thank you," she said, "for sharing and not immediately throwing me out of your wondrous abode."

Knowledge is to be shared. Only the greedy keep it to themselves.

A scroll awakened when Eshani walked past. "Can I interest you in chemistry?"

"In architecture?" another offered.

"Biology?"

"Tales of princesses?" one giggled, adding, "And their steamy romances."

Eshani laughed, shaking her head.

"Adventures of great warriors?"

"Sailing the high seas?"

A thick book fluttered out, its pages like wings. "Botany is what she wants."

Eshani bit her lower lip, lured by the knowledge. She gritted out, "No. You can tell me anything, correct?"

"If it has come past us by way of the traveling souls," a book replied, "then yes, we can."

"How do I defeat the Shadow King?"

A touch of blood alongside rising darkness. A perfect pairing.

"What does that mean?"

Your blood… paired with the rising darkness. We cannot be any clearer.

Eshani groaned. "You could be, actually, and it would help a lot. Tell me the Shadow King's weakness."

He is very strong. Protected by the crown, which is connected to the realm. But now there is you, a new venom beneath a blood sky. Just know that if you kill the Shadow King, the Nightmare Realm will dissolve and all those within it will perish, for the realm needs a royal.

Eshani gasped. "*Hiran.* Yes. That makes sense. He's a royal, an heir. Everything's aligning!" she said excitedly. "We can weaken the Shadow King and Hiran can take it from there… But he doesn't have amrita."

Then he should be very careful.

Eshani shivered. Hiran could die. They could fail. This would all be for nothing. Letting out a harsh grunt, she decided that if they died, they would die trying their best. She would have to help weaken the Shadow King and protect Hiran so he could kill his brother, take the crown, and save the realm. She could do that, and with celestial saffron, she could heal Hiran if he were to be wounded. A far-fetched plan where the odds stacked higher against them, but a plan nonetheless.

"How do I return?" Eshani asked, her voice quiet and unsteady.

Down the long, curved hall flanked by blooming walls, a glow appeared. Eshani thanked the ecosystem and went through the door illuminated by lime-green fruit, emerging in a grand room with statues larger than life. One was draped in flowing robes and capes with many hands, each holding a symbolic item, including scales for judgment.

Were the dead truly judged? If so, by whom? But answers did not magically appear, and Eshani had little time. She moved on, entering a seemingly endless room. Ruhi stirred awake, raising her sleepy head in curiosity.

At first, the grand hall appeared empty, but as Eshani narrowed her eyes, images appeared. Until the entire scope of the room was filled with neat rows and columns of floating marble slabs. Upon each slab lay a body dressed in white. Were these the dead?

Curiosity took hold of Eshani as she carefully walked around several bodies. They were not solid but transparent as they slumbered. How strange.

A glint of green in the otherwise-white room caught Eshani's eye. A slender vine rose up toward a slab, as if it were a pillar for which the marble rested upon. Eshani, always moved by plants, reached out and touched it. A colossal wave of information washed over her.

The extraordinary vine sang through her fingertips, *These are unconscious souls, yet to determine whether they shall live or journey through death. But this one? Ah, she is special. For she has clung to life for five mortal years, so long that we have grown beneath her. Even we wonder how she remains alive.*

"Show me," Eshani whispered, her breath catching in her throat as her fingers tingled with information.

She saw mirages and illusions of a house catching fire in a storm, struck by lightning, and doused in tarry blood under attack. A boy hiding with her in a cellar before they were separated by soldiers. A girl traumatized by events and sheltered in a palace. A court ripe with politics and snares, of strangers who'd determined her worth—and her fate. A girl who'd desperately wanted to run away with her brother, a boy sent to slay monsters. A girl who'd heard ancient whispers in long-lost underground libraries with gilded books. A girl who'd deciphered too much and was sent away to marry a nobleman's son. A girl who'd escaped her fate only to find herself trapped another way. A girl named Pritika.

Eshani saw the girl as she lay in the mortal realm, entombed in a strange glass apparatus to preserve her.

Someone else appeared, tapping away on the glass coffin. A message. Not for the girl, but for—

Eshani stumbled away and gasped for a breath. "Sithara?"

She wanted to know more, but the vines withered. In a fading echo, they sang, *She is awakening.*

THIRTY-TWO

HIRAN

"There you are." Holika's worried tone roused Hiran awake. Which meant he was still drifting in and out of consciousness. "Shit," he muttered.

The dark silhouette of the Gloom stood closer than ever, his eyes piercing white and the cobalt designs around his eyes shimmering. He grinned. When he spoke, he sounded like Hiran, but older, darker, gravelly. "This is us. Shadow behind the boy. Shadow *within* the boy."

"No," Hiran snapped. "I am not like my father and my brother."

The darkness tilted his head. "Neither am I."

And then he broke apart. The Gloom, once contained as a shadowy apparition in the corner of Hiran's mind, had dissolved into a whirlwind of dust and ash amid gale-force winds. Particles lifted to the skies, working them into roaring turbulent clouds.

"Your darkness is rising," Holika strained to say.

"It's probably tired of getting knocked out by Tarak." Hiran rubbed his shoulders but felt no injury where his wings had been violently cut away.

"You have to face him. And kill him. You know that. Don't you?"

Yes. Hiran knew. He looked at the Gloom and said, "I am ready."

"You'll be the last Shadow King standing," Holika said.

It was natural for Hiran to say he didn't want the crown. After all, he'd been saying it since he was a boy, and it had been drilled into him from birth. He did not deserve the crown, had not been declared the future King. But the truth was . . . he desired the crown the way it desired him. He felt the realm calling to him.

The truth was, the crown had been kept from him and given to an inferior leader. Tarak was not for the realm, whereas Hiran was willing to perish in order to save it.

Holika pressed her nose against Hiran's so that her eyes bored into his. "No matter what happened with the nagin, this thing inside you will not be satiated until you take back what is yours."

The realm needed a royal asura to feed from, and Tarak had to die if anyone was going to survive.

"Do not take your beatings like some borderland child! Whether you like it or not, you are much more. Your true self—this tenebrosity—is going to rip the scared little boy open and be bolder than you'd like if you don't ease it out." She stepped back. "Your true self will no longer take these blows sitting quietly inside your soul. You are not separate things; there are not two of you in your head. You are one. Do not deny this part of yourself. You can be in control and powerful, or you can be mad and powerful."

Holika twirled around, sparks flickering from her fingertips and falling as burnt embers wrestled away by the wind. She spoke loudly to be heard over the wind. "I enjoy mad, to be honest. But I don't think I'm mad. It's just what all these people call me in their dreams."

"Well, you *are* giving them nightmares, so . . ."

"Don't say that," she snapped, her hair flapping wildly about. "Don't ever sound like one of these delusional men crying out that I'm evil and crazy because I make them see themselves for what they really are. It's called *accountability.* You know the only ones who don't call me mad? The ones who have nothing vicious lurking in their heads. I'm crazy to the ones who see their own madness reflected back at them. I can be a delight."

"You've lost touch with reality a bit, don't you think?"

"No. I absolutely do not think so," she yelled louder as the winds grew louder. "You know one reality; I know multitudes. What you think you know or believe is a social construct. I'm *free.* A free woman is dangerous—that's why they trapped me here and give me titles like *dreamreaver* to the Court of Nightmares. Or *demon.* You've yet to be freed. I'll make sure you are. And once you're free, sweet brother..."

She gripped his jaw and hinted at a small smile. "You'll see there are blurred lines between good and bad, sanity and insanity."

He could only believe her since she'd been exposed to the realities of the realms and knew all sorts of secrets and truths. Because of this, Holika was more educated than him, wiser, more knowledgeable. She hadn't simply obeyed the Court of Nightmares during her forced imprisonment. She hadn't lost her way in solitude as others had before her.

His sister went on. "I speak the truth, now harsher than ever, because you are on the verge of death, and I will not let you die! There is no wholly good or bad, only shades of in between. Sure, there's a point where a person is truly evil, but people are the result of their own choices. Make hard choices—embrace your true self if you wish to save the realm. You are not a lowly child. You are a powerful being. You speak to the dead and can either save or destroy this realm. You can be freed from tyranny or be forever imprisoned by fear. The road to freedom and great things is paved in blood. But it won't be *your* blood, dear brother. Oh, no. Not if I have anything to do with it."

"Are you antagonizing the Gloom? I have already accepted it!" Hiran yelled over increasingly turbulent winds.

"You must unleash it! There is no subduing those too strong to remain in chains. You cannot bend Tarak. Kill him or be killed by him. The choice is yours, but know this: This darkness, the real you, will not go down without a fight. Let the darkness fill you. Become who you were always meant to become."

Hiran grunted, accepting the truth as ribbons of shadow poured into his pores, strengthening him. He accepted the Gloom, let it fill him and become him. Two halves to one complete being. A true Shadow King.

Holika blinked as Hiran became shadow. Realization dawned on her features. "This isn't from our father..." she rambled, putting something together, some unknown trinket of knowledge that Hiran had yet to figure out.

Her eyes sprang wide just as Hiran felt the vague awareness of the truth, of what the Gloom in the corner of his mind had been all along. It was not darkness but shadow. It was not his father's lineage being called by the realm.

He drifted away.

Hiran was awakening.

THIRTY-THREE

ESHANI

The Vermilion Mahal exuded exquisiteness, the sort of riches kingdoms would go to war over. Encrusted with sunstones and diamonds, rubies and opals...gems of all colors but mostly red-orange to vermilion. A dazzle of pomegranate flowers burst across the pillars lining a hall so tall that the ceiling was lost to the clouds and so wide that one could roam for eternity.

Cream-and-pink marble floors welcomed Eshani. A breeze swept across courtyards that vanished into a sparkling silver fog. Grand pillars had been sculpted with animals and trees and blooms, some creatures that Eshani could only dream of. Blue-and-gold butterflies fluttered around, sparks of light flashing from their bioluminescent wings.

There was a distinct calmness within this place, an intrinsic understanding of what was to come. Here, many walked about, strolling along, a few conversing with others. By the look of their garments, they'd known each other in life, or maybe they'd died together. Some, those closer to the entrance and just outside its gates, carried scars and wounds. Their faces were wrinkled and weighed down by old age and the diseases or injuries that had taken their lives. Many grim and grisly, but never as gruesome and tortured as the dead in the Blood River or the Passage of Bones. These ones might have died horrible deaths, but they were free of pain. And as they ventured farther into the Mahal, closer to the towering gates on the other end, their wounds subtly vanished, their confusion eased, and their souls were appeased.

Some were brilliantly created beings of elegantly twisted horns or translucent wings, large eyes or suspended hair taking shape, taller than trees or robust as houses. . . . There was simply too much to take in.

Eshani didn't know much about the afterlife, but she was happy to know they would come here, have their broken bones mended and their spiritual bodies renewed, and hopefully enjoy whatever lay beyond the vast gates of gold and jewels.

On the other hand, what would happen to those who fell into the Blood River, or those who'd been fished out and staked to the wall in the Passage of Bones? Would they never cross to their eternity? Maybe she could help those poor souls wailing in agony. Maybe she could let their corpses down and take them to the ferry for an expedited, tranquil ride to the edge. Maybe the Ferryman would grant her this one wish if she could bring down the Shadow King.

Since Eshani wasn't dead, she didn't go toward the gates with the crowd who healed as they advanced toward their peace. She went left, toward the courtyards.

Amid the soft conversations, a singular, familiar voice rose above the rest. A distraught man fought against the current of serenely floating people. They kept their focus straight ahead, but eyes drifted toward the man who interrupted them. No one else interrupted the flow, not even those chatting in small clusters. If recognition dawned on anyone, they were quiet and calmly moved on. Unlike this man, who spoke loudly and stopped everyone coming through the entrance.

Everyone shook their heads at him. Some expressed apologies and empathetic expressions.

Curiosity drew Eshani to the man. Memories rose and billowed up from the recesses of her mind from long ago. This voice assembled the pieces that had faded too far away, a puzzle of remembrance, clarifying the nebulous images.

Her heart skipped a beat as she rushed through the throngs, her steps growing quicker, more ardent as the memories aligned. No. It couldn't be!

"Excuse me," she muttered. "Please, let me through."

She was a pair of outreaching arms over a wall of bodies, desperate to see the man.

"Have you seen them?" the man asked, stirring her heart.

Eshani pushed through, forgoing consideration, but no one shoved back or yelled. They simply glanced at her.

"Please, help me," he pleaded.

The crowd finally parted for Eshani as she stumbled through. They'd parted around the man, too. She could see his back as he reached out to stop others. He was dressed in the same cream-colored clothes he'd worn the day he walked into the plumes of war. The day he handed her that last pomegranate.

Eshani's breath hitched and she hiccupped on her words, words that choked into silence.

"I'm looking for my family," he said, half turning to the side so that his profile glinted in the soft light between the palace and its courtyards.

Eshani's chest ached and her heart pounded so painfully against her ribs that her breath caught on every shuddered inhalation. She ran faster, closing the distance, tears clouding her vision.

"My wife. Her name is—is Padma," he told a woman walking by. She shook her head without stopping.

"My daughters," he went on, pleading with another in passing. "I—I have three. Twins named—"

"Papa." His name fell off Eshani's quivering lips.

He turned to her, bathed in the velvety white light of the gloaming between life and afterlife. His hair was messy, his expression weary. Soot was smeared across his face, but some parts had blurred in the eventual cleansing of his soul. Hard lines were caked with dirt and crusted blood while other lines were smooth and renewed.

Eshani faltered, her gaze drifting down. A wound oozed on the other side of a long gash in his chest, his sodden shirt curling over the tear made by a sword.

"Papa," she said again.

He squinted, taking several strides toward her.

He used to tower over her. She was younger then, much smaller. He was still taller than her, but not by nearly as much. She must've looked so different to him. Would he recognize her?

"Eshani?" His voice sounded like a wonderful dream.

She nodded, fervently hoping this wasn't a cruel deceit.

He walked to her, cupped her face, and gazed into her eyes. His had once been golden brown, the color of gulab jamun syrup, now drifting toward gray. He should've smelled like death, but he didn't. Papa was in limbo. Papa was real.

He ran a hand down the top of her head. Tears pooled in his eyes, and a few streaked down his cheeks. His voice hiccupped. "Beta?"

Eshani cried, embracing her father after so long and forgetting his wounds. She hugged him tight, clutching the back of his shirt in her fists and weeping enough tears to fill entire palaces. She would never let him go.

Papa wept with her, cradling her head against his chest.

They stood like this, embracing and sobbing, while the crowd flowed around them.

Papa pulled away and searched her face. "Are you really here?"

She nodded, biting her cheek to hold herself together.

"Oh, beta. You've grown so much." He cupped her face again, studying her features. "You were just a young girl when I handed you a pomegranate before going off to war."

"Don't think of that awful time. I grew up. It's been almost four years."

He nodded. "Ah. I'm sorry you met your demise at such a young age. I hoped you would have grown old."

She managed a smile. "Papa, I didn't die."

He furrowed his brow and looked around. "How are you here, then?"

Blowing out a breath and wiping her cheeks, she confessed, "It's a long story."

He smiled so that his eyes crinkled at the corners. "I have all the time for a long story."

Eshani beamed, longing to spend time with her father. Her heart ached knowing she couldn't. She clenched her eyes shut, resisting the urge to stay with him. It was not an easy battle. In his presence, after all this time, knowing she might never see him again, Eshani faltered. She took his hand and told him her story.

Papa walked her to the edge of the courtyards and sat on a smooth marble bench with mosaic designs in sapphires and emeralds. All around, soaring trees burst with full blooms. The cassia trees showered yellow petals in the breeze, swept away by those entering the palace. A tamhan tree showed pride in vibrant purple and pale pink, reminding Eshani of Papa's favorite color.

By now, others had gathered to listen, mostly naga. She supposed Papa wasn't the only one waiting for loved ones.

"So you must return? And battle this cruel, powerful man?"

"Hah," Eshani confirmed.

He let out a breath. "You are stronger than you know."

She found that difficult to believe at the moment. She wasn't even sure how she could return. "Papa?"

"Hah?"

"Did...the war change you?" she asked, worried that her path could forever alter her in deplorable ways.

"Yes," he replied. "I would sacrifice anything for my family. War changes a person. We see things, do things, compromise morality that we otherwise would never do. But if we keep the truth alive, our fire bright, our reason for fighting at the forefront, then we will be stronger for it. War made you grow up faster, did it not?"

She nodded.

"Instead of breaking, you emerged stronger. It pushed you to dig deep inside yourself. It tested you, and you prevailed. You do what needs to be done, and the destruction of this Shadow King and the mortal King...well, beta..." He rubbed her head the way he had when she was a child. "No man is too powerful to escape the blade of your vengeance. But...it is not just about vengeance. Your journey is about healing. Healing yourself, our family, our people, entire worlds."

He tapped her armband where the celestial saffron sat and smiled with recognition of what he'd taught her. "Do you know what must happen to infested trees in a forest in order for new saplings to grow?"

"Burn the trees. The ash will return to the ground and the saplings will meet the sunlight." It made sense now, what he was saying. "Restorative power sometimes must come from destroying the issue so a healthy, new generation can grow."

"You can give back in so many wonderful ways."

"You believe I can do this? They're not ordinary men."

"You are no ordinary girl."

Eshani let his words sink in. After a moment, she asked, "Why are you still here? Why haven't you moved on?"

"Do you think I would leave without my family?"

"But, Papa, you can't wait for us. It's been years."

He sighed. "Time is nothing here, beta. It doesn't exist. What has been years for you feels like minutes to me. Here, there's no sleep or food or water. There is no work or school or building. We are utterly free of any needs. I'm allowed to wait here until I'm ready to pass on. And I will wait an eternity for my family."

"Papa," Eshani said, tears once again brimming. "Please, find peace and end the pain."

He gently kissed her forehead. "I have peace and am in no pain."

She stared at his wounds. "If you walked farther into the palace, your wounds would disappear."

"And so would my resolve to wait for you."

Eshani's words came out shaky. "Mama would want you to go on. I want that. I know Sithara and Manisha would want that as well."

He closed his eyes in relief. "Ah, my beloved ones are alive. I take great solace in this."

"Hah. We fought and survived and are going back to end it all."

"Do you see? My purpose isn't over. I . . ." He looked off at the yellow blooms and concentrated on his thoughts. "If I move closer to the other side, I'll forget my purpose."

"What is your purpose?"

"It evades me at the moment."

She rested a hand on his arm. "Your purpose is to move on knowing that we're alive and well. We'll meet you when the time comes. I've seen this journey. It's not so scary after the Blood River."

He scowled, perplexed. "The Blood River?"

"Hah. The ferry took you down the river, didn't it? To the Bloodfall at the end. How did you cross?"

"I, and many naga who were slain that day, traveled on a pleasant boat down a beautiful river. And at the end, a bridge of rainbows took us the rest of the way. Is that not what you saw?"

She smiled, her eyes misting. The dead meant for a peaceful afterlife experienced a nice journey.

"How is your mother? And your sisters?" he asked, eager to learn everything.

They were in better situations than what he'd left them in, and they would reunite with Manisha soon.

"How will you get back to them?"

Eshani shrugged. "I've yet to figure that out."

He tapped her head. "You are an intellectual connected to nature. If anyone should figure out how to cross the uncrossable, it will be you."

"Papa." She blushed.

Papa frowned. He stood and offered Eshani a hand. He pulled her up, and they walked beneath the blooming purple trees.

"It's time for you to go," he said.

Tears prickled her eyes. She might never see him again. "I want to spend more time with you."

"No. There's no more time for you."

"You said time meant nothing here."

"It means nothing to the dead. You have family waiting for you, friends who need you. Besides, the King won't rest until—" He stopped himself.

"I know what he wants. Why didn't anyone tell us the truth?"

"It's a ridiculous thing to believe. The King wanted us to give up our daughters."

"What?" Eshani asked.

"The King demanded that we send him every girl and woman from the city of Anand to *inspect*." He spat out the last word. "He said he was searching for someone special. We agreed to no such thing. How detestable of him to even ask! Then he promised war and annihilation. We welcomed it; we prepared for it. We discussed matters with every woman of age, and every woman agreed that we would fight, flee, or die."

"But they killed women and girls, too. I saw it."

His chest expanded with a sorrowful sigh. "Things spiraled out of control, but retribution is at hand."

"He'll pay."

Papa pressed his lips to her forehead. "Then you must go now. Time continues onward beyond the rainbow bridge."

"I'm not sure how to get back."

"We can figure it out together."

Like old times. But there were no books or scrolls or teachers to go to. Even if the library had an answer, it wouldn't give up the knowledge. All she truly knew was that this realm would not allow what it did not want.

Eshani went past the courtyards to a harrowing cliff. Water from streams ran down the edge into the silver fog. She really didn't want to fall over another cliff, but she'd probably end up here again.

She dropped rocks down, only for them to fly back up and land where she'd taken them from.

She tossed rocks across, only for them to be thrown back into place.

She dared to reach out with her foot and felt nothing except the cold wind.

She gathered an armful of petals and tossed them out, hoping they would land on the invisible bridge, but they scattered back into place behind her.

She sighed, trying one thing after another, adding calculations, and then wondering if the ferry activated the rainbow bridge—she could potentially cross that way.

But the ferry never came.

THIRTY-FOUR

ESHANI

Hiran believed that Eshani could form a bridge of brambles and thorn and simply walk across, bypassing the rainbow bridge and the whole "being thrown back" issue that had thwarted the asura for so long. She stood on the edge of the cliff, taking a look around, and wondered if this was the sort of view Manisha beheld on the floating mountains. Crisp air high above with a splendid building and gardens and a view straight down into clouds.

Soon. She would reach her sister soon. She could only hope that Manisha had evaded that awful General.

Eshani closed her eyes and let out a breath, calling down the meditation rites of the naga to venture, for once by choice, to the ancestral plane of her people.

"Help me, great ancestors..."

Her foremothers were waiting, weaving baskets straight from plants. Instead of using prepared strips of leaves and fronds, the trees themselves wove baskets. Without using their hands—just their minds—the women asked vines to intertwine themselves into beautiful baskets complete with blooms.

The plants sang across the air, a thrum against Eshani's skin, a tingle in her hands, a drowsy force in her head, and an echo in her heart. A jasmine plant offered itself to her whims, just as the pomegranate tree had given itself for her armbands. A rangoon creeper joined with its lovely red flowers. Instead of a basket, they wove a belt. One strip became two, becoming a dozen, then a hundred, drawing out roots and sturdier jungle vines until a road lay out in front of Eshani, stretching into the vast ancestral plane.

As she stepped onto it, the sides continued weaving themselves into waist-high handrails. The ground beneath the road gave way. She yelped and clutched the rope on both sides of her. Below her, there was nothing but air and clouds.

The plants writhed around her, crawled up her back, and extended from her hands as if they were her own limbs. She felt every segment of bark and vein and root, the tethering of one into another, the twisting and strength, the solidification.

A leaf all on its own was fragile.

A mass of grafted vegetation, layered to form a cantilever structure as solid as a wood-and-iron bridge, was strong. And an architectural feat.

The sensation of the first nagin's abilities ran through Eshani's veins, called from her blood, mixing with the primordial elements now present within her, and enhanced her gifts.

Her palm twitched, then curled around a weapon. A bow made of intertwined vines and roots slithering over one another, braiding, strong but with the right amount of pliability, the string made from interlocking strands of durable hemp and resilient vegetable fibers. In her other palm, she felt an arrow, a rudimentary but sturdy wooden arrow with one sharpened end.

Sweat beaded down her temples, and when Eshani opened her eyes, returning from the ancestral plane, she gasped at the sight of roots dislodging themselves from the precipice of the cliffs beneath her feet. They snapped and shot through the air, intertwining with one another and snaking toward the white fog beyond. The bridge of brambles formed into a sturdy overpass. In one hand, she held a bow, an arrow in the other, and across her back hung a quiver sagging with the weight of many more arrows.

Eshani took a tentative step forward. The bridge supported her. It didn't falter or sway, nor did the realm push her back.

She giddily looked over her shoulder to find Papa watching her proudly. He nodded, as if to say, *What did I tell you? You will conquer all.*

Behind him, a crowd had formed. Many were naga.

Dread collided with joy, and she blinked away tears. It was time to say farewell, and this time it would be for good. A raw heaviness burdened Eshani's heart.

She ran to her father and swung her arms around his shoulders, nearly knocking him back. Embracing her, he asked, "What is this, eh?"

"I have to go," she said through clenched teeth, fighting through the tears. "I don't want to leave you."

Papa ran a hand over her head. "Beta, you will live, and I will meet you here again when your time has come. This is not farewell, huh? This is a happy send-off. We shall see one another when you're returned to me, and our family will be whole."

Eshani choked back a sob and hugged her father perhaps too tightly. Her chest burned with emotion as she wondered if the amrita prevented her from uniting with her family after death. She could walk through portals, but she couldn't walk into the afterlife if she couldn't die. She shoved away the thought.

"Tell your sisters I love them dearly."

She nodded.

"Kiss Manisha on the forehead and tell her she is strong. Hug

Sithara and tell her she is dauntless. Even if she says she dislikes embraces, we know she loves them the most."

Eshani nearly cried when a laugh broke through her. It was true. Sithara loved hugs more than anyone.

"Take care of your mother. Tell her that I have loved her from youth and will love her into eternity."

Blinking away tears, she sucked in a sobering breath and released her father. Stepping back, she nodded.

His eyes glistened. "I am forever grateful that your journey brought you here. That you should know what became of me, and that I should see you as a lovely young woman. You, just like your sisters, will always be my little one. I was blessed to have your mother and blessed threefold with my daughters."

He brought her forehead to his lips. When he spoke again, his voice quivered. "I am so proud of you, my beta, my firstborn, my little goddess of spring. No matter how hard you are knocked down, you will always rise."

He stepped away, blinking back his own tears. "Go. Meet your fate and be its fury."

"I love you, Papa."

"I love you, my precious one."

With another large breath, Eshani turned and marched across the bridge, confident it would hold her weight, and disappeared into the white fog.

The bridge continued to form beneath her feet, and Eshani refused to look down into the white abyss that had claimed her once before. The smell of clean air and sweet blooms mixed with a metallic tang. The white flirted with pink mist. The calm sound of light breezes faded against the din of the Bloodfall.

She wasn't walking directly toward the Blood River, but to the right, toward the cliffs nestled between the shore of bones and the forest.

As the fog parted, as the light breeze and clean scents faded, shadows appeared. There was no shadow dome here, no solid barrier of darkness, simply a haze. Ruhi stirred, protectively rising and hissing as a figure appeared. Then two, four, ten, twenty soldiers—all waiting for one girl to return from the dead.

Eshani refused the fear wanting to coil around her, even as her next few steps faltered. She focused on the bridge. If she could just get across, the bridge would dismantle itself and whoever else tried to pass would fall, getting tossed back to the cliff to stay in the realm they belonged.

Fully grown men, trained soldiers, armed asuras, aimed arrows at her. They ordered her to come to them.

She was still holding the bow and arrow. Papa's words came to her thoughts. She was a different girl now. She was stronger. No one, least of all *these* men, was going to order her around again. They were powerful, but she was no ordinary girl.

Eshani exhaled, her heart beating fast, her skin thrumming and heating, her pulse quickening in her ears as all noise wilted away.

"I am the daughter to a great man, a naga warrior," she told herself.

She continued on her path, the blood of her people coursing through her veins.

"I am the daughter of Padma, granddaughter of Padmavati, part of a lineage of great queens."

Her fingers pressed into the grooves of the knotted bow.

"I am a walker of worlds, linked to the first of our kind."

She marched forth, the whispers of her people resounding in her ears. Her ancestors, her father.

"I am a goddess of nature."

The wails of the slain naga on the walls of the Passage of Bones reached her.

"I am retribution."

Her pace steady, the gap between her and her enemies shortened, their bowstrings pulled taut.

"I am primordial poison and venerated amrita."

The men ordered her to stop where she stood. When she did no such thing, an arrow sliced across her arm. A warning shot. Eshani flinched, hissing at the sting. Blood smeared her fingers as the cut, incredibly, healed itself. The glistening red streak sang of her ancestors, of the winter-steel arrow tips coated in the blood of her foremothers, of the naga in the Passage of Bones.

Her mother's voice sang through her, reached her like prowling shadows breaking open the mist of her nightmares. Her mother's voice was ethereal, ghostly whispers speaking directly into her ears.

Mama had often said, *We have the tradition of dipping arrowheads in the blood of our foremothers to grant a quick death to our enemies. A poison, potent and deadly. The blood of your foremothers flows through your veins.*

Eshani smeared her blood on the sharpened end of her arrow, then reached over her shoulder and touched the sharpened tips of every arrow in her quiver.

They'd known, and now she knew. She had the blood of her foremothers, mixed with halahala.

"I am Eshani."

She nocked and pulled back the arrow glazed in her blood and released.

"I am a nagin."

Her arrow slit through the archer's hand before he could nock his next arrow. He screamed in pain, and then, as if he were underwater, his movement slowed. His eyes were wide, terrified just as Eshani had been in the palace. His mouth gaped open as his entire body stilled in mid-movement. He convulsed, dropping to his side and ripping off his mask as various fluids oozed from his eyes and nose and mouth. Soldiers stepped away from him, both bewildered and fearful.

"And I. Am. *Venom*."

The soldiers cried, "Drop your weapon, nagin! You are out-numbered!"

"No! She is *not*!" a voice rallied behind Eshani. She jolted.

Papa's wispy figure emerged through the fog, one foot in front of the other, armed and prepared to go to battle once more. Except he no longer looked mostly repaired as he had in the courtyard; he was slightly decayed like a fresh corpse.

"Papa! What are you doing?" Eshani asked, terrified that the realm would hurl her father back to the cliff, or worse, send him to the Blood River as one of the dead who refused to meet their fate.

"You will never stand alone," he told her, a hand on her shoulder. "Not if I can stand at your side."

"You have to return," she pleaded, but he had the same intense resolve he'd had when he left Anand that morning.

He walked around her and roared across the expanse, "You shall step away from my daughter!"

The soldiers gulped, unnerved, never having seen the dead walk, much less return from the beyond. Still, they were asura soldiers and believed they were the strongest and the worst of threats. "Or what?"

"Or welcome back the dead," replied another, a naga who'd fought in the war.

One and then another, until the bridge was filled with naga return-ing from the dead. Eshani didn't think this possible, or allowed, and urged them all to return. No, no, no! They would all suffer in the Blood River!

"Young one." An auntie missing an eye placed a loving hand on the top of Eshani's head. "You have a bigger battle. Let us have this small one."

An uncle with an oozing wound in his chest touched her head in the same gesture of elder love and said, "Let us fight one more time so others may live."

"Our honor," another said in passing.

"Our duty," another crowed as they walked past.

"Our right."

"For us and for the next."

"For the naga!" others cried, a call to battle, a charge across an unimaginable bridge.

The dead took their chance at surprising the asuras, who didn't expect corpses to cross. A vicious fight ensued, with the sounds of clanking of swords and metal and unleashing arrows.

Eshani released her arrows faster than ever. Even though the naga fighting alongside her were already dead, she didn't want to risk anything. Some of her arrows were blood-tipped, but not all. Some were made of razing fire and gnashing teeth. When the naga crossed the final feet of the bridge, Eshani winced, expecting them to be hurled back to the cliff or into the Blood River. Neither happened, and there was no time to question.

A soldier ran a blade into a naga but was stunned into place when the naga kept fighting, as if the wounds didn't hurt. Maybe they didn't. The naga surely didn't die a second time, but the asura died a first time.

Papa fought with the ferocity of a young warrior, all in the name of his people and for his daughter who would not fight alone. A soldier pounded Papa's head with a harsh blow, taking him down and inciting a rage within Eshani that she hadn't felt since the Fire Wars.

In close combat, Eshani swung her bow over a shoulder and used two arrows as stakes, lunging at the soldier when another asura lunged at her. Ruhi hissed, her jaw wide, her fangs dropping. She catapulted from Eshani's neck, sinking her fangs into his temple while Eshani sliced through her father's attacker. The soldier yanked off his helmet and mask and roared at her, unleashing a long forked tongue between sharp teeth in a mouth that was too big for his face. Taken by surprise at his gruesome features, Eshani failed to dodge as another soldier punched her in the stomach.

Eshani saw his fist fly toward her before she could process what was happening. In that split second, she braced for impact. But it was the asura who howled in agony, holding his broken hand to his chest. Her skin glowed a golden-bronze iridescence, hummed like the soft cadence of a song. Eshani didn't feel the punch nearly as much as she should've, hardly anything really.

Battle left no time for bewilderment. Eshani punched him in the throat. The first soldier—the one who had taken Papa down—swung for her, and she ducked, punching his gut and then side-kicking his head. There was a luscious darkness sparking inside Eshani, and she let it rise, let it devour her. In a shadow world, she finally welcomed the darkness.

She grabbed the asura by his collar and growled, "Do *not* touch my father." And promptly headbutted him, cracking his skull.

The scholar in her wanted to know what was happening and how any of this could be, but the warrior in her wasn't going to fear these monsters sent to drag her back so someone else could gain power he didn't deserve. *She* was power. No one could take that away.

Inside her, opposing forces of life and death balanced each other, letting the darkness flow. Darkness didn't run, didn't cower. Darkness devoured.

After a flurry of limbs and swords, the naga were the only ones remaining.

Eshani's shoulders slumped as Ruhi found her way to her. "Thank you," she told her as she picked up Ruhi and cradled the serpent to her chest.

"Please, return to your peace," Eshani told her father and those with him.

"When the Mahal wants us back, it will take us. Let's not waste time. Let us leave a wake that changes the tide."

There was no fighting against the naga who had taken up arms to defend their people. Eshani couldn't force them back, and it seemed the Mahal was on their side.

"Go ahead. We will catch up. I promise," Papa said.

Eshani nodded.

"Wait," someone called after her. She returned to the uncle as a few naga warriors slipped off pieces of their uniforms from the Fire Wars. "Take this. We can't be killed; we're already dead. But you need protection."

"Thank you," she said, reverently holding many items that created one set of armor with an insignia of a cobra. Eshani donned their armor with pride. They gave the choice parts of their garments, strong remnants. As a child, she hadn't been able to wear these pieces because they were meant for warriors, then for other adults going into battle. They never fathomed children would go to war, so she'd never had this.

An uncle said, "Let me clean that off—the blood of my wife who died before me."

Sorrow cleaved through Eshani. The weight of the armor, of bronze and winter-steel, was heavy on her frame. These weren't just the harvested materials from carts and homes from Anand repurposed for protection . . . these were from the slain warriors themselves. A sense of deep appreciation flowed through her, a mutual respect. Some of these were the brave men and women who went out to fight before the scholars and farmers took up arms. They were among the first to fall, and surprisingly, some fought a valiantly long time. They were the reason some of the naga had time to flee early on, why the rest had time to forge weapons and teach fighting skills to younger ones, to children like her and her sisters.

The day many of these standing before her went to war, a strong breeze had washed over her face as she stood tall and proud and nodded at the brave warriors marching forward to their deaths all in the name of her freedom. She had wanted to remember them all, but she couldn't. She didn't even know most of them.

She had always wanted to honor those who had fought and died for her freedom, her safety. And now she had the chance. She would know every name and document their legacy, somewhere, somehow.

As the uncle lifted his hand to clean his wife's blood from the arm guard he'd given her, Eshani pulled his hands into hers. She looked into his milky eyes, his hunched back lowering him to her eye level.

"No. Leave it," she told him. "It would be my honor if I could take her memory into battle with me. A part of her will be present for the reckoning of our people. A part of her will see what's to come."

He nodded.

"Please be careful," she told everyone.

"We're already dead. What can happen to us?" Papa asked.

Her thoughts flitted back to the Passage of Bones. The Shadow King could do plenty to the dead.

THIRTY-FIVE

HIRAN

When Hiran came to, his wrists were in shadow chains above his head, and blood streamed down his back. At his feet lay his wings, a mockery of his brutal disfigurement. He trembled from pain and loss, and then rage. For he and the Gloom were becoming one.

Tarak approached him, his heavily embroidered jacket off, his sleeves rolled up his forearms, and a sadistic smirk on his face. A soldier gave him a torch. Tarak tipped the flame to the broken wings and watched them burn. He took in a long breath and laughed.

"Now *that's* what I expected to smell that day you and your sister and your whore mother were set on fire."

Hiran clenched his jaw, siphoning his anger. His fingers twitched, feeling the flow of the shadow chains.

"You want to know a secret? Eh?" Tarak tilted toward Hiran and looked left, then right as if he were confiding in him, as if they weren't surrounded by a dozen guards and elder dakini.

Tarak clucked his tongue. "Everyone thought it was my mother who ordered the immolation."

Hiran's eyes went wide.

"But it was me," Tarak confessed with a laugh. "I killed your mother and your sister. How did you survive? Was it these wings? Did they cover your weak little body and save you?"

He lifted the torch in between them, asking, "What will save you now?"

Tarak shoved the flames into Hiran's stomach. The fire burned his kurta and seared his flesh. Hiran trapped his screams behind gritted teeth. He glared at his brother, maintaining eye contact as the Gloom inside him hissed to be set free. Ribbons of his dreams crept in and out of his memories, fragments to complete the realization of what had been inside him—part of him—all along.

Tarak laughed maniacally. "I love the smell of cooked meat! But I won't kill you yet. I have some questions. First, where were you hiding all this time? On that ferry? Smart. Well, it's your fault I had to burn the ferry of the dead down. Not that I care about what happens to those from other realms when they die. Or how the true realm will retaliate. Because I'll get the nagin and get out before then. Oh, and I let your friends burn on the boat."

Hiran roared, bucking toward Tarak and fighting the chains. Three elder dakini struggled to hold him back.

"Don't fret, dear brother. Their screams were drowned by the river."

Rage swelled in Hiran. Trickles of shadow skittered across his wrists as fiery as the torch to his gut, igniting his memory as he fought to recall the very last moments of his dream.

"What were you going to do with the nagin, huh? Use her for yourself? You don't have what it takes to be immortal, to rule a realm, to walk through a gateway."

But wasn't Hiran the Gatekeeper? Wasn't he meant to protect the portals, decide who walked through them?

"When we retrieve her, I'll have my way this time. Fast, furious, no time for her to squirm away. This time, I simply won't care if I break her."

"Do *not* touch her," Hiran growled, every word a razor blade down his throat.

"Ah. Do you...do you *like* her?"

Hiran's nostrils flared, his expression otherwise stoic, menacing.

Tarak chortled. "You're as stupid now as you were when we were children. Only a king can wield that sort of power over her. Besides, I doubt you've seen her as I have."

Hiran had never hated a man as much as he hated his brother in this very moment, as he described how he paraded Eshani in a diaphanous gown in front of the entire court, berating and humiliating her. And how after he retrieved her, he would imprison her at his side as he conquered one realm after another.

The Gloom was far beyond writhing. It exploded, teeming into Hiran's veins. And Hiran, for once, welcomed the Gloom as part of himself. It connected to the shadow chains, the ribbons around his wrists, and drew them into his pores. The shadow tried to fight back, to stay out, but the Gloom—and Hiran—weren't having it.

"Well. I suppose I didn't have any questions for you after all," Tarak concluded. "Before I shove this torch down your throat, any last words, *brother*?"

Hiran swallowed and leaned toward Tarak, curling his lip over elongating fangs. His claws lengthened, and the line down his face broke open. Even his brother stood back, almost aghast, surprised as Hiran's face pulled back his skin from the bone, showing gray slate and gnashing teeth drenched in shadows and darkness.

Yesssss, the Gloom inside him purred. The silhouette that had sat in the corner of his mind hummed through him, all the way to the particles of his bones.

We are not your father, the Gloom reminded him. The final remnants of his dreams came crashing into him, the moments of realization that had nearly fluttered away. The Gloom was neither evil nor cruel. It was a connection to this realm, a calling. It came not from his father's lineage, but from his mother's. In a realm where everyone looked to paternal bloodlines, no one had paid attention to maternal gifts.

Hiran's connection to the shadows, the realm itself. His markings. His mother had the blood of powerful dakini. Dormant gifts combined with powerful asura royalty ignited within Hiran. He was no longer afraid of what the Gloom meant, for now he knew.

When Hiran spoke, he didn't sound like the small child who knew to keep to himself whenever Tarak, the anointed Prince, was around. He didn't sound like the scared boy hiding on the ferry. He didn't sound like the boy slaughtering monsters to find himself. He didn't even sound like the boy commanding corpses from the ferry during their last battle.

Be the madness; feed the darkness.

Hiran growled, feral, his voice reverberating. "I will rip your throat out and feed your corpse to the river. My throne will be made from your bones, and your stripped flesh the rug at my feet."

Unknown things trilled around them. Every dakini and guard skimmed the area with unease.

"You haven't *seen* true darkness, *brother.*"

Every flame in every torch around them flickered. A gush of air ravaged the crowd of soldiers. The trills turned into screams. The elder dakini lost their hold on the shadow chains. And the shadows moved into Hiran.

THIRTY-SIX

ESHANI

Eshani ran parallel to the river, kicking up dirt and rocks between the shore of bones and the forest. Ruhi stayed around her throat, her little head tucked between coils and growing heavier by the minute.

As Eshani sprinted faster than she thought possible, she couldn't help but wonder if her newfound speed, like her healing properties, was a result of the amrita or her naga blood come to full force.

Her breath came out in swift, steady pants. Her feet hit the ground without sending a jolt up her legs and back, practically gliding.

Her ears picked up new sounds from near and far: each pebble crunching beneath her soles, malicious insects buzzing near shrubs and nibbling on leaves, the fading march of the naga behind her, and the wings of something familiar. Another of the army's flying beasts!

Eshani slid, holding Ruhi to her throat. Talons as large as her entire body knocked her back and pinned her to the ground. A soldier slid off the creature's back.

Eshani squirmed, trying to push the beast off, but it was too heavy.

A talon curled into her shoulder. She bit down a scream as her skin tore.

The asura clucked his tongue mockingly, looking down at her with great pride. Squatting beside her head, he stroked her face. She jerked away, which only added to the gripping agony of her wounds. Something slithered over her neck, falling to the ground opposite the soldier. Ruhi! Oh, thank the stars she hadn't been crushed by the beast.

"Get it off!" Eshani cried, calling upon the vegetation to come to her aid.

He laughed. "The Shadow King will reward me handsomely for this."

Ruhi rustled in the leaves against the mess of Eshani's hair. She was bigger than she'd been at the pomegranate tree, now the size of a well-grown cobra. She rose, her hood spreading wide, her ruby scales glinting, and her emerald eyes a deadly warning. She hissed, baring a set of sharp fangs dripping with venom. Magnificently menacing. Viciously protective.

But she was still small in comparison to the beast, who could easily end her. Eshani worked faster, drawing roots and vines toward her.

"What sort of thing is this?" the soldier asked, unafraid.

Ruhi launched herself at the asura, her mouth unhinged. She clamped down on his eye. A burst of viscous fluid exploded from his eye socket. The air shriveled with his screams.

Eshani flinched and turned her head as drops splattered across her neck. The beast screeched and its rider fumbled back. The soldier grabbed Ruhi, attempting to pull her off. And when he couldn't unlatch her, he went for his blade.

"Ruhi! Let go!" Eshani ordered.

Ruhi fell at once. His blade sliced the air where her body had been, and instead bit into his own throat.

The beast shuddered with animosity, its grip crushing. A scream tore through Eshani.

There was a rustling of leaves and snapping of twigs that alerted the beast. It stilled and lowered its head to glare into the darkness of the forest. Two white eyes glowed, followed by a low growl so resonant that Eshani felt the ground rumble.

Ruhi appeared several feet from Eshani, slithering toward her leg behind the beast while its attention was ensnared by the unseen creature in the forest. Ruhi was fearless. Eshani had to be the same.

The creature stepped out from the dark forest, one giant paw after another, her head low, prowling.

"Lekha!" Eshani cried.

Lekha didn't acknowledge Eshani, much less look at her. Her eyes remained fixed on the beast, her body shuddering, her lip pulled over her fangs.

The flying beast cawed a warning, and Lekha cared not one bit. She unleashed a primal, deafening roar and the beast flinched, although it did not retreat. Lekha pounced, claws out, fangs glistening, eyes wide and wild. She went straight for the throat, her powerful jaws locking, her sturdy neck snapping to the side and ripping out a chunk from the strange arachnid-bird-type creature.

The beast staggered back, bleeding. Eshani grabbed Ruhi and scuttled away as Lekha ripped apart the flying creature. By the time the fight was over, Eshani was on her feet and partially healed, Ruhi coiled once more around her neck. She willed her furiously beating heart to calm as the flying beast twitched, splayed across the ground, its long neck slumped against the trees.

Lekha roared once more and clawed the monster's chest wide open. She slowly turned toward Eshani. Eshani didn't dare move.

"Lekha?" Eshan intoned. "Do you remember me? My sweet girl."

Please remember me.

Ruhi raised herself but didn't hiss.

Lekha glowered at Eshani with cloudy, lost eyes. Eshani's heart broke. "Please," she said, offering a hand and praying Lekha wouldn't attack. "You can fight this. I can...I can save you!"

The large golden tiger of lore paced back and forth, slowly, contemplatively, methodically assessing her next move. Her lip curled over her teeth; her muscles rippled. Gloriously deadly.

Eshani resigned herself to the truth. Lekha wouldn't attack, but she wouldn't go to her, either. Eshani nodded, understanding, and blinked back tears. "I wish you well. May your pain be gone and your future great. I'll always love you, my sweet girl."

Lekha blinked, and Eshani knew there was still light inside her. She knew Lekha fought for her life, and she had a choice. With slow, deliberate movements, Eshani withdrew a saffron from her arm shield and cupped it in her hands. She moved ribbons of communication through it so that it flourished and grew. And when she opened her palms, a beautiful, healthy purple flower showed her its healing, red-orange stigma.

Eshani placed it on the ground, never losing eye contact with Lekha. She backed away. With each step Eshani took, Lekha took one step forward. She snarled at Eshani and then dipped her large head to sniff the flower.

Eshani waited with bated breath. Finally, Lekha's white infection-striped tongue licked the flower off the ground and ate it. Eshani let out a breath of relief. She didn't know how long it would take to work, or that it would indeed heal the white plague, but she believed.

Lekha shook her head in wide sweeps, blinking and grunting before she stilled. Her ears pulled back. Many feet padded over rocks and leaves. The brush behind Lekha rustled, and she swung her head to face Papa.

Eshani gasped, gesturing for her father to stop. But he hadn't seen her yet, only Lekha.

"Lekha?" Papa called, a smile on his face. "You're here, too?"

"Papa, no!"

But Lekha was already prowling toward a confused Papa. Eshani hurried toward Lekha as Lekha quickened her steps. She head butted Papa, practically knocking him over...but *playfully*. Nuzzling her nose against him to demand petting, and when he complied, she purred.

Eshani paused, mere feet from them.

"What's wrong?" Papa asked.

Eshani bit the inside of her cheek and told him what had happened.

Lekha calmed beneath his worried touch, and Eshani longed to pet her, too.

"Go," Papa told both Lekha and Eshani. "We haven't time to waste."

Upon that command, Lekha went to Eshani and pinned her with a cloudy stare. She grunted and shoved Eshani with her forehead, nuzzling her. Eshani hugged Lekha as Lekha pawed at her. She knew, thanks to amrita, that Lekha could not infect her.

"Is it working? Or are you still partially you and fighting?" She wept her apologies into Lekha's soiled coat, her kurta sullied with the flying beast's blood. They both needed a bath.

With the naga warriors marching past them, Lekha offered herself to Eshani, lowering herself so that Eshani could climb on and ride.

Lekha might've been undead, but she was still extremely fast. She zipped alongside the river, a blur of gold, the ground smashing beneath her thunderous paws. Eshani leaned low, gripping Lekha's fur, and felt the wind in her hair as they dodged low limbs, whipped around shrubs, and evaded warning cries from guards stationed along the way, ones Lekha went out of her way to maul.

Ahead, the ferry appeared. Eshani alerted Lekha, and she seamlessly went toward it. The crunching of pebbles and twigs turned into the pounding of bones. The ferry was docked close to the shore and most likely had guards keeping her friends as prisoners.

Two nearby soldiers called to each other, but Lekha was already on them. Eshani tightened her grip as Lekha pounced, knocking the closer soldier down. She raised herself onto her hind legs, lifting Eshani high into the air, and promptly hammered him, pulverizing him into the bones beneath him. The second soldier ran toward them from the right, spear in hand. Lekha swung her massive front leg out; the back of her paw crushed his face. He had essentially hit a wall of fur and muscle and dropped.

Lekha snorted, annoyed, and gave herself a running start, leaping across the expanse of bloody river water and landing on the ferry deck with grace.

Eshani slid from her back and ran to the other side, around the cabin, to find two guards watching the Eternal Rann, unaware of her approach. She withdrew a blood-tipped arrow from her quiver. The guards barely had time to register her padded footsteps before her cuts came swiftly. They were not deep enough to kill, but they were deep enough to insert her venom. First, the guards' movements stalled, slowing until they were convulsing. Their eyelashes batted in bewilderment. Their mouths gaped in horror.

She stepped closer, unafraid but wholly inquisitive. There were different venoms for different serpents, and she wondered which kind she possessed.

Eshani removed their masks, and this time their ghastly appearance didn't startle her. Their veins pushed to the surface, and clotted blood gushed from their orifices. Their flesh turned pallid, quickly decaying. Eshani watched it all. She looked them in the eye, undaunted.

Asuras. Demons. Men who stood so much taller and broader than her, with such frightening appearances and menacing strength. Next to them, she was a little girl. They'd made sure she'd known that from the beginning. Insignificant and weak. An ant among giants.

Her stoicism remained unflinching, even as she said, "Meet your fate," and shoved them over the railing into the river of no return. The corpses below quickly covered the soldiers in a mass of arms and legs and sank into the bloody waters.

Eshani crept into the cabin and down its many long halls, finding Hiran's room. It was empty, as were hers and the dakini's. She found Rohan, Shruti, and Vidya tied and gagged in Rohan's room. They were unconscious on the bed. Eshani carefully checked the room, but there seemed to have only been the two guards on the ferry.

As she removed Rohan's gag and used her winter-steel blade to cut through his bindings, he stirred awake, groaning, "What happened?"

"I happened," she said.

He smirked, coughing on a weak laugh. "I'm wearing off on you." His eyes went wide and he scrambled back, demanding to know what was on Eshani's neck.

"My friend," she assured him. "Ruhi won't hurt you." She smiled and worked on Shruti. "Are you all right?"

Rohan fell onto his side and attempted to help Vidya. He said, "They knocked us out hard. Something is in these gags to keep us sedated. Holika found us. Hiran is with the Shadow King being tortured."

Shruti's eyelids fluttered awake. She drowsily sat up as Eshani climbed farther onto the bed to unbind Vidya. Eshani remarked, "It would make sense to keep you asleep if Shruti and Vidya can use shadows to get free."

"How are you alive?" Vidya groaned, sitting up only to lie back down.

"I'm singularly magnificent," Eshani joked, handing them each a clean washcloth from the basin on the table before fetching water.

"Seriously, how did you survive?" Shruti asked, gulping her entire cup and taking a second.

Eshani quickly explained her treacherous fall, her walk across worlds to the Mahal, and the creation of the bridge. She omitted the amrita and celestial saffron but briefly mentioned Ruhi, who sat around her neck and calmly watched everything. Before her friends could ask questions, Eshani said, "You rest. Do you know exactly where Hiran is being kept?"

Rohan lurched out of bed.

"Where are you going?" Eshani demanded.

"Have to help my brother."

"You're in no condition."

"I am, too."

"So are we," Vidya said, carefully standing.

There wasn't time to argue, and Eshani could use all the help this realm would give her. "Don't die, okay? I can't bring you back."

"Your father?" Eshani asked Rohan as the group emerged onto the deck.

"I'm fine," the Ferryman said, peering around the corner. He had several dark bruises on his face. "I'm the Ferryman, after all."

"They didn't even tie you up?" Rohan asked.

Lekha slowly walked around the cabin, the space too small for her, and spat out binds.

"I had some help," the Ferryman admitted.

"Is that Lekha?" Rohan barked as the dakini oohed over their first sighting of a tiger.

"You should probably wear your masks," Eshani reminded them, and climbed onto Lekha. "Can you make it there on your own? I don't think Lekha will let you all ride her."

Vidya squinted into the forest. "There are keshi tied to the trees. Where are the soldiers?" Her gaze scanned the shore. "Oh! There they are. Lekha's work?"

Eshani nodded.

The Ferryman lowered the ramp and the band dismounted. They took the weapons and keshi from the mauled soldiers and rode into the next battle.

THIRTY-SEVEN

ESHANI

With the Blood River far behind them, Lekha had left the keshi in her wake. She found the Shadow King's camp, pouncing on unsuspecting enemies. Eshani's friends and the naga warriors weren't far behind.

Ahead, a sprawling tent of tapestries had been erected in a clearing guarded by just two elder dakini. The Shadow King would not be expecting rebels, much less a small army.

Eshani had to get to him before too many engaged in battle. She wouldn't be able to carry the loss of the naga if they were dismantled or staked to the walls of the Passage of Bones, or if her friends were tortured or killed.

The fight began as soon as she was spotted. Yells and cries rang through the air, but the asura did not assemble to properly fight. They yelled for her to stop and surrender. When Lekha showed no signs of slowing down, archers aimed for the tiger instead. She zipped one way and then another, avoiding arrows. Behind them, a new cry rippled through the air. Rohan, Shruti, and Vidya riding while simultaneously shooting arrows was a spectacular thing for Eshani to glimpse over her shoulder. Beyond them, the naga deftly ran across tree limbs out of sight.

Needing every bit of help possible, Eshani called to Ashoka, so far away. A distant pulse returned her call.

An arrow cleaved through Lekha's shoulder, and she stumbled, knocking Eshani off and sending Ruhi into a bush. Eshani hurried to fight back. She used her primitive arrows first, saving the metal-tipped ones—stolen from the dead soldiers—for the Shadow King.

Metal clashed against metal and arrows shot through the air as the naga and the band of friends dove into the fight. A fight for their lives, a fight for vengeance, and a fight to stop the cruelty of this reign.

"What is the meaning of this?" a familiar voice roared. The High Lord shoved aside soldiers, standing with feet apart, chest out, as commanding as a high lord could be.

Even though Eshani was stronger, the sight of him made her tremble. He smirked the second he saw her. Stray hair flapped furiously around her face, but she didn't budge. He took that as a sign of fear, as if she were a fawn paralyzed by fright in the face of a predator.

Rohan appeared beside Eshani with bow in hand, prepared to face the High Lord at her side. She looked at her friend and shook her head. The High Lord belonged to her. Rohan clucked his tongue in acknowledgment, falling back into battle to save a nagin from a confused soldier who lamented, "The dead have risen!"

Eshani trained her nocked arrow on the High Lord, but she missed as he'd dodged and lunged for her. She kicked him away with the strength of a boulder, taking him by painful surprise. She went for a sword on the ground, knocked out of the hand of a dead soldier.

The High Lord chuckled, as if she hadn't just broken his ribs. He was asura, and he would not show defeat.

"Little mortal girl," he said, like it was a slur. He leaned to the side, the side she knew hurt him the most. "Will you submit?" His words became labored. He was surely bleeding internally. "Or shall I defeat you as easily as I did before?"

Oh, how Eshani welcomed a rematch.

"It would be fun, although short-lived," he said with a wince. "You are too weak to be worth much effort."

"You look a little wounded." Eshani swung. He moved out of the way, taken aback at first, but he hadn't become a close companion to the Shadow King without knowing how to fight.

They dueled, sword against sword. She put every ounce of strength into her lunges. But one miscalculated step, and she stumbled. He caught her, twisting her wrist back and disarming her. She yelped as he slammed her to the ground, flipping her onto her back and straddling her. Right here, in the middle of a battle where several had taken notice and tried to get to her. They were held at bay by the elder dakini.

Eshani struggled for air as he choked her, her strength leaving her body. She kicked, one hand on his trying to pry his fingers off, the other punching his broken ribs. Which only made him angrier. He slammed her head into the ground. Pain radiated from the back of her head to her shoulders. She nearly passed out.

Her fingers desperately dug into the dirt and commanded the vegetation to come to her. Ribbons of communication poured into the roots below the ground, and every last one rumbled. The ground shook. Even though the roots were close, her strongest connection careened toward her. Ashoka had arrived.

The High Lord gasped, one hand still on Eshani's throat and the other on his own throat. Vines whipped around his neck and tightened. He struggled to breathe, his face contorting as he lost hold of Eshani. She scurried back, catching her breath and rubbing her tender neck. She grabbed his face and jerked him toward her, his eyes bulging and his mouth gasping for breath.

"Know that a little mortal girl killed you." She whispered for only his ears to hear, "Although I'm a mortal no longer."

And with that, the vines gave a great twist, decapitating the High Lord.

"Harm only the soldiers who rise against us," Eshani told the vines hungering for flesh. "Protect my people and my friends."

She snatched the High Lord's head by his long hair—as heavy as she imagined an inflated head to be—and marched toward the looming tent in the distance. Whoever attempted to stop her was deftly met with arrows, blades, and the gnashing vines with their blood-splattered blooms.

THIRTY-EIGHT

HIRAN

Hands pressed against the wall of the tent, corpses moaning and groaning to get inside. The faint chorus of battle rang in the distance, but these corpses had known to come around to the back.

"Your tricks?" Tarak's gaze swept across the sturdy fabric holding back dozens upon dozens of hands.

While the dead kept his brother's attention and the elder dakini raised shadow shields to protect him in case of a breach, Hiran soaked in the remaining streams of shadow from the cuffs. Inside his body, shadows met the Gloom, and they were one. At long last, he embraced the dakini lineage buried deep inside him.

Tarak shrugged with the confidence their father had raised him with, asserting, "By now, I'm sure my vigilant and skilled friend has found the nagin and is dragging her back as we speak, and your end will be here. But I want you to watch as I use her so you, my inferior brother, may see your futile ambitions thwarted."

"Do you mean this friend?" Eshani's voice called, her words alerting every guard and dakini in the tent, who had been so focused on the corpses clawing at the wall that they hadn't noticed her walk in.

Hiran's heart raced. She was alive! He couldn't understand how or why, except that Eshani was simply magnificent. *Of course* she could walk across worlds, survive halahala, survive the Vaitarani, and fight her way back.

She stood at the entrance of the tent, her hair wild and coming undone from her braid, her emerald eyes a beam of colorful light in this dreary realm. She was covered in blood, but not from the river. By the smell of it, the blood belonged to soldiers. She left carmine steps in her wake. Blades of grass turned toward her as she passed; roots beat against the ground for her; leaves fluttered up and danced in her breeze.

The mere sight of her dulled the pain in his back and the burns on his stomach.

Her small fist gripped the head of Tarak's beloved friend.

"How?" Tarak snarled.

Simple. Eshani was a goddess.

She threw the head at Tarak's feet. It hit the ground with a flat thud and rolled once with a splatter of blood. She raised a brow and sweetly asked, "Did you miss me, *moonflower?*"

Behind her, a tiger prowled into the tent with many wounds, smeared in blood, her eyes cloudy and feral. Lekha was infected with the white plague, yet she lived.

Every guard pointed swords and arrows at them. Eshani flashed concerned eyes at Hiran, but he nodded reassuringly. She returned Tarak's glare. This was not the girl who had first stumbled into this realm or even the girl who had stowed away on the ferry.

Eshani took several confident steps toward Tarak, a bow in her hand. In a manner befitting the greatest kings and queens, she spoke. "Know that *you* brought this upon yourself."

She plucked an arrow from her quiver. "You should not have come for the naga."

Tarak laughed. *"You,* little girl? The scared mortal who couldn't even cut me when you stood a foot away?"

Lekha snarled. When a guard crept toward her from behind, she snapped her jaws and chomped his arm off. For an undead beast, she was lightning fast. An arrow cut the air and hit the tiger's shoulder.

Quicker than a blink, Eshani shot the guard in the throat, and then nocked another arrow and aimed at Tarak.

"That girl died in the river. I'm reborn. But most importantly, I am naga." She unleashed the arrow at the moment an elder dakini erected a barricade between Eshani and Tarak.

Hiran pulled down his hands, the cuffs now fully dissolved.

A snake fell from the roof onto the dakini as the guards engaged in battle with Eshani and Lekha. The dakini cried out and thrashed about to get the serpent off, but the snake had already zipped around to the dakini's face. When the dakini lurched back and screamed, the serpent darted into her mouth and disappeared down her throat. She choked for breaths that would not come and tore open her garment to her inner shirt where her stomach writhed and pulsated with ungodly terror. The bulge stretched her skin before ripping it open in a fountain of blood, squelching guts, and the birth of a fanged serpent.

"Subdue her," Tarak roared, "and kill them all!"

Yes, kill them all, the Gloom whispered, uniting with shadow particles in Hiran's blood. His veins bulged and beat black, pushing up against his skin. Tarak had to do a double take before he stepped back.

"No tricks," Hiran promised. *"Brother."*

And with that, a shadow sword flashed into existence in Hiran's grip. Tarak immediately grabbed the sword at his waist. But here was the thing about shadow weapons: They were invincible as long as they could be held in solid form. The shadow blade skewered Tarak's sword, the broken piece clanking to the ground. Their father's blade lay in pieces, just like Tarak's legacy.

To the right, a semicircle of dead yanked the tent up from the bottom and crawled through, gnarling and gnashing their teeth. Soldiers fought them, but one couldn't kill what was already dead.

Tarak craned his neck, his eyes growing wider. His skin slithered, and tentacles crawled out of his pores, little horns that became larger. His claws elongated into talons and his mouth pulled back into an ear-to-ear cavernous void of teeth. He launched himself at a surprised and disgusted Hiran, knocking him back with a punch. Hiran had never seen his brother like this. The facade of a royal in control had been hammered into him so well that no one had known what sort of monster Tarak truly was.

"I will *eviscerate* you!" Tarak howled, hunching over Hiran like a beast and slashing him with one swipe after another.

Hiran cried out as black fluid wept from his wounds instead of blood. Shadows layered him with a second skin, one of armor. Hiran could only block his brother's blows. And although he was stronger and better skilled than when they'd last fought, Tarak dragged him back to their childhood, where the elder brother had always been viciously victorious.

Above them, the tent had been torn asunder as the vines from the Court of Nightmares swung wildly overhead like a maniacal, tentacled beast.

Hiran glimpsed Eshani between blows. She was in the middle of close combat with a dozen soldiers, giant asuras compared to her mortal form. Lekha was being wrestled down by elder dakini.

Unleash me, the Gloom demanded, *for we were meant for this singular moment.*

There was no choice, even if it meant his own demise.

It consumed Hiran fully. His vision went dark. His bones splintered and realigned. Wings of shadow bolted from his shoulder bones. His fangs descended and his arms skittered with armored flesh.

He'd been born from chaos and secrets, bathed in nightmares. As it turned out, all nightmares had breaking points and came to an end. And what a glorious end this would be.

Hiran blocked blow after blow before catching Tarak's claw and growling, "This is for my mother."

He snapped Tarak's talon back, dislodging it so that it hung from its socket. For the first time, Tarak howled in pain.

A spike protruded from Hiran's elbow. "This is for my sister."

He jammed the spike into Tarak's wrist, cutting off his hand. Tarak bellowed, but Hiran kept him close, yanking Tarak toward him by the neck. "And *this* is for Eshani."

Hiran hung on to Tarak's neck with every ounce of anger in him. And then he gave his brother—his childhood tormentor, his mother's killer, a traitor to this realm, and Eshani's oppressor—a powerful twist. Tarak's neck bent in an unnatural way, the crunch of bones loud in Hiran's ears.

If Hiran were to die consumed by shadows, he was determined that his brother would die before him.

THIRTY-NINE

ESHANI

Everything had descended into chaos within the billowing tent. Eshani staved off enough guards and sent both Ruhi and Ashoka to help Lekha. Catching her breath, her body exhausted, she bent over to wheeze a few more precious breaths. Her clothes hung as rags from her body, her shoulders and arms bearing gashes, her sides bleeding but healing.

Rohan and Vidya had fought their way through. Without Eshani having to ask, Vidya confirmed, "It's under control out there. We're winning."

Rohan's gaze stilled at the sight of the Shadow King ramming against Hiran, who was on the ground covered in blood. Whose blood, though, was hard to tell. Both were injured.

"We have to help him," Rohan said as Hiran ripped out part of the Shadow King's throat.

"It can't be!" Vidya said. "Are those shadow wings?"

As Hiran pushed the Shadow King back, he sat up with a pair of massive black wings with obscure smoky edges.

"This is going to kill him," Rohan said. "We have to hurry!"

With that, Rohan and Vidya surged through the fight.

The shadows would kill him? Eshani didn't understand, but she knew she did not want Hiran to die.

Her many wounds left streams of blood down her leg and arms. She plucked the last arrow in her quiver and coated the entire sharp end with her blood. She hadn't much energy left. Amrita might heal her, but it wouldn't prevent her from passing out from exhaustion.

Her vision blurred, her head dizzy. Sweat, blood, and grime trickled down her temples, stinging her eyes. The cacophony of battle rang in her ears and then went quiet as she tried her hardest to focus. Her steps were too wobbly to move forward, and another attempt would send her crashing.

As she nocked her arrow, Eshani knew several soldiers were coming for her and no one was left to protect her. She stood alone, embers and dirt suffocating the air. She aimed, her arms trembling from fatigue.

The Shadow King and Hiran were grappling and moving with heavy strikes and the sudden push-and-pull of brawling.

If she missed, she could kill Hiran. If she didn't try, then Hiran would die from the shadows growing from his body.

She swallowed, telling her arrow to hold true, to find the Shadow King and only him.

With soldiers closing in on her left and right, she unleashed before her body crumpled. The arrow catapulted across the air, slipping into the space between others fighting, narrowly missing Rohan when he dodged a sword, cutting through the shadowy air of Vidya's quickly forming shield, and carving into the exposed, meaty part of the Shadow King's face, right through the too-wide mouth of too many teeth.

Eshani thudded to the ground, onto a bed of grass that sprang up to catch her, her eyelids clamping shut. All sorts of roots and moss protectively arched over her body, cocooning her so that she disappeared into the ground.

She fell knowing her arrow had made its mark. Perhaps not a fatal blow by any normal standard, but enough to inject venom. *Her* venom.

FORTY

HIRAN

Bone-chilling cold seized Hiran's bones, freezing his blood and consuming his entire being. He felt the edges of death calling to him, the sweet cradle of eternity. His mother's voice beckoned, coddling his descent. Even the dead sang a chorus of welcoming.

A few more inflections and Tarak would be wholly eviscerated, disemboweled like the late Queen Mother. A fitting end.

Hiran's muscles ached with odd gratification, hurting but wanting more. He knew this was his end, and he gladly bowed to the whims of fate.

But, as kismet would have it, Hiran didn't fight alone. He heard the calls of Rohan, muddled by the shadow pounding in his ears. Then a buzz, swift and brutal, collided with Tarak's face, piercing his gaping mouth from cheek to cheek and shattering teeth.

Hiran went to bite him again, but something about the bloody arrow gave him pause. The arrow smelled of something highly toxic.

His head jerked to the left where Eshani had fallen, his vision returning as grass and moss and roots rapidly grew around her body.

Eshani! This was *her* arrow.

Hiran shoved Tarak off. His brother clutched his face, not with simple irritation but with dread. His skin transformed and blood wept from his eyes, nose, and ears and gurgled out of his mouth. The gush of blood from where Hiran had taken a chomp clotted and bubbled over.

The Gloom inside Hiran abated, releasing its hold on him. He didn't waste a moment of time. He pressed his katar blades into Tarak's neck, yet Tarak didn't resist. He had become immobile.

"Long live the shadows." Hiran grunted as the blades not only pierced Tarak, but went all the way through, fortified by shadows. With a great twist, his brother's head slipped to the side.

The crown of shadow and ash called vehemently to Hiran, and he went to it.

The realm needs a king.

He picked up the crown, featherlight in his hands.

Welcome to your destiny.

An unseen power writhed out of the crown and twisted around his wrists, up his arms, and to his chest. It wrapped him in glory. It was not simply a crown, as it had been for Tarak, their father, and those before them, but one that connected to the Gloom and thus the shadows. He felt the entire realm in his heartbeat. He was a true Shadow King.

As he stood upright, his presence turned into a physical aura demanding attention. The battle stilled and the remaining soldiers muttered, confused.

In an abandoned shield propped upon a fallen guard, Hiran saw not a crown of shadow and ash, but his horns gilded like a crown.

The dead reached out to him, wailing, *"Gatekeeper."*

Rohan's mouth dropped open. He came out of his stupor to look around, ordering the remaining army, "What are you waiting for? Bow before your King."

Rohan was the first to drop to his knees, then Vidya and Shruti, and finally, the soldiers. Knees to the floor, foreheads to the ground, and palms against the soil. The deepest of bows—the deepest of respect.

"This battle is over," Hiran declared, "and I am its victor."

He marched toward Eshani, where the tiger and serpent stood to guard the coffin of grass, roots, and blooms. They did not attack him, and the ground opened itself to him.

Eshani lay in torn and bloodied clothes, her skin caked with dirt. A coronet of red hyacinth and brambles perched atop her head.

"Eshani." He said her name as if to savor the word.

Her lips parted when he leaned down to pick her up, ignoring his own pains and wounds. He carried her out and was met by a small army of people he didn't recognize. They couldn't have been asuras or dakini, but they were too coherent to be the dead.

A man hurried toward him, frantic. "Beta?"

"Are you Eshani's father?" Hiran asked, perplexed.

"Hah. Give her to me."

Hiran did as he asked, even though her father had been weakened in the fight and struggled to carry her. "Where are you taking her?"

"To the Mahal."

Hiran swallowed, tears burning his eyes as his friends gathered behind him. His words came out despondent. "Wait. She's not dead. She can't be."

"Of course she's not dead," her father called back as others like him—naga, Hiran presumed—gathered around her.

"I don't understand," Hiran said.

"She can rest in the Mahal, and we promised her we would return."

"Let me carry her."

"No. She is my daughter. I will carry her," the man insisted, even as he limped and had slowed.

The tiger nudged him with her forehead, but he told her, "No, Lekha. This time, I will carry her."

Lekha understood and walked alongside him, the serpent flinging itself from the tiger onto Eshani with her father's approval.

They walked a long while, slowly, and Hiran wasn't sure what would happen once they reached the Bloodfall. Eshani couldn't walk across if she wasn't dead, and she wasn't awake to conjure a bridge. Even as the new Shadow King, he wouldn't argue with her father, but he wasn't ready to say goodbye. He *couldn't* say goodbye. Not yet. This wasn't how things were supposed to end. She was never supposed to die. But she *was* fated to leave this realm. And this truth utterly gutted him.

FORTY-ONE

ESHANI

"There you are! Sometimes I can't do anything but pace and wonder what in the realms is happening out there. Well? What happened?" Holika exclaimed, her eyes wide and gleaming with excited curiosity.

Eshani sat up. "Am I dead?"

Holika waved her off and stood akimbo, bending at the waist so that her face was closer to Eshani's. "You know the dead don't dream! Go ahead! Tell me what happened! It's been such a long time since I've been able to contact you. How is my brother? Is he . . . is he alive?"

Fragments rushed back to Eshani as she explained the battle, ending with "I shot an arrow into the Shadow King's face. He's as good as dead."

Holika's expression fell flat. "An arrow to the face doesn't kill an asura, my dear."

"One tipped in my venomous blood does. I've killed many asuras with it."

Holika's brow arched. "Interesting. I will ask for details later. So, my brother will be the new king? The realm just might survive."

"Ahem," someone said with an exaggerated clearing of their throat.
Holika rolled her eyes and sidestepped to reveal Sithara.

Eshani shot to her feet. "What are you doing here?" Her gaze immediately went to her twin's head. "And what happened to your hair?"

Sithara tilted her chin up. While her thick hair fell over one shoulder, the opposite side appeared shaved. She touched the short hair there, tapping a scar, and asked, "Do you like it?"

Eshani stumbled over her thoughts. Before she could utter a word, Sithara—the sister who theatrically lamented her abhorrence of hugs—flew into Eshani's arms, hugging her tight. "Hello to you, too!"

Eshani returned the embrace, taking in the scent of her sister, even though she knew this wasn't real. She touched her twin's shaved head. The two had much to talk about. "Did Holika connect us through our dreams?"

"I did find this one for you," Holika boasted, blowing on her nails.

Sithara pulled away and scowled. "You came into my head." Her hand lengthened into a blade. "Do that again, and I'll sever yours."

Holika snarled, baring her fangs. "If you can find my body at the bottom of the pool, go ahead. I'd love to stop this madness."

Sithara tilted her head. Eshani knew the look of Sithara formulating a plan. The empty space around them shook.

Sithara took Eshani's hand and said, "There isn't much time. You're waking up. We'll meet soon and I'll tell you everything. Just know: That *was* my voice in your head those times before. I can do much more than that now."

"How?"

"I'll tell you another time, when you're awake and rested and we can have a *private* conversation." She eyed Holika. "I'll see you soon. I know it."

As Eshani began to awaken, leaving her sister, Sithara told Holika, "Get those watery legs ready, dreamreaver. I have an idea."

"PAPA?" ESHANI ASKED, OPENING HER EYES TO FIND HER father carrying her beneath an agitated red sky.

"Beta?" he said, surprised.

"Why are you carrying me? What happened?"

He gently put her down, and Eshani found herself surrounded by an anxious and perplexed crowd. Lekha nudged her, and she hugged the tiger's neck. Ruhi curled up beside her, and Eshani ran a hand over the serpent's head.

Hiran squatted at her side, and Eshani threw her arms around him. He chuckled, returning her embrace.

"You're alive," she muttered, holding him tight.

"Thanks to you." He sighed against her neck, holding her to him longer.

Shock ricocheted against her insides in a pleasantly surreal way. Ugh, this boy...

"I thought I'd never see you again," he said, gripping her waist as if letting go might be a final farewell.

"It takes more than an epic battle with demons to get rid of me." She pulled back and took in his bare face, those harsh angular lines, the swirl of his eyes, and...gilded horns? "They're beautiful."

"I thought I should enhance my appearance," he joked, his mouth tugging into a smile. "You're alive."

"Why wouldn't I be?" The crowd rustled around her. "Did someone stab me?"

"Well..." Hiran scratched the back of his head. "You fell unconscious and the ground wrapped you up. Your father was taking you to the Mahal."

"Papa," she said, touching her father's worried face. "You know I'm—" She stopped herself and stared at Hiran.

His expression contorted and then relaxed as he understood. "You found it."

She nodded, wondering if he would demand it. He did not.

"Did I kill the Shadow King?"

"You're looking at the Shadow King," Vidya said.

"Does that mean the other one's dead?" Eshani asked.

"Never heard a girl so happy to hear someone died," Hiran teased. "But yes. And no one will hunt you ever again." He cleared his throat, and his brows knitted in such a serious, forlorn way. "I'm glad that I am able to at least say goodbye."

"Where are you going?"

He smiled warmly, although he couldn't hide the sadness in his eyes. "You're leaving, aren't you? Walker of worlds. To the gateway that will take you back to the mortal realm, leaving us forever."

She swallowed. That was what she wanted. To return to Sithara and find Manisha and reunite with their mother and rebel against the mortal King. "I feel that there are some things left to do...."

Hiran shifted, his knee pressing into the dirt and his finger inadvertently grazing hers. Eshani stilled from the sudden shock ricocheting against her insides, even more aware of her father and a dozen others watching. "You've helped destroy a tyrannical legacy. What else is left?"

Her gaze swept between Hiran and his—*their*—friends. Her eyes met Papa's and he nodded. She looked to Lekha. A sliver of honey appeared beneath the cloudy eyes. Eshani had the ability to destroy, to exact terrible vengeance. A great gift with immeasurable responsibility. But she also had the ability to heal. She'd done so her entire life with vegetation, and now she could share her gift in a new way.

She slipped open the armband and held its delicate, invaluable contents in her palms. Closing her eyes, she let the ribbons of communication flow, bringing resurgence to the celestial saffron threads and fabricating new blooms. When she opened her eyes, she found everyone waiting with bated breath. Unfurling her hands, Eshani presented a purple flower with red-orange stigmas that could heal this world and all worlds.

FORTY-TWO

ESHANI

Eshani couldn't just leave a fragmented world behind when she had the ability to heal it. She supposed she was like Papa in that way, who would've run back for injured soldiers and animals alike, even if it meant risking his own life. He watched with great pride as Eshani cultivated the celestial saffron grafted onto the realm's most potent botanical power—Ashoka.

"I am entrusting you with this valuable gift," she whispered to Ashoka.

We are honored.

Eshani smiled at the vines before carefully harvesting the colorful stigma into jars.

Vidya and Shruti took the items with reverence, packing the jars into padded satchels.

Chintan, the little boy Eshani had met in Amreli, was one of the first to receive the thread. His sister nodded, encouraging him to partake. In a matter of time, the lightning streaks down his chest and shoulders began to recede.

"It will take some time," Eshani told him. She glanced at Lekha, whose eyes were now a mix of plague white and rich honey. She had not fully healed yet, and Eshani couldn't risk bringing her back into the mortal realm with such a severe disease. She would have to wait a little while longer before heading back.

"I trust you to spread the medicine to all," Eshani said to Vidya and Shruti.

They nodded from atop their steeds. Shruti said, "We have reliable friends to help with the work."

"What will you do?" Rohan asked, on his own keshi. Behind him were several soldiers from the final battle who had sworn allegiance to Hiran after having witnessed his powers. They would escort the group, fighting off dangers on their behalf.

"Once Lekha is healed, we'll return to the dark forest and portal back."

"But the monsters..." Vidya contested.

"Between my gifts with vegetation, Lekha's teeth, and perhaps a small army of soldiers...we'll make it through."

"And leave us?" Shruti asked, saddened.

Hiran appeared at Eshani's side, and she thought she might never get used to his magnificent wings and intimidating crown. "Once I gain control of the shadow dome and stabilize it, I'm going with you."

"What do you mean?"

"I have dakini blood in me. The crown amplifies my connection to the realm, and my bloodlines to the shadows. I can help fix it for now."

"That's wonderful! But I meant...well, why are you coming with me?"

He took her hand in his, gently stroking the back of her hand with his thumb. "You said there was an unresolved war. My father started it, and my brother kept it going. I need to make it right."

"You would go to war for us?"

He tilted his chin to the side and touched her cheek. "I went to the end of the world for you, and I would go to war for you."

In the near distance, Papa clucked his tongue and did a little head bob, as if silently saying, *What talk! This boy is good. I approve.*

Eshani's cheeks flushed. She expected Hiran to clear his throat and back away, but he'd changed during that battle. He was no longer an awkward boy hiding his lineage, but a confident ruler. He was, finally, who he was meant to be.

And who was Eshani meant to be? She watched Chintan smile at his sister. She was meant to be a healer and a leader. Papa had been right; war had changed them, but they came out stronger.

"If the portal allows it," she said.

"I'm the Gatekeeper," he replied with such haughtiness that it made her laugh.

"Well, Gatekeeper," Rohan said, leaning forward on his keshi and avoiding the lashing lavender tendrils. "You're not going without me."

"Are you allowed to leave?" Vidya asked Rohan.

"My father said as long as he is alive, I'm not tied to the river. He would want me to go. Besides, Hiran needs me."

"Do I?" Hiran asked, one brow cocked.

"And us," Vidya added.

Hiran swept his gaze toward Eshani. She nodded. The more friends, the better, especially ones with their particular skills.

"We'll meet at your village," Eshani told them.

And with that, Vidya, Shruti, Rohan, and the soldiers left to distribute the saffron. Hiran returned to the highest point to connect to the realm. His work would be exhausting, but he alone could fix the dome.

AFTER CLEANING UP, ESHANI DRESSED IN GARMENTS GIVEN to her by her friends and met Hiran where he worked endlessly on a cliff overlooking the southern end of the Blood River. Here the land was unsettling, barren with sparse, burnt shrubs and plenty of crags for creatures to hide within. Still, with Lekha nearby and Hiran ahead, Eshani had little to fear.

Eshani's breath hitched at the sight of him tugging down the jacket to a black sherwani. Metallic red thread had been woven at the cuffs. The fine clothes and crown made him appear regal. His tall stature when he stood straight, wings out, made her heart flutter.

"A royal must look the part when first presenting themselves to their people," Hiran said sheepishly when he greeted her.

"I thought the royals wore blue?"

"I prefer red." His gaze swept the length of her body, and her skin turned hot. In Anand and on Kurma, she'd always been fully covered, but the custom of this realm had draped her in a black-and-red dhoti that was loose around her legs and a glimmering, midriff-baring black choli.

"I adore red."

He touched her cheek. "I know."

Warmth blazed in her chest as she stepped closer to him, her palm flat on his stomach. It was strange to feel a gushing connection to him amid the horrific landscape.

As if to remind them, a trill shivered across the desolate land. Eshani clutched Hiran. "What is that?"

"Do not be afraid." He held her close. "They are the creatures of the borderlands. They bend to me now."

She looked around. Although she couldn't see anything in the darkness, she sensed them. Hundreds of creatures crawling against the ground, in and out of crags. She swallowed hard. "What are they saying?"

"That the true Shadow King is connected to the physical realm." He let out a sigh of relief. "It will be saved for now."

The trilling increased and Eshani flinched. They might bend to Hiran, but they still sent shivers down her spine.

"They say one more thing," Hiran added, his cheeks burning bright. "All know the cure is here and who is responsible for it. The queen with a crown of bramble and thorn."

She frowned. "How can I be a queen?"

He touched a knuckle to her chin, sending pleasant flutters through her. His lips parted to reply when someone cleared their throat.

Eshani yelped when a girl spoke. "Why are you still there?"

She stared wide-eyed at her twin floating like a ghost, eyes glowing green and a crown of shattered glass on her head. "A little dramatic, don't you think?"

Sithara grinned, and Eshani longed to hug her. "You knew I could project myself into your mind, but guess what other new talents I have acquired?"

"I meant the crown."

"Am I seeing a ghost?" Hiran asked. "You are not dead."

"You can *see* her?" Eshani asked.

Sithara winked at him. "Oh. Hello. You must be the boyfriend."

"Sithara!" Eshani hissed, her skin flushing hot.

Sithara rolled her eyes. "I jest. Sort of. We can talk long into the night about boys later. You need to hurry up."

"I have to wait for Lekha to heal. She's almost ready."

"It's been weeks since your battle."

"That can't be." Eshani looked to Hiran.

He nodded. "Time passes quicker here than in the mortal realm."

The passing of time had felt like nothing without a sun and moon.

Sithara frowned, her image flickering, her voice solemn. "I have terrible news. It's about Manisha...."

MEANWHILE...

SWATI INHALED THE SALT AIR, THE WIND RISING AND FALL-ing like waves over her skin. Sea spray misted her lashes and dotted her lips. She perched on a boulder on the edge of Kurma, her weapon at her feet. The naga elders had been away for many days, gathering allies and formulating plans. They would never go quietly into the night or forget what had transpired.

"They should just find a new home," her mother mumbled from below.

Swati had once believed that, until the twins left, taking on the unsettling world of the kingdom on their own. Finding peace was a fine thing, according to the teachings on Kurma, but could she so easily forget and move on? She knew, if the situation were turned around, the twins would not let her fight alone. She knew, even if her situation were not as dire, the twins would aid her. So how could she let them stand alone?

Divided, they would never rise. United, they could thrive.

Ahead, the nose of a boat appeared, breaking through the heavy fog like curtains pulled back for the rise of morning. A new dawn. At the helm stood the twins' mother, a goddess of war who could not rest in peace. She raised her trident in triumph. Reckoning was at hand.

Swati heaved. She felt their determination brewing in her bones, a sweetness burrowing into her, for their fight would be her fight. She would finally stand for something.

The spear at her feet sang with bloodlust. A song of reckoning hummed through the air as another boat breached the fog. Then another. And another. Until the sea was covered with allies rocking on the waves. Makara and yakshini, mortals and beings she'd never seen before. A percussive rhythm floated across the water—a cadence of drums and conches, of chanting that reached into her soul and made the very fibers of her being thrum.

The Fire Wars were not over.

A world built in blood shall drown in blood.

The kingdom would dissolve with a taste of chaos.

EPILOGUE

SITHARA HAD ACQUIRED MANY SKILLS OVER THE YEARS, BUT her newest obsession could not be taught. She stood at the rotund arena of the Court of Nightmares, glowering at the statues who were neither dead nor alive, and who were unaware of her presence. They wouldn't have detected her, the same way a dreamer couldn't detect Holika unless she made herself known. Thus was Sithara's newly minted gift.

She floated toward the pool, parts of her ghostly body flickering as she concentrated on journeying just a bit farther.

"It will never work," Holika had told her.

"Think of this as repayment for helping Eshani and easing Manisha's nightmares."

Holika had waved her off, stating, "No girl should carry such a burden. You should thank me for passing her nightmares on to the General so he may experience his crimes himself, since *he* was the one who caused her nightmares in the first place. Oh, what fun that was."

"Let me settle the debt."

"And if something goes wrong? Should I spend my quiet days listening to your incessant complaints trapped in an eternal abomination of a prison?"

"At least we'll be together," Sithara had joked dryly.

"No thanks."

Yet here she was, skirting the impossible as she had done so many times. It had been inconceivable to go to war as a child and survive, to inherit the gifts from her ancestors, and to cast her image into the minds of others. Sithara had never attempted anything like this before, a full bending of the mind.

With her physical form worlds away, she stood at the lip of the pool, mist rising and falling like breaths. And in she dove. Deep into the waters, where sparse light showed her very little. She swam for what felt like miles into the abyss, toward the faceless entity of chaos. Amid stones and ancient ruins sat a perfectly preserved body of gray against gray, hair floating in an unfelt current.

Holika's remains were a sad sight, but she was wholly intact.

Sithara slipped into the dreamreaver's physical body, aligning with it head to head, arms to arms, and feet to feet. With incredible exertion and the will of great warriors, Sithara sank into bones and forced them to move. With each grunt and silenced scream, she crawled up the stone wall of the abyss where whispers rippled across the water.

Light shimmered above, signaling the surface. Holika's hands broke through the water, piercing the mist, and felt for the edge for the first time in a very long time. From the pool of the abyss, bathed in the displeased glow of awakening statues, rose the dreamreaver freed of her bonds.

Once Holika's body was fully out of the water, Sithara lurched out, separating herself, panting and flickering amid flashes of lightning bathed in the roar of thunderclaps.

Water streamed down Holika's face, her eyes narrow and hungry and darting to the towering statues, which she loathed with all her soul. They had fully awakened, setting the arena aglow. A chorus of voices rumbled as one, an angry echo against echoes. *"Chaos."*

Holika scoffed, her gaze sweeping toward Sithara. A wicked smile curved her lips as she said, "They're referring to you."

ACKNOWLEDGMENTS

WHEN I WAS IN MIDDLE SCHOOL, I SELECTED LATIN AS MY foreign language class with the hopes that this would help me understand the etymology of medical words—for my future as a doctor, of course. Latin class came with prospects of joining the very cool Latin Club. We embarked on state-level academic decathlons and competed *in Latin*. I excelled in mythology and was exposed to the gripping, petty world of Greek and Roman gods. My obsession with mythology only grew.

When I finished writing *A Drop of Venom*, the story did not simply cease to exist. It grew into wondrous tales for three siblings. Worlds within worlds. A universe where each sister traversed her own epic journey to find her true self and embrace the breadth of her full potential.

I continued combining my favorite Greek myths with Indian lore to create something unique yet familiar. The naga and the sisterhood endured a realm ruled by cruelty so they could one day unite, more powerful and more venomous than imaginable, and take down the system.

Eternal gratitude shall always be bestowed upon my agent, Katelyn, who has been with this series from the very beginning. She is the champion who has guided me through the exciting and arduous journey of publishing.

Endless appreciation goes out to my editor, Christine, who is dauntless and incredible, with the sharpest editorial eye that I've ever seen. We've been in sync since day one and I cannot imagine another editor I'd rather be working with on the Venom series.

Thank you, Rick Riordan, for welcoming the world of Venom into the Rick Riordan Presents family.

I want to thank the entire Rick Riordan Presents team for making this possible, as there are a multitude of people and moving pieces that go into publishing a book. Many thanks to Phil and the art team. To the incredibly talented Khadijah Khatib for bringing Eshani and Ruhi to the cover in the same beautiful way as she did with Manisha and Noni. To Virginia Allyn for another amazing map to obsess over.

I can't express enough gratitude to my husband for his encouragement, because writing is a tough business with many ups and many, *many* downs. You never lost faith, even when I lost sight of my own.

To Rohan, who read the early draft and immediately demanded more. Your approval means this book must be truly special.

To Meet, who promotes my works like it's his job. I adore your enthusiasm.

To Parth, who continues to be a blazing source of support. You are cherished.

To my parents, who tell every auntie and uncle about my books.

And to the readers, who keep reading.

I hope you've enjoyed Eshani and Hiran's adventure. And I hope you'll join me for the next story. Whatever it may be...